HEARTLESS GAME

A DARK COLLEGE HOCKEY ROMANCE

KINGS OF REINA UNIVERSITY
BOOK 2

JO BRENNER

HIGH RISE PUBLISHING

Copyright © 2025 by Jo Brenner

All rights reserved.

No part of this book may be reproduced in any form or by any electronic or mechanical means, including information storage and retrieval systems, without written permission from the author, except for the use of brief quotations in a book review.

This is a work of fiction. Names, characters, places, and incidents are the product of the author's imagination or are used fictitiously, and any resemblance to actual persons, living or dead, business establishments, events, or locales is entirely incidental.

Trademarked names appear throughout this book. Rather than use a trademark symbol with every occurrence of a trademarked name, names are used in an editorial fashion, with no intention of infringement of the respective owner's trademark(s).

No part of this book was created or produced with the use of AI. No part of this book may be used for AI or Machine Learning.

Editing provided by Brittney Mmutle, Lit and Knits Literary Services.

Photography provided by Michelle Lancaster.

Cover design provided by Qamber Designs.

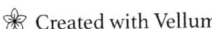 Created with Vellum

For everyone who dreams of being edged in a hockey locker room...

...I can't make it happen in real life, but I <u>can</u> write it for you.

ALSO BY JO BRENNER

Bad Heroes
 You Can Follow Me
 Lose Me In The Shadows
 Meet Me In The Dark

Tabb U
 Butterfly: a dark college hockey romance

Kings of Reina University
 Brutal Game: a dark college hockey romance

NEWSLETTER, BONUS EPILOGUE, AND A SPECIAL GIFT

Want to read about what happens with Tovah and Isaac after "The End"? Join my newsletter for the epilogue, updates, and other goodies! **Click the link below to join and read the bonus epilogue:**

Read the bonus epilogue here!

And make sure you read to the very end for the preorder/release week signed art incentive!

PLAYLIST

Bad
Bishop Briggs
The Fall
Michael Sanzone
You Don't
Sadie Jean
The Beginning
Snow Patrol
Down Bad
Taylor Swift
imgonnagetyouback
Taylor Swift
Beautiful Things
Benson Boone
vampire
Olivia Rodrigo
Shameless
Camila Cabello
dirty dishes
KiNG MALA

Daylight
David Kushner
Way Down We Go
KALEO
You're Somebody Else
flora cash
Creep
carolesdaughter
Colorblind
Counting Crows
exile (feat. Bon Iver)
Taylor Swift
evermore (feat. Bon Iver)
Taylor Swift
Yellow
Coldplay
Born to Die
Lana Del Rey
Cut Deep
Matt Maeson
Darling It's Over
A Great Big World & Jason Mraz
Like Real People Do
Hozier
Tell It To My Heart (feat. Hozier)
MEDUZA
DAUGHTER
Beyoncé
I Gotta Feeling
Black Eyed Peas
Fuck You
Cee Lo Green
Billy Jean

The Civil Wars
Chasing Cars
Snow Patrol
Rolling in the Deep
Adele
RUSSIAN ROULETTE
Nessa Barrett
flatline
Sam Short
Matches (alt version)
Jonah Kagen
My Body Left My Soul (feat. Pusha T)
USERx, Matt Maeson & Rozwell
Red Flag
Natalie Jane
Scream My Name
Thomas LaRosa
Runrunrun
Dutch Melrose
Angel by the Wings
Sia
AFTERCARE
Nessa Barrett
PASSENGER PRINCESS
Nessa Barrett
False Confidence
Noah Kahan
Angel
Toby Mai
Cities
Toby Mai
Hangman
Chris Pureka

Super Villain (feat. Kendyle Paige)
Stileto & Silent Child
I Will Wait
Mumford & Sons
Carry You Home
Alex Warren

IMPORTANT CONTENT NOTE

Content Note! Please Read

This is a dark bully romance, with dark themes and plot points that may be sensitive to some.

Please, please, please read the content warnings on my website, jobrenner.com. I'd add them here, but the River Platform (IYKYK) could get big mad if it sees the list, and then bye bye, book.

Joking aside, please do visit my website. Your health—mental, physical, spiritual, emotional—matters.

1

Isaac

"You might want to get on your knees, Jones, because you're about to blow a good game," my opponent, Colson U's center, chirped at me as we faced off on the ice.

I snorted through my cage. The guy was deluding himself if he thought some uninspired shit-talking would throw me off my game. I ignored him, my eyes trained on the ref—and the puck in his hand. There were only four minutes left in the third period, and the Reina University Kings, my team, was tied with Colson, 4:4. Colson was known to win all their games that went into overtime, and I was determined not to give them the chance.

It had been an exhausting but exhilarating match so far, and I was determined to win. Not only because I wanted to give the victory to my team and my school, but because hearing the horns go in our favor would drown out my father's voice in my head and erase his recent voicemail from my memory.

Enjoy the rest of the season and your senior year, Isaac. Because the second you graduate, your life belongs to this family. It's time for you to become who you were always meant to be: Ruthless. Violent. Cruel. Everything you claim to abhor. That was our deal, remember?

No. *Fuck that.* There was no goddamn way I was going to become the man my father wanted me to be. I was the only member of my family who'd never killed anyone, and I was keeping it that way. More importantly, I was the Reina Kings' first line center on the ice and their moral center off it. I kept these assholes in line.

I certainly didn't respond to dumb chirps.

"Hey, Jones…" Colson's center started again.

"Don't bother," his teammate said nearby. "Isaac Jones is unflappable. No one's ever been able to get him to throw his gloves. Asshole's a saint."

The ref blew his whistle in warning.

"Can it!" he said.

Colson's center stared me in the eyes.

"Maybe you aren't the one who should get on your knees," he started. "Your mom, on the other hand…"

Heat pooled on my neck, my mother's face flashing in my mind, but I forced myself to take deep breaths and stay calm. It didn't matter that he'd hit his target. Or that losing my mom had been the lowest point in my life. Although there was a well-hidden monster inside me that wanted to punch his teeth out, Good Guy Isaac prevailed. The jackass would eat his words when we won the puck drop—and then the game.

Judah Wasserson, the Kings' left defenseman and one of my best friends, was not so calm.

"His mother's dead, you goddamn asshole. But you're

welcome to blow my blade—" he started as he began to strip off his gloves.

The ref blew his whistle again.

I put my hand up.

"Judah, don't," I said calmly, stopping him before he threw the game into chaos.

Anyone else, Judah would've ignored. But for me, he lowered his hands reluctantly, leaving on his gloves.

"Fuck, man, I'm sorry," Colson's center said. "I didn't know."

"That's okay," I said, grinning at him through my cage. "You're just used to your own mother being on her knees, aren't you? Easy mistake."

"You motherfucker—" he roared...

...just as the ref dropped the puck between us. Grinning harder, I caught it with my stick before passing it to Jack Feldman, our left wing and my other best friend.

"I don't know why they ever bother," Jack said as he skated away with the puck.

I turned my attention back to the game, aware of the pissed-off offenseman who had me in his sights. As he headed down the ice toward Jack, I skated beside him, putting out my elbow and—accidentally—knocking him into the boards.

"Whoops, my bad," I called behind me, gliding quickly across the ice toward his team's goal. As I did, I passed the penalty box—and *her*.

Tovah Kaufman. The currently pink-haired distraction sitting one row behind the penalty box. The girl I hated so fucking much, I followed her home every night, sitting outside her apartment in my car with the lights off, daring some slick motherfucker to buzz her door.

If anything was going to distract me from winning, it *would* be Tovah.

Head in the game, Jones, I reminded myself.

Just in time, because Jack caught my eyes through his cage. He then deked to the right, distracting Colson's defensemen, before passing the puck to me.

I caught it with my stick, charging toward the goal.

We were down to ten seconds left of the game.

One, two, three, four...on the fifth glide, I slapped the puck straight into the net, an inch over the goalie's right glove.

The horn sounded, signaling the goal, and our win. As the crowd roared, chanting, "*Jones, Jones, Jones,*" my team surrounded me, knocking chests and slapping me on the shoulder. In the past, the crowd's ecstatic celebration as they cheered for me would've been all I needed to be happy. I loved the game. The feeling of the ice under my skates, the competition and challenge of pushing myself harder than my opponents, the joy of winning and being one with my team—it meant everything.

Lately though, it dimmed in comparison to *her*. My compulsive obsession with Tovah Kaufman was fucking with my equilibrium. My happiness. And my control. I hated it, which made it easier to hate her.

Like right now. I tried to celebrate with my teammates, but it was half-hearted. I was too distracted. As I took my perfunctory victory lap, I pulled my helmet off my head, brushing back my sweaty hair, and zeroed in on her.

Tovah was typing away on her phone. Probably working on an article for *The Daily Queen*, Reina U's newspaper. Tovah was the sports editor, but I'd heard they were short-staffed so she was taking on story assignments that usually would have gone to someone else. I couldn't take my eyes off the little journalist, or her big tits and lush hips. Some might have called the aspiring journalist fat. I called her a pain in the ass—a gorgeous pain in the ass. She was curve after curve after curve, and it made me crazy how badly I wanted to carve my name into every single one of them.

She'd dyed her hair a hot, daring pink since I'd last seen her.

I fucking hated that color.

As if she'd heard my thought, Tovah looked up at me. I couldn't see the color of her eyes from this far away, but I knew they were a soft brown. I'd seen them in my dreams too damn often. She tilted her sweet, heart-shaped face to the side as her friend Aviva leaned over and said something to her. Then her eyes shot forward, catching mine and holding them. Pink lips, the same in-your-face color as her hair, turned down and she shook her head at me.

I hate you, she mouthed.

Then smirked.

Fuck, I'd give anything to wipe that smirk off her face.

Ideally with the crown of my cock before I shoved it down her throat and choked her with it.

What was it about this woman? What was it about her that brought out the darkness I'd buried deep—so deep I didn't recognize it?

Lost in my head and her eyes, I skated toward her. I didn't have a plan, didn't know what the hell I was doing, just wanted to drive the point home that she meant nothing to me.

You're the fucking worst, she mouthed, clearly not done.

I'll show you the fucking worst, I mouthed back and winked, making sure to smile so she could see my dimples. For whatever reason, seeing them always seemed to piss her off, and I planned to take full advantage of that discovery.

Even from ten feet away, I could see her cheeks flush pink. Now, *that* was a pink I liked. That was a pink I wanted to see all over her body when I tied her to my bed and—

Holy fucking hell. What was wrong with me?

But then she'd had this effect on me since the first time I'd seen her.

"Isaac Jones! Isaac Jones!" a young voice called from behind the glass, redirecting my attention.

A kid, about seven or eight, was jumping up and down, holding up a white cardboard sign that said, "Jones is the boss." The woman next to him waved at me timidly. She was pretty, with curly blonde hair and blue eyes, and usually I'd consider flirting my way between her thighs, but unfortunately these days, my cock only got hard for one woman.

I skated over to them.

"Hey," I greeted the kid.

"Ohmygodohmygod. Mr. Jones, you're my idol. My hero. I want to be you when I grow up!" the little kid cheered. He was so excited, tears filled his eyes.

"Well, thank you. What's your name?" I asked.

He puffed out his chest. "Charlie. Will you sign my poster?"

Feeling eyes on me, I turned my head. Tovah was staring —no glaring—at me. Knowing she was watching made me stand up straighter, smile bigger, and become the best, most charming version of myself.

"I'll do you one better," I said. "If you come to the locker room in about thirty minutes, I'll sign a jersey for you."

His eyes went wide. "For me?"

I grinned. "Yup."

I turned to the woman I assumed was his mom. "I'll make sure they let you back there, just tell a security guard named Bill that Isaac said Charlie's VIP."

"Oh my god, thank you," Charlie's mom said on one grateful breath.

"Don't mention it. I love my fans, young or...still young," I said, winking at her. She blushed, but it wasn't nearly as captivating as Tovah's, which was fucking bullshit.

"See you in thirty," I said, jerking my chin up at Charlie, who, after a second, copied me.

Smiling to myself, I skated away. Tovah might bring out the worst in me, but to everyone else, I was still Isaac Jones, Good Guy. As long as it stayed that way, I'd be fine.

Judah, and his twin, Levi, appeared, bumping me from both sides. Levi was the other defensemen for the Kings, and my other best friend. Together, he, Judah, Jack and I made up what everyone at Reina called "The Core Four"— the four best players on our hockey team...and the four biggest players on campus.

Or we had been, until Jack met Aviva.

Judah's long hair was down, a rarity since he usually wore it in a man bun. He slapped me on the back, pulling me out of my thoughts.

"Good game, Jones. That was a nice goal at the end."

Levi, who was more of an insightful Loki to Judah's brash Thor, but with glasses, cleared his throat.

"You're distracted," he said. "What's going on?"

I didn't want to answer either of them, so I smiled.

"Nothing."

Judah shook his head. "Don't pull that bullshit with us. We know you too well for you to pull a Dr. Dimples on us," he said, calling me by the irritating nickname he'd come up with when we were freshmen.

"Right, Jack?" he added.

But Jack ignored us, focused on his fiancée, Aviva, as she made her way down to the ice. The second she put a foot on the ice, Jack lifted her up, spinning her around and kissing her. There was a familiar burn in my chest. I'd admit this one to myself: jealousy. Not for Aviva, but for what they had. I was alone, and okay with being alone. I couldn't bring a woman into my life, not when it didn't belong to me. My world was too dark for love, and loving a woman would be a death sentence for her. I knew that, which was why I had fun with girls but never got serious with any of them. No, I was fine with being alone.

But sometimes, it fucking sucked.

Especially with Tovah Kaufman glaring down at me, like I'd committed some huge crime by my mere existence.

I smiled at her, giving her the full-on *Dr. Dimples*.

She rolled her eyes, shaking her head. But I could tell she was pissed.

Good. Her very existence pissed me off. It had since the first day I'd seen her, and it had rocked my very foundation. When seeing her woke up a monster inside me I'd never known existed, I'd had to confront a darkness, a violence, that was too much like my father's.

I hated that side of me.

But not as much as I hated her.

And she should at least feel a little of what I felt when I was in her presence.

Hey, she might take over my brain and haunt my dreams —including the ones where I woke up and immediately needed to jack off. But I'd won this round.

Judah whistled. "Oh, I see how it is."

"No." I shook my head, heading toward the locker room. "You really don't."

2

Isaac

I was this close to being free and clear of Tovah, when I felt a tug on the sleeve of my jersey. Even in the cold, I could smell her: lemon and sugar. I'd never been able to identify the exact brand of perfume she wore, even though I'd once embarrassingly spent an hour in a department store sniffing so many perfumes, I got a headache.

Stopping, I turned, making sure to loom over her.

"What do you want, little snoop?" I asked.

She glared, but flipped her hair like she didn't care about the insulting nickname, or the way it questioned her honesty and integrity. Close up, the pink color was even more distracting.

"You never responded about the interview."

Goddamn it, that fucking interview. She'd emailed me three times to schedule it, and I'd ignored every single email. I wasn't giving her an interview. That would require spending time with her, facing her, being surrounded by her sharp and sweet scent and having to look into those daring brown eyes. There was no fucking way.

I moved my eyes to the right, like I was trying to remember. "Didn't I? I'm sorry, I thought I responded. My bad. The answer is *no*."

I winked again, just to annoy her.

She shook her head, like I was a silly toddler. "Isaac, this interview is to help your team. Don't you need some good press? Why would you turn something like that down?"

I hated that she wasn't wrong. Last fall, Aviva had transferred to Reina to get revenge on our coach on her brother Asher's behalf. In the process, she and Jack had met, fought it out, and fallen in love—and our coach, who'd turned out to be an abusive asshole, died. The team had been shrouded in scandal ever since.

But I doubted that Tovah *really* wanted to help the team look better in the public's eye. No, I called bullshit.

"Doesn't the offer of 'good press' go against your journalistic ethics? I'm ashamed of you, Ms. Kaufman. I expected better. Maybe you're a hack *and* a snoop."

This time, *she* raised an eyebrow. This time, *she* smirked, like she'd caught me.

"So you *don't* want me to write a piece that features the Kings in a good light? Interesting. Is that on the record?" she asked.

Damn it.

"Why are you doing the interview, anyway? You're the editor. Shouldn't one of your underlings be doing the interview?"

Her cheeks colored. "The editor-in-chief wants me to do this one. Lucky for both of us."

Interesting. Once again, her blush distracted me. Captivated me. I wanted to see that color all over her. Particularly on her delectable heart-shaped, curvy ass as I delivered hard slap after slap to it. In fact, I'd turn *those* cheeks redder than her current blush. My cock stiffened from that thought alone. Fortunately, she wouldn't notice. Unfortunately, it hurt like hell in my cup.

My breathing had picked up. So had hers. I wasn't sure when it happened, but the two of us had moved in closer, narrowing the distance between our bodies so her big, juicy tits brushed against my chest.

Were her nipples hard?

Fuck, I wanted to bite them until she shrieked from the pain—and pleasure.

I shook it off, taking a step back. I'd never had these dark, almost violent inclinations with other girls. Sure, I'd played a bit—some light spanking here, some easy bondage there. But I'd never wanted to make a girl scream from pain as she struggled to get away from me, but I just pulled her closer and made her take whatever I fucking wanted to give her until she—

Holy fucking hell. Get your head out of her pussy, Isaac, I scolded myself, alarmed by my dark fantasies. I *didn't, couldn't* want her. She brought out my worst instincts, and not only sexual ones. I wanted to bruise her soft skin, spank her until she sobbed...and some part of me wanted to protect her from harm from anyone *but* me.

"Tovah Kaufman," I mused. "What is it about you that makes me fantasize about doing such fucked up things?"

"Oh, Isaac," she batted her eyes at me. "Because I'm the only one who sees the real you—and that scares you."

I stilled. "And why do you think there's a 'real me?'"

"Because I know what it's like to have to hide who you really are," she murmured, like she didn't even realize she was saying it, so lost in the daze of this intense...energy between us.

Her soft brown eyes had darkened, her breathing accelerated. Was she fantasizing about me, too? No way. Tovah Kaufman wasn't a prude, but there was no way she'd want it as rough as I wanted to give it to her.

Before I could entertain that intriguing, terrifying thought further, a throat cleared.

Glancing over, I spotted Coach Philip. He'd replaced our former coach, Joshua Jensen, after he'd died. From what I knew, Coach Philip had coached for Harvard before coming here and was considered the best hockey coach in the NCAA. I wasn't sure how much Reina had paid him to convince him to leave Cambridge, Massachusetts for Gehenom, New York, but it had to have been a fortune. He seemed like a good guy—if a hardass. He pushed us harder in practice than our former coach had, and didn't take any shit. He'd also enforced a "no partying before game day" rule, which pissed off some of the guys. But not me. I wasn't afraid of a little hard work, not if it meant we won the Frozen Four and I could prove to myself that I was meant for hockey. That I was meant for the lights of the arena, not my father's darkness.

The second you graduate, your life belongs to this family, my father sneered in my head.

I shoved the dark thoughts about my future away, focusing on the present.

"Hi, Coach," I greeted with a charming smile.

"Jones. Ms. Kaufman," he greeted both of us, surprising me that not only did he know Tovah's name already, but that he'd said it with such respect. Yeah, she *was* Reina's sports editor, but he hadn't been here long enough to be familiar with her. Regardless, hearing her name in his mouth, even her last name, even with only respect and no innuendo, pissed me the fuck off. I was the only one who got to call her Ms. Kaufman, even if I only said it to annoy her.

My hands tightened into fists, and I had to force myself to relax them.

"Ms. Kaufman, is there something you needed?" he asked.

Tovah exhaled slowly, turning to look at Coach. "I was asking *Mr. Jones* if he was able to finally find time in his schedule to be interviewed for a feature on the Kings."

"And I was giving her some helpful advice on her approach," I added cheerfully.

"Hmm," Coach Philip said. To me, he barked, "Jones, locker room."

Fuck. He must have seen through me. I was about to be reamed out, and it was completely *Ms. Kaufman's* fucking fault.

Pissed, I leaned down and whispered in her ear, "You're getting nothing from me, little *snoop.*"

This time, the insult must have hit, because her face went white, and her eyes narrowed. I should've felt satisfied, but there was just a sick, angry feeling in my chest. Because I wanted to give her something—my cock shoved down her throat, in her pussy, or so far up her ass she'd feel me forever...

With that fucked-up image haunting me as much as Tovah did, I followed Coach Philip into the locker room, where the rest of the team waited. Multiple players slapped me on the shoulder, congratulating me on the winning shot. My friends watched me, Judah smirking and Levi staring like he could read my every thought. When I joined them at my locker, Jack looked like he was about to say something, opening his mouth before shaking his head.

"What?" I snapped.

"That," he said. "This surly, sullen shit isn't like you."

"Girl trouble," Judah offered.

"Nah," I said, forcing an easy smile.

Before they could push me further, Coach interrupted once again.

"Good game, all. You worked together as a team, which is what we need, especially in the face of this increased scrutiny. For those of you who are juniors and seniors, this means that scouts are going to be extra critical. Anything *any* of us can do to re-establish the team in a good light will benefit the team and your teammates." He looked at me meaningfully.

Shit. Even though I would never get to play hockey professionally—my father had seen to that when we made our deal —I still wanted my team and friends to get the futures they deserved.

"Alright." Coach cleared his throat. "Feldman, the press are waiting for you. Jones, my office."

"What's that about?" Judah asked.

I shrugged. "Maybe he wants to congratulate me on a good game," I said, forcing a laugh and a grin.

But my gut sank as I followed Coach Philip into what was now his office. All traces of Coach Jensen were gone, like he'd never existed, which was for the best. The office was stark, except for a few photos on the wall of our new coach with his arm around a man and two young boys.

He watched me, like he expected me to be some homophobic douchebag. "Problem?"

"Absolutely not, sir. Nice looking family."

He made a *hmph* sound, but my response must have satisfied him because he changed the subject.

"Jones, why don't you want to do that interview?"

Curious, and a little skeptical, I asked him, "How do you even know who Tovah is?" He'd only been on campus for a couple months.

He smiled. "My husband is a professor in the journalism department. Tovah is one of his students, and he always speaks very highly of her." He cleared his throat. "Now, why don't you want to do that interview?"

I looked away, wracking my brain for a good excuse. *Because if I spend even a second alone with the little snoop, we're both going to end the interview bare assed with me pumping between her insanely hot thick thighs* wouldn't go over well. *Because I hate the rude, nosy bitch for no real reason beyond the fact that she fucks with my head and equilibrium, so I refuse to give her the upper hand* also wouldn't fly.

I settled on, "I don't like interviews, sir."

He snorted. "Jones, even with Feldman as captain, everyone knows you're the real face of the team. You've done interviews in the past. You'll do this one, too. Like I said, the team needs a new narrative, and it's your job to create it. Use that easy charm and confidence and answer her questions truthfully."

I raised an eyebrow. "And if she asks questions that, if I answer honestly, put the team in a bad light?"

She would. There was no doubt that Tovah, clever as she was, had hard hitting questions ready that most guys would stumble over.

"Then you answer them the best you can, while making sure to present the team well and distance us as much as you can from your former coach."

"And if I say no?" I asked, already knowing the answer.

"Then you're benched for the rest of the season," he said. "It would be a damn shame. We need you. But I'm not going to let whatever personal issues you have with Ms. Kaufman keep this team from getting back its good standing in the league."

"I don't have any personal issues with Tovah," I said.

He raised an eyebrow. "Then this should be easy. Right?"

"Right," I muttered.

"Alright. Good game, again, Jones. You're a solid player and teammate, and it's going to mean a great future in hockey for you."

The praise slightly softened the blow, but his reference to my future was rubbing salt on an open, secret wound. Because I wouldn't be playing hockey after college. The invisible noose around my neck pulled tighter.

Time to go face the little snoop and let her know she'd won the battle, even though I'd win the war.

Whatever it took.

3

Tovah

God, he was *such* an asshole.

I stood outside the locker room door that Isaac had slammed in my face, glowering with frustration and helplessness. I hated feeling helpless, and Isaac always made me feel that way. He reminded me of the past, and the ways I couldn't protect my mother and me from the villains in the shadows. Equally bad—or worse—he made me feel physically helpless, because I was so intensely attracted to him. I was like that Pablo Neruda poem, except toxic instead of romantic. Everything in my body wanted his body, even though I hated him and loathed his family more.

I guess no matter what you do, you can't get rid of a childhood crush.

Even if your childhood crush—the first and only boy you ever thought you loved—didn't remember you.

"That didn't go over so well," Aviva, my best friend,

commented beside me. She brushed her brown curly hair out of her face, the light catching on her engagement ring.

I bit my cheek.

I was *not* jealous. I was happy for her, even if I still didn't trust her fiancé.

Okay, fine. A good journalist was honest, so I would be, too.

I wasn't jealous...but sometimes, late at night, I wondered what it would be like to be able to belong to someone else.

I never would be free to love someone and have them love me. Not when I had so many secrets to hide. Not when life had taught me that no one could protect you but you.

But when the nondescript dream lover's face I imagined turned into Isaac Jones' obnoxiously attractive one—with his dark, wavy hair a weaker woman would want to run her hands through; strong, sharp jaw, and high, sculpted cheekbones that would make *anyone* swoon, and piercing brown eyes that promised retribution in a way that made my thighs clench—I stuffed my head into my pillow and screamed. Not to mention his towering height, broad shoulders, and abs upon abs upon abs...

Stop it, Tovah.

"I think it went fine," I said, shrugging and tossing my curly hair. This month, it was a bright hot millennial pink. Everyone thought I was some rebel, but I dyed my hair to keep those from my past from finding me and exacting their revenge.

It was being-in-hiding 101. Most people would choose a basic, natural hair color, figuring that they wouldn't stick out and therefore no one would notice them. But I knew better: sometimes hiding in plain sight was the best approach. I changed my hair color regularly, opting for big, bold, sometimes neon colors, with the rationale that no one would look at a girl with bright pink or green hair and think, "Oh, she must be hiding from the mafia."

Besides, I liked it. It was fun. It made me feel like I at least had a little control over my life.

Aviva shook her head lovingly, seeing right through my denial. She knew I was attracted to Isaac.

"You know, if you showed up wearing one of the many jerseys you have of his, he might be more willing to give you the interview. You'd look real cute with JONES written across your back, don't you think?"

"Stop matchmaking," I growled, even as I could feel my entire face go pink, matching my hair. "It's never going to happen."

Aviva didn't know *why* Isaac and I would never happen. It wasn't only that he hated me—I assumed because he didn't trust journalists, given his family's notoriety.

I knew why I hated him, though. Or why I was supposed to.

Even though Isaac had forgotten me, I'd grown up near him. I'd always had a crush on the dark-haired little boy with the dimples, who was kind to everyone, including me, even though my mom—who didn't trust his family—made me promise to never tell him my name. The crush was one from afar, for the most part: He was the boy prince, heir to his family's criminal Brooklyn dynasty. And I was just the lowly maid's daughter.

That was, until his father's closest friend and second-in-command decided to marry my mom when I was six, raising us up from the lowly "help" to...well, still the help but less lowly. Mark Berner had seemed like the perfect stepfather...

at first. It didn't matter that I was no longer the maid's daughter: my mom refused to let me tell Isaac who I was. She didn't trust the Silvers or the people who worked for them, not even Mark—and she was right not to.

It didn't take long before fists started flying, and my mom started wearing long sleeves and cover up. Even at six, even though she'd tried to hide what was going on from me, *I knew*. I knew what the crying and begging at night meant, and why she'd become so timid and would tremble as soon as he got home from whatever violent work he did for Abe Silver.

My mom did her best to protect me, until she couldn't anymore. Until the abuse got worse and worse. Until he started threatening to kill us.

And that's when she—when *we*—took drastic measures to make sure he couldn't hurt either of us anymore. That's when we changed our last names and went on the run.

Before we'd left, there'd been Isaac. We'd only played together once or twice, only spoken a few times, but I never forgot any of them—especially the last.

I promise to protect you, bashert, as long as you promise to always be here.

I promise, Isaac.

Then why won't you tell me your name?

Because I like when you call me your soulmate.

I shook my head. That had been a long time ago. I'd learned quickly that Isaac was a Silver through and through. The Silvers were our enemy, chasing us for so long we'd never be free.

But Isaac? If I could corner him, and get him to confess to his father's crimes, I'd finally have the evidence to get Abe Silver put away for good, destroy their dynasty...and my mom and I would finally, *finally*, be free. I knew it wouldn't be easy, that Isaac had been trained by his family to keep their secrets close to the chest. But I had an ace up my sleeve —a good one.

"Tovah?" Aviva placed a hand on my arm, looking concerned. "What did I say? Where'd you go? You had that million-miles-away look on your face again."

A million miles and fifteen years. I cleared my throat.

"Just planning out the interview," I said brightly.

"Riiiiiight," Aviva said. "I'm onto you, Tovah Kaufman. You're hiding something, and I'm going to find out what it is."

I laughed, like I had no idea what she was talking about. I hated lying to my best friend, but she couldn't know the truth. She couldn't know what my mom and I had done; she couldn't even know my real last name. Not only would she hate me for it, knowing would get her killed. She was the only real friend I had. I refused to be the reason for her death, even if that meant I had to hide the truth from her.

At that moment, the door to the locker room opened, the team filing out in regular clothes. Jack nodded at me, before turning his attention to Aviva.

"Wife," he said.

"We're not married yet," she protested, laughing.

"Don't care," Jack said, bending down and scooping Aviva up in his arms like a bride and carrying her down the hall and out of sight.

Leaving Isaac standing there with a glower on his face, holding two signed jerseys with JONES, 37 on them. A jersey I had three of in my closet, because I hadn't been able to kick that crush, no matter how much I tried.

He started to speak, when a little kid came running down the hallway, tugging a pretty, embarrassed-looking blonde woman behind him. I recognized them; Isaac had talked to them after the game. Beaming, glower gone, Isaac sauntered over to them. He bent down, handing one jersey to the little kid, who immediately and eagerly pulled it over his head. It was so big on him, it practically hit his ankles, and the sleeves hit the floor. Kneeling, Isaac patiently rolled up the sleeves on the jersey until the tips of the kid's fingers reappeared.

Slowly rising to his feet, he handed the second one to the kid's mother, who blushed.

"For you," Isaac said.

"Oh, you really didn't have to," she said, tucking a piece of golden hair behind her ear. She looked like a fairy tale princess—unlike me. I doubted that fairy tale princesses had pink hair and big curvy asses. I didn't have an issue with my appearance, usually, but when Isaac quickly glanced over at me, shook his head, and leaned in to whisper something in her ear, my stomach dropped.

That's what he liked, right? Petite blondes?

Tovah, stop. I scolded myself. *You hate him, remember? Who cares who his next conquest is?*

But I couldn't help but watch as Isaac handed her his phone and she typed on it, probably giving him her number. Then, he bent down one more time to the little kid and gave him a high-five, handshake, and hug, making the kid squeal before he and his mom headed back down the hall.

I shook my head. Isaac Jones might be a good guy charmer, but Isaac Silver had a hidden dark side. If only the rest of the world knew.

I squared my shoulders. I was going to make sure they did.

He approached me.

"Well, little snoop, seems like you're going to get your way," he drawled.

My stomach dropped down to my toes. "What do you mean?" I hated that my voice trembled, hated that I was afraid.

"Coach Philip said I have to do the interview. Something about the team needing good press and knowing you'll treat us with respect." He snorted. "I don't believe for a second you'll give us an ounce of respect, but I'm nothing if not a team player."

The fear receded, leaving space for almost incredulous triumph. Was I really going to be able to do this? Get time alone with Isaac "Jones"? Reveal that I knew he was Isaac Silver—as well as everything else I knew about him and his team? Blackmail him into giving up his family's secrets to protect his team and his own personal interests?

Trying to school my face and hide my excitement, I nodded. "Your coach is right. I'm nothing if not respectful... you just refuse to see it."

"Respectful, huh?" he murmured, setting off violent butterflies in my stomach. A dark, secretive look came to his eyes, but he quickly hid it before I could try to read what it might mean.

Clearing my throat, I offered him what was hopefully a white flag of a smile. I needed to trick him, get him to lower his suspicions so he'd follow through on meeting up with me.

"Tomorrow night at the Stacks? I won't bite, I promise," I offered.

He leaned down, whispering in my ear, like he had with the little kid's mom, his lips so close to my sensitive skin it sent shivers down my spine.

"No, but I might," he practically growled, shocking me down to my core. "And if I do, I'll make sure it hurts."

He straightened. The dark devil was gone and the golden god was back.

"See you tomorrow, Tovah," he said cheerfully, whistling down the hallway as I tried to calm my pounding heart.

If he meant what I thought he meant, I was going to have to be the smartest, cleverest, and bravest I'd ever been.

Or I was in deep, deep shit.

4

Tovah

I was on my way back to my apartment, desperate to take a freezing shower before getting into bed and screaming into my pillow, when my phone buzzed with a text.

> Meet me at my apartment. I have the info you need.

"Oh my god," I said in my car, excited and afraid, as I made a U-turn and headed back the direction I'd come in. If this was the evidence I needed to blackmail Isaac, I'd kiss my source, even though Sebastian and I weren't remotely interested in each other.

Reaching the fancy apartment building that only the wealthiest Reina students' parents could afford, I found a guest spot and parked. I shook my head as I got out of my car and locked it. Compared to all the nice, expensive cars that surrounded it, my car looked like a trash heap. There was no reason to lock it; no one was going to steal it. Still, old habits die hard, and I never, ever risked that one of Abe Silver's "employees" could be waiting in my backseat. It was unfortunately more than possible.

Walking down the sidewalk to the front of the building, the back of my neck tingled, like someone was watching. I pivoted around, scanning the street once, twice, three times. There was no one and nothing there besides the already parked cars.

"Tovah," Sebastian said in the shadows, making me practically jump out of my skin.

"You scared me!" I gasped.

He shook his head, a small smile playing across his lips. "Sorry. I wanted to wait outside for you to make sure you were safe."

I shivered, still feeling like there were eyes on me. "I appreciate that."

Glancing behind him, he wrapped an arm around my shoulder and guided me inside his building.

"Did you see someone?" I asked, still on alert.

"No, but you can never be too careful," he said.

Sebastian should know. He was in a secret society on campus, not to mention connected to the Gold dynasty—the Silver crime organization's biggest enemy. He had a lot to watch out for.

I finally relaxed when we reached his huge, modern apartment and he locked the door.

I took a seat on a bar stool in the kitchen.

"Want anything?" he asked.

"Water," I said, realizing how thirsty I was. But then the stress of thinking I was being followed and spending time with Isaac "Jones" would do that to a girl.

Nodding, he grabbed a bottle out of the fridge, handing

it to me. I gulped greedily, before capping the bottle and asking, "So what do you have for me?"

He smiled slowly, teeth flashing like a shark. "Video footage of one of the Kings dealing Vice and Vixen at a party. It's old, from the beginning of the semester, but it's solid."

My throat tightened in anticipation. Vice and Vixen were two black market sex drugs, one for men, and one for women. They didn't work the same, but both drove the people who took it into sexual frenzies. For guys, it was like an aphrodisiac—they were fully aware of what was happening, just hard and horny. For girls, it was glorified roofies—lost in a sexual daze, they had no sense of what was going on.

I'd had a hunch that the hockey team participated in Vice and Vixen's distribution, based on some things Aviva had said, but I didn't have *proof*.

Until now.

"Is there any evidence that Isaac's involved?"

My stomach hurt. I needed Isaac to be involved to blackmail him, but I didn't *want* him to be—because I hated what that might say about his character.

"Silver?" Sebastian scowled. He knew Isaac's true identity. "There's no footage of him dealing, but one of the guys in Fire and Hail was a dealer and can testify to working with Isaac Silver and Jack Feldman last year."

Disappointment filled me. That wasn't enough. "Will he testify?" I asked.

Sebastian nodded. "I have a recording of his statement."

He handed me his phone, and I watched the video, excitement bubbling within me. *This was it.* This was exactly what I needed. Proof that would destroy Isaac and Jack's future hockey careers, as well as their team's. For a moment, guilt raised her timid head: Messing up Jack's hockey career would hurt Aviva, too.

As if he sensed my hesitation, Sebastian reminded me, "What's more important, that Feldman and Silver get to go to the NHL, or that your mom gets to be safe...and you get to be free of this bullshit?"

As if she'd sensed him talking about it, my phone flashed with an incoming call from "LOML" (love of my life). It was both true—I loved my mother most in the world and owed her everything—and a way to keep her identity hidden. Aside from Sebastian, everyone thought Hana Lewis was dead...and that Tovah Kaufman was an orphan.

"Mom?" I said. "What's wrong?"

She never called unless it was an emergency.

"I don't want you to panic, honey," she began, of course making me immediately panic. "There was a black Escalade outside of work yesterday. Now, I work at a big hotel, so of course there's going to be an Escalade every once in a while." She laughed, but it sounded forced. "I'm sure it's nothing, but I just want you to be careful."

Her voice broke at the last. My mother was as tired of running as I was. It had been a fight to convince her it was okay for me to go to Reina U—and she didn't know that there was a Silver on campus.

The Silver. The most dangerous one, the primal wolf in a sheep's designer clothing.

Isaac.

"Tovahleh," she started, using the diminutive of my name. "I think it's time for you to leave Reina and come back to California. It's warm, and you can take online journalism classes..." she trailed off, knowing what I'd say.

"No, Mom," I interrupted.

"Honey, I know becoming a journalist is your dream, but

my dream is that you're safe. I'm worried for you. For both of us."

I sighed, but kept my voice steady. "No, Mom. I'm not leaving. I'm an adult now, and I need to see this through."

"See what through?" Her suspicion and worry came through the phone.

Shit. That gave too much away. "College," I said.

She sighed. "You've always been so stubborn. Please, think about it."

"I will," I lied. "Be careful, okay? Make sure no one's tailing you on your way home."

She laughed shakily. "I know, honey. I taught you, remember?"

Oh, I remembered. The long, dark, terrifying drives on highways, trading in one shit car for another, leaning on old friends for new identities, always on the run. It wasn't until we got to California when I was in high school that it seemed like the Silvers had forgotten about us, but I always watched over my shoulder.

I liked LA, and I knew my mom loved it. She'd even felt safe enough to send me to summer camp as a scholarship student, which was where I'd met Aviva. She made some friends. Settled in.

But we were living on borrowed time.

And now it was my turn to do everything in my power to make sure my mom never had to run again. That we were safe, and I could live out my dreams as a journalist who traveled the world, and she could discover hers, whatever they might be.

"I love you," I told her, and after she said the same back to me, I hung up, sliding my phone into my jeans pocket and rubbing the back of my neck.

"Assuming that was Hana," Sebastian said.

"Yes," I said. "Can you send me the video?"

He seemed concerned. "You know it's a major risk."

I nodded. It *was* a risk, but I had no other option than to trust my plan and my ability to think on my feet.

He sighed, relieved. "Good. I'll watch out for you the best I can, and so will the rest of Fire and Hail." That shark-like smile reappeared. "We're going to finally take those assholes down, aren't we?"

"We are." Although, in reality, *I* was. But I didn't tell him that.

From my memories, and from all the investigating I'd done, I knew Isaac loathed his father. He was only involved in the Vice and Vixen distribution game because he had to be. His team came first, always. So, if he had to choose between Abe and the Kings, he'd choose the Kings. I'd bet my life on it.

This was my only option. I squared my shoulders, took a deep breath, and committed myself to my plan. Based on my mom's call, our time was running out.

I needed this to work.

Our lives depended on it.

5

Isaac

I seethed as I watched Sebastian Greene walk Tovah to her car before kissing her on the forehead. Sebastian led Fire and Hail, a secret society at Reina. Rumor was they were into some truly fucked up shit. No one was supposed to know, but I knew everything that happened on this campus.

Why was she always visiting this dick?

Tovah leaned into him as he hugged her tightly, and I had to restrain myself from getting out of my 1986 restored Aston Martin Vantage and ripping the secret society nerd's arms off his body and punching his face in so he could never kiss any part of her, ever again.

Pulling away from him, Tovah opened the door to the driver's side. It made a high-pitched scratching sound, like it didn't want to open. Sebastian said something and she laughed, before getting in her car. I hated seeing her laugh. Hated knowing he was the one who put that joy on her face. Not that I ever wanted to make her happy.

Sebastian closed the door and waited for her to drive off before he headed back inside. As he walked past my car, I ducked down, grateful for the dark screened windows that made it possible for me to see out but impossible for anyone else to see in.

Once the douche was inside, I turned on the car but kept the lights off, slowly following Tovah as she made her way home. This had become a habit of mine for the past god knew how many months—tailing her, waiting in the shadows as she went up to someone's apartment, and then following her home so I know she made it there safely. I was stalking her, plain and simple, and although at first I had loathed myself for it, now it was a normal part of my life.

My phone buzzed, and my car's infotainment system read the text out loud to me. It was from me and my friend's group chat, which used to jokingly be titled the Core Four, but now was called "Core Four + 1" because Aviva's brother, Asher, had joined.

> Judah: Where are you, asshole?

> Judah: For once, there are too many girls to go around. We need Dr. Dimples to distract them, especially the ones that are trying to climb all over Jack before Aviva kills one of them and Jack helps her hide the body.

> Asher: My sister is not violent, you idiot.

> Levi: I'm the only one who gets to call him an idiot.

> Judah: Isaac, get your ass over here.

I dictated my text to the car.

Heartless Game

> Me: Can't. Busy.

> Judah: What the hell? What's gotten into you lately? You're all moody and pissy. Did you and Feldman switch places? What happened to the sunny fucker we all know and love?

> Levi: It's not what's gotten into him, it's who he hasn't been able to get himself into.

Levi was always too insightful for his own good. Both twins were, but at least Judah was funny about it.

> Judah: Ah, girl trouble.

> Judah: Well, a certain curvy pink-haired troublemaker isn't here, but I'm sure we could track her down and invite her...

I rolled my eyes as Tovah made a left down her street and I followed, responding.

> Me: No clue who you mean. And I'm the same sunny fucker I've always been.

> Judah: Then get your ass over here. I'm drowning in pussy and I need a life raft.

As Tovah found a parking spot on the street, I watched carefully, making sure no asshole tried to accost her. She needed to live somewhere safer. But it wasn't my business. I didn't give a shit. Really. For a moment I considered heading to the party once Tovah was inside and getting lost in warm, tight pussy in order to stop thinking about her.

But the truth—one I would take to my grave—was that I

hadn't been able to get it up for anyone but Tovah in fucking months. Yeah, I'd flirted with other girls, took them back to their home, even got them off—but it did nothing for me. I'd bide my time, be a gentleman, and then go home and fuck my fist, imagining it was Tovah's throat or cunt or ass, until I came all over myself like the pathetic dipshit I'd become.

So I ignored Judah. Ignored everything but Tovah pulling open the door to her apartment building, waiting until I saw the lights switch on in her bedroom before driving away.

She was safe. I was free for the night.

But as if I didn't have control of my own car, my own body, my own fucking *mind*, I found myself turning around and heading back to Sebastian's building.

I needed answers. And if that meant giving this asshole a glimpse of the monster buried within me, so be it.

It didn't take much to get into Sebastian's supposedly secure building—just a little flirting with two sorority girls who were on their way to a party. They immediately knew who I was, and when I said I was picking up a friend and hell yeah, I'd love to meet them later at the mixer at Kappa Alpha Theta, or whatever it was, they giggled and let me right in. Oh, and did they know which apartment Sebastian was in? He wasn't texting me back, the asshole. Probably in the shower. I showed off my dimples and without hesitating, they told me he lived in the penthouse.

Of course the fucker did. I couldn't talk, of course. This level of lux was something I'd grown up with. But I preferred my bedroom at the hockey house—and the house I owned situated between the edge of campus and the forest that surrounded it.

I knocked, twice.

"Coming," Sebastian called.

Idiot.

He pulled the door open...and I shoved him backward as I stepped into the apartment. It was modern and clean and lacked any personality, but I ignored the boring space and focused on the douchebag in front of me, his dark hair wet, his jaw locked, and his eyes pissed.

Too bad. I was pissed, too.

"Get the fuck out of my apartment, Jones," he spat.

"Nah." I grinned at him. "I think I'll stay for a while." I pretended to glance around. "Your daddy buy it for you?"

"I could ask you the same thing," he said, pinging an alarm in my head that he might know more than he should, but then he added, "Oh, please. You didn't get that Tag Heuer on your own," he said, nodding at my watch.

So he didn't know who my family really was. Of course he didn't.

I shrugged. "Sponsorships."

He shook his head. "Fucking jock. I don't know what the hell you're doing here, but I do think it's time for you to leave."

I didn't have time for this bullshit. "What was Tovah Kaufman doing here earlier?"

His eyes widened. Just for a second, but I caught it. "I know you're just a dumb jock, but even you know stalking is illegal," he drawled.

I raised one shoulder. "You didn't answer my question."

"And what if I tell you she was here for exactly the

reason you think she was?" He stretched, twisting his neck both ways before adding, "Gave me a real workout, too. Worth it."

A red haze filled my vision, and then I was on top of him, my hand around his throat, squeezing. And his face was turning the same color red.

Fuck.

What the fuck was wrong with me?

Catching myself before I killed the fucker in my jealous fury, I took a deep breath, released it, and forced my grip to loosen. The red haze began to clear, and as it did, the realization of what I'd done dawned upon me. I prided myself on being the only member of my family who hadn't killed someone—even though I'd been exposed to so much violence. But here I was, Isaac Jones, Good Guy, choking the fuck out of a guy for insinuating he'd fucked the woman I hated. I'd completely snapped. Just because I thought someone had touched a girl who wasn't even mine.

The monster within was winning.

Her fault.

Sebastian gasped, but I didn't fully release him.

"Was that true? Did you touch her? Did you fuck her? Because if you did..." I began to tighten my grip again.

"And so what if I did?" he taunted on a cough. This asshole must have a death wish. "What, are you going to kill me? What happened to Isaac Jones, everyone's best friend? Has he been an unhinged, violent maniac this whole time? It'll be fun to leak it to all of Reina."

An unhinged, violent maniac.

Just like my father.

Feeling sick, I tried to release Sebastian's neck, to back away. But the word "leak" made me think of newspapers, which made me think of Tovah, so I maintained my grip on his neck.

"Answer the question, or you won't be around to leak anything," I threatened, my voice low and menacing.

Wheezing, Sebastian said, "No, man, I didn't fuck her. She's like a sister to me."

Before I could respond, Sebastian's phone started buzzing in his pocket. Still gripping his neck, I reached into his jeans and pulled it out.

A name flashed on the screen.

Tovah L. calling.

L?

Why had he put L as her last initial?

Because I know what it's like to have to hide who you really are. She'd said those words to me at the arena earlier, but I'd been too distracted by thoughts of fucking her into the ground to really consider them.

What was she hiding?

"What's the L for?" I asked him, voice thick.

"What do you mean?"

I tightened my grip, letting the monster show in my eyes. "Tovah *L*. What is the L for, Sebastian?"

He swallowed beneath my hand but didn't speak.

"Here's how this is going to work," I said. "You're going to stop doing this bullshit prevarication thing you think you're so good at. Instead, you're going to tell me exactly why she's listed that way in your phone, or I'm going to fabricate evidence that *you* are dealing Vice and Vixen—believe me, I can. And then there goes your entire future. Got me?"

"You think I'll give her up to you?" he glared at me.

The fact that he was protecting her pissed me off even more. No one was getting between Tovah and me. Certainly not this fucking nerd.

"No, but I think if you have to choose between her and your brotherhood, you'll choose your brotherhood. And so I'll up the ante: I'll make sure it looks like Fire and Hail is behind the Vice and Vixen distribution on campus, so that you and *every single one of your 'brothers'* winds up in prison. How does that sound? Knowing that you could've saved them, but you chose an outsider instead?"

Sebastian didn't speak for a moment, shutting his eyes.

When he opened them, and I saw the pain and guilt there, I knew I had him.

"Don't hurt her," he said.

Oh, I was going to hurt her. I was going to leave the kind of wounds that remained long after the scars faded away.

"You aren't in the position to make requests," I said instead, squeezing his throat again. "Now, tell me. Why 'Tovah L?'"

He coughed. "Tovah's last name isn't Kaufman. It's Lewis."

He watched my expression, like the last name was supposed to spark something. I kept my face blank, but my brain was spinning.

Tovah Lewis.

I knew all about fake last names. *I* had one, after all. I'd chosen "Jones" because I wanted no association to my crime lord of a father, or the "organization" I was going to inherit when I graduated Reina.

But what was Tovah hiding? Who was Tovah Lewis?

I released him. He leaned over, gasping.

"Don't. Hurt. Her," he repeated.

"Don't you fucking get near Tovah again," I told him. "Whatever it was you *are* doing with her—it ends now. Or I really will ruin you and your brotherhood. Don't test me,

Sebastian. As far as you're concerned, Tovah *Lewis* no longer exists."

He glared at me. "Heard."

Exhaling slowly, I turned and slammed out of the penthouse. As I walked to the elevator, I grappled with everything I'd just learned. It was possible that Lewis was her dad's last name, and Kaufman was her mother's. But if that were the case, it wouldn't have been some big secret. Also, Aviva had once said that Tovah was an orphan, so it wouldn't make sense she used different last names.

I froze a step from the elevator.

Could Kaufman be her maiden name? Was Tovah *married*?

The red haze that had only just cleared reappeared in front of my eyes. It took every bit of willpower I had to keep myself from storming back into Sebastian's apartment and demanding more answers.

I didn't recognize myself.

I *wasn't* violent.

I *wasn't* ruthless.

I *wasn't* the man my father so badly wanted me to be.

I solved my issues rationally, peacefully. I was the mediator, not the instigator.

I'd managed to keep the monster inside locked away tight.

Until now.

Until Tovah *Lewis*. Whoever she was, whatever reason she had for pretending to have a different last name, she was like the trigger for the sleeper agent inside me. If I was wise, I'd stay far away from her.

The elevator was waiting for me when I pressed the button to call it, doors sliding open. I walked inside, leaning against its cool, metal wall as it descended to the ground floor and ejected me from this hell I'd volunteered for. This, here, was why I couldn't have Tovah. Or anyone. Feelings and passion like this turned men into monsters. I'd seen it happen with my father after my mother was murdered; and with countless other men like him when there was a woman involved. Not only did I know that bringing someone into my world meant death for them, but it would also mean death for me as well—the death of the man I'd always promised myself I would be.

No, I needed to stay as far away from the little snoop as possible.

Too bad she called to me like a siren to a sailor—right before he crashed his ship on the rocks.

I already had my phone out when I reached the ground floor, googling "Tovah Lewis."

There were a bunch of entries, but all of them were for much older women.

It was like she didn't exist.

Without hesitating, I texted my sister Liza.

> I need you to get some information for me.

She responded immediately.

> Dad said you won't return his calls. He wants you home for Shabbat dinner soon.

I couldn't even respond to that right now. I had no interest in seeing my father or hearing what he had to say, what new Faustian deal he had ready for me. I'd already agreed to oversee the distribution of Vice and Vixen with Jack, knowing it could jeopardize our entire team's futures. What was next, performance enhancing drugs? No fucking way. I was staying as far away from Brooklyn and the Silvers as I could, until I got dragged back to take up a role I dreaded.

I could feel that figurative noose growing tighter.

> I don't want to talk about dad. Can you help me get this info or not?

I'd clearly piqued her interest, because she responded.

> What do you need?

> To find out whoever Tovah Lewis is.

> On it. Is this some girl you're dating?

I snorted to myself as I walked out of the building and toward my car. I didn't want to date Tovah. I wanted to return to a time when I didn't even know she existed. Barring that, I wanted her on her knees in front of me, tears dragging makeup down her face as I shoved my cock so deep down her throat she couldn't breathe. Or on her hands and knees as I fucked her so deep, the little snoop forgot what it felt like when I wasn't inside her.

My silence clearly had answered the question for my sister, because she sent back.

> Just don't be stupid. But I'll look into her for you. Be good, little bro.

I rolled my eyes, smirking despite myself. Liza was only a year older than me, but she acted like she had all this life experience on me. I loved my brilliant sister, even if I wish she didn't take my father's side. But then again, she'd always wanted what I dreaded: to lead the family.

Getting in my car, I headed home. As I drove, I realized something that made me grin.

I might not know why Tovah was hiding her identity.

But I knew she *was*, which meant I finally had leverage over her. I didn't know what I planned to do with it yet, but the knowledge made me feel better than I had all night.

"Good luck, Tovah Lewis," I murmured to myself as I steered the car home. "You're going to fucking need it."

6

Tovah

The next night, I stared at myself in the mirror. My pink hair was curled into mermaid waves, my eyelids were painted a soft rose gold and lined with bronze liner, and my lips were painted in my favorite pink gloss. My cheeks were a soft pink, and not from blush—but there was nothing I could do about that.

I was wearing black leggings and a tight black button down that emphasized my chest and ass. And yeah, all the other bumps and swells society liked to shame people over having. "Plump," "fat," "plus-sized," "curvy," or whatever the hell they wanted to call me: it didn't matter. In my opinion, these extra curves added to my appeal.

Society could suck it.

I looked amazing. Like, hot as hell. Hotter than hell, even.

And I was disgusted with myself.

"Damn it," I told my reflection. "You're trying too hard, Tovah Kaufman. Why are you trying so hard?"

Kaufman wasn't actually my last name, but I'd trained myself to respond to it, so I answered to it—and only to it. Even when I was alone and talking to myself.

That didn't matter right now. What mattered was that I'd put in a ton of effort for a meeting with the last man in the world I wanted to find me attractive.

I pointed at myself in the mirror. "Liar."

Because I *was* lying.

Regardless, I brushed my hair to mess up the waves and curls, and put makeup remover on a cotton pad, rubbing at my eyes and lips until my face was bare.

Better.

Now he'd know I didn't care.

Even if I knew I did.

I turned to leave the bathroom and find something else to wear—maybe a hoodie and sweatpants, when I stopped in my tracks.

Why was I putting so much effort into *not* looking cute? What was I trying to prove? It was a Saturday night, and I was going out after the interview with my friend Lucy, so we could bitch about men together and dance our asses off. Was I really going to come all the way home to change when I could just meet her after the interview?

Glaring at my reflection, I pulled out the makeup I'd just taken off and the curling iron and started over from scratch. I would be late to the bar where we were having our meeting but not...that late. And the asshole could learn patience—it would be good for him.

The Stacks was the bar I worked at. It didn't open for another couple of hours, and I was the only one who was supposed to be there from now until opening time. I could have a private conversation with Isaac without anyone overhearing, in a mostly neutral location—but one where I was in control.

And, as my fallback plan: The Stacks' giant bouncer, Alex, lived above the bar. If things got...tricky with Isaac, I could always text him to come down. Isaac might be the big bad mafia prince, but Alex was 6'7" and weighed three hundred pounds—practically all muscle.

There. *Sorted.*

A half hour later, I was made up, hair done, a coat and scarf wrapped around me. It was a cold night, and I hoped my car didn't take forever to warm up.

My car did me one worse. When I got in and turned on the ignition, it sputtered a few times before giving up entirely.

"Fuck!"

I tried again, but now it refused to do anything.

Checking my phone, I groaned, realizing I was already five minutes late. I couldn't afford an Uber, and the next bus wouldn't come for thirty minutes.

Guess I was walking.

I didn't have Isaac's number to text him, and emailing to say I was running late just annoyed me, so I got out of my car and ran-walked the five blocks to the bar. Fortunately, I had been the captain of my high school's track team, and even though it had been a few years, I could still run.

When I arrived, it didn't matter that I'd put on makeup or done my hair. I was sweaty, my face was bright red because of the cold and physical effort, and who knew what the wind had done to my hair.

Pulling the door open, I found an annoyed Isaac leaning against the bar, typing on his phone.

He looked good. Black jeans, black long-sleeved shirt

that defined his pecs, arms, and abs lovingly, like it was a girlfriend—or the sculptor who'd created him.

When he looked up at me, he scowled, dimples hidden, dark hair falling in his darker brown eyes before he pushed it back.

"I'm sorry I'm late," I said, even though I hated apologizing. "Something distracted me."

Something like the mindfuck of wanting to look good for him and hating that I wanted to look good. Not to mention a dead car, but if he made a joke about me being poor, or worse, if I saw pity in his eyes, I'd have to scratch them out, and my nails weren't long enough for that.

Isaac looked me up and down. I fidgeted. Heat rose in my chest and my breathing went shallow as I realized he was checking me out and not even bothering to hide it.

"I'm sure it did," he murmured, and fuck it, I was going to scratch his eyes out anyway.

The insinuation was clear. There'd been a rumor last year that I got around, started by a vindictive former friend. At first, I'd hated the reputation I'd gotten, and all the cruelty that accompanied it. The stares and the whispering, all the times someone called me a slut behind my back or to my face. I'd come home from class with my face red from shouting at someone one too many times. Aviva and Lucy had threatened to kill "any other motherfucker who dares say one bad word about you."

Like most wounds, the pain from the rumors and slut-shaming faded, turning from a raw blister to a sore scar. It still hurt, and it was still complete and utter fucking bullshit that my sex life, real or fabricated, could create so much judgement. But there were benefits to people misjudging you. Just like with my changing hair color, no one would suspect the "girl who got around" to have deep, dark secrets.

Heartless Game

And it made it easier to meet up with my informants, too. No one questioned where I was going so late or what I was doing. The only person who knew that I actually was a virgin was Aviva, and that was fine with me.

So then why did it bother me that Isaac also thought I was a slut? Fuck him. I wasn't going to bother defending myself.

I crossed my arms.

"I agreed to this interview under the impression you'd be respectful of my time," he drawled, practically purring the word "respectful," his eyes lighting up.

Immediately, a wild, horrifying image presented itself to me: naked, arms tied behind my back, kneeling in front of him as he told me to be "respectful" as he unzipped his jeans and pulled out his—

I cut off the fantasy before it could continue, aware that I was blushing—again. Even worse: I was wet, my breathing was shallow, and my nipples hurt like they'd gone hard. I hated this man, and I hated how much I wanted him. It was the absolute worst.

The *worst*.

I sat next to him, ignoring the glass of beer he pushed toward me. I knew better than to drink anything someone offered to me that I didn't pour myself. Aviva had hammered that lesson into my head, and besides, with Vice and Vixen on campus, there was no way I would trust anyone with my drink—least of all him.

"You know," I said, clearing my throat, hating how husky it had gotten, "you come off as this easygoing charmer to everyone else. Why do I get this grumpy asshole whenever we talk?"

In response, the grumpy asshole grunted.

It was bullshit. I had real reasons to hate him, but he had

no reason to hate me. He didn't even fucking remember who I was.

But I knew who *he* was, and I was about to use it to my advantage and get the evidence I needed to save my mom and free myself from the cage of perpetual fear.

"See!" I said. "I don't know what I did to hurt you, Isaac, but—"

Before I could finish my sentence, he interrupted me. "So what's the content of this interview? You never sent me questions."

I slowly exhaled, trying to quiet and calm my pounding heart.

"I didn't want to give you a chance to figure out a lie," I said, watching his response.

He gave me almost nothing, face blank, eyes shuttered—except there was a small twitch in his cheek, just to the right of his left dimple.

A tell.

"What would I have to lie about?" he asked calmly, as if he hadn't given himself away.

Steeling myself for an intense reaction from him, I stated, "Why you're pretending your last name is Jones, for one."

My breath roared in my lungs while I stayed still and tried to pretend I hadn't just dropped a bomb on him. Under the table, I tapped on Alex's name on my phone, just in case.

He narrowed his eyes, and said slowly, the threat clear, "If you know my real last name, you know better than to threaten me, little snoop."

Little snoop. I hated the diminutive, the clear derision in it, the hatred.

I straightened, annoyed. "I don't know who you're calling little, Isaac *Sil*—"

Before I could finish saying his last name, his hand was on my mouth, shutting me up. His fingers dug into my cheek painfully, like he could control me. Control my words, my everything. Shock filled me at his touch, and the blatant violence in it. Had I been wrong about Isaac? Disastrously so?

But no fucking way would I let him shut me up. The reason I wanted to be a journalist wasn't only because I wanted to take his family down and free my own. It was because I had one calling in this life: speaking truth to power.

Growling low in my throat, I bit him, hard.

It didn't work. Still gripping my face with his big hand, he leaned forward, his dark eyes intent on mine. "You like to play rough, huh?"

I glared at him, enraged. I tried to bite him again, but was distracted when he dragged my chair closer to his with his free hand and then draped a casual arm over it, his hand closing around the back of my neck...

...and squeezing.

Like I was a pet, and he was my owner. Like he was in charge.

My body agreed, heat traveling from his hand on my neck down my spine before pooling at the small of my back just above my ass. I was already wet from my earlier fantasy, but his dominance did something to me—I got wetter.

Angry, frustrated, helpless, and turned on, I shuddered at his touch.

His voice lowered, the threat in it like a caress. "You might know my last name, but that doesn't come close to what I know about you."

And then his next words shot terror through me.

"That's right," he continued, staring at me with triumph.

"I know *your* secret. And while you revealing mine would be an...inconvenience at best, if I revealed yours, it would blow up your entire life, wouldn't it? I could take it to the police, to the dean...*even tell Aviva.*"

No. No, he couldn't know. There was no way. We'd buried our tracks, kept the past hidden. And if he really, truly, knew the truth of who I was, then why were we sitting here? Where were his father's men with guns, ready to kidnap and torture me to find out where my mother was? And why now?

I didn't even realize it, but I'd been jerking my head back and forth beneath his hand in denial of what was to come.

But I couldn't stop the inevitable. Especially when he said, "After all, if you know my real last name, it's helpful that I know yours...Tovah Lewis."

He knew.

He *knew.*

Oh god, I was dead. Worse, my mother was dead. I'd had a whole fucking plan, and he'd destroyed it in an instant.

Without a second thought, I typed *come down to the bar now!* to Alex and pressed send.

Unaware of what I'd just done, Isaac smiled, and the light in his eyes and bright white of his teeth petrified me. It was more terrifying when he finally released my mouth, only to tuck a wayward strand of hair behind my ear—the same ear he'd whispered into before. I shivered uncontrollably, fear—and desire—overwhelming my ability to think. To get out of this mess.

"Now, here's how this is going to go," he began.

But my inner rebel, the part of me that was sick of being controlled by outside forces, by his family—it wasn't about to let me be controlled by him. I'd been helpless almost my entire life, and I refused to be helpless anymore.

Shoving away from him in my chair, I stood, still trembling, but lifting my chin and calming my voice despite my fear.

"No, let me tell *you* how this is going to go, Isaac Silver. You may know my last name, but I know something bigger: You and the Kings are distributing Vice and Vixen for your father, aren't you? I have evidence that you're in charge of the entire set up here at Reina, and the nearby schools like Tabb, as well as where it's coming from."

"And what's your proof?" he asked calmly, but his right cheek twitched again.

Pulling up the video, I pressed play on my phone and showed it to him. He watched until the video ended. Then he looked up at me, and this time, he couldn't school his expression. Shock, rage—and sheer hatred shone in his gorgeous dark brown eyes, revealing the monster underneath.

The monster I'd known was there all along.

Triumphant, I ignored the threat in them, too excited about my checkmate in the game we were playing.

"Here's the deal," I said. "Either you give me the evidence to put your father away for life, or I'll expose you and the team for dealing in date rape drugs. You're under enough scrutiny as it is, this will ruin all of your futures. No hockey career for you—or for any of them. What do you think's going to happen to your teammates, to the rest of the Core Four then?" Sweetening up my voice, I added, "It's an easy choice, Isaac. I know how you feel about your father. I know how you feel about your team. Just give me what I need…and all of this goes away."

I exhaled, my heart racing from exhilaration, anticipation, and yes, underlying fear. But my mother's terrified face flashed in my mind. I was doing this for *her*.

Slowly, Isaac rose to his feet, towering above me. He stepped forward, and then again. I held my ground, even though I had to crane my head back to look at him. He wasn't going to intimidate me, not this time. I was done with being intimidated by the Silvers.

He was so close we were breathing the same air, our legs touching, my chest brushing his six pack and sending sparks through my body.

"You've done your homework, haven't you, little snoop," he mused, and there was a hint of admiration in his voice. "Unfortunately, you got two things wrong. First, that video's old: the team isn't in the Vice and Vixen game anymore. We learned the harm it can do." He blinked, and the monster disappeared for a moment, leaving behind a man filled with regret.

But then he blinked again, and the monster was back. "Second, I'll do anything for my family—and my team. *Anything.* You may think you've won, you may even think this is mutually assured destruction, but one phone call and you're dead. And then how are you going to expose any of this? Not only that, I will make sure anyone you love, anyone you have left in the world...they're dead, too."

My heart froze.

"You wouldn't," I said. "Even you're not that big of a monster."

He leaned down, his lips almost on mine. I caught his scent: earthy and dark, with a hint of something fresh and surprising. Something that always stuck with me, long after he was gone.

"You bring out the monster in me," he said. "And he's thirsty for blood—yours."

7

Isaac

I was bluffing, of course. I knew her last name, knew she had some reason she wanted to destroy my family. My sister had gotten me little to nothing about Tovah Lewis. There *had* been a police APB out on someone with the same name once, but whatever the case had been, it went dead. I'd thrown the threat out there as a test. Based on her reaction, I was onto something.

Not to mention, if she knew who my father was, she knew I wasn't bluffing. I could get her killed. And maybe I should. I meant what I said: I'd do anything to protect my family, and I considered my team my family, too. I might hate my father, but I had siblings to protect, cousins I cared about. If my father fell, then so did the entire dynasty, leaving them easy prey for the vultures who would come. Tovah had revealed herself as a true threat, and as my father always said, threats had to be put down.

No.

Everything in my body rejected the idea of a world

without her in it. I loathed that I felt that way, but it was the truth. Death wasn't what I wanted for the fucking snoop. Not when she brought out the violence I tried to hide from. Not when I wanted her so badly I couldn't think about anything else except hockey—and sometimes, not even that. So, I was going to make her life hell and finally get what I wanted from her. Extract my pound of flesh, in a way that would make my cock happy and finally end this obsession for good. When I was done with Tovah Lewis, she'd be nothing more than a broken shell. And I'd be free, no longer haunted by her face, her voice, her goddamned scent.

Oh, this was going to be *fun.*

Placing a heavy hand on her delicate, rounded shoulder, I began to push down firmly. I wanted her on her knees, but for now, forcing her to sit back down in her chair would do. Especially because, short as she was, it put her at nose level with my cock, and with her gazing up at me with that wild fear and even more wild defiance, it made it easy to imagine her in this position for other reasons.

My cock picked up on that, straining in my jeans like it could pop through the zipper and make its way into her hot mouth.

All in due time.

"Like I said earlier, here's how this is going to go. First, you're moving in with me. Can't risk you trying to publish the story."

"I'm not moving into the hockey house," she protested. "I have no interest in being surrounded by you fucking slobs, partying all the time, and—"

Offended, I put out a hand. "I don't know who you're calling a fucking slob, but we keep things clean. We have a maid."

"Of course you do," she scoffed.

"Careful, or I'll put you in a maid costume and nothing else. Make you clean my floors with your tongue," I threatened.

Fuck. The image of her on her knees with her ass exposed, bent over as she cleaned what was going to be my cum off those floors made my cock hurt. Too bad the bar was opening soon, or I'd make that fantasy a reality.

Holy fuck, what was wrong with me? I was as bad as Jack had been with Aviva. I knew better than this, couldn't be this person. But Tovah's lemon and sugar scent and big brown eyes were turning me into him, no matter how hard I fought it.

Shoving that thought away, I continued. "I have my own house on the edge of campus; you'll live there with me, so I can keep an eye on you. You don't go anywhere without me knowing, or without me or one of my teammates accompanying you."

"But I have class! And newspaper meetings!"

"Should've thought of that before you tried to blackmail me," I said smoothly.

She glared. "Aren't you doing the same thing to me?"

I winked, loving every second of this. "Yes. But I do it better."

She growled. It was cute.

"And what, people are just going to believe we're happy to be around each other that much? All of Reina knows we hate each other."

I moved in even closer. I could feel her breath against my jeans.

Fuuuuuuuck. Could she tell how hard I was getting?

Forcing myself to focus, I bent down, sliding my thumb under her chin and lifting it so she had to look directly at me. "Then you better hope you're a good fucking actress, because everyone is going to have to buy that you're happy with our new...arrangement."

Her eyes widened. "I'm not going to pretend we're dating."

I scoffed, ignoring the way her rejection sliced into me. "Who said anything about dating? You wouldn't be the first girl willing to be my *toy*."

Of course I'd never forced another girl to live with me or tracked her every move. But Tovah didn't challenge me on that point.

"Is that all?" she practically spat.

I cleared my throat. This last part...I hated myself for what I was about to say, but the anticipation outweighed the realization that I was about to act like a complete animal.

But then, maybe it was time to let the beast out if its cage.

"Finally, you're mine. However I want you, for however long I want you for. I say jump naked, you say, 'yes sir, how high?' I say get on your knees...well, you know the rest. And you won't go near another man when you're with me. I don't care about your history, or whoever else you're seeing. I. Don't. Share."

"That's not what I heard," she countered, sickly sweet in her helpless anger.

"Let me rephrase then. I. Don't. Share. *You*. Got it?"

"I got that you've legitimately lost your mind if you think I'll go through with any of this," she said, rolling her eyes. But she licked her pink lips, chest heaving. She may hate the attraction, but like me, she couldn't help herself.

"Or I can call my father right now," I said. "How does that sound?"

She glared. "Hockey players. Thinking you own everything and anyone and can get away with whatever you want. You are an entitled piece of shit, and I hate you."

That was fine with me. "I don't particularly like you either."

She seemed to consider something, and her eyes lit up. I didn't know what had just occurred to her, but I didn't like it, whatever it was.

"Fine," she said. "I'll come home with you, stay with you, let you and your dumb friends escort me around campus like my own personal entourage. Pretend I like you." She flipped her hair. "But I'm not sleeping with you."

"Who said anything about sleeping?" I made sure to look her up and down.

"I mean it, Isaac. I am *not* fucking you."

That made me laugh.

"We'll see about that," I said. Her nipples were hard, and it wasn't cold in the bar. Tovah Kaufman—no, Tovah Lewis—wanted me, badly.

She started to argue with me, when the door to the bar swung open.

Without even thinking about it, I turned around, shoving her behind my back like I was her shield from whatever harm might be coming our way.

But it was only the bar's bouncer, Alec or Alex or something.

Fuck. There wasn't even a real threat and the first thing I'd done was protect her. Which was bullshit, since she wanted to destroy me.

The giant bouncer filled the doorway, his concerned eyes on Tovah.

"Everything okay?" he asked her, before looking at me and doing a confused double take.

"Jones? What's up, man? Great game last night." To Tovah, he said, "I thought something was wrong."

Why would he ...

...she was clutching her phone in her hand.

The clever journalist must have texted for reinforcements when I'd threatened her. I couldn't help admiring her for her fast thinking, even if part of me wanted to throttle her for getting someone to interrupt us just as things were getting good.

Fortunately, Alec/Alex knew Isaac Jones, Good Guy, and had no reason to think I would hurt Tovah, even if she had asked the bouncer to come.

"We're good," I said, flashing him an easy grin. "Tovah wanted to see if you could cover for her so she could ditch work and leave with me."

"He's never going to believe you," Tovah hissed from behind me. "There's no way I'd ditch work, much less to spend time with *you*."

Ouch. "He will if you sell it," I murmured back. "And it's in your best interest to sell it, Tovah. Even better if you sell *us*."

"You want to ditch work and go hang out with Jones? I thought you two hated each other..." Alec/Alex trailed off, looked confused and a little suspicious.

Tovah stepped out from behind me, her voice high and bright. "Yeah, we're good now! No more hate." She flipped her pink hair.

"So what, y'all are," he gestured between us. "Hooking up?"

I didn't have to see her face to know she was blushing. "Just...talking," she said.

Talking. Like she was embarrassed that anything else

could be happening between us. Overwhelmed by a ridiculous urge, I slowly sat back down in my chair, pulling her onto my lap. I rested my chin on her head, wrapping my arms around her waist. It was supposed to look tender, but it was so she couldn't get away.

"We're calling it talking now, baby?" I asked, hugging her close to me, and staring straight at Alec/Alex, daring him to interject.

I expected her to drop the acting, to fight me, to tell him she needed his help, to rat me out, anything. Yeah, I'd threatened her and told her she had to sell us getting along, even implied it was better if she sold us as "together," but I didn't expect her to actually listen to me and follow my lead.

So I was shocked when she leaned into me, sighing sweetly—so sweetly it made me harden under her delectable ass, even though I knew the sound was fake.

Her giggle was even faker. "We can call it whatever you want, *baby*."

Nicely played.

She surprised me further when she twisted around on my lap, wrapping a hand around the back of my neck.

And kissed me.

It didn't matter that it was fake, or simple, or close-mouthed. Just the feel of her soft lips pressed firmly against mine made my blood roar, my heart pound, the floor beneath my feet rumble. That lock in my chest shattered, releasing something feral and terrifying. In that moment, as I tasted her lips, lost in a cloud of pink hair and citrus scent, my entire world shifted in ways beyond my understanding or control.

And then I was taking over the kiss, over *her*. One of my hands cupped her cheek, the other wrapped around the back of her hair, fisting it, as I tilted her head to an angle that satisfied me, dominating her mouth with mine and demanding she *let me in.*

With a gasp, she did, and I took advantage of her temporary surrender to taste her, licking her cheeks, her teeth, tangling with her tongue. I could taste the lemon and sugar on her. She tasted like shocking sweetness and sharp danger. Because this woman *was* dangerous. To me, in unfamiliar ways I'd be wise to stay away from.

But in this moment, I wasn't wise. I was too captivated by her taste, her scent, the feel of her in my arms, the little gasps and whimpers she made into my mouth as she gave in, chasing my tongue with hers, just as lost as I was. At that moment, nothing mattered—not that I hated her for who she was turning me into, or that she was trying to destroy *both* my family and my team, or that everything about her including that goddamned pink hair drove me crazy. Nothing and no one could've separated me from her. I'd like to see someone *try.*

Tovah was the one who tried. She bit down on my lip—hard. The taste of copper exploded in my mouth. She'd broken skin.

Too bad for her I liked that kind of shit.

Ripping her mouth away from mine, she gasped two words:

"Game. On."

Trying to regain my equilibrium, aware of that bouncer still watching us, I smiled at her indulgently, licking the blood off my lip.

"That the best you've got?" I taunted under my breath.

"You haven't seen my best, Isaac *Jones,*" she taunted back.

I rose with her on my lap. She had no choice but to wrap

her legs around my waist and grab onto my shoulders or she would've crashed to the floor.

"Isaac, put me down. You can't carry me anyway, I'm too heavy—" she started to argue.

I snorted. "I could bench press five of you. But if you want me to pretend otherwise and drop you, I will."

"Tovah, you sure you're okay?" The big bouncer's voice betrayed his uncertainty.

He glanced down at his phone, then back up to us. I could read it in his eyes and the tightness in his body: she'd likely texted him that she needed his help, or something along those lines, and he couldn't reconcile her need for backup with who she needed backup from.

But I was smiling easily at him, like I didn't have a care in the world, like there was no monster inside me rattling his cage. Channeling the message that I was a decent guy who wanted time alone with his girl.

Needing to send that message loud and clear, I pinched the dimple between Tovah's hip and waist—and immediately wanted to bite and suck the skin there. Leave my mark on her.

"All good," she craned her neck around and assured him.

The tightness in Alex/Alec's shoulders loosened. "Y'all are cute," he said. He'd bought it.

Tovah growled.

Reaching into my pocket, I withdrew my wallet, pulling out a hundred-dollar bill and dropping it on the table.

"Have a good night," I said as I passed by him. He let us through. As Tovah, clearly not trusting me, tried to jump down, I caught her with my free arm, wrapping it tight so she couldn't escape.

"Let's go home, *baby*," I said. "Do some more *talking*."

As I exited the bar with her reluctantly wrapped around me, satisfaction filled me. Finally, I had what I wanted, even if I wasn't supposed to want it.

Game on, indeed.

8

Tovah

What the hell was I doing?

This wasn't like me. I didn't get turned on by assholes, didn't make out with guys I hated. Even though I could still feel Isaac's lips on mine. Once upon a time, Isaac Silver kissing me was all I'd ever wanted, ever dreamed of. Now, it represented a nightmare I couldn't seem to wake up from.

Or an opportunity, my mind supplied.

Right, an opportunity.

When Isaac had listed out his "rules" for me, every part of me wanted to protest. Even the parts that were attracted to him—and there were a lot of those parts. I couldn't let him control me like that, *own* me like that. I refused to act like I liked him. I already felt trapped by his family, I couldn't literally be trapped by him, too.

Until I realized what being around him that often would mean.

He'd called me "little snoop," and he'd been right.

Because being in his space would make it so much easier to snoop on him and his family, so I could find the evidence myself to take him down for good. He'd be watching me, but even Isaac needed to sleep and go to hockey practice. I'd find what I needed, write an article, publish it, and put his father behind bars.

And my mom and I would finally be *free*.

I know it shocked him when I went along with his little game, snuggling into him and giggling, but I had a game of my own to play. Which meant being the best actress I'd ever been. And it didn't matter that he was an athlete. This one, I was going to win.

There was no other option.

One of us had to lose, and it wouldn't be me. Losing would mean death for me, and discovery for my mom... which meant death for her, too. And I wasn't letting that happen. I loved her too much, *owed* her too much, for that.

As I thought through this, Isaac was still carrying me down the street. It was around seven p.m., still too early for students to be out on Bar Row, so the sidewalk was empty. *Thank god*. I would be so embarrassed to be seen carted around by Isaac Jones like a child. Or worse, one of his—

I refused to use the phrase "puck bunny," even in my own head. It was offensive to the girls who were labeled that way, and I wasn't about to play into the misogynistic bullshit that surrounded the hockey team.

One of his many girls, then.

When he reached his car, he set me down so he could unlock the door. But he surprised me, no, terrified me, when he backed me up against it, the cool metal against my back. He braced his arms on either side of me and leaned in so I was, once again, trapped.

"You're going to pay for that bullshit back there," he said.

"What bullshit?"

"Biting my goddamn lip. *Giving* me lip, especially in public. I never was into...punishment. But with you?" He seemed to think, and then his voice went thick, and he said, "I bet I could get into it. What do you think? Does pain get you off, little snoop?"

Oh, *fuck* this shit.

I hated the way my breathing sped up at his insinuation. I might need to get close to him to get the evidence I needed to free my mom and myself from our years-long nightmare, but that didn't mean I'd let him talk to me that way. He thought I was going to let him fuck me? "Punish" me? *Hell no.* If I let him touch me that way, if I gave into my darkest desires...he'd destroy me. And it was that fear, more than anything else, that caused me to lean further back against the car and blink up at him.

"Maybe it does," I murmured, intentionally wetting my lips with my tongue.

His eyes went hazy, and just as he leaned in, I raised my knee and shoved it into his dick.

With an *oomph,* he bent over, moving his arms to cover himself. I used the momentary distraction to shove him backward.

And *ran.*

I didn't even look behind me. Even though I was a little out of shape these days, my body knew how to run. This time I wasn't racing to win a medal for my team. I was getting away from a man who had the resources to kill me—or do worse.

Muscle memory kicked in, and I sprinted down the sidewalk back toward the bar. All I had to do was get inside and Alex would protect me.

Wait.

Shit.

If I went back into the bar, Alex would want to know why I was running from "Good Guy Jones," when I'd just put on a loving girlfriend show minutes earlier. I'd have to tell him the truth. Alex was a friend and deserved to be safe. Now that Isaac was onto me, it no longer would be Alex vs Isaac, it would be Alex vs the entire Silver criminal enterprise. I couldn't let that happen.

Frustrated, I ran straight past the bar. I was a sprinter, not a distance runner. Isaac had probably recovered by now, and it wouldn't take long for him to catch me. Playing hockey and training regularly meant his stamina was better than mine. I'd never make it home safely.

But up ahead, two and a half blocks away, was a bus stop. I glanced at my watch. There was a bus arriving in two minutes. All I had to do was get to the bus stop and then Isaac would be shit out of luck.

Only two and a half blocks. I could do it.

Behind me, feet pounded the pavement. Based on the sound, he was only about a block behind and gaining quickly. Exhaling, I increased my speed, pushing my legs and lungs to their limits and putting more distance between us.

Half a block down. Only two to go.

The sound of him following me got louder, his pounding feet roaring in my ears.

I pushed myself harder. All I had to do was breathe and let my muscle memory do its thing.

One block now.

He was closer.

Was that his breath on my neck, or the wind?

Lungs burning, chest aching, I tried to push harder.

Only half a block now.

And here came the bus rolling down the street, headlights dispelling the shadows surrounding me.

Holy shit, I was going to—

—A thick, muscular arm snagged me around the waist, dragging me backward. I opened my mouth to scream, and his other hand shot out to cover it, muffling the noise.

As he lifted me off the ground, I turned feral, scratching and kicking and biting, doing anything to get free. Doing anything to survive.

As we disappeared into a pitch-black alley, the bus continued past the stop and down the street, oblivious to the woman in desperate need of rescue.

But then I'd always rescued myself, hadn't I? I'd never been able to rely on anyone but my mom.

I only prayed I could do it again.

Isaac shoved me up against a rough brick wall of a building, the pain and shock of it reverberating through my body. The only thing that kept me from a broken nose was his hand between my face and the wall.

What, was I supposed to thank him for that?

Behind me, he tsked in my ear. "You shouldn't have done that. I was going to go easy on you, but I'm not feeling particularly merciful anymore." Thoughtfully, he added, "But I guess I am a little grateful."

"Why?" I gasped against his hand.

Cupping my breast with one hand and thrusting his hips against my ass so I could feel how hard he was, he said, "I never knew how much fun chasing down and catching my prey would be. Fuck, I'm going to like this."

He leaned down, dropping a gentle kiss on my neck and surprising me.

And then he surprised me further when he bit my neck, so hard I screamed into his hand.

He must have broken skin, because when he backed up, spun me around, and kissed me violently, I could taste blood on his lips.

And, as truly and beyond fucked up as it was—I kissed him back.

9

Isaac

I had let the monster out of its cage. I'd avoided this side of myself for so long, I was almost shocked by how goddamn good it felt to let the feral, obsessed animal *free*.

I'd felt fairly calm about taking Tovah home with me. I wanted her, but I could control it. Until the violent little brat kneed me in the nuts. Between the pain in my balls and my surprise that *she'd* had the balls and bravery to hurt me like that, it took me a moment to gather myself and chase her down. At first, I thought I wouldn't catch her. She was fucking fast, graceful in her speed and determination to get away, like a gazelle—if a gazelle was a short, curvy, pink-haired demon of chaos in human form. But, like a gazelle, she was prey, not predator.

I didn't recognize this side of myself. I'd never, not once, chased a girl down the street before, in the dark or otherwise.

Wait, that wasn't true.

An image appeared in my mind, briefly slowing me down: me at age seven, laughing as I chased a giggling brown haired little girl through the massive backyard of my family's enclave. I never even knew her name, but playing tag with her was the most fun I'd ever had.

I used to call her my bashert. My soulmate, my destiny.

Until she'd disappeared.

But I couldn't think about that little girl from the past. Not when the woman in my present, who fit so perfectly in my arms as she kissed me, made me feel more alive than I had in a long, long time.

I'd fucked up, though. Hadn't realized that the mix of lemon and sugar and the hint of copper would be the sweetest thing I'd ever tasted, that I'd need it endlessly, more than I needed air to breathe.

It didn't help when the madwoman started kissing me back.

I lost track of everything for a while. It didn't matter that we were only steps away from the street and anyone walking by could see us, or at any moment Tovah could yell for help. Who cared that I was supposed to be making her pay instead of kissing her like my fucking life depended on it? All that disappeared with the feel of her soft tits against my chest, the perfect weight of her in my arms as I lifted her off the ground to change the angle, the way she moaned and gasped as she licked and bit and sucked my lips and tongue, surrendering to me and surrounding me in some perfect goddamn dream I never wanted to wake up from.

Until I heard a car alarm go off somewhere down the street and common sense returned.

She was so fucking dangerous. She was a mystery, and I hated mysteries. My father always said mysteries meant you lacked the leverage you needed to win, and even though I hated most of Abe Silver's "wisdom," this piece of advice I agreed with. I'd dig up all her secrets. But first I needed to get her to a location where I was the one in control and didn't have to worry about her destroying my life or my very soul.

But I couldn't release her mouth.

I needed more.

Still kissing her, keeping her steady with one arm and gripping her hair in my hand with the other, I walked out of the alley and back down the street toward my car.

So caught up in the taste of her, I lost sight of where I was going, nearly tripping over a crack in the pavement. Quick reflexes saved both of us as I caught myself before I fell, tightening my grip on Tovah's hip to keep her steady.

The movement must have pulled Tovah out of her reverie, because she wrenched back from me with a gasp, staring at me with needy confusion.

"Why do you keep carrying me everywhere?" she asked.

"Because you never go where you're supposed to," I answered.

That pissed her off. "Fuck you, Isaac Silver, put me down."

"Gladly," I said, releasing my grip on her hair to pull my keys out of my pocket and hit the button to unlock the trunk of my car.

"Wait, what the hell are you—"

The top of the trunk raised automatically, and once it was high enough, I dumped her inside.

"Isaac, I swear to god I'm going to kill you so hard," she cried out as I reached into her pocket and grabbed her phone so she couldn't call for help. The rest of her attempted threat was cut off when the trunk closed on her.

For a moment, I worried that she'd suffocate in there.

Ah, well. It was only a ten-minute drive to my house. She'd survive that long.

Whistling, I opened the driver's side door and got in, starting the car and backing out of the spot before making a left off Bar Row, back toward campus.

In case Tovah watched enough action movies to know what to do when someone locked you in their trunk, I took the back roads. They'd be empty, so no one would see her if she figured out how to kick the taillight out.

And certainly no one could hear her scream.

No. That screaming was for me, and would only be for me, later.

Distantly, I realized that I was descending into darkness I'd managed to avoid for most of my life. Was I turning into my father?

Shaking off the thought, I made a right and drove through the woods toward my two-story colonial, grateful for the privacy of my home, and the surrounding quiet.

Once we got there, she could scream all she wanted.

I couldn't fucking wait.

10

Tovah

Holy shit. He'd put me in the trunk of his car.

Like full on threw me in the trunk of his goddamned car.

I reminded myself to breathe. Usually when someone who was part of an organized crime family put you in the trunk of their car, it meant you were about to die. But I doubted I'd pissed him off *that* much.

I wasn't risking it, though. And I'd watched enough movies to know that older cars were built so if you were locked in the trunk, you could kick out the taillights. It wouldn't actually get me out of the trunk, but I could wave my arm around and scream for help and someone would see me. I hoped so, anyway.

Taking a deep breath, I kicked out my leg, hard, directly at the taillight. Nothing happened, so I did it again, and again. Finally, on the fourth kick, I heard a crack and then cold air greeted me.

I did it!

Turning around in the tiny trunk wasn't easy. I had to slither on my stomach, which hurt. I was going to have rug burn on my stomach later. After a few tries, I managed to turn around and stuck my arm out the hole where the taillight had been. I started to scream for help at the top of my lungs. I couldn't see anything, had no idea if there was anyone around, but it didn't matter, it was my only chance.

As I continued to scream, the car slowed to a stop.

Oh, shit. Had Isaac heard me somehow?

I pulled my hand back into the car, preparing to run.

The car stopped, a car door slammed, gravel crunched, the locks beeped, and then the lid of the trunk was being raised and I was exposed to fresh air, moonlight, and Isaac's cold expression.

"That was clever," he said, sounding amused, not irate like I'd expected him to be. "Fortunately, I already knew how clever you are."

Crap.

I shouldn't have appreciated the compliment, but Isaac's admonition did stir up a little satisfaction in me. Or would've, if it hadn't screwed me over. Because from what I could tell, we were alone.

Isaac reached into the trunk, grabbing me by my armpits and hauling me out. We were front to front for a moment, and the proximity to the heat of his body made my breath stutter. He slowly slid me down his body until my sneakers hit gravel. I expected him to release me from his hold, but he just gripped me tighter. His hands were so big, the tips of his thumbs teased the edges of my breasts. Inhaling sharply, I forced myself not to react, looking up at him.

"Let me go," I said softly.

He jerked his head to the side. *No.*

"Isaac, let me go. You're hurting me."

"You agreed to this," he said, also softly—but there was a danger in the quiet of his voice. "And then you kneed me in the balls and ran. Leaving a few bruises on your arms is the least I'm going to do to you."

"Really?" I scoffed, hiding my fear. "What would the students at Reina think if they could hear you threaten me right now? What would your teammates or your new coach think?"

I expected him to release me, but a smirk played on his face, illuminating his left dimple in the moonlight.

"It doesn't matter what they'll think, Tovah. They won't ever know."

And then he was releasing me briefly, only to grab my left wrist and drag me behind him down the gravel path to a house a few hundred feet ahead of us.

Huge oak trees surrounded us, the darkness and shadows only broken up by the dim light of a crescent moon. It was mostly silent, except for the nearby hoot of an owl as it observed me stumbling after Isaac as he took long, angry strides toward the house ahead of us. In the dark, it was an ominous gray, with closed shutters and a large porch. *Old Colonial*, my brain supplied, but the fear and frustration eclipsed it.

"Are you seriously kidnapping me?" I huffed.

Isaac ignored me.

"You know that's a crime, right?" I continued.

"According to you, I'm already a criminal. What's one more felony?" But he didn't sound as blasé as he was trying to be. I'd hit the target, but it didn't mean he was releasing me.

When we reached the house, he hauled me up the five steps to the porch, withdrawing a key from his pocket and unlocking the front door. I managed to pull in one more breath of fresh air before he was slamming the door behind me and locking it. Finally, he released me, only to play with his phone, and with an ominous beep, a robotic voice spoke.

"House locked down. Alarm on."

That was it.

I was all alone, with the dark, dangerous, hockey-playing mafia prince.

And there was nowhere else to run.

The house was beautiful. With muted grey walls, original beams and wainscotting everywhere, and big picture windows looking out on the forest, it was everything I ever could have wanted in a home. Too bad I didn't want to be here.

"Where are we?" I sassed.

"My house," he said simply, watching me.

His house.

"I thought you live in the hockey annex?" I asked, curiosity getting the better of me.

"Sometimes. Sometimes it's easier to be alone. And *this* is one of those times."

Although his quiet admission brought out an understanding in me, I shoved it away. What was more important was I was in Isaac's *home*. A home where he probably stored secrets that I could use as evidence. Curious, I followed him through the living room into a big, sparkling, modern kitchen, with Shaker cabinets and a big black farmhouse sink. It was exactly how I'd design a house, if and when I would be able to afford my own. My mom and I had spent years living in temporary rentals and even motels. Did Isaac even get how lucky he was?

"Must be nice," I muttered, then jumped when Isaac asked:

"What must be nice?"

"Being rich as fuck," I said, tossing my hair.

I expected him to grin, to preen, to rub in my face everything he had that I didn't. What I did not expect was the way his jaw went tight and his eyes flashed.

"You might be surprised," he said. "When all that wealth comes with strings attached, it feels more like a trap than a golden ticket."

"I'm playing the world's smallest violin for you," I told him.

He rolled his eyes, pulling out a bar stool and pointing to it. "Sit."

"I think I'll—" I started.

"Tovah. Sit."

I glared at him.

He picked me up by the waist, depositing me on a bar stool, then braced his arms on both sides of me on the island countertop. My chest burned with anger and helplessness.

"Let's try this again," he said slowly. "I don't think you understood the rules the first time. One: You don't go anywhere without me or one of my teammates accompanying you. Two: All of your internet time is monitored. Schoolwork only. I'm not risking you notifying your editor or sneakily publishing something on *The Daily Queen*'s site. Three: Whatever I tell you to do, you do. Whatever I tell you to wear, you wear."

The burning in my chest grew. I crossed my arms over my chest. Shaking his head and tsking at me like I was an unruly child, he lifted one of his arms from the countertop, grabbing my left wrist and pulling my left arm away from my chest, then my right one.

"Leave them," he warned.

"Fuck you," I said slowly.

He paused, staring me down. The words were unnecessary, because the implication was clear: *Oh, you're gonna.*

He continued. "Little snoop, hear me loud and clear: If you don't follow my orders to the letter, if you break a single one of my rules, I will have absolutely zero qualms calling my father and telling him I have Tovah Lewis in my grasp. How long do you think you'll survive?"

Not long. But that wasn't the only issue. Isaac didn't seem to realize that my mother was alive. I didn't want to follow his bullshit "rules," but it wasn't just my life on the line—it was hers.

Which meant going along with what he wanted.

For now.

He'd made a mistake. He'd brought me into his home. His *life.* He might know I was clever, that I was smart, but if he knew just how smart or clever I was, he wouldn't have risked letting me get so close. They said keep your friends close and your enemies closer, but that didn't apply to journalists.

I was skeptical when it came to his plans, though. "How the hell are you going to pull this off? You think no one's going to be suspicious that we're together all the time, that you can't stay away from me, that your friends are always around me—when before it was pretty obvious to everyone that we can't stand each other? People are going to think you're pussy whipped."

Isaac threw back his head and laughed. I was entranced in spite of myself: by his deep, husky chuckle, the way his Adam's apple moved in his throat, the way his dark eyes warmed with humor. The experience was like a seductive caress; a temptation I neither needed nor wanted.

"Do you know how much pussy I've played with?" he taunted. "Your cunt could be entirely made of diamonds and gold, and it still couldn't control me. Nah, everyone on campus will think you're dick drunk." His eyes narrowed, his hand squeezing my right wrist. It didn't hurt, but the warning was there. "And you're going to *make* them believe that, aren't you, little snoop? You're going to follow me around with big heart eyes, sit on my lap and toss your hair and giggle like you did at the bar in front of your friend, and let me touch you however I want to. Make everyone think you're in love with me."

"And you?" I countered, hating how breathless I sounded. "Are people going to think you're in love with me?"

A look came to his eyes I couldn't read. "They'd be idiots if they did."

It shouldn't have hurt. I didn't care what Isaac Silver thought of me. But the memory of who he'd been as a boy was stronger than I'd realized, because his outright hatred burned almost as badly as my chest did.

"You'll come to my home games," he said. "Away games are negotiable depending on good behavior."

"I can't! I have work!" I protested.

"Not any more you don't. I'll quit the bar for you."

"I need that money, Isaac." I was at Reina on scholarship, but I still had to pay for textbooks and rent.

He waved a hand, releasing my wrist. "I'll pay for whatever you need. You aren't working at that damn bar in that tight little tank top while douchebros hit on you."

"*You* are a douchebro," I muttered.

He raised an eyebrow. "You'll come to every single one of my games, here and away, and you'll wear *my* jersey. We're not playing games where you wear some other player's number and make me look like a fool."

"What, are you jealous, Isaac Silver?"

He smirked. "Why would I be jealous of anyone else, when I know you're going to end every night in *my* bed?"

I gulped, my throat suddenly dry. It grew drier as his eyes lazily tracked me as I swallowed.

"This is a big house," I protested. "Why would I sleep in your bed?"

"Because I don't trust you in my home. I don't trust you alone. And you're going to have to get used to me touching you, so we can sell this fake thing between us publicly. And," he added with dark silk in his voice, "because I want you in my bed, and I'm getting what I want. From now on, I say 'suck,' you ask, 'how deep?'"

The angry burn in my chest made it hard to breathe. I hated his words, and I especially hated the feelings they sparked in my core.

"If you get your dick anywhere near me, I'm biting it off," I threatened. "That deep enough for you?"

What happened next was almost too fast for me to track. With a growl, Isaac lifted me off the barstool he'd set me on earlier, flipped me around, and threw me face down on the kitchen counter so my legs dangled off. A slap rang out and a moment later, my right ass cheek *stung.*

He'd hit me.

Spanked me.

As if he had the fucking right.

"You fucking asshole," I seethed, lifting myself off the counter, only for him to push me back down with a hand between my shoulder blades.

I struggled against him, but I was no match for the big hockey player here in his own house. He peppered my ass with hit after hit, not tempering his strength or restraining himself in any way, just delivering pain. It *hurt.* It stung. It *burned.*

And then something horrifying happened: it started to feel good.

The more it hurt, the wetter I grew. I could feel it, on my pussy and between my thighs, and thanked fate that I was wearing jeans so he'd never know.

I'd barely had that moment of gratitude before he was lifting my hips and unbuttoning the top of my jeans, slowly pulling down the zipper. Cool air brushed against my panties.

"What the hell are you doing?!" I shrieked.

"Taking your pants off. What does it seem like I'm doing?" he countered as he dragged my jeans down my ass and legs, letting them crumple between my ankles, making it impossible to kick him.

My pink panties followed, his fingers tracing bare skin and leaving aching shivers in their wake. If I wasn't imagining things, his breathing was becoming heavier, rougher...

...especially when he shoved one of his hands between my pussy and the counter, and his thumb came in direct contact with my bare lips.

My wet, bare lips.

He froze. His hand, his body, his breath, everything.

And then:

"Fuuuuuuuuuuck." he rasped, his breath tightening and quickening. "This turns you on, you little snoop? Me beating your ass makes you hot and wet? You like pain, don't you?"

"No," I gasped.

He delivered another slap, this time to the underside of my ass. "Don't fucking lie to me. I can feel how much you like it. I don't care that your name means 'good.' There's nothing *good* about you, bad girl." He delivered another slap, this time between my thighs. I screamed from the combined pain and pleasure. "And I'm going to make sure you feel it."

11

Isaac

I was fucked.

Completely and utterly fucked.

I thought I could keep my shit together with Tovah in my space, even with the smell of lemon and sugar goddamn everywhere. Sharp and sweet, just like her. I was only getting the sharpness from her right now. She was pissed I was taking over her life, and I didn't blame her, but it didn't matter. I needed to, to keep myself, my team, and my family safe. And my cock didn't hate the idea of her having to bend to my every whim, either.

Even when she said that everyone would think I was pussy whipped, and I worried she was right. But could I be whipped by a pussy I'd never seen, touched, tasted?

She'd warned that people would think I was in love with her. I didn't explain that there was no way—I could and would never be in love with anyone. It was easier to insult her.

I continued delivering big, heavy, hard spanks to her

denim-clad ass, just so I could feel in control again. It wasn't enough. I craved the feeling of her hot skin under my hand, and who was going to stop me? There was no one here but Tovah, me, and my currently quiet and watchful conscience, waiting to see what I'd do next.

Taking her jeans off was the biggest mistake I'd ever made in my life—and the greatest discovery. Not only because the feeling of her bare ass under my hand shattered any notion that I was in control of anything right now. But because when I'd given into my need to feel the pussy I was apparently going to be whipped by, I'd felt how wet she was.

Sloppy wet. It spread over her pussy, her lips, her inner thighs, bathing my hand in *her*. I bet if I licked my hand, I'd taste the same sharp sweetness I could smell everywhere.

I tried to keep a handle on my actions, taking deep breaths to rein myself in. But how the fuck was that possible when she was getting off on the pain I was delivering to her? How the hell was I supposed to be Isaac Jones, Good Guy, when I finally had the girl who'd been driving me fucking insane in my home, under lock and key—and in goddamned hand? I'd blown so far past the good guy version of myself, he was probably little more than ash, miles back.

And, more importantly, why would I rein myself in when I didn't have to? She was here now. Mine now, for however long I wanted her. I could do whatever the fuck I goddamn wanted—

—don't do something you'll regret, my conscience warned.

I told it to shut the fuck up. The monster was hungry, and I was finally going to unlock his cage and let him loose.

Starting with licking Tovah's wetness off my fingers. If I was wrong, if it was nothing more than normal girl pussy juice, I'd regain control and she'd lose the power over me. But I knew better.

"You smell like lemon and sugar," I grunted at her. "Let's see if you taste the same."

"Isaac—" she gasped, but I'd already stuck my wet fingers in my mouth and licked.

Fuck.

Fuck fuck fuck.

Fuuuuuuuuuuuuuuuuuuuuuuuuuuuuuuuuuuuuuuuuck.

Sharp. Sweet. And raw. Tovah tasted like every fear I'd ever had, and every desire I'd ever ignored. She tasted the way the sun must taste on your skin, when you know it's going to burn you painfully but you want it to bathe you in its rays anyway.

She tasted like *mine*.

Making a novel sound low in my throat, I gripped her thighs and lifted them as I bent my head down, biting her bare ass cheek hard in reprimand for making me feel so out of control.

And then I got my face between her thighs, buried my nose in her pussy, and, well, I don't know how else to describe it.

I ate.

It was a slaughter and my last meal, all in one. I hunted for her taste, licking it off her mound, her lips, biting into her thighs as if it might be there, searching deep inside her with my tongue for every last drop. And when it seemed like I'd run out, I made sure there was more, using my fingers to draw circles over her clit, thrusting them inside her and teasing her G-spot until she convulsed and with a low, throaty, satisfying-as-fuck moan, came all over my face.

Just like I'd wanted.

Her orgasm wasn't for her. It was for me. I'd discovered

the best fucking tasting thing I'd ever gotten on my tongue, and I wasn't giving it up for anything. I licked up her cum, without finesse or gentility. This wasn't a wine tasting. This wasn't even chugging a beer. This was a bloodbath. I didn't know what would be left or if either of us would survive after I was done with Tovah's cunt, or if I'd ever *be* done with Tovah's cunt.

The girl in question was struggling against me. Maybe. I couldn't tell if she was trying to get away or get closer, and I didn't really fucking care either way. The Isaac Jones who gave a shit over concepts like consent didn't exist anymore. Isaac Silver, on the other hand, didn't give a fuck about anything but figuring out how to permanently attach Tovah Lewis's pussy to his lips so he could drink down her cum and taste the essence of her sassy strength whenever he goddamned wanted. Oh, and maybe getting a recording of Tovah's wild screams as she came multiple times, her thighs clamped around my head like my own personal pair of X-rated ear guards.

"Isaac, stop, please, I need—"

I bit her thigh to shut her up.

"Don't fucking interrupt me when I'm eating," I growled like a fucking madman.

"It's too much!" she cried.

"Sounds fake," I said, before diving back into her cunt, in case there was a complexity to her flavor I'd missed the first time.

Finally, after a few minutes or a whole hockey season, I stopped. I hadn't nearly had my fill, but sanity was slowly returning to me, reminding me that the woman attached to the pussy I was eating might need a break, based on her gasps and trembling thighs. The moment I released her, she slithered onto the counter in a heap like a rag doll.

"No more," she cried brokenly against the counter. "Please, Isaac, no more. I can't—it's too much. It hurts."

It's not too much.

It'll never be enough.

When it comes to you, I'll always need more.

I swallowed down the words. What the fuck had gotten into me? The plan had been to keep Tovah from fucking up my life, not turn her into my new favorite meal. How many orgasms had I given her in my momentary lapse of sanity?

How had I lost control?

I stood back, crossing my arms over my chest to stop myself from reaching forward and helping her as she climbed down from the kitchen island. Standing on shaky legs, she turned around to look at me. Her face was flushed, her hair a sweaty, tangled mess.

I'd made her that way. The monster inside me practically snarled with triumph.

Instead, I sneered at her. "Go take a shower. You're a fucking mess."

Tovah stared at me like I'd grown two heads—and she'd happily decapitate them both.

"I'm sorry," she said slowly. "You just made me come four times *without my permission*, without listening to me when I told you to stop, and I'm the one who's a," she made air quotes, "fucking mess?"

I ignored her—the point she made, the validity of it, the guilt it stirred up in my gut.

"Bedroom's on the second floor—first door to the right of the stairs. It has an en-suite. It should have everything you need for now but make a list of what you want and I'll order it for you tomorrow. Or we can just go pick it up from your apartment."

I didn't mention that I knew where her apartment was or

that her ever setting foot back in that unsafe building made me want to break something. I'd shown enough of my hand tonight. God forbid she figure out she had any control over me, even just her pussy. She would think I was whipped. And I couldn't prove otherwise.

"You're a fucking asshole," she said, stomping out of the kitchen and down the hallway.

As soon as I heard the squeak of her sneakers on the wooden staircase, I slumped over, burying my head against the once-cool marble countertop that had been warmed by her body. I could still smell her here, and god knew I'd never be able to make myself food in this house again without seeing her plastered against it, crying out as I tried to turn her inside out with my tongue. I could still taste her, too, and I knew that lemon and sugar flavor would haunt me for the rest of my life, even after she'd finally gone.

"Fuck!" I yelled, slapping my hand down on the marble, relishing the sting in my hand from the hard slap.

I'd never felt this unhinged before.

And the worst part?

I didn't hate it.

Not when it meant that Tovah Lewis was upstairs, naked in *my* bathroom, water pouring over her as she cleaned herself with *my* soap, knowing she'd end up smelling like *me*.

Sighing, I leaned back against the fridge, preparing myself for what I knew was about to be the next fight of the night.

A fight I was *also* determined to win.

12

Tovah

O*h.*
My.
God.

I stood under the hot water in Isaac's shower, letting it soak my hair and body and hopefully wash away the past hour.

My whole body was ice-hot, cold flashes and heat rushes making me tremble and sweat. I felt feverish, insane, my skin too tight, my heart racing. And I ached everywhere, especially my pussy. My clit was sore, pulsing weakly between my legs. The fact that my clit even *had* a pulse was a whole new worry I didn't have room for right now.

No man had ever given me an orgasm before.

No man had ever even *touched* me between my legs, much less attached his mouth to my vagina like he was a demonic vacuum trying to suck out my soul. I wasn't just a virgin—I had never let a guy get that close to me. I didn't trust men. Well, I didn't really trust anyone, but men especially.

Guess that didn't matter to Isaac. But then why would it? He assumed I'd been with a ton of guys, and as far as I was concerned, he could keep assuming that.

But god.

God.

That had felt like nothing I could have ever imagined feeling. Amazing and terrifying, shocking and perfect, surreal and raw. I'd been overcome, overtaken, overwhelmed...over-*everything.*

I hated that Isaac Silver had been the one to give me my first non-self-induced orgasm—but part of me, the part that had swooned over him as a little girl—loved it.

I groaned, sliding down against the warm shower tiles until I was sitting on the floor, the water pelting over my head.

What was I doing here? Yes, I had a plan: snoop, eavesdrop, get evidence, expose the Silvers, finally make it so my mom and I were safe and free. But no part of that plan included "get your rocks off courtesy of your enemy's firstborn son's tongue."

At least, not last I checked.

I couldn't let that happen again. I knew better than to let some hockey star with a chip on his shoulder the size of Australia distract me from my goals—even if when we were children, he'd called me his destiny.

The only thing we were destined for was to ruin each other's lives.

With that depressing thought, I turned off the water and stepped out of the shower, wrapping a big, fluffy white towel around my body and hunting down another one for my hair. I really needed my stuff: my hair towel, my diffuser, my gel and mousse.

Make a list of what you want and I'll make sure to order it for you. Or we can just go pick it up from your apartment tomorrow.

Like what I wanted mattered to him. Like we were dating, like there was a *we* at all. I didn't know why Isaac was pretending to care about what sort of toiletries I wanted, when he didn't give a shit about me. But I'd make sure to get my hair stuff...and whatever else I could use against him. I'd hide my interview recorder in my shampoo bottle, if that's what it took.

Locating an unused toothbrush, and hating that he had an unused toothbrush, and then hating myself for hating it, I spread some toothpaste on it and brushed my teeth, staring at myself in the mirror. My skin was flushed, and I could pretend it was only from the shower, but I knew better. My eyes were big and dark and confused. Scared.

Who would I be when I finally got out of this madhouse?

"Tovah," he called from outside the bathroom, his voice annoyingly, enticingly husky. "You done?"

I froze.

I wasn't ready to see him yet. I'd basically ran out of the kitchen after yelling at him for making me come without my consent.

I should be angrier about that. Should be fucking *livid* that he'd taken my choice away from me.

So why wasn't I?

"Tovah," he called again.

You're strong, Tovah Lewis. Smart and clever and tough. More than even he realizes. You can do this.

With that short silent pep talk, I blew myself a kiss in the mirror and opened the bathroom door, letting the steam out and facing Isaac.

And then immediately regretted it when I spotted him there, framed in the door in grey cutoff sweats and no shirt, his delectable abs on full display.

But when I went to slam the bathroom door back shut, he stopped me, putting out a hand and catching it.

"Hiding?" he commented.

I straightened my shoulders, aware that they were bare, that there was nothing separating him and my naked body but the towel. His towel. Pretending I had no such awareness, or just didn't give a shit, I tossed my wet hair. "No, but your bedroom is cold. Can I borrow some clothes?"

He stared at me in his towel, his throat working.

"Fuck no," he muttered.

"Excuse me?" I raised an eyebrow, trying to control my breathing. "There's no way I'm sleeping naked with you. So I can either go sleep in another room or you can give me clothes."

He sauntered over to his armoire, pulling out a big t-shirt that said Reina Kings on it and tossed it to me. "You can sleep in that."

I rolled my eyes. "I need underwear."

"No, you don't."

"Isaac." My voice broke.

His eyes narrowed, and whatever else he was going to say got cut off with a snarl. A pair of man's boxer-briefs sailed toward me, and I caught them.

"I need the bathroom," he muttered, walking toward me, grabbing me around the waist, and moving me out of the way like I was an annoying piece of furniture. The bathroom door slammed behind him.

I heard the water turn on.

Hell, now was the perfect time to snoop.

Keeping my eyes on the bathroom door, I pulled on the huge shirt and boxer-briefs. I walked around the bedroom, opening the drawers on the right nightstand, but other than a huge box of condoms and a pair of metal handcuffs I dropped immediately back into the drawer like they'd burned me, I found nothing.

The door opened and I turned toward it like I hadn't been doing anything sketchy.

Isaac came out, a towel wrapped around his waist. His dark hair was wet, droplets trickling down his face, his neck, one sliding between his clavicles to make its way between his pecs...

"See something you like?" he said wryly.

I jerked my head up, hiding my embarrassment by glaring at him.

"Says the guy who had his head locked between my thighs only half an hour ago," I taunted.

He shrugged. "Not denying that I like looking at you. I can hate you and still know you're the fucking hottest thing I've ever seen in my goddamned fucking life."

Oh. My. God.

I gaped at him.

He smiled, dimples appearing for the first time since the bar, and for a moment he became Isaac Jones, charmer.

"Time for bed," he said, taking a step toward me.

"I'll just go sleep in another room."

"You will not," he told me. "Like I said, I don't trust you alone. You're spending the night in bed—with me. You're spending every night in bed with me for the foreseeable future, so get used to it."

"I'm not fucking you," I said immediately.

He raised an eyebrow. "Who said anything about fucking? You have to earn my cock, little snoop. So far, you haven't come close to it."

I snorted. "I'm never going to want your cock, so you're fine."

"Whatever you say," he hummed, pulling down the bedding. "Get in."

"I really—"

"Fuck this," he muttered, and then he was picking me up again and depositing me on the bed. I bounced, and began to scramble off, but he was on me two seconds later, the pair of handcuffs dangling from his hand. He closed one around my left wrist, shocking me when he closed the other around his right wrist, before clipping them together.

"Did you just handcuff me to you?"

"Yup. This way you're really not going anywhere. Now, go the fuck to sleep."

And then we were both lying flat next to each other, nothing touching but our pinkies. He did something on his phone and then the lights were out and the room was dark.

"Do you snore?" I asked the dark room. Because what the fuck else was there to say? My childhood crush turned nemesis had become my sexual tormentor-slash-captor-slash-fake-boyfriend (maybe) so fast I had whiplash. And now I was literally handcuffed to the asshole.

I heard him laugh. "No, I don't snore. Do you?"

I paused. I had no way of knowing. "I don't know," I admitted.

"What, none of your ex-boyfriends told you?" he asked dryly.

The truth was, I'd never spent the night with someone else other than my mom, and that had been years ago, but I wasn't about to tell him that.

"What about you? Do the girls tell you if you snore?"

It was quiet for a moment before he admitted, "I've never spent the night with one of them, so I have no idea."

A sweet feeling took hold of my chest. I shouldn't care that Isaac hadn't spent the night with a girl before. I *couldn't*.

But I did.

"Well," I finally said. "Don't. Or I'll kidney punch you."

He laughed again, but didn't say anything else.

And even though my mind and heart were both racing, even though I was somewhere strange and unfamiliar and deeply unsafe, even though there was a metal handcuff attached to my wrist and that couldn't be fucking comfortable, my body somehow didn't get the memo that we were in danger. Instead, I relaxed in the soft warmth of Isaac's bed, liking the graze of his fingers against mine. As his breathing deepened and slowed, so did mine—until I was fast asleep.

13

Isaac

I woke up in the dead of night to soft snores in my ear and the warm weight of a woman in my arms.

Tovah.

I couldn't resist pulling her tighter against me. We had gone to sleep lying side to side, but at some point in the night, one or both of us had moved, and she was sprawled out on my chest, her curly pink hair tickling my chin and nose. Our cuffed arms lay connected across her back. My wrist ached from the way the handcuff dug into my skin, but I couldn't lie—I liked the assurance of knowing she couldn't go *anywhere*. Her captivity satisfied the monster, who was frustratingly obsessive over this woman I truly couldn't stand.

What was it about her? There was no plausible reason I should be so compelled, so obsessed. There'd been plenty of pretty girls over the years, but none of them got my cock hard the way she did. None of them were here in my bed, handcuffed to me. None of them made me want to know them, inside and out, mind, heart, and soul. The monster had slept through all of them. There was something about her: the rebellious, I-don't-give-a-fuck attitude toward other people, her compassion and care toward her friends, her intelligence and savvy, her strength and sass when she stood up to me and fought me, which no one did. Or maybe it was her determination to find the truth and share it with the world, no matter how it hurt her—even while she hid her own truths.

Speaking of which.

I reached out with my free arm, fumbling around on my nightstand until I grabbed my phone, holding it up to my face to unlock it in the dark. Once it was open, I pulled up my texts and messaged my sister.

> Any info on Tovah Lewis?

> Why are you awake? It's late.

> Can't sleep.

> Girl trouble. I never thought it could happen. For Reuben? Sure. For you? Never.

I smiled despite myself. Reuben was my second youngest brother and was always getting into some mess with a girl.

But Tovah breathed in my arms, reminding me why I'd texted my sister in the first place.

> Info, please.

> Nothing. Whatever there is on her is buried deep and locked down. I keep hitting a brick wall. Maybe you should try your friend Jack's brother, Micah? He's an expert hacker, he should be able to find something.

I sighed. That would mean telling Jack more than I needed to, but maybe it would help if he knew where my head was at. Not to mention he and the team were going to have to help me babysit my captive, so he was going to have to know sooner rather than later.

> Okay.

> Love you. Stay out of any messes I'll have to clean up later.

I didn't respond. I did love my sister, but I couldn't say it. Hadn't been able to say those words since my mother was killed.

Tovah murmured something in her sleep. I put down my phone and leaned in closer to hear her.

I was shocked by the word that came out of her mouth, on a breathy moan.

"Isaac..."

Was she dreaming of me?

Fuck. Was she having a sex dream about me?

My cock, trapped by her bare, silky thigh, went hard in my sweats. I curled my free hand into a fist to keep myself from reaching between her thighs and testing to see if my hunch was right and she was wet.

I couldn't do it. I'd already crossed so many fucking lines when I'd let the beast out and had eaten her into multiple orgasms without her consent. I couldn't touch her in her sleep.

But...

Couldn't I?

She was here. Asleep. Helpless. In my arms.

And there was no one to stop me but *me*.

On that realization, I slipped my hand between her thighs, gently swiping my thumb on the boxer briefs of mine she was wearing.

And grunted in pleased shock.

Wet.

She was dreaming of me.

And I was going to make her have an even better dream.

Sliding my fingers under the elastic, I began to play. She was mostly hairless, with just a small triangle of short curls. The idea that she waxed for anyone else made my heart roar with frustration. But it didn't matter. She was here now, with me, and wouldn't be touching or touched by anyone else as long as she was mine. I stroked my fingers up and down her slit, gathering some of her wetness before focusing my middle and index finger on her clit, hiding under its hood. Slowly, carefully, gently—maybe even tenderly—I started tracing small, light circles around it, barely rubbing. I was rewarded by more wetness as her arousal grew.

I was rewarded more when she moaned my name again.

Fuck.

All I wanted to do was slip my cock inside her pussy, but I'd meant it when I'd told her she had to earn it. And while I could excuse myself for touching her, I wasn't sure I could rationalize full on fucking her while she was asleep. Instead, I appeased myself by playing, drawing more circles, patterns, even tracing my name on her pussy as she moaned and shifted in my arms.

That's right, little snoop. You come for me. *And* only *me. Whenever I want you to.*

I sped up my circles, following her breathing patterns and movements, this time not so lost in her cunt that I couldn't pay attention to what she liked and didn't like. She was perfect this way, vulnerable, open, unaware and unable to fight me. And when her thighs tightened and she inhaled, somehow still asleep but close to coming, I stuffed two of my fingers inside her while playing her clit with my thumb, and oh fucking god, the way she squeezed them so tight when she orgasmed.

It made me do something I hadn't done since I was a teenager: come in my sweatpants.

Some-fucking-how, doing nothing but playing with her pussy was the hottest sex I'd had in years. Maybe the hottest sex I'd ever had.

Yeah, I wasn't fucking turning Tovah Lewis over to my father to be killed. Not when she was such a perfect little plaything. Not when she was the only bit of light in the darkness.

This was the moment where I should've unlocked the handcuffs, gone to the bathroom and cleaned myself up. Maybe even slept in another room to get distance from her and this uncomfortable feeling in my chest, like something had been cracked open and was leaking out. I couldn't risk feeling about her this way, about feeling anything about her at all. Not when I knew that she wasn't for me, long-term. No one was. I'd learned that the hard way as a young boy when my mother was killed right in front of my eyes.

So yeah, I should've gotten the hell out of that bed, washed away the reminder of what Tovah did to my body, and put a wall between us, literally and figuratively.

Instead, I rearranged Tovah so she was curled into the nook below my arm, her head resting on my chest, and closed my eyes, reveling in a feeling that would never, ever last. And swiftly fell asleep, and slept better than I had since my mother was killed.

14

Tovah

I woke up, groaning. My underwear was embarrassingly wet, my shoulder hurt, my back ached, and my wrist stung.

But at least the weight of the metal handcuff was gone.

Was I free? Had Isaac changed his mind?

And why did that thought make my stomach drop like a lead weight?

Stretching, I sat up. Isaac stood at the edge of the bed, holding a steaming mug of what I assumed was coffee. I didn't drink coffee, even though like any good journalist, I subsisted on caffeine (in the form of chai lattes), chocolate peanut butter cups, and determination—and not much else. Isaac probably didn't care. Or the drink was for him.

Except he leaned over, holding out the mug. The delicious scent of cinnamon, ginger, cardamom, and cloves teased my nostrils.

How did he know that was my drink of choice?

"Here," he said, passing it to me. After a moment of hesitation, I took it, lifting it to my nose and sniffing.

"Did you poison it?" I asked suspiciously.

He snorted. "I'm saving that for if you really piss me off."

Well, that certainly put a damper on things.

"How'd you know I like chai?"

"I know everything about you," he said.

Not everything. If he did, he would've mentioned my mother when he threatened me.

"Have you been stalking me?"

He nodded.

"Wait, what the hell?" He'd been stalking me?

"For how long?"

"Since we met."

"Over a year?!" This was insane. *He* was insane. And the real question was:

"Why?" I asked, completely confused.

He glared at me but didn't answer, his eyes catching on my wrist, which had been rubbed raw from wearing the handcuff all night. His jaw went tight, some look coming to his eyes I couldn't read. If I didn't know better, I'd say it was regret. But there was no way. Isaac didn't care that he'd hurt me with the handcuffs.

"Why is your wrist so red?" he demanded.

I glared.

"Why do you think?" I retorted.

The strange look in his eyes disappeared, and they went blank and cold.

"I need to go train. You don't have class until eleven—yes, I know your schedule, too—and usually I'd bring you with me, but you're not coming to the gym."

"What, you don't want me around your shirtless, sweaty

teammates?" I fluttered my eyelashes. "That's too bad, it sounds like a good time."

His eyes narrowed. "You won't be seeing anyone shirtless but me," he stated. "I'm leaving you here but taking your phone with me. The office door is locked and the WiFi is disabled anyway. The doors will be locked, the alarm on, and if you try to escape...well then, poisoning you sounds like a good alternative to keeping you under lock and key." He lowered his voice. "Don't get into trouble, little snoop, or I'll find a new way to punish you...since you liked your spanking so much."

I growled, but didn't deny it.

"Drink your latte," he ordered.

I took a sip, moaning. It was fucking delicious, the best one I'd ever had—and I was a chai latte connoisseur.

"Where did you get this?"

He shrugged. "I made it."

"What?!" I gaped at him. "Since when do hockey playing billionaire mafia princes make their own drinks? Or anything?"

"I may know a lot about you, Tovah, but for a reporter, you really haven't done your homework. Might want to work on those investigative skills," he tsked. "I'll be back later to take you to class."

With those final, obnoxious words, he sauntered out of the bedroom. A minute later, I heard the alarm go on.

I smiled.

He might shit on my investigating skills, but I was about to prove him wrong. He'd locked the fox in the hen house, and I was going to use this time alone in his home to find every fucking piece of evidence I could against him and his family.

"Freedom, here I come," I said to myself, humming "Tiny Dancer" from *Almost Famous* as I headed into the bathroom to shower and brush my teeth before embarking on my fact-finding mission.

15

Isaac

"You don't call, you don't text. No one's posted on social media lately about you saving old ladies or helping puppies cross the street. Where the hell have you been?" Judah asked me as we sat on the bench, lacing up our skates.

I tugged them extra tight in frustration. "I can't be a hero every day," I said, but winced at the strain in my voice.

Levi joined us, dropping down on the bench to put on his skates, too. "You know, my brother likes to give you shit for girl trouble, but there's girl trouble and there's girl crisis."

I sighed, rubbing my temples. "Sometimes I wish you weren't fucking psychic."

"What fun would that be?" Judah asked.

I hesitated. I tended to be a closed book around most of my friends, because it was safer that way. But I could tell them what was going on without telling them who I was. So I cleared my throat. "Tovah Kaufman is living with me."

Levi raised an eyebrow like he was impressed. "That was fast."

Judah laughed. "He's been hyperfocused on her for over a year now. Doesn't seem that fast to me. How's the sex? I've heard she's—"

My hand fisted. "Don't talk about her that way."

Judah raised his own. "No harm meant. Girl has a reputation, that's all."

I forced myself to relax my fingers. *Fuck.* Why was I defending her this way? Had the little snoop gotten under my skin that quickly? But then Judah was right; she'd crept her way under there long before she tried to blackmail me.

Speaking of which, I needed to talk to the team about that. Give them a heads up and get their help.

"Gentlemen, what's with the dawdling? Practice started five minutes ago," Coach said, blowing his whistle. Jack stood beside him, eyes trained on me.

Ah damn. Lowering my voice, I said, "the crisis applies to all of us."

"Let's talk on the ice," Levi said, and rising, we entered the rink. The four of us found each other, doing hip and quad stretches.

"What's going on?" Jack asked.

"Tovah knows about Vice and Vixen."

Judah and Levi glanced at each other. Jack looked pissed.

"We're out of that game," he said. "I thought we'd agreed on this already."

"We did," I said, continuing to stretch. "But Tovah got evidence of it and was planning on writing an article about it. So I uh, kind of kidnapped her and blackmailed her into living with me so I can keep an eye on her."

It was almost comical, the way all three of my friends'

mouths dropped open. Judah had frozen in a lying quad stretch, like a statue of a hockey player mid hump.

"I'm sorry," Jack said in a choked voice. "You 'kind of' kidnapped her? How do you 'kind of' kidnap someone?"

"You kind of chase them down on the street, throw them in the trunk of your car, drive them home, lock them in your house, and handcuff them to you at night so they can't get away from you," I mumbled under my breath, but given the acoustics of the arena, all three heard me.

After another frozen moment, my friends started stretching again.

"Well, I guess that's one way to court someone," Judah said.

"She was going to write an article exposing all of us. It's less of an issue for those of you who were already drafted, but for the younger guys...well, it could fuck up everything for them. Not to mention for the Kings going forward," I said, somewhat defensively. "I did it for the team."

"Sure, for the team," Judah repeated, raising an eyebrow.

"It is a major issue," Levi argued.

"Doesn't mean we can't call his motivation into question," Judah argued back.

Coach blew his whistle for laps. Jack skated over to me and helped me up.

"She's really done a number on you, hasn't she. Talk to me about what she knows."

As we skated, I walked him through everything that had happened since stalking her to Sebastian's apartment. Jack listened without interrupting, his blades moving on the ice.

When I was done and we'd moved onto drills, he said, "What's the plan?"

I shook my head as we practiced some stick handling. "I need the team to take turns watching her, escorting her to class and newspaper meetings when I'm unavailable. I don't trust her." I passed him the puck.

Jack nodded, but he didn't pass the puck back. "As a heads up: The more time you spend with her? The more you're going to want her and the harder it's going to be to let her go."

He finally passed the puck back to me and I caught it, turning in a circle and shooting the puck toward the net, where Asher stood, waiting.

"That's what I'm worried about," I admitted. "But I don't see a way around it."

As we set up to scrimmage, I didn't add that it was probably already too late.

After practice and I showered and changed, I headed back to my house in my car. On impulse though, I made a left and not a right, headed to the sleazy sex shop in town. If I was going to have Tovah underfoot, and always on my mind, I needed a way to get some of my control back.

As I drove, my infotainment system alerted me that I had an incoming call from my father.

Fuck.

There was only so many times I could ignore the man I hated so completely. Memories appeared: Being forced to learn how to shoot a gun, watching my siblings kill our enemies at young ages. My father having his men beat them for speaking out, talking out of turn, fighting back. Starving me for days when I refused to pick up a gun; hurting my siblings in front of my eyes when I was helpless to stop them. Liza crying in the bathroom as she administered to our cuts and burns and bruises, saying fiercely, "One day, I'll be in charge. One day, I'll change everything," and the rest of us being in too much pain and having too much doubt to even respond to her wild fantasies.

Refusing to kill the son of the man who'd murdered my mother and being punished for it—in ways that left no physical scars, just internal wounds that would never heal.

I refused to be like my father. But that didn't mean I could avoid him forever.

I finally answered. "Hello, Dad."

"A real man does not shirk his responsibilities," my father said immediately.

Guess we weren't exchanging any pleasantries.

"We made a deal," I reminded him.

"Yes, and you've reneged on your end of it. Refusing to distribute Vice and Vixen is a real issue for the family business. Do I have to remind you what the consequences are?"

"What else can you take from me?" I asked him angrily. "I already have to give up hockey. What else is there?"

He laughed darkly, and I could hear a hint of wild mania in it. My father had never been completely sane. "You might think right now that losing hockey is the worst thing that could ever happen to you. But there are such bigger, more important things and people to grieve."

Tovah's pink hair, nose stud, and the strength in her eyes when she refused to bend all flashed in my mind. Was he threatening her? Did he know about her? I swallowed.

"Heard." I said. "But Vice and Vixen—"

He interrupted. "I'll let that go. But there are other things you can do for this family, now. Perhaps it's time to start considering marriage—the kind of business merger that will fortify our family and its legacy."

Tovah's face flashed in my mind again.

"I won't fucking go along with an arranged marriage," I told him point blank. "That's absurd."

I wasn't marrying anyone. He knew that. There was only one woman I wanted, and even though she was currently locked away safely in my house, I'd promised myself it was only temporary.

Abe sighed. "Believe this, son. I will do everything and anything, no matter how extreme, to make sure you take your place in this family. You don't want to push me."

"Oh, I know," I said bitterly. "You've taught me how little you care about who you hurt to get what you want."

My father chuckled. "One day, you'll understand why. I'll be seeing you for dinner soon, son."

I hung up without replying.

Damn it.

Pulling into the sex shop, I parked my car, turned it off, and knocked my head against the wheel. The pain helped mitigate some of the frustration.

No, I might not have control in my life outside Reina.

But here, I was king. And I'd make sure to keep it that way.

Starting with Tovah.

16

Tovah

I had failed to consider one important fact: I had no clean underwear. There was no way I was wearing my pink lace panties from yesterday; just the idea made me cringe. And I wasn't going to class sans unmentionables, either. Or wearing a pair of Isaac's boxer-briefs. *Ugh.*

I was about to collapse back on the bed in frustration, when a thought came to me, filling me with glee. Isaac might have given me rules, and I might have to play by them for now, but that didn't mean I couldn't find ways to get him back. I needed to show him I wasn't a doormat he could walk all over, and I knew just the way to do it.

Grabbing my bright pink lace panties off the ground, I spotted his laundry hamper and carried it downstairs, searching until I found the absolutely ginormous, pristine laundry room.

"Rich people," I muttered in annoyance.

I didn't even have laundry in my building; I had to lug my dirty clothes all the way to the nearest laundromat. The huge difference between our lives had never been more clear. Isaac and I were polar opposites. My goal in life was to speak truth to power, he hid the truth so he could maintain his power and control. I'd spent my whole life poor, he was so wealthy he'd never known a day of struggle in his life. I only had my mother as my family and hadn't even gotten to be around her for my teenage years, he had a huge family he could rely on—even if his father was an evil asshole. I tried to stick to the background in order to do my job without too much attention, he lived in the spotlight—and loved it. And I dressed like a pop punk princess—multicolored, ever-changing hair, torn jeans, nose stud and attitude—whereas Isaac looked completely preppy and straightlaced...until you saw all the tattoos he was hiding.

And there were a lot of them. There was a whole sleeve on his left arm, although I hadn't gotten the chance to really study them. All I'd seen was a man with a gun for a face... horrifyingly, the mysterious violence drawn on his skin only made Isaac hotter.

Anyway, we were polar opposites. Who would *not* attract, even if I had to fight myself every single day until I got free of here and of him.

Opening the washer, I dumped his clothes inside. They were mostly faded jeans, white t-shirts and button downs. Then, with more than a bit of savage, vengeful glee, I tossed my pink underwear on top, threw in some detergent, closed the lid and hit start.

"Millennial pink one, Isaac Silver, zero," I said with satisfaction.

That done, I turned to my next task.

Isaac said he'd locked his office door, but he obviously didn't know that I had learned how to pick a lock at a young age. I didn't *have* my lock picking tools with me, or even a bobby pin, but I was sure there was something in his house that would be a good substitute. Heading into the kitchen, I went through the drawers, looking for a thin, pointing object, and settled on two metal skewers he must use for grilling kabobs. Or his housekeeper did; I still didn't believe that Isaac was self-sufficient enough to cook for himself.

I wandered the house, testing each locked door. I didn't know how much time I had until Isaac got back from practice, so I listened carefully for him as I used my makeshift lock picks to open all the doors. Bedrooms, a gaming room, a workout room—I wasn't sure why he'd locked them all, but I didn't care about the rest. Finally, I found his office. It was modern—white walls, white, L-shaped desk with two monitors. The bookshelves were filled with foreign language and linguistics books and novels in their original languages. It made sense: I'd learned that Isaac was a linguistics major, with minors in French, Spanish, Italian, Portuguese, Hindi, Urdu...the man was a polyglot, and I assumed it had to do with the work he was planning on doing for his father down the line. It did force me to respect him; he was by no means a dumb jock.

There was nothing on the walls, except an MVP plaque for the Kings and a photo of him, Jack, Judah, and Levi, arms slung around each other. The Core Four, ruling over Reina without a care in the world. They looked casual and happy, Isaac's dimples out on full display.

An annoying part of me wished he'd direct those dimples at me.

But I knew it would never happen, nor did I really want it to. He was my enemy, and chai lattes aside, I needed to remember that before I did something stupid. Like forget my mission and act like a lovesick idiot.

Turning back to my task, I started carefully opening

drawers in his desk, only to be stymied by how empty they were. No paperwork, no bookkeeping, nothing. On some level, I'd known it was stupid to expect that he'd have papers with obvious ties to his father's business, but I certainly had hoped.

The bottom drawer was locked with a code.

Jackpot.

There had to be something useful in here. Maybe even his laptop. Unfortunately, I had no idea what the code could be. I started testing a few options: his birthday, the day his mother had died. Neither worked. I was wracking my brain for other ideas when the alarm beeped off.

"Shit, shit, shit," I muttered.

"Honey, I'm home," Isaac called. I heard footsteps.

Oh, fuck.

Abandoning the locked drawer, I made sure all the others were closed before hurrying out of his office, locking the door behind me just in time.

He appeared at the top of the steps as I stepped out into the hallway.

"Miss me?" he asked.

"Like a toothache," I said.

He snorted. "Nice to still see you in my clothes, but I brought home some of yours. Here," he said, handing me a small duffle bag.

Unzipping it, I found jeans, hoodies, tank tops, a dress, two bras...and no underwear whatsoever.

"What the hell, Isaac?" I said, appalled.

A sly smile slid across his face. He knew exactly what I meant. "You don't need them."

"Fortunately, I washed mine," I told him, so annoyed I decided to spoil my surprise. "And I was nice enough to wash some of your clothes, too."

His smile dropped away, his gaze suspicious.

"What did you do, Tovah?"

I shrugged, unable to conceal my grin. "See for yourself."

Isaac headed back down the stairs, and I followed him, needing to see his face. He walked into the laundry room, opening the washing machine. And like I'd planned, every single item either had pink spots on it, or had turned completely pink.

"You. Goddamned. Brat," he said slowly.

"What, is it not your color? I think it brings out the evil in your eyes," I said innocently.

He turned toward me, holding one of his hockey jerseys. Although the majority of the jersey itself was still red, the white lettering had turned pink.

"Tovah..." he began.

"Oopsies," I said, then collapsed into giggles at the sight of the shocked anger on his face. And, if I wasn't wrong, there was even a little bit of respect there, like he was impressed by my ballsiness.

I was, too.

"...run," he finished.

Still gasping with laughter, I turned on my bare feet and raced out of the laundry room, down the hallway, and up the stairs. His feet thudded after me as he followed.

I ran into his bedroom, slamming the door shut—or trying to, but his hand shot out, catching the door and forcing it open.

As he advanced on me, I retreated, my next plan to lock myself in the bathroom. But before I could reach it, I was being lifted in the air and thrown on the bed.

Oh no, not this bullshit again.

I tried to crawl away, only for Isaac to grab me around

my right calf and drag me backward. Shoving a hand between my shoulders, he delivered hard swat after hard swat to my bare ass—because my underwear was still in the dryer.

His slaps *burned*, like yesterday's spanking had been nothing more than a prelude to the real thing. He went at my ass brutally, like it had personally offended him and the only possible response was to leave painful handprints.

I screamed and fought, kicking and trying to get away.

He just spanked me harder.

"This is what you get for being a smart ass brat," he said sternly as he peppered my ass with pain. "And it's only the beginning. You're going to hurt when you try to sit in class, and you're not going to forget what happens when you try to fuck with me. I know you like it, though, don't you? I don't even have to touch your pussy, I can smell how wet you're getting."

"Fuck you," I said, even though it was muffled against the comforter.

"Oh you'd like that, wouldn't you?" *Slap.* "But you certainly haven't earned my cock yet." *Slap slap.* "You're going to be begging for it like a little whore before I give it to you." *Slap slap slap slap slap.*

"Stop!"

"Say you're sorry."

"No!"

"Then you're going to miss class," he threatened. "And I'll turn your ass black and blue."

"Fine, fine. I'm sorry," I cried.

Immediately he stopped, cupping my ass like he was trying to contain the heat that centered there.

"Stay there," he ordered, disappearing for a moment.

The burn in my ass had relocated to my pussy, my core

clenching with the need to come. I tried to ignore it. I certainly wasn't going to let him know how good it felt and how badly I needed his touch.

When he reappeared, fabric brushed my ankles. He was working underwear up over my legs. I relaxed slightly, until elastic strings swept over my ass, only to settle around my hips.

A thong?! Who the hell still wore thongs?

He pulled the elastic, releasing it so snapped back into place, making the burn worse. I yelped from the shocking pain.

There was a weird bump at the front of the panties, right over my clit.

A moment later, I heard a buzz.

And the panties started *vibrating.*

All the arousal I'd tried to dampen returned with a vengeance, driving me up toward the cliff I was terrified to fall over. My core tightened, a coil of need within me...

And then it stopped. Right before I came.

"What the fuck, Isaac?"

The vibrations started again.

"On my way back from hockey practice I stopped at that sleazy sex shop," he said conversationally, over the buzzing and the horrible pleasure. "I realized that even if spanking wasn't a real punishment, edging you—in public—might be. Congratulations, Tovah, you're about to slut it up in journalism class today."

"You wouldn't," I gasped.

Pain lashed through my scalp as he gripped my hair in a ponytail and pulled me up and backward, until I was kneeling up on the bed, my body arched in a bow, my head craned back to look at him.

"Oh, I would, little snoop. You don't even know the

beginnings of what I'll do to put you in your place and keep you there."

Releasing me so I fell forward on the bed, he walked toward his closet. "I guess I'm going to be matching your hair today. What color pink is that, anyway?"

"Millennial pink," I said, flipping onto my back and glaring as he ripped his shirt off over his head, exposing delineated muscles on the most beautiful back I'd ever seen. The sleeve tattoos on his arm of shadows, guns, blood and death stopped, interrupted by a stone wall with a dying vine crawling across his back. I was curious what it meant but didn't want to ask. The tattoos were just more proof that the good, straightlaced guy he presented in public wasn't who he was in private. I hated to admit it, but they were also fucking hot.

He pulled one of the now pink long-sleeved shirts over his head, and the tattoos disappeared like they'd never existed. It felt like a secret between us. They weren't, obviously—his teammates would've seen him shirtless, and so had probably plenty women when he'd fucked them. But I couldn't help but feel like I held the keys to Isaac Silver.

Turning to me, he rolled his eyes. "That's stupid."

I'd lost track of the conversation. "What is?"

"Millennial Pink. You're not even a millennial."

I rolled my eyes right back at him, trying not to show that his insult hurt. I hated being called stupid. "Well, sucks for you, because now you look as stupid as you think I do."

He paused. "Tovah, I don't think you're stupid," he said. "Or look stupid. Far from it. I just think it's a dumb name for the color."

"Oh."

It was actually the nicest thing he'd ever said to me. But then the bar was in hell.

He nodded to the duffle bag he must have brought in here at some point. "Get dressed. We're going to be late for your class."

I gaped at him. "We? You're not actually coming with me."

"Oh, I am. I've always wanted to learn about journalistic...ethics. Especially because I'm not going to learn them from you."

Ouch.

Like I said, the bar was in hell.

17

Tovah

In my time at Reina, I'd been mostly invisible. Yeah, students knew who I was, mostly from my byline, but no one noticed me when I was walking across the arts and sciences quad to class or eating in the cafeteria or studying in the library or getting a chai latte in the café.

So it was a strange and deeply uncomfortable experience to be walking through campus with Isaac next to me. *Everyone* noticed him, everyone said hi, congratulating him on his win for the last hockey game, or sending him flirtatious glances. It was like a giant spotlight followed him, bathing him in the most flattering light. *Even* in the pink shirt he wore.

He responded to everyone easily, a charming grin on his face, dimples in place, nodding to some, saying hello to others, giving fist bumps to guys and gentle shoulder squeezes to girls. But even though no one else noticed, I could see a slight strain behind his smile, like maybe Isaac wasn't such an extrovert and being so social and friendly drained his energy. It made me feel sympathetic toward him, because I knew what it was like to wear a mask. And I hated that. I didn't want to feel sympathetic toward the asshole. I didn't want to feel anything but well-deserved animosity.

The worst part? Was that for once, people were noticing *me*. Some of Isaac's spotlight was trained on me, and not in a good way. Students were elbowing each other and whispering, confused and trying to figure out who the rebel with the pink hair was, and why Isaac was walking so close to her. I could feel their scrutiny, and I hated that, too.

"Tovah, slow down," Isaac ordered, catching up to me in relaxed strides.

I'd been trying to hurry ahead of him, hoping to put some distance between us and get people to stop looking at me. It didn't work, his legs were too long and he was too fast. And I wasn't exactly going to run across campus and let him chase me, even if a part of me got lost in the fantasy of him grabbing me and shoving me to the grass and—

Stop it, Tovah, I admonished myself. *You absolutely cannot want him.*

"I'm going to be late for class," I offered as an explanation over my shoulder.

His eyes narrowed. "Bullshit, we have plenty of time."

Reaching out, he caught my hand in his, engulfing my small hand in his big one. Interlacing our fingers, he brought my hand to his lips, dropping kisses on my knuckles.

My heart stuttered in my chest. The sweetness took me by surprise, and each kiss sent tingles through my body.

"What are you doing?"

He smirked. "Selling the act."

My heart started beating normally again. Of course. This wasn't real. Isaac felt no tenderness toward me. He was making it look like we were intimate as rationale for why he was spending so much time with me, and vice versa. It was going to be humiliating when he finally released me from his blackmail and it looked like he'd dumped me like yesterday's trash.

No, I reminded myself. It wasn't going to be humiliating for me. It was going to be humiliating for him when I got to the bottom of his father's illegal activities, exposed his whole family, and Isaac was led away in handcuffs.

Speaking of handcuffs. My wrist still stung—the same wrist attached to the hand that Isaac was holding. The same wrist Isaac was glaring at, like it had harmed him in some past life.

"What's wrong with it?" he asked.

"With what?"

"Your wrist."

"The handcuffs fucked it up," I told him.

"What the fuck?" he growled.

I stopped, turning to face him, trying to tug my hand out of his. He tightened his grip.

"Why do you even care?" I asked. "The handcuffs were —" I lowered my voice, aware of the people around us. "They were your idea."

He grunted. It was funny; everyone else got conversation, I got grunts and growls as the barest of acknowledgment that I'd spoken.

"Also, people are staring."

"Of course they are," he said. "They've never seen me hold a girl's hand before. You should feel special."

I snorted. "So special."

We'd reached the steps outside of the Language and Literature Building, which was where my journalism class was. Resigning myself to my fate, I tugged Isaac up the stairs, and he followed, finally dropping my hand to pull the door open for me.

"How chivalrous," I said as I stepped inside, waiting for him as he held the door open for the girls following us.

"Hi, Isaac," one said. "You played so well the other night."

"Thanks," he grinned, dimples popping out. "Couldn't do it without my team—and the support of my fans."

"You look good in pink," the other girl giggled.

"Yeah?" he winked. "I think it brings out the brown in my eyes, personally."

Annoyed, I left him there. If he wanted to flirt with other girls and ruin our cover, then that was on him, not me.

Moments later, he'd caught up to me. "Where'd you go?"

"You seemed busy, and I have to get to class," I said, trying to make my voice casual, even though I wanted to punch him.

He chuckled. "You're jealous."

"Am not."

"Are too."

"Are you a child?" I scoffed. "I don't care who you flirt with, Isaac. I don't care about anything you do."

"Really. So if I took those girls, found a closet, and fucked them both, you wouldn't be upset?"

I stopped, and, aware that people were watching us, stood up on my tiptoes, wrapping my arms around his neck. His arms came up around my waist, gripping my hips. Pressing my lips against his ear, I whispered, "You can stick your dick wherever you want, because you'll *never* be sticking it in me."

"Never say never," he taunted.

I released his neck, but he didn't release my waist. "It's going to be so sweet when you finally beg for my cock."

I looked up at the clock on the wall. Class was starting in five minutes.

"Can those absurd fantasies be taken to go? I'm going to be late."

He released me, only to drop an arm over my shoulder and guide me down the hall to my Ethics in Journalism classroom.

"How do you know where my class is?"

"I know—"

"Everything about me. Yeah, yeah," I muttered.

When we entered the classroom, everyone's heads popped up. There was more murmuring. Isaac took it in stride, just like he'd taken the pink shirt. He scanned the room, choosing a row about five back from the lectern, and nodding to the seat next to the aisle.

Sighing, I slid in. He dropped into the seat next to me, his legs so long he had to stretch out in the aisle. The whispering grew louder.

"Ugh, do you *have* to be here?"

"Yes," he said.

The professor, an older man in a wrinkled suit, passed by our row.

"Sir," he addressed Isaac. "I don't believe you belong here."

Isaac grinned. "Couldn't let my best girl go to class alone, could I?" he said, slipping an arm back over my shoulders, making me hunch. "She hates when I'm not with her," he continued, making my chest tighten.

Oh god, he was about to humiliate me.

"He can leave," I started. "I'll—"

But Isaac wasn't done. "You know the clingy type. She even dyed my shirt pink and insisted I wear it today so we match. And I'd feel too guilty making her cry, so here I am.

You don't mind, do you?" he finished, dimples on full display.

There was silence, and then laughter rang out in the room. It echoed, haunting me. I tried to slump down in my seat, my cheeks flaming, but Isaac moved his hand to the back of my neck, gripping it to keep me in place.

And then he turned and dropped a *falsely* sweet kiss on my lips.

The professor cleared his throat. "Well, as long as you don't cause too much of a distraction, you can stay."

"Thank you, sir," Isaac said with his usual bullshit charm.

Once the professor had moved on, I turned my head to Isaac.

"I'm going to kill you," I hissed.

He released my neck, pulling his phone out of his pocket. "Oh, you're *really* going to want to kill me soon," he threatened with a deep laugh.

The professor began his lecture on the code of ethics most journalists sign when they start working at a media outlet. I tried to pay attention, but Isaac clearly had other ideas, because as I began taking notes, there was a quiet buzzing sound and my fucking panties began to vibrate. I jumped, then glared over, shaking my head at him. He winked, playing with his phone. The gentle vibrations grew stronger. I'd done my best to forget about the vibrating underwear on our way to class, and had succeeded, until now. How was I supposed to ignore them, when they massaged my pussy in all the right—no, wrong—places? The thickest part moved in rumbling vibrations against my clit, waking it up and making it ache for more.

But I couldn't want more. I couldn't get off *here*. People

would figure out what was happening, and I'd be even more of a laughingstock.

Or worse, get kicked out of class. Maybe out of school. Goodbye, journalism dreams.

It didn't matter. The more I tried to ignore the pleasure in my core building, the more intense it got. I couldn't ignore Isaac's dark gaze as he watched me try with all my might not to come.

I was so, so close. My breathing had sped up, my nipples were hard, and I was biting my lip to hold in my gasps. Was I going to moan or cry out when I came? Was there any way I could hide it?

"Let it happen," Isaac murmured.

And I had no choice. My whole body coiled tight, the wire to orgasm about to be tripped and—

The buzzing stopped. So did the vibrations.

I slumped back in my seat, breathing heavily. I'd been so close, about to come and completely destroy my reputation, but Isaac had given me a reprieve.

Was the vibrating underwear just meant as a warning not to disobey him? Was this it?

"Thank god," I gasped.

"I wouldn't thank god just yet," Isaac murmured again, and the vibrations returned.

So did the coiled tight feeling. I was closer this time, because of how he'd teased me earlier. Tense and terrified and, worse, wanting it, I hovered on the precipice of the orgasm...

...only for Isaac to dial back the vibrations again, tugging me back from the brink.

And then he did it again.

And again.

And again.

And again.

By the fifth time he'd edged me, my pussy *ached* with the need to come, and I was no longer capable of even minutely ignoring it or hiding my fortunately quiet moans. I no longer gave a shit if I came in front of the whole goddamned class and got expelled. I needed, truly needed, *desperately* needed to finally come and release the painful tension in my body.

My skin hummed from the vibrations, so aroused I was sure there was a wet spot on my wooden auditorium chair. My chest was heaving and I was biting my lip so hard I could taste my own blood. I pulsed, my pussy trying to grip something that wasn't there. Closing my eyes, I got lost in a fantasy of Isaac pulling me onto his lap, ripping off my jeans, panties, and shoving what had to be a huge cock inside me. It didn't matter that I'd never had sex before, or that I hated him. I needed him to quell the ache he'd created.

"Ms. Kaufman? Ms. Kaufman," the professor was calling my name, aggravation in his voice.

My eyes shot open.

Oh, shit.

"Ms. Kaufman, did you fall asleep?"

"N—no," I said weakly. "I was just concentrating on what you were saying."

"And what was I saying?"

I cleared my dry throat. I had no idea, and what's more, I was terrified to speak, especially when Isaac ramped up the vibrations so high my clit was pulsing. Someone must be able to hear it.

"Um," I started, when Isaac spoke.

"You were talking about the importance of protecting

your sources," he said. "That their anonymity and privacy matters more than the story itself."

The professor smiled, impressed. "Thank you, Mr.—"

"Jones," Isaac said easily, as he began to trace figure eights on my knee. The gentle, barely there touch over my jeans was more arousing than the vibrations, or maybe it was the combination and his casual display of ownership that shoved me so close to the precipice. I teetered there, my clit throbbing, my insides clenching, a whimper trapped in my throat, because *ohgodohgodohgodIcouldn'tstopitIwasaboutto—*

Isaac lifted his hand, and said, "It's Tovah you should thank. She's taught me a lot about journalism since she first started following me around—" the whole class laughed at this, and I would've been embarrassed and livid if I wasn't about to have the biggest orgasm *of my life*—"and it's been... enlightening."

The vibrations stopped.

I didn't hurt any less. I didn't throb any less or stop clenching.

But at least I didn't scream in tortured denial.

"Well," said the professor. "That's our class for the day. Please do the reading. Ms. Kaufman, if you could come to my office? Alone?"

Isaac stiffened beside me as students gathered their stuff and rose to leave. "She won't be going anywhere alone," he stated firmly.

The professor raised his eyebrow. "And Ms. Kaufman is the clingy one?"

I would've laughed, if I didn't want to cry.

Isaac scowled.

"I'll leave you to say goodbye to your...friend, Tovah. I'll be waiting for you in my office," the professor said, departing and leaving us alone in the lecture hall.

"You don't say a word to him about what's going on," he warned. "You will not like the consequences, Tovah."

"Heard," I said, relieved as the tension in my body began to ease.

"I have an Italian test, so I won't be able to come with you to your newspaper meeting, but Judah and Levi will be escorting you. Do *not* cause them any trouble."

With that, he bent down, wrapping a hand in my hair and tugging my head back so he could kiss me. It wasn't a light, gentle kiss like before. No, this was all tongue and teeth and ownership, a declaration to anyone watching that I was *his*. And god help me, but it felt so fucking good, and he tasted so good, the orgasm he'd been teasing me with exploded, so intense and sharp I saw stars and swooned. I probably would've fallen if Isaac hadn't caught me, tugging me tight against him and capturing my cries in his mouth, growling against my lips in response as the orgasm crashed over me, wave after wave after mind shattering wave.

Finally, it ended, leaving me sweaty, shaking, trembling in Isaac's arms.

He pulled away, looking down at me with what would've been awe in another man's eyes.

"You're so damn responsive. Coming from a kiss?" He was about to say more, when something caught his eye and he released me so fast I stumbled backward. Clearing his throat, he chuckled, even though it sounded forced. "Playing with you is going to be fun as fuck, little snoop. Don't you dare touch yourself."

With that, he inexplicably picked up my chafed wrist and dropped a kiss on the pulse point before swaggering off.

I turned to see Judah and Levi standing there, Judah's

hands in his pockets, Levi's arms crossed. Judah had a shit-eating grin on his face. Levi looked like he was seeing right into my soul, and he didn't like what he saw.

Judah whistled. "You two put on quite a show there, Tovah Kaufman."

I relaxed slightly at the implication that Isaac hadn't told them who I really was. Trying not to blush, I took slow, deep breaths, then gathered my notebook, textbook, and pen and shoved them back in my bag, lifting it to my shoulder and walking past the twins.

"I need to go to my professor's office so I can get yelled at for zoning out during class, and then I have a newspaper meeting. I'm not waiting for either of you, so hurry up."

Judah threw his head back and laughed. "Isaac has his hands full with you, doesn't he?"

Levi said nothing, readjusting his glasses so he could watch me more closely.

"He has no idea," I said with saccharine sweetness, heading out the door as Isaac's teammates laughed and followed.

18

Tovah

Like I'd suspected, my professor had called me into his office to give me shit for not paying attention during class. The retired elderly investigative reporter had probed me with question after question to figure out why I'd acted so strangely today. Was I sleeping alright? Was it my boyfriend? He wasn't treating me poorly, was he? Because if he was, there were options available...

I sidestepped all of his questions. I certainly couldn't tell the professor the truth. It would make him a target, too—and risk my safety and my mom's. Instead, I told him I was tired and stressed with my workload, and he reluctantly let me leave.

I was a good liar, after all.

The conversation with my professor made me late to my newspaper meeting with the other editors. Our editor-in-chief, Toby, glared at me. We didn't have the best relationship. He was a pretentious douche with a stick up his ass, but his great grandfather had founded *The Daily Queen* in

1872, which meant that the board would let him get away with anything. Including making me senior sports editor when I'd wanted to be managing news editor—and letting people believe we'd been sexually involved when I wouldn't touch him with a thirty-foot pole.

It didn't help that Veronica Lucas, the vindictive former friend who'd started the rumors about me, had badly wanted the senior sports editor position and felt like I'd stabbed her in the back when I'd gotten it...even though I'd never in a million years wanted to steal it from her. If I hadn't accepted the role, Toby would've kicked me off the paper entirely—and then no news outlet would hire me after I graduated. All I'd ever wanted was to be a journalist, to search for the truth and bring it to light so powerful men were brought to justice. It was the one thing my mother and I had never been able to do—yet—and I was determined to build a life around helping people in that way.

Veronica didn't believe that, though, no matter how hard I tried to explain it. She thought I was just an "opportunistic ho," as she'd told me multiple times.

In the present, she glared at me, glancing at my two giant babysitters standing in the corner of the room.

"I heard you were fucking Isaac Jones. I didn't realize you were fucking the whole hockey team, but then I guess I shouldn't be surprised. Especially when you fucked Toby to get sports editor," she hissed.

Judah's and Levi's faces turned thunderous.

Toby, the asshole, didn't even come to my defense. He'd never dispelled the rumor, and even though I'd wanted to punch him multiple times for it, I told myself that it was fine. It was all fine. It didn't matter that people thought I was fucking every guy on campus, right? Who cared what people thought, if it served my purpose? One day I'd have a

Pulitzer, and all this college social hell would be nothing more than an ugly memory.

But for some reason I didn't want Judah and Levi to think that. Like their opinions of me mattered.

I didn't know why they looked so pissed off. Were they that upset by the idea that I'd supposedly slept with my boss? Were they judging me? Were they going to tell Isaac?

Shit. I could just imagine how that would go. Isaac had made it clear that while we were "together" no other man was allowed to touch me. For someone who didn't give a crap about me, he was weirdly possessive.

At least I wasn't on the edge of an orgasm anymore. On the way to the newspaper offices, I'd stopped in a bathroom and taken off the vibrating underwear, tossing them in the trash. I wasn't letting Isaac put me through that hell again, and even though he was taking a test, I wasn't sure if the app on his phone could control the panties from far away and wouldn't put it past him to not fuck with me during my meeting.

My meeting that was *not* going well.

"Tovah, can I talk to you?" Toby asked, ignoring the way Judah and Levi straightened. "Alone?"

"Not gonna happen," Judah said. "Whatever you can say in front of her, you say in front of the two of us, too."

I could feel my face turning crimson. This was becoming a pattern, one I *hated*.

Getting out of my chair, I followed Toby out of the bullpen where we'd been meeting and into his office. Judah and Levi, who'd been busy propping up the wall with their backs, stood up and followed.

"They don't actually think they're joining us, do they?" Toby said, sounding worried.

I understood. Separately, each of the Wasserson twins

probably outweighed him times two. Together, they could flatten him into a newspaper, or something resembling one.

"Tovah, what is going on? Why do you have bodyguards? Or are they babysitters?" he continued, holding his office door open for me.

I followed him in, and as Judah started to step inside, I slammed the door shut in his face, locking it.

He shook his head slowly at me.

"Isaac's not going to like this," he said through the door.

I pulled down the shade in reply, turning to Toby.

"What's going on?" I asked him.

He exploded. "Tovah, what the *fuck*. You were supposed to send me an interview with Isaac Jones, but I checked the Dropbox multiple times last night and this morning and there was nothing. You didn't respond to a single one of my texts and emails."

Of course I hadn't responded. Isaac still had my damn phone.

Toby continued. "Then, I hear you're dating the guy? Don't you hate him? There's no integrity to the feature if the writer is the subject's girlfriend," he whined in his nasally voice.

I was still stuck on what Toby had said. Girlfriend? Isaac and I had gone to *one* class together, and yeah, Toby was a journalist, so it was his job to know things, but still. It had gotten around campus *that* quickly? And Isaac had made it pretty clear in class it wasn't a girlfriend-boyfriend situation so much as a clingy hookup situation.

"Am I going to have to assign someone else the interview?" Toby prodded.

"No," I said. "I'll get you the feature." I would, and Toby didn't know it yet, but the story he was going to get was going to be so much more than he'd ever expected.

"Good, because I don't want to regret giving you the sports editor position."

"I didn't even *want* to be sports editor, Toby," I pointed out. "I wanted to be managing editor. You just made me sports editor because you hate Veronica."

He shrugged. "She's a bitch. You know that."

"You made her bitchier," I said. "You so easily could make my life easier and instead—"

"—and instead I did what made *my* life easier," he said agreeably. "And you're just going to have to suck it up and deal with it because—"

The door to Toby's office banged open liked someone had kicked it.

Because someone *had*. Isaac stood there, hands fisted as he planted his right foot back on the floor and stared at me.

"Excuse me, did you just kick open my door?" Toby looked shocked.

"It never should've been closed in the first place," Isaac said, and although his voice was calm and easy, the flash of anger in his eyes and his fisted hands were not.

"Tovah, maybe when you write your piece on the hockey team, you can talk about how they must all be taking drugs that have turned them into roid-ridden psychopaths," Toby said, clearly not caring or aware that he'd just taken his life in his hands.

Because at the mention of drugs, Isaac, Judah, and Levi all went solid. Isaac's dark, accusatory gaze searched mine, like he thought I'd been talking about the team's control of Vice and Vixen to Toby, or worse, had made up something about them using performance-enhancing drugs. I shook my head, once. Isaac relaxed somewhat, but the suspicion was still in his eyes.

"Toby, steroid use isn't really a thing in hockey," I said. "That's more football and—"

He waved a hand in the air. "I don't really care."

Isaac crossed his arms in front of his chest. "Are you this disrespectful to all your editorial board? Or is it only Tovah who gets to experience your dickishness?"

My jaw dropped.

Was Isaac defending me?

There were murmurs around the bull pen. Toby's cheeks flamed.

Veronica cleared her throat. "Tovah's *very* familiar with Toby's dick," she said, giggling.

Jesus fucking Christ, was everyone trying to destroy my life today? What had I done to deserve this?

I was stressed, and annoyed, and tired, and just wanted my bed and a bag of Flamin' Hots and a whole season of *House Hunters International* to watch. I was so done with all of this, including the way that Veronica was eyeing Isaac like he was a tree she wanted to climb.

"I am *not* familiar with Toby's dick," I said to her, too pissed off to watch my tongue anymore. "Game's getting old, Veronica. Don't you have anything better to do than to spread rumors about me? Like, I don't know, learn how to be a better journalist?"

Laughter broke out in the bullpen, and I couldn't even tell who the other editors were laughing at anymore.

Isaac glanced at me.

"Rumors?" he asked. "What rumors?"

Damn it. I wasn't supposed to care what he thought of me, or what anyone thought of me.

"How dare you!" Veronica cried, rising to her feet and sticking a hand on her hip. "And you should talk. You wouldn't even be an editor if you hadn't sucked Toby's dick."

Violent images—ones I usually ignored—came to me, including the urge to rip Veronica's hair right out of her head. Before I could act on them, or, hopefully, shove the image away, Isaac had crossed the room to her and was picking up her hand in his.

My heart dropped like a lead balloon.

I shouldn't feel so disappointed and betrayed, but for Isaac to turn to her so quickly, especially after the ways she'd insulted me...well, it showed just how little I mattered to him. And the knowledge stung like a million papercuts.

"Veronica, right?" Isaac said. "That's a pretty name."

"Oh," she blushed, fluttering her eyelashes at him. "That's so sweet of you, Isaac. We know each other, by the way. I used to be the reporter in the front row on the left after games, remember? You always said you liked my questions."

He smiled, a dimple showing. "I try to be sweet. You know what isn't sweet, Veronica? When you're so pathetically jealous of my brilliant girlfriend—"

Girlfriend? Since when was I his girlfriend, even his fake girlfriend?

"—that you make up rumors to undermine her talent and authority on campus, even though you know rumors about a woman's sexual history, especially with her boss and coworkers, can have far-reaching consequences. That's not a good example of journalistic integrity or honesty, is it, Veronica? I didn't know who you were then, but I do, now—and I promise, in this instance, you don't want me to."

Veronica's lips pinched, her eyes got big, and she tried to tug her hand out of Isaac's, but he didn't release her. He didn't squeeze tight, or hurt her, but the threat was there.

"Got it," she sniffed.

"Aren't you forgetting something?" he said calmly.

"I—" she seemed confused.

"An apology," he said, that same calm patience in his voice. "I think you owe my brilliant girlfriend an apology for starting rumors about her and Toby and then repeating them to me—because you were hoping that it might impact our relationship."

"I'm sorry," she muttered, eyes flashing.

Judah put a hand to his ear. "What? I couldn't hear you."

"Say it with meaning," Levi suggested.

I covered my mouth with a hand to hide my laughter. I felt like a bitch for enjoying this, but Veronica had been causing me issues for months now, and it felt good to get mine back—and to be supported this way by the hockey team. By Isaac, especially.

"I'm *sorry*," Veronica said, louder this time, her face pale with rage.

"I'm sorry, Tovah," Isaac prompted.

"I'm sorry, Tovah," Veronica spat, and finally, Isaac released her hand.

She moved away from him, her eyes trailed on the ground.

Turning to Toby, he said, "You clearly went along with it, which is a dick move, but I'll make you a deal. You set the record straight that Tovah got the senior sports editor position because she's a talented journalist and manager, and never say a word about her again—or I will happily defenestrate you."

Toby gaped at him. "Defenes—"

"It means toss you out the fucking window," Isaac added helpfully. He smiled at Toby, his dimples fully on display. He'd never looked so terrifying—or so sexy.

"I—" Toby swallowed. "I don't—"

"You will," Isaac told him. "Or I will." To me, he said, "Ready?"

I grabbed my bag, ready to be done with this place—and this day.

"Ready."

But as we left together with the entire newspaper staff watching us, my shoulders drew back and my head felt higher than it had in a while, like a whole weight had been lifted—and Isaac was carrying it for me now.

19

Isaac

Anger usually wasn't an issue for me. Part of being Isaac Jones meant not letting irrational feelings like *anger* or *jealousy* get in the way of being a chill, pleasant guy. But as I followed Tovah out of *The Daily Queen* offices and into the parking lot where my car waited, I had to work really, really fucking hard not to give into my anger, storm back inside and up the stairs, and toss the sniveling little editor-in-chief out the window like I'd threatened.

"Keep it together," Levi murmured to me. "There's a time for rage and retaliation, and that time isn't now."

"Eh, rage and retaliation are fun," Judah argued from behind us, slamming his hand into his fist. "Let's break some editor faces!"

"Shut up." Levi rolled his eyes.

Leaving him behind to deal with his twin, I caught up with Tovah in the middle of the parking lot.

She spun around, pink hair flying, as she pointed a finger at my chest.

"Why did you do that?" she cried.

"Do what? Stand up for you? Tell that envious bitch and your pathetic excuse for a boss to stop picking on you?"

"Yeah. That. *Why?*"

I opened my mouth, then shut it, because I didn't know how to answer her. Why *had* I done it? There was no need for me to support her or protect her; it didn't make it easier to keep her from exposing my team, and it's not like I actually cared. So then why did I kick in a door and threaten two strangers who'd never done anything to me personally?

You were jealous, my brain offered. *That's why the door.*

My brain was right. The idea of Tovah alone in a room with another man had sent rage through my veins like oxygen, lighting my whole body up with the need to dominate and defend. When Judah texted me to let me know there might be a problem, I ran out of my Italian test so fast I could've won a record. Finding Tovah dressed hadn't helped, not when she'd looked so upset.

And then when Veronica had accused Tovah of slutting it up with her boss, I'd seen red. Not even because I was jealous that it might be true, but because it so clearly wasn't. She had hurt Tovah, had wanted to hurt her more, and it didn't matter that I didn't threaten women as a rule, or that I wasn't supposed to care about Tovah's feelings. The only person allowed to fuck with Tovah was me.

So I'd threatened the bitch. Hadn't physically hurt her; hadn't had to. My voice and words and the look in my eyes had done the trick.

"Why, Isaac?" Tovah asked again, interrupting my thoughts.

Her breathing was shallow and aggravated, her hair a

mess, her eyes so big and brown as she stared up at me in confusion and what might be...

...hope.

"Why do you let people think you fucked your boss?" I asked her instead.

She blanched. "I don't let people think that..."

"Bullshit," I scoffed. "The rumor around campus is that you only got the senior sports editor position because you were fucking Toby. Why let it go on for so long?"

She inhaled, her face going pale.

Quietly, so that only I could hear her, she said, "Because no matter how much I denied it, no one would've believed me. In fact, the more I denied it, the more people would've thought it was true. So why fight it? Why not use it in my favor? People can believe what they want to believe about me, Isaac. Including you. Their opinions of me don't matter. All that matters is *my* opinion of me. And I think I'm pretty fucking fantastic."

I smiled, my dimples popping out. Usually I did it intentionally, but her words made it happen naturally.

"I like that," I told her truthfully. "I like that you like yourself. That's pretty rare."

She blinked, then smiled back at me.

"Your turn," she said. "Why come to my defense like that?"

Because the thought of anyone hurting you makes me want to burn down the whole fucking campus, I thought. *Because I can't stand the thought of* anyone *making you cry.*

Instead, I said, "Because no one gets to hurt you but me."

Her face fell. Seeing her look so sad was like getting hit in the face by a puck. But I couldn't tell her how I really felt. It would give her power over me, and worse, it would give her the wrong idea of how I felt, or how things could be between us if we stopped hating each other. I wasn't the protective boyfriend type, even if I was good at pretending to be one. I wasn't the boyfriend type, period.

Caring for someone like that meant signing their death warrant, and I wouldn't do that—to anyone.

"Ahem." Judah swung an arm around my back, and another around Tovah's.

A snarl rose in my throat the moment his hand touched her back, but I silenced it. I'd been jealous enough.

"So that Toby's a real douchenozzle, isn't he?" Judah commented.

Tovah rolled her eyes, lifting Judah's arm off her body. "He's been like that since we were freshmen newswriters."

"Has he been into you since you were freshmen, too?" he asked conversationally.

Tovah rolled her eyes. "Toby doesn't like me. I don't think Toby is capable of liking anyone other than Maureen Dowd. He just likes the way us supposedly having slept together makes him seem like less of a prude."

That snarl came back. Realistically, I knew that Toby wasn't a threat. But he and Tovah had one major interest in common; what was I other than a dumb jock with a violent family? Not that I gave a shit.

"It doesn't matter if he likes you," I said gruffly to Tovah. "He won't be touching you. Not for the foreseeable future, anyway."

Tovah rolled her eyes. She clearly thought I was being an idiot. That was fine; so did I.

"Like I'd *let* him touch me," she said.

I addressed Judah. "Was there any talk about her writing an article about the team? Exposing us?"

Judah turned serious. "Nothing concerning." He flashed

Tovah a flirtatious smile. "No, she's been a good girl. Haven't you, Tovah? That's what your name means, after all."

Before I was aware of what I was doing, I'd backed the bigger man against a nearby car, my arm on his throat, blocking his air. The car's alarm started going off.

"Isaac, stop!" Tovah cried.

She was trying to protect him? Absolutely the fuck not. It didn't matter that Judah was one of my best friends, or that logically I knew he wasn't interested in Tovah and was just fucking with me to get a rise out of me. It was like my brain had switched off and some sleeper agent had taken over, and all it thought was that Judah was the enemy and was trying to steal what was *mine.*

Judah didn't fight me, though. His hands were already lifted in surrender. Awareness returned, the car alarm screaming in the otherwise quiet evening. I backed away from my friend, feeling like an out-of-control asshole.

Once again, Tovah had brought out the beast in me, and I didn't like it.

"Why the fuck?" I asked him.

He grinned. "Shit stirring."

Levi came around the side, helping his brother stand.

"You need to accept your emotions around her, or they're going to keep biting you in the ass," Levi said quietly so only Judah and I could hear him.

Pulling my car key out of my pocket, I hit the unlock button, and my Aston Martin's locks beeped from where I'd parked it out of the sun.

"We're going home," I told Tovah, turning back to grab her hand in mine and tug her toward my car, not bothering to respond to Levi's warning.

"You *are* jealous," Tovah said, disbelief in her voice.

I didn't respond, just opened the passenger door for her,

waiting for her to slide in before reaching over her and securing her seatbelt, closing the door, going around to the driver's side and locking the doors, finally satisfied that she was safely inside and couldn't go anywhere unless I wanted her to.

Only then did I look at her.

"I am, little journalist. I'm fucking territorial and possessive, even though I shouldn't be. There's a part of me that wants to piss a circle around you, so no other man will come near you. I'm jealous as hell, and it doesn't matter who flirts with you or touches you, so I suggest you be the good girl you were named for."

Her beautiful brown eyes were wide. I wanted them wider, full of tears, with her mouth around my cock and her throat stuffed full. Maybe then this roaring in my ears would go away.

"I don't even know what to say to that," she said. "You're crazy. You've completely snapped."

I started the car and pulled out of the parking lot. "Seems that way."

20

Tovah

When we got back to Isaac's house, I undid the seatbelt. Isaac, for all of his anger at Judah earlier, had been gentle when he'd buckled me in, and the care for me and my safety—coupled with his confession of jealousy—had undid something inside me, something soft and vulnerable that petrified me. I couldn't be feeling soft toward Isaac, not when he was my enemy and had threatened both my life and my mother's, if the latter unknowingly.

Speaking of my mother, I needed my phone back from Isaac. Although he hadn't said anything, and my phone was locked, I was worried she'd texted and hadn't heard back and was freaking out by now. I needed to get a burner phone somehow so I could get in touch with her and let her know I was okay.

But was I?

When I went to get out of the car, my door was still

locked, and I couldn't unlock it. Could you even put child safety locks on the passenger side door?

Isaac got out and came around to my side, opening the door and helping me out by grabbing my hand and lacing our fingers together again. He didn't release me as we walked up the sidewalk to the front porch. I couldn't understand why he was holding my hand. The only audience we had were the trees from the forest that butted up against his property, so there was no need for him to pretend we were a couple who held hands. His big hand engulfed mine, making me feel safe and extending the cared-for feeling that had begun when he buckled me in, and I hated it, and the way it confused my brain—and my heart.

"Let go," I said, tugging at my hand.

"No," he said, typing the keycode into the door, disengaging the locks and opening it.

He still didn't release me when we were inside, leading me down the hallway to the kitchen. Then, he finally let go of my hand, only to boost me onto the kitchen counter—the same spot where he'd spanked me and gotten me off the night before. My nipples went tight at the sordid memory.

Isaac, of course, noticed. His eyes went dark with lust, and a feral smile took over his face.

"Don't worry, little snoop. I'll give you what you want later but first I need to feed you. How's spaghetti and meatballs?"

He was cooking for me?

"That's fine," I said.

As he made his way around the kitchen, pulling ingredients out of the huge fridge and pantry and setting them up near a chopping board and the stove, I watched him, flummoxed.

"I didn't know mafia princes knew how to cook," I finally said. "Don't you have like, staff to do that for you?"

He looked at me. He smiled slightly, but his eyes were sad.

"My mom taught me how to cook, before she was killed," he told me. "After she died, I cooked for me and my siblings. My dad is an old school chauvinist and has always given me shit about it, but it made me feel closer to her. I don't know." He shrugged, and then his voice turned bitter. "But I guess if you know so much about me already, you already know she was killed."

I did. I knew Louisa Silver had died in a tragic accident, but the night she'd been killed was the same night my mother and I had made our escape. I'd been young, and terrified, and determined to help get me and my mother out from under my abusive stepfather's thumb and had never bothered to learn exactly what happened.

"I'm so sorry," I said. "How did she die?"

"She was on her way to the opera," Isaac said as he started mincing garlic. "My father wasn't accompanying her, but she was meeting her sister. Her car had barely pulled away from the curb when gunshots rang out. They shot up her car with her inside, killing her on the spot. I've never seen so much blood in my life."

He closed his eyes at the memory, and my heart squeezed in sympathy. I'd liked Louisa. She'd always been kind to me and my mother, even though we were only the help. But I couldn't say as much to Isaac, or he'd realize who I actually was.

"My dad went running out of the house, pulling her out of the car. He was covered in her blood. He made a sound I'd never heard before and I've never heard since. He was always a maniacal asshole, but he loved her. That night, he told me you couldn't love anyone when you were a part of our family. Loyalty, yes. Love, no. Because love meant death." Isaac started chopping an onion furiously, making my eyes sting with tears. "And he was right."

I didn't know this side of Isaac, the part that thought he didn't deserve and could never have true love in his life. It wasn't something I wanted, either, but my reasoning was different: My mother had loved my stepfather, at first, and look how that turned out. I couldn't trust a man long enough to believe he'd take care of me, instead of trying to destroy me. No, my love was reserved for my friends and my mother. That was it.

"I'm sorry, that sounds terrible," I said.

"You know what I sometimes think is worse?" he mused, as he finished chopping the onion and pushed it with his knife into the big pot with the garlic, pouring in some olive oil and setting it on the stovetop to sauté. "There was a little girl who lived on the property. I never learned her name; I think she was the daughter of one of the maids or my father's men or something. She refused to tell me. But even when I was young, I cared about her a lot. Actually thought I loved her, that we were meant to be together. I called her my bashert, my destiny." He scoffed, and I had to look away so Isaac couldn't see the pained shock on my face. "Anyway, she disappeared around the time my mother died, didn't even come to the funeral. I was an idiot; her family was clearly involved in my mother's death."

I caught the denial in my throat. My mother and I had had nothing to do with Louisa's death. I'd been devastated for Isaac, but my mother had thought that the chaos going on with the Silvers was a good opportunity for us to take care of my stepfather and disappear. And she'd been right.

But I hadn't realized that Isaac had looked for me at the funeral.

Isaac had grabbed a can opener and was using it on a can of tomatoes, like he wished it bodily harm. "Anyway, that was the last time I gave my love to anyone. It's better this way."

I swallowed. What could I even say? All I wanted to do was to wrap my arms around my enemy and tell him that I was here, that I cared, that I hadn't left him by choice. But I *had* left him, and he thought I was involved in his mother's death. If I told him who I was, what was to stop him from using the big chef's knife on me?

"I'm so sorry you lost her," I said, and I wasn't sure if I was referring to his mother or to me. "That's a horrible thing for anyone to go through, especially when you were so young. Do you know who did it?"

"The Golds," he said shortly. "Which made it kind of awkward and inconvenient when Jack got involved with Aviva, but she's only a distant cousin and isn't involved at all in the family's actual business. They've been our enemy forever."

Aviva *was* a Gold. But the wealthy, dynastic family had never wanted anything to do with Aviva or her brother, Asher. The connection had concerned me, at first, but Aviva knew nothing. And I needed to keep it that way, to keep her and Asher safe.

Isaac stirred the sauce, and the smell of garlic and onions filled the kitchen, making me salivate. "In fact," he added, "I bet that little girl was a plant or a spy of theirs. Just goes to show the kind of taste I have in women."

Ouch.

"She was just a kid, wasn't she?" I said, defending myself even though I needed to leave it alone. "Do you really think she'd plot against you that way? Or was she just an innocent bystander with no control of her own?"

Isaac turned away from the stove, his eyes landing on mine—and narrowing. "Why do you even care?"

Shit.

"As a journalist, part of my job is to both expose the bad guys and defend the innocent from slander. I guess I feel some sympathy for her, when it's unlikely she's the villain you think she is."

Isaac nodded. "Go get a pot from the bottom left cabinet and fill it up with water. Usually I'd make pasta from scratch, but I'm starving, so we're going to have to go with the boxed kind."

I grabbed the change of subject with both hands. "Boxed pasta is my favorite pasta."

He smirked, but it didn't reach his eyes. "That's because you haven't had my pasta."

Dinner was quiet, broken up by my helpless moans as I ate the best spaghetti and meatballs I'd ever had in my entire life. And each time I moaned, Isaac watched me, a dark look in his eyes as he gripped his cutlery so hard, white showed around his knuckles.

"You know," I finally said, patting my stomach. "If hockey doesn't work out, you could easily become a chef. This was delicious."

His eyes shuttered. "Hockey's not going to work out," he said.

I sat up. "What do you mean?"

He hesitated, like he wasn't sure he wanted to tell me.

Then he shrugged. "You might as well know. I'm going to have to take over for my father one day. Can't really be the head of a criminal empire and play for the NHL at the same time. I made a deal with him a while back; he'd let me go to college and play hockey as long as I came home to take up my position in the 'company' after...and agreed to run Vice and Vixen distribution in Gehenom."

I digested his words, almost feeling guilty for the assumptions I'd made about him in the past. "So that's why the hockey team oversaw the dealers," I guessed.

He nodded, watching me. "We're out of the game now," he said. "We'd always known how dangerous it was, but what happened with Aviva and Jack really drove that point home, so we decided as a team to be done."

"How'd your father take that?"

He snorted. "The old man was pissed. He hasn't acted on it yet—and I've been avoiding him anyway. But there will be retribution. There's always retribution," he added darkly.

I swallowed, hating that I felt bad for him, but I did. "Is what happened to your mom partially why you don't want to work for your father? Is that why you want out?"

Isaac rose, taking my plate and his.

"I can wash up," I said.

"I've got it. Can't have you thinking you're here for your maid services. And no. It's because unlike my family, I'm not a killer, and I'd like to keep it that way. Unfortunately, that looks like it's not in the cards for me. Sometimes you just don't have any control over your own fate."

I sat there quietly, because how did you respond to something like that? Or how devastatingly resigned Isaac sounded to his future?

"I'm sorry," I finally said. "That fucking sucks."

Because what else was there to say? I might hate him, but I *was* sorry.

He shrugged. "It is what it is," he said. "What about you?"

"What do you mean, what about me?"

"Why do you want to be a journalist so badly?" he asked. "Does it have anything to do with the way you lost your mom?"

Because Isaac thought my mom was dead.

"Something like that," I said.

He watched me from where he stood, plates in hand. "That's it? I just told you all sorts of deep, dark shit about me, and you can't even be bothered to share beyond a 'something like that?'"

But I couldn't tell him more.

So I shrugged, getting up from the table. "I really can help with the dishes."

He shook his head back and forth slowly, placing the dirty dishes back on the kitchen table.

"The dishes can wait. If you won't use your mouth to talk, you can use it in a better way. Get on your knees, Tovah."

I glared at him. "No."

He raised an eyebrow. "No?"

"No, Isaac. No one is here, we don't have to pretend. I'm not going to blow you."

He chuckled. "Oh, calling it a blow job doesn't even get close to what I'm about to do to you. Remember: I say get on your knees, you *get on your knees.* I fed you dinner, now I'm going to feed you my cock. *Kneel.*"

Glaring at him, I kneeled. Because what other choice did I have? But one of these days—

"I'm going to bite your dick off," I told him.

He laughed again. "This better be one of those times where you're all bark, no bite. If I feel even the hint of teeth, I'll strip you down, drive you to campus, and tie you to the statue of the founder. How does that sound?" He caressed my face. "I don't want to hear another word out of that pretty mouth. Open up, little snoop. That's all you're good for, after all."

21

Isaac

I was being an asshole and I knew it, but I was pissed the fuck off. I'd opened up to Tovah, exposing vulnerabilities I never even looked at myself, they were so painful, and she couldn't be bothered to match me with her own secrets. For all I knew, she was storing them away for some future exposé on me. I had let my guard down and forgotten I couldn't trust her.

So even though I saw the hurt in her eyes for telling her she was useless beyond her holes, and even though part of me hated myself for it, at least I could make her feel *something*.

And I wasn't going to deny how hard my cock was, seeing her kneeling there in front of me with helpless rage in her eyes. Dinner had been torture, listening to her moan as she ate the food *I'd* made for her. I'd never known how sexually satisfying feeding someone else could be, but watching the food disappear between her lips, watching her enjoy it, knowing I'd provided for her, that she was no longer hungry because of *me*—it appeased the monster inside me. I'd taken care of her. Served her.

And now she was going to serve me.

Scanning the kitchen, I spotted a dishtowel. I walked behind Tovah, making short work of tying her wrists together.

"Isaac!"

I ignored her, walking back around to face her and slowly unzipping my jeans so she got the whole show. I pulled down my boxer briefs and revealed my cock in all its hard, desperate glory. I felt pretty damn beastly right now, my cock so excited to finally get off in one of her warm holes and test out the object of its desire's tight throat for the first time. Edging her all day had kept me on the edge too, but the best things took patience, and my patience was finally going to be rewarded.

The first time I'd touched her, I'd been afraid of how out of control she made me feel.

But she'd already changed something within me— because now I relished it.

Fisting it in my hand, I slapped my cock against one of Tovah's cheeks, than the other, leaving a trail of precum on her skin, painting it over her lips like a white, perverted gloss.

"Open," I ordered her again, my voice deep with desire. "And remember, no teeth."

Glaring at me, she opened her mouth in a small "o." It wasn't wide enough for how thick my dick was, so I leaned down, hooking two fingers into her mouth and pulling it wider so I could slide my cock into the open hole.

"Isaac," she tried to cry out, but my cock plugged her mouth and blocked the sound, so it was just a faint garbled protest.

"Fuck," I groaned, the heat of her mouth practically doing me in like I was a teen getting his first blowjob. "Suck," I told her.

Closing her eyes, she sucked. It was sloppy, and, if I didn't know better, unpracticed. But maybe she was just messy.

Something about the seeming inexperience was a huge turn on, though. I could pretend that she'd never sucked a cock before, and I was her first. But sucking with her eyes closed wasn't working for me.

"Eyes on me," I barked. "I want to watch your humiliated helplessness as you lick and suck me, little snoop."

Her eyes popped open, and yeah, there was the hatred I expected in them, but also the need I'd wanted as she bobbed her head, licking the shaft and sucking the crown, her hesitant movements hotter than the most confident blowjob I'd ever received. I let her stay on the shallow end for a bit, the feel of her tongue and lips against my cock a heady experience I'd only fantasized about a million times.

"This turning you on?" I groaned, watching her as she rubbed her thighs together. "Being helpless, wrists tied, forced to lick my cock? Probably freeing in a way, because you don't have to admit how hungry you are for it. You can pretend you don't want this, but we both know that's a lie. But then you're a good little liar, aren't you?"

She tried to say something that sounded like *fuck you*—or would've, if my cock wasn't effectively gagging her.

"Oh, this isn't enough for you? Well don't worry, there's more where that came from." Keeping my fingers hooked in her mouth, I grabbed the back of her head with my other hand, forcing her forward on my cock, until I hit the back of her throat.

Her eyes got wide and teary and she tried to shake her

head, but I held her still, tilting her chin at the perfect angle, pulling out, and thrusting back in, slowly, so slowly, so that I sank, inch by perfect inch, into her throat.

"Holy fucking shit, who knew this tight little throat would feel so sweet squeezing my fat cock? I was right, wasn't I? You were made for this. Your mouth, your throat, all of you was created to be my little plaything and make me feel good," I rasped, my voice dropping several octaves from how good she felt.

My balls hurt from the need to come, which I was going to stave off as long as I could. Pulling out slightly, I thrust back in, pulling out and then shoving back in again, setting up a fast and brutal pace until I was blatantly fucking Tovah's face. Tears ran down her cheeks as she gasped for air every time I withdrew, only to shove deeper, holding still so her nose was pressed against my base.

"That's right, choke on my cock. You're lucky I'm letting you breathe at all."

She moaned around me, like the idea of my stealing her air turned her on even more.

Fuck.

I was close.

I slowed down, not wanting to come yet. I wanted, no needed, for this to last as long as possible. It wasn't only how good her throat and mouth felt. It was the way our eyes had locked on each other, the connection making my heart race in my chest. She might absolutely loathe me, but in this moment, she was mine, trapped by my hands and my cock and unable to look away.

"I own you," I told her harshly. "Not just your mouth or throat. I own *all* of you, amore mio. How does that feel, bella ragazza, knowing you'll be owned by me forever? Possederò la tua anima proprio come tu possiedi la mia."

Amore mio. My love.

Bella ragazza. Beautiful girl.

Possederò la tua anima proprio come tu possiedi la mia. I'll own your soul like you own mine.

I barely knew what I was saying. I'd switched to Italian and absolute nonsense was pouring out of me, words I'd take back if I had any real awareness of how I felt. I couldn't be blamed, not when her throat was squeezing my cock so damn tight, like a fucking vise, and not when her eyes were a dark, passionate, angry and lustful brown, filled with tears and wet like her pussy must be by now.

I inhaled, trying to force myself not to come, shoving my cock in impossibly deeper, gripping her wretched pink hair tight in one hand so she had to take me. She spluttered and choked, unable to breathe, trying to pull away, but with nowhere to go. The monster, angry at all she'd made him feel, leaned into his evil inclinations, pinching her nose closed with his free hand so she couldn't breathe at all. A dazed shock filled her eyes and I realized she was about to pass out with her throat closed tight around my fucking cock. I'd never had this much control over anything or anyone, but my girl was about to black out because of my cock and fingers, and the knowledge won against the effort not to come.

With a groan, I released her nose and hair and withdrew my cock from her throat. She gasped, falling backward, but I was already coming all over her hair and face, shooting lines of white cum across her forehead, closed eyes, nose, mouth, down to her chin and neck, until she resembled an abso-fuckinglutely filthy toaster strudel.

And I wanted to eat her just as badly.

Falling to my knees, I crawled over her, pulling her legs free and descending on her soaked cunt, sucking her clit and stabbing my tongue inside her pussy until she came all over my face with a desperate, exhausted cry.

Fuck.

Catching my breath, I stuffed my cock back into my jeans and zipped them closed.

"Isaac?" Tovah searched my gaze, seeming worried and vulnerable. I'd never owned her more than I had in that moment, tied up and naked, exhausted and trembling, face covered in my cum. I relished my possession, as much as I did her soft uncertainty. If I didn't know better, I'd think she was looking for reassurance that she'd done a good job. And she'd done an excellent job, but I couldn't tell why she seemed so shaken up and needy. I just knew I fucking *liked* it. Seeing her like this made my cock begin to thicken all over again.

A thought occurred to me, awful and inspired. Grabbing my phone, I unlocked it, snapping a few photos of her as she stared at me, confusion turning to cognition, and then all-out rage.

"Did you just take pictures of me?! Like this?!"

I shrugged, putting my phone back in my pocket.

"Spank bank material," I explained, giving her the full-on Dr. Dimples.

"Isaac Silver, I'm going to kill you," she seethed.

I tilted my head. "Are you? Or are you going to do *exactly what I say*, unless you want these photos emailed to Veronica's and Toby's inboxes—along with the rest of campus."

"You wouldn't."

"Want to test me and see?"

I was lying through my teeth, of course. No fucking way would I ever let anyone see her looking like this. No, Tovah Lewis, naked and covered in cum, was an image for my eyes and cock only. I'd kill anyone else who even tried to imagine it. She didn't need to know that, though—not if it hurt her. Not if it kept her in line.

You're being a real asshole, Silver, my inner voice said uneasily.

I ignored it. I'd given the monster full control.

Still, I walked behind her, untying her wrists and checking for any sign of strain. Her right wrist was still red and chafed from the handcuff the night before, and seeing it made me want to punch someone—myself, namely. I'd ordered a new set, leather and fur-lined, so she'd be comfortable when she was chained to me. They were arriving later this week. Tonight, I'd bandage her wrist after she showered so she could heal. And try to ignore the fire in my chest—guilt from knowing I'd caused her physical harm.

It was truly insane, how one second completely humiliating her turned me on, but the next, seeing that I'd caused her pain made me want to shove *myself* into the boards. Being around Tovah was like being on an emotional rollercoaster. Even though I knew the right choice was to exit while I still could, all I wanted to do was to hang on tight and enjoy the ride.

Tovah jerked away from me, rising to her feet and tossing her cum-covered hair. Unsteady, but still somehow defiant.

"I'm showering," she said. "And then I'm sleeping in the guest room."

I laughed. "You're not very good at your job, are you? Did you fact-check with your source? If you had, you'd know your sleeping arrangements hadn't changed." Turning serious, I stared down at her, noting the way her nose stud winked in the light. "You'll sleep with me, chained to me, every night, until I'm done with you. There's no negotiating or getting around it, Tovah Lewis. You belong to me, and you better start acting like it."

She shook her head. "I'll fact-check you in the balls," she tossed over her shoulder as she turned down the hallway and headed up the stairs.

Laughing, I followed her. "Oh, and we're going to dye your hair back to its original color," I added. "I brought all your hair dye boxes from your apartment. I'm sick of this pink."

At the foot of the stairs, she stilled, turning to me, fear muting some of the defiance in her eyes.

"I'll dye my hair any damn color I choose, Isaac Silver. Get this: You may control me sexually. You may even be able to humiliate me publicly. But *I* decide what I do with my hair."

I whistled. "We'll see about that." Slapping her ass, hard, I added, "I've never seen a girl dye her hair before. Sounds fun."

"Fuck you."

I laughed again.

"Patience, little snoop. Patience."

22

Tovah

"Shit," I muttered, wiping sweat off my forehead. "Why is there nothing incriminating in this fucking house?!"

I had been snooping top to bottom through Isaac's home for hours while he'd been at hockey practice. Pulled papers out of filing cabinets, searched the trash for old receipts, tried every password I could think of on his laptop. I'd tried the code on that drawer in his office again, but after multiple tries, I'd given up.

All I had to show for my hours of work was exhaustion from painstakingly removing possible evidence, only to replace it when I realized it wasn't evidence after all. Oh, and sweat. And tears, because I felt like I was going to cry. I'd been living with Isaac for a week, and I was no closer to finding answers that would put the Silvers in prison and set my mom and me free.

A good journalist never gave up on a story. I knew that.

And this was more than a story—it was life or death. But I was getting absolutely nowhere but discouraged.

Glancing up at the mirror across from the desk in Isaac's office-slash-workout-room, I frowned at my expression. The purple-haired girl in the mirror—which I'd dyed this morning because fuck Isaac and the Zamboni he rode in on—looked a little pissed off and a lot defeated.

"Don't you give up," I told her, tossing my head. "You're Tovah fucking Lewis, future Pulitzer Prize winner. You don't give up; you just get creative."

I sat at the desk, running my fingers through my violet-colored hair. I'd dyed it with the only box of old, fun color dye I had among a range of new boxes of browns. Isaac must have accidentally brought the purple from my apartment when he'd brought the rest of my stuff over. He'd think I'd dyed it as a fuck you to him, and that had been part of it, but mostly it was because I was starting to feel twitchy, which was the sign it was time to change my hair color again so no one recognized me.

There had to be some other way to get either evidence or some sort of confession, I just had to keep thinking.

At that moment, the alarm announced that the door was unlocked and Isaac was home.

Crap, he was early.

Quickly, I scanned the office to make sure nothing was out of place, but before I could exit, the door began to open.

Shit, shit, shit.

I dove out from behind the desk, landing in a heap on the workout mat.

Isaac stood before me, framed in the doorway, his face thunderous.

"Find what you were looking for?"

"No," I said, a little out of breath. "Why don't you have a yoga mat? Or foam blocks?"

His face was unreadable. "They're in the closet."

Oh, damn.

"You do yoga?" I asked, momentarily distracted by the thought of Isaac doing downward dog.

"It keeps me limber. I do Pilates too—it helps protect me from injuries. But I like yoga the most, it keeps me emotionally centered and calm."

I rolled my eyes. "You should probably do it more, then."

He walked toward the mat, until he was looming above me, his arms crossed over his chest. A paper bag dangled from his fingers.

"I should," he agreed. "Since my emotional equilibrium was thrown into chaos the moment you moved in."

"I have an easy solution for that," I said amiably. "Let me move back out."

He shook his head. "And let you publish some article that will destroy my family? No, little snoop. I know better than to trust you. Here." He dropped the paper bag on the floor next to me. "I got you something to wear. There's a big party at the hockey house tonight, and you're going to be helping serve and clean up after our guests."

Alarm bells went off in my head. I looked over at the paper bag with concern. Based on his tone, poisonous snakes could come slithering out of it at any moment, and I wouldn't be surprised.

He grinned, a little viciously. "Look at what's inside."

"What if I don't want to?" I asked truthfully.

"Then I leak those photos I took of you on social media. Open the bag, Tovah."

This fucking guy. Why did someone so fucking evil have to be so fucking hot?

I opened it, pulling out some lacy, frothy fabric and holding it up to the light.

Dear god.

"No," I said immediately.

There was no way I was wearing this thing.

Wicked satisfaction flashed in Isaac's eyes.

"Yes," he said. "I gave you a heads up about this, after all. Remember?"

Careful, or I'll put you in a maid costume and nothing else. Make you clean up my floors with your tongue.

Lost in horror, I said absently, "There's no way I'm touching my tongue to the hockey house floors."

He shrugged one sexy shoulder. "Of course not. I wouldn't want you to do something—so unsanitary."

"You're really going to humiliate me like this? Make me be the help for the night?"

My breathing sped up. The shock of almost getting caught was wearing off. Isaac didn't know this, but the maid costume was giving me flashbacks to my childhood. My mom had never had to wear something so skimpy, but she *had* worn a formal maid uniform, and she'd been treated like crap in it. When my stepfather had set eyes on her, we'd thought it meant no more mistreatment by the Silvers.

We'd been wrong.

And now I was going to have to parade around in the slutty Halloween version of her uniform while Reina students laughed at me and whispered and made me do god knew what. And I'd have to suck it up and deal with it, because otherwise Isaac would leak those horrible photos of me naked and covered in his cum. Or, worse, much worse, he'd tell his dad about the little fake maid living in his house, which would become Abe Silver finding his *real* former maid, and then—

I stopped my mind before it could go that far. All I'd get out of it was a panic attack.

"Fine," I said, scrambling to my feet. "I'll wear the stupid costume. I'll let you embarrass me in front of all your friends and all our schoolmates. It'll be a grand old time."

I stormed toward the door.

"Aren't you forgetting something?" he called smoothly.

I stopped, turning back to look at him. He held the frilly maid costume and matching thong in his big, beautiful hands, and I hated how, in that moment, even though I wanted to kill him, a part of me wanted to crawl over to him on my knees, pull out his cock, and suck.

What had he done to my brain?

Was there a cure?

I stormed back toward him, trying to hide the way my hand trembled with want as I grabbed the costume from his hands.

If he wanted a damn maid, he'd get a maid.

But I wouldn't go down without a fight.

IN MY THREE AND A HALF YEARS AT REINA, I'D ONLY BEEN TO the hockey house once—with Aviva. I'd promised myself I'd never go back, but then I'd been breaking all sorts of promises to myself.

I followed Isaac inside, wrapped in my raggedy, worn pea coat. The party had already started, and people were on their way to getting drunk and high, if they weren't already there.

Everyone was dressed normally, in jeans and t-shirts or cute skirts and skimpy dresses. I'd hoped that this was a costume party and that I wouldn't stick out, but no such luck. Although his teammates and their friends eyed me curiously, no one said anything.

The only thing that kept me even a little calm was the fact that no one could see what I was wearing underneath.

Until we reached the kitchen, and Isaac held out his hand, that same dark, wicked look in his eyes. I was beginning to loathe that look.

"Why don't you give me your coat, Tovah? You must be warm," he said, full Isaac Jones Good Guy charm—and dimples—on display. We were back in public, so the mask was back on.

I hesitated, crossing my arms over my chest. I might pretend I didn't care what people thought about me, but their judgment still stung. And they were going to judge my outfit, no question.

Isaac apparently didn't have much patience for me, because he uncrossed my arms and started to remove my jacket, pulling off one sleeve and then the other like I was a petulant child. I felt the warm, recycled air of the house caress my bare skin as he pulled away the wool of my coat and my pretty fucking scandalous, pretty fucking ridiculous costume was revealed.

There was shocked silence, and then laughter broke out. I wanted to disappear.

"Tovah agreed to serve everyone's drinks tonight. Said she was in the mood to help out the team," Isaac called out to everyone around us. "She's going to clean up the mess after, too, so don't feel like you have to be mindful of where you put things."

"All the messes? Because these parties tend to get... sticky," Nick McPherson, a junior and the Kings' backup left wing joked, and the girls around him giggled.

"She can clean me up if she wants," Bryan Marks, another junior on the team, added.

One of the girls whispered something to the other. I didn't have to hear them to know it wasn't something nice.

Isaac's gaze went hard. "Make a joke like that again, Marks, and you're off the team."

The room got very quiet in the wake of Isaac's threat. He wasn't defending me, he was marking his territory, and I was sick of it. Sick of the way he ping-ponged between protecting me and hurting me. I could feel how red my face had turned; my cheeks and neck were hot, and I wanted to hide from all the eyes on me. All their speculation, their taunting, their ridicule...

...but then this wasn't anything new, was it? I'd been speculated about, taunted, and ridiculed ever since Veronica had started those rumors about me. I hadn't lied to Isaac when I'd said their opinions of me didn't matter. All that mattered was my own opinion of myself. And maybe there were moments, like now, where that was hard to remember, but it didn't make it any less true. I was fucking amazing, and if I had to deal with being exposed in some slutty maid costume and try to pretend it didn't make me think about my mom and all she'd endured and all we'd lost, then I'd deal with it.

Squaring my shoulders and tossing my hair, I glanced around the room, catching people's gazes, making it clear that not a single one of them intimidated me. When I finally ended on Bryan and Nick, I winked at both of them playfully.

"I can handle a mess or two," I told them. "The stickier, the better."

The girls who'd been whispering froze, their eyes widening in shock.

Yeah, I went there, I thought, grimly satisfied.

Raising my voice, I called out, "Guess I'm working tonight. Who needs to be *served* first?" I made the insinuation as obvious as possible, rewarded when Isaac's eyes darkened and his jaw got stiff.

"Tovah—" he warned.

"What? You said it was my job to serve at this party, *Jones*. So I'm serving," I said sweetly, making sure to sway my hips as I headed in the direction of some of his teammates to take drink orders or whatever inane bullshit he wanted to get up to.

I was livid. Completely livid. But I'd die before I showed him how much he'd angered and embarrassed me. And if I was right—and I had the gut instinct of a news reporter, which meant I was almost always right—Isaac was already regretting what he'd done.

Good. Let him stew over watching his teammates hit on his...whatever I was to him.

Let him fucking *burn*.

"Jack, man, you're here! Hey, Aviva!"

My head lifted, and I scanned the room. I hadn't seen my best friend since the hockey game, before all this blackmail and bullshit had started with Isaac. God, what was she going to say when she saw me? I wanted to tell her everything, so badly...but I also knew I couldn't. Because if I told her Isaac was blackmailing me, she'd ask why, and I'd have to tell her about his family. I'd have to tell her the truth, and not only would she never look at me the same way, it would also make her unsafe. Isaac's dad would come after her and Asher, too, and I couldn't let that happen.

Which meant I had to lie. *More.*

"Tovah? What the hell?" Aviva spotted me across the

main living room, headed in my direction, tugging Jack along with her.

When she reached me, she released Jack's hand and grabbed me in a tight hug, and I let myself hug her back, taking refuge in my loyal best friend, even as I worried the aspiring therapist would do some psychoanalyzing magic on me and figure out what I was hiding from her.

Finally, she pulled away, her eyes narrowing as she looked me over.

"Was there some costume party you went to before this?" she asked. "Or is this the costume party, and the rest of us missed that line in the invitation?"

Fuck. I had no interest in defending or making excuses for Isaac, but I didn't want her digging too deep, either.

As I tried to think of a way to explain the current situation, while also berating myself for not planning for seeing Aviva earlier like I should've, she laid into me.

"I'm so mad at you, Tovah. What the actual hell. I've texted you multiple times, messaged you on literally every platform that exists and some that probably don't, and *nothing*. You haven't responded once, not even just to tell me you're alive. The only thing I have to rely on is the rumor mill that claims you're either dating Isaac or you're his live-in fuckbuddy?! You've apparently spent more time with the *Wasserson twins* than you have with me lately."

"Princess—" Jack interjected.

"Don't *princess* me, Jack. This doesn't concern you." Aviva waved him off.

I watched as Jack raised an eyebrow at her. "Are we really back here? Everything about you concerns me. Maybe we should let Isaac and Tovah handle what's going on with Isaac and Tovah. Although..." he looked at me with those Jack-Feldman-lie-detector-eyes. "Are you safe?"

Aviva scoffed. "It's Isaac. Of course she's safe. But she's been avoiding me and I *want to know why.*"

Jack just watched me.

I considered. Was I safe? Isaac had threatened me numerous times, and somewhere, not far away, his father waited in the shadows. But at the same time, Isaac hadn't actually hurt me. He'd even been bandaging up my wrist every night before putting on the handcuffs...

...oh god. I'd been Stockholmed. Aviva had told me the supposed syndrome had been fabricated to discredit a woman, and yet here I was, emotionally connecting with my captor.

Goddamnit.

"I don't know," I answered Jack truthfully.

Aviva gasped. "If you aren't safe, then you don't get to be around him. And if he's *hurt* you, I'll kill him." She turned to Jack. "And I don't care if he's your best friend, *you* get to bury him. He's too heavy for me."

I put a hand on her shoulder. "No, I'm safe, I misspoke. Aviva, I'm fine."

Her eyes grew wet. "If you're fine, then why have you been avoiding me? What did I *do?*"

She hadn't done anything. She'd been perfect. It was me. I was the liar.

But before I could say any of that, or come up with anything reasonable *to* say, there was a hand wrapping around my good wrist.

"We're going upstairs to my room," Isaac gritted out between his teeth as he began to drag me away from Aviva and Jack.

"Hang on," Aviva said. "You aren't taking her anywhere, Isaac Jones."

Isaac completely ignored her as he pulled me through the center of the living room.

"Isaac, why—"

"Hang on," he muttered, stopping at the edge of the room and dropping my wrist so he could pull his long-sleeved Kings shirt off his head.

I gaped at him.

The whole room gaped at him.

And his abs.

He ignored them all, dropping the shirt over my head and pulling my arms gently but firmly through the sleeves, so that it draped over me, hanging all the way down to my thighs, and hiding the maid costume and my bare skin.

Oh.

That done, he grabbed my wrist again and started dragging me up the stairs, clearly not giving a shit about the whispers that broke out at his actions.

Even I couldn't care, or parse, what the hell was going on. I was too busy jogging up the stairs so I didn't trip and fall. I hurried to keep up with him as he stormed down the second floor hallway, stopping at a room that said Jones on the door and unlocking it with a key he produced out of nowhere before he picked me up, carried me inside, locked the door, crossed the room in three strides, and threw me on the bed.

I stared up at him, eyes wide.

"You think you're cute, Tovah? Flaunting yourself, displaying your tits for every single asshole here, showing off that pretty skin? Well, the game's over, and you've had your fun. Congratulations: you get to be my personal maid for the rest of the night. And I'm about to make things really fucking goddamn messy in here—and you are going to clean it up with that sweet little tongue of yours. Now, get on your goddamned knees and open that smartass little mouth."

My mouth *did* drop open, but not to take his cock. No, I had *shit* to say.

"I'm sorry, you're blaming *me*? It was your idea to dress me up in some slutty costume and parade me around in front of your friends. Did you expect me to cower and cry? To let you humiliate me in front of everyone? Clearly you don't know me at all."

"I *do* know you, unlike the rest of those fucknuts," he muttered. "I know you like your showers scalding hot. I know that you change your hair color when you get antsy, even though you pretend it's a fuck you to everyone. I know you're stubborn as fuck, especially when it comes to finding out the truth. And I know despite your reputation, you don't *actually* go out of your way to flirt with assholes. You did it to fuck with me, and I don't like it."

Oh.

Oh.

He was jealous.

That should've amused me, or settled me in some way, but I was still fucking angry at the way he'd treated me tonight.

"There's only one reason why you'd react this way, Isaac Silver. You're feeling territorial. I should have seen it before. Is it because you're starting to care?"

I was aware I was taunting him, but I was too pissed off to give a shit. He was acting like a little boy during recess who shoves the girl he likes because he can't admit his feelings. Except *worse*. Isaac was so determined to pretend to be someone else, he'd turned *like* into lust and loathing.

Both lust and loathing were clear in his eyes, which had darkened to a burning black.

"You really think," he said slowly as he unzipped his jeans, "that I *care*? That you're anything other than a pain in my goddamn ass? I'm not jealous. Why would I be?" He climbed on the bed, shoving my legs down, and crawled on top of my prone body. "I'm the one who fucks that beautiful face. I'm the one who makes you come and sees you at your softest. I'm the one who turns that delectable ass red." I struggled against him but lost as he straddled my arms and chest. *Trapped.* "I don't have to care about you to own you, Tovah Lewis. And I think it's time to give you another demonstration. Now, *open that smartass mouth* so I can put it to use."

"You get your dick near my mouth, and I'll bite it off," I threatened.

Pulling out his cock, he slapped it against one cheek, then the other.

"If I even feel your teeth, I'll follow through on tying you naked to the founders' statue and leave you there. Anyone could find you. Will you think I'm jealous then?"

I shut my mouth, glaring at him.

He pinched my nose shut, watching me. I tried to keep my mouth closed, but my lungs burned and I opened it. The second I did, he released my nose and surged forward, shoving his cock deep inside. From this angle, with my arms trapped under his thighs, and him on top of me, I couldn't control anything. Not when he pushed his hard, thick cock down my throat and stayed there. Not when he stared down at me in angry triumph. And not when he slowly, almost tenderly, stroked my face, his touch belied by his next words:

"Oh, little snoop. I bet you're already soaked. You love

being treated this way. This time I'm going to fuck your face so hard, you'll learn your mouth is only good for one thing: pleasing me."

And then he did exactly that.

As I tried to ignore him.

Tried not to come.

Even though I worried I'd fail.

23

Isaac

I'd severely miscalculated.

When I'd been pissed at Tovah the other night for her reticence in sharing about herself—and at myself for the way her presence had turned me completely pussy-whipped—I'd decided I needed to punish her. And from the way she'd reacted in her journalistic ethics class, it was clear public embarrassment was the best punishment for her. Sure, it got her off, and she seemed to have something of a humiliation kink, but if anything, being turned on by her own shame made her hate the experience even more.

So even though the purchase of the sexy maid costume had originally been meant just for me to enjoy, I'd decided to make her wear it to the hockey house party.

But what I hadn't considered was what having her wear something so damn slutty in public would do to me. It somehow hadn't occurred to my moronic ass that putting her in a skimpy, frilly little outfit would mean that every fucker at the party would be able to stare at her bare skin.

That her gorgeous, heavy tits—usually only on display for me—had been served up for all my teammates and whoever else had shown up at this damn party.

It only took twenty or so minutes before I was dragging her out of the room and up the stairs, determined to get her under me and remind both of us who she belonged to.

You're jealous. Is it because you're starting to care?

I wasn't. I *couldn't be*. Jealousy and caring would mean I wanted her long-term, and I couldn't have her long-term. Not with my family and the danger that followed us. No, I wasn't jealous. And I'd fucking prove it to her.

But first I was going to come down her tight little throat and remind her of her place. Coming might happen faster than I'd intended, because the feel of her throat squeezing the sides of my cock was almost more than I could take. Couple that with knowing she couldn't fight me, and fuck, my spine was tingling, and my balls were as heavy as rocks. I'd only thrust a few times, and I felt out of control.

What was it about this girl that made every time feel like the first time? Not just with her, but the first time, period. Like I was a virgin all over again.

I stared down at her, lost in her angry but turned-on brown eyes. I stroked her face, marveling at her silky skin, needing this contact between us. It must have been too much for her, because she closed them.

Nope.

I wasn't letting her stay distant from me, from this. The more I got my hands on her, my cock in her, the more I needed her open, vulnerable.

Mine.

"You open those pretty eyes and keep them on me," I ordered. "Or I'll shut your nose again and you'll pass out with my cock down your throat."

Her eyes popped back open, and the helpless rage in them made me even harder.

But it wasn't enough. No, I wanted her truly helpless, wanted her to fight her body and lose.

Withdrawing, I rose off her chest. It took some awkward maneuvering, but moments later I was turned around, with my back to the headboard, still on top of her, but this time facing her pussy. She'd started struggling again, trying get away, but I surrounded her, covered her. She wasn't going anywhere. I pulled up the frilly skirt of the maid costume. And yeah, I'd been right; the little black thong was soaked. It only took one pull to rip it in two. There was her bare, glistening pussy, just begging for me to get my mouth on her.

Ah yeah, I was hungry.

But first.

Some more awkward maneuvering, but then my cock was back in her mouth.

"You ever done sixty-nine before, Tovah?"

She gurgled something around my cock, making my spine tingle again.

The thought that she had made me ragey.

Nope.

I wasn't angry. I wasn't jealous. She was wrong. So I felt a little territorial, so what? It was normal, probably—even though I'd never felt that way before.

Besides, no one made her come the way I did. And when I was done with her, no one ever would.

With that thought, I shoved my face in her cunt at the same time I thrust my cock deeper in her mouth, sliding down her throat. My balls rested on her nose and cheeks. I went to town on her, alternating between licking gentle circles around her clit and shoving my tongue deep in her pussy, over and over but with no particular rhythm, surprising her each time. She began writhing underneath me, so I moved my arms, gripping her thighs and holding her still. I was rewarded almost immediately by a flood of arousal from her as she soaked my face and filled my mouth with her taste, sharp, sweet, and raw. And when she started moaning around my cock, making the whole thing vibrate in her throat—well, I gripped her poor thick thighs tighter in an effort not to come.

I'd probably leave bruises. Good. She'd be reminded of me for days after.

Her little clit was like a tiny, hard cherry, ripe for picking. Sucking it between my lips, I forced it out of its protective hood and then began stabbing and lashing at it with my tongue, working it so hard, her whole body stiffened, and then I heard a muffled scream.

Ah, yeah. She'd come.

She wasn't done, though.

I kept up with torturing her poor clit, adding in little nips with my teeth, knowing I was hurting her at the same time I was pleasing her. She came again, her throat working around my cock, and I must have had some superhuman strength because somehow I didn't follow her over. Her thighs were quaking between my hands, but she was pliant enough that I could remove one hand from her thigh and slide it between her legs, stuffing two fingers, then three, inside her pussy. I was in the wrong position to fist her, unfortunately, but she was still clenching tightly around my fingers, and that had to be enough for now.

It was; she came again, a third time, and then a fourth, and then a fifth. I was distantly aware I was thrusting wildly into her mouth, and my body was possibly crushing her, but based on her clenching, trembling cunt and throbbing clit, she hadn't passed out or died, so we were okay.

Besides, the muffled sobbing sound, and whatever begging words she was trying to say were vibrating my cock so hard I didn't have a goddamn chance. Lifting my head from her clit so I could focus on my own orgasm, I shoved my cock even deeper down her throat, my balls and spine literally burning. The little brat's teeth closed around my cock. It wasn't painful. In fact, the extra pressure and the threat of it unleashed me. Losing all control, I released everything inside me, including one, terrifying word:

"*Mine.*"

Dazed, I withdrew from her mouth and dropped a soft kiss on her mound—a bit of tenderness I couldn't resist giving her. Rolling off her body, I collapsed on the bed, trying to slow my rapid, heaving breaths.

Fuck.

As I recovered, two thoughts occurred to me:

She'd bit me, even after I threatened her. And that meant a punishment that fit the crime. The fact that I'd also bit her didn't matter.

And, worse, I'd called her *mine*. And I had to do everything I could to prove to her that wasn't true. I might own her, but that *mine* had meant more than ownership—because what I hadn't said, but I'd thought, was, *yours.*

She was going to hate me for what came next. But as my father said, you can't warn people about consequences and then not follow through, or they'll think you're full of empty threats.

Climbing back off the bed, I pulled my boxers and jeans over my wet cock before reaching for her. She was half asleep. The multiple orgasms had taken a lot out of her.

Even though I shouldn't, I gave into what *I* wanted, leaning down and pressing my lips to her hair.

"You okay?" I asked her.

"Mmmhmm," she mumbled against my chest.

"Good. Because you used your teeth, little snoop, and you know what that means. I warned you about your punishment, and I can promise you this: You really aren't going to like this one."

And with that, I scooped her up, and carried her out of my bedroom, down the back stairs, out of the house, and into the night, ignoring the party still happening and the loud voice in my head warning me that I was about to make a huge mistake.

I'D HAD TO THROW HER IN THE TRUNK AGAIN. FORTUNATELY, I'd tied her up her arms and legs with a couple shirts, and gagged her with that little black thong. I just had my car fixed and my taillights replaced; I wasn't going through all that again. It had been hard enough to explain the first time.

When we arrived back at campus, it was midnight. The quad was empty and almost pitch-black, so I had to use the flashlight on my phone to light my way as I opened the trunk and boosted a struggling Tovah into my arms, carrying her down the path to the statue of the founders.

Reina University wasn't the first Ivy to accept women. That was Cornell. But Reina was the first, and only, of the Ivies to be founded by women. No wonder why we'd been named queen in Spanish.

Arms linked, heads thrown back in frozen laughter, the statue stood in the middle of campus. Right now, their stone eyes watched me, creeping me out as I lowered Tovah to the ground in front of them. If I believed in ghosts, I wouldn't be surprised if the long-dead women decided to haunt me for what I was about to do.

Grabbing a Swiss Army knife I'd had in the center console, I sliced down the middle of the maid costume, tearing them off her body until she was naked and shivering before me. Restraining her with one arm, I worked the rope I'd had in the trunk around her waist, one, two, three times, before tying it off so she was trapped between the two stone women, facing the quad—and whoever might pass.

I doubted anyone would. There was no reason for anyone to be around this late at night. The goal wasn't for her to get hurt, but it *was* to scare her into obedience. And prove that I wasn't jealous, that I didn't care. Because if I was, if I did, I'd never do something so heinous, would I?

This is a mistake, the voice in my head warned again, louder this time. I did my best to ignore it.

I tried to ignore her, too.

"Isaac, don't you dare fucking do this," she warned through the wet thong I'd stuffed in her mouth. I had to lean in to understand her. "I swear, you leave me here and I'll never fucking forgive you."

"You should've thought of that before you bit me," I told her.

If I were honest, I wasn't only doing this to scare her. I was doing this because she'd scared me. Sixty-nine shouldn't have been so intimate. I'd done plenty of it over the years. But when I'd had my cock in her mouth with her pussy on mine, it was like she'd sucked out part of my heart and soul, and I'd lost not just physical control, but emotional control, too. For fuck's sake, I'd called her mine. Thought of myself as hers. I didn't know where it had come from, but I had to put some distance between us and regain my power, my control.

The beast inside me was pissed. He didn't like this. He did not want anyone else to see her naked, not even stone statues. He agreed with Tovah. Her naked body was for me alone, no one else. He didn't want her hurt, either.

Which was why I had to do this. To prove to myself I didn't care.

I walked away, trying to block out her screaming after me, making sure I was out of sight, before I went to find a place to hide. Not that I cared, but just to be cautious, I'd stay in the shadows, watching to make sure she was safe.

For a while, no one came. I shivered, shirtless, knowing that Tovah was probably freezing. Every part of me wanted to go untie her and carry her away, take her somewhere warm and safe. But I didn't let myself. This was as much a punishment for me as it was for her. Because it made my chest hurt, knowing how scared and helpless she must be right now. Because I'd been in her position, once: tied outside in punishment, not knowing who might pass by or what they'd do. Knowing that my inner voice was right, and this was not something I'd be able to come back from. She and I had been growing closer, and this would only succeed in pushing her away—for good.

I waited, watching. No one came by, but the seconds ticked by, slowly and torturously. Twice, I'd had to stop myself from going back to her. Untying her. Dropping to my knees and begging for forgiveness.

She must be cold. It was still early spring. What if she got sick?

Finally, eons later—although it was only ten minutes—I decided I'd had enough. I'd proven my point. She knew I didn't care. And it was time to take her home.

But I heard a voice.

A *male* voice.

"Well, what do we have here? Some dumb little senior prank? Or a gift? Don't mind if I do," some asshole said.

"Help!" Tovah screamed below her gag.

"Help," I'd screamed, tied to the tree and forced to watch as my father held the gun on the young boy whose father had killed my mother. His men jeered at me, and I'd never felt so helpless or ashamed. I couldn't get free, couldn't do anything, trapped under rope and my own powerlessness as my father raised the gun.

"Real men shoot," he said. "Babies watch."

And then he pulled the trigger, and all there was, was blood.

No.

This was not the man I was. And I wouldn't put her through the same kind of pain I'd been put through.

Who had I become?

"Help!" she cried again.

It didn't matter if she was yelling for help from me or from the assholes in front of her or from someone else. I was already running toward at a breakneck pace. I didn't even take a second to look at the guy who had dared to even *taunt* my woman, much less touch her.

I tackled him to the ground, throwing punch after bloody punch, more vicious than I'd ever been on the ice. This guy was my enemy, he'd threatened her, and he was going to fucking *pay*. I didn't see what I was doing, because my vision was in a red haze.

"Don't." Punch.

"You." Punch.

"Ever." Punch.

"Fucking." Punch.

"Touch." Punch.

"Her."

Someone was screaming.

It was Tovah.

I looked down. I was covered in blood—my fists, my bare abdomen. The guy beneath me was groaning and begging for me to stop.

So at least I hadn't killed him.

Rising to my feet, I tried to ignore the carnage in front of me, immediately going to Tovah and untying her.

She was freezing. I covered her in the shirt I'd tied around her ankles, lifting her in my arms and carrying her toward the car.

"Isaac, what is wrong with you?" she cried. "You—you hurt me and then, and then...you have to go back. We have to go back. He's not okay."

"I'll call 911 from the car," I said. I didn't give a shit about the guy I'd beaten. I should, and on some level, I was concerned about how little I cared, but that was an issue for later. Taking care of Tovah was for now. "I need to get you home before you get sick."

Opening the passenger door, I carefully placed her in the seat and buckled her in, hating the way her body was wracked with shivers. Hating that *I* was the reason she was shivering. I'd never fully accepted myself, but I'd never loathed myself like I did in that moment. If anyone deserved to be beaten to a pulp, it was me.

No time for that right now. Going around to the driver's side, I cranked the heat to its highest setting, letting the car warm up.

I'd never known I had a heart until those quiet minutes in the car, because as Tovah sobbed quietly in the passenger seat, my heart shattered into tiny, painful pieces. I reached my hand out for hers automatically, and she snatched hers away, moving as far into the passenger side door and as far away from me as she could, like she needed distance between us.

The small shards of my heart stabbed into my chest at her understandable rejection of me. I'd gone too fucking far, and I had no idea how to make up for it.

Someone tapped on the driver's side window.

Shit.

I turned to address whoever it was...

...only to see Aviva standing there, glaring at me with utter disdain and disbelief in her eyes.

Double shit.

24

Tovah

I was numb.

Frozen everywhere: my skin, my bones, my heart. Maybe this was shock? I wasn't sure. I'd been trussed up almost naked in the middle of my university's campus for anyone to see me. And someone had, and Isaac had lost his goddamned mind and beaten the guy half to death like he hadn't put me there in the first place. So I welcomed the numbness, because I knew it was the only thing keeping the pain at bay.

Isaac clearly didn't give a shit that I wanted to be numb. He'd turned the heat up as high as it could go, and the warmth in the car melted my frozen heart into tears that spilled from my eyes. I hated that I was crying, that this asshole knew he'd hurt me. And when he reached his right hand over the console to grab mine, as if he could *make it up to me*, I pulled my hand away and huddled against the door, needing as much distance as I could get.

For a moment, I even contemplated unbuckling my seatbelt, opening the door, and getting out, but I didn't relish the idea of walking around campus barefoot and half naked, in the dark.

Better the devil I knew.

And he was the devil. I'd thought I'd known how deep Isaac's darkness went, but I hadn't fully realized until I'd watched his fists fly and blood splatter everywhere while I stood, helpless and tied to a fucking freezing statue of two women who I knew wouldn't have put up with this shit for a hot second.

I needed out. How, I didn't know. Maybe it was time to listen to my mom and disappear for a while. I'd hate to give up college and my dreams, but I didn't need to be tortured by the boy I'd loved as a child because he was more fucked in the head than I was.

While I was lost in thoughts and desperate plans, someone knocked on Isaac's window. I turned my head, only to see Aviva standing there, Jack behind her.

Oh, thank god.

All I wanted was to cry in my best friend's arms.

Unlocking the passenger door before Isaac could stop me, I burst out of the car and ran around the front, and then Aviva was grabbing me and holding me tight.

"I don't know what he did to you, but I'll fucking kill him," she was saying.

"How—how did you find me?" I asked, trembling.

"Jack saw Isaac carry you out. We've been driving around, trying to find you, and we happened to be driving past campus when we saw Isaac carrying you back to his car. Why are you only wearing his shirt? What did he *do*?"

"Give her back to me." Isaac's voice broke on that last word.

Aviva released me but kept a hand on my shoulder as

she whipped around to face him. "Absolutely the fuck not. She's standing here, barely dressed and shivering, with *you*. You have blood all over you. I'm shocked and ashamed of you, Isaac. This is not the man I know. I don't understand what the fuck has gotten into you, and I don't give a shit. You don't *get her back*. Jack and I are taking her home with us."

"I—" Isaac started, but Jack put a hand up, interrupting him.

"Aviva's right. Whatever the hell is going on between the two of you is not okay. Tovah's spending the night with us, and you can talk to her in the morning."

"Absolutely the fuck not," Isaac parroted Aviva as he advanced on Jack, bloody fists clenched. "She doesn't go anywhere without me. You try to take her, and I'll kill you."

"Tonight, she does," Jack said, voice even. He lowered it, saying something to Isaac I couldn't hear, but it must have worked because Isaac unfisted his hands, only to scrape them angrily through his hair. His eyes were wild, desperate, seeking mine in what...an apology?

Like he and Aviva had said, absolutely the fuck not.

God, I thought that stranger was about to rape me. And I couldn't have done anything, and Isaac had left me there to be hurt...and it was worse than anything he'd ever done to me. Tears welled up in my eyes as I tried to contain a sob.

It broke out anyway.

Isaac let out a terrible sound I'd never heard from him before, moving toward me. Jack caught him by the shoulder and tugged him back.

With his free hand, he tossed Aviva his keys. "Take her home. I'll deal with him."

Through a blur of tears, I saw Jack holding Isaac back as Aviva guided me toward the car, gently sat me in the passenger side of Jack's car, and buckled me in. As we drove away, I heard an anguished, almost animalistic roar—so loud, it could have shaken the trees.

I WAS CURLED UP UNDER THE COVERS IN JACK AND AVIVA'S guest room, lights ablaze, watching *House Hunters International* through dry, burning eyes when Aviva knocked on the door.

"You can come in," I called.

The door opened. She entered the room holding a mug of hot chocolate.

I glanced over at the bedside table, where two other mugs of hot chocolate sat, both near-full, both cold.

"You know, you don't have to keep bringing me new mugs."

"Well, you haven't drunk the old ones," she scolded half-heartedly. "And you need to get your blood sugar up. Please, Tovah, have some."

Sitting up, I held out my hands for the mug, and she handed it over. I took a few sips under her watchful, worried gaze, before finding a spot for it on the bedside table.

"Tovah..."

"I'm okay," I told her softly. "Really."

I wasn't. But I didn't want to worry her any more than she was already worried. Worrying would just lead to questions, and I couldn't give her real answers. Because if I told her what Isaac was holding over my head, and she did anything about it, it would get her killed.

"You don't seem okay," she said. "Don't think I couldn't hear you crying. Tovah, what did he do to you?"

I shook my head. If I told her, she'd drive back to

campus and try to take Isaac on. And I couldn't let her. Partially because I didn't want her getting hurt, but also because—and I hated that I felt this way—I didn't want her doing anything to hurt him, either.

I buried my head in my hands.

She pulled my hands away.

"What—" she started. I cut her off.

"What the hell is wrong with me? He humiliated me at the party and…and then he did other awful things, has done terrible things, and I should hate him. I should want him dead. But…"

"But you don't," she said understandingly.

"But I don't," I finished, feeling pathetic.

She sat on the edge of the bed, grabbing my hand in hers, and squeezed. I squeezed back.

"I get it. Truly. Jack did—things he should be in prison for life for, truly. I should never, ever, have spoken to him again. But somehow, the good he did and that he's still doing outweighs the bad from when the whole messy thing began between the two of us. Logically, it makes no sense. But I've given up on logic. I love him, and he loves me."

I laughed. "Isaac doesn't love me. And I don't love him."

She raised an eyebrow. "Are you sure? Because it seems like these boys do the absolute craziest things when they start to fall. I'm not excusing it, to be clear. But it being horribly wrong doesn't make it any less true."

God, if she was right…and why did I want her to be right so badly? Because I did, I wanted it, I longed for it—even though I should hate him. Even though I never, ever, wanted to see him again, unless it was at his funeral.

"I still want to kill him," I told her.

"Oh, believe me, me too," she assured me, and we both laughed.

"I missed you," I said.

Her face turned serious and accusing. "Well then why did you disappear? I haven't heard from you in days."

This at least I could tell her—right?

I groaned. "He took my phone."

Her hand tightened painfully on mine. "He what?! Why?"

I answered more or less truthfully. "He doesn't trust me not to write an article or make a post about what's going on."

She loosened her grip but didn't let go. "And what *is* going on?"

Looking her in the eyes, I admitted, "I can't tell you. I really, really wish I could, but I can't. It wouldn't be safe for either of us."

Her voice rose. "Fuck safe. All I care about is that you're okay."

I knew that. Which is why she couldn't know anything about the Silvers, or my past. I didn't want to use previous conversations against her, but in this case, I had to.

"Aviva, remember a while back, when you were dealing with stuff with Jack, and you asked me to give you space and not push for answers?" Her eyes narrowed, and even though it hurt me to bring this up, I pushed ahead. "I'm asking for the same thing."

There was silence between us as she processed my words, remembering. After a moment, she nodded.

"I don't like it, but I guess I have to give you that. Just promise me one thing, okay? Don't disappear on me. I won't judge you for being with him or making sacrifices for... whatever or whoever it is you're protecting, but I need you around, and to do whatever I can to make you as okay as you can be."

"Promise," I said, not mentioning that she was one of the people I was protecting.

"Good." She scooted up on the bed, sitting next to me, back against the slatted wooden headboard.

"What are you doing?"

"Watching TV with you until you fall asleep. I'm here, okay? I'm here."

Her words made me cry all over again. But I settled back against the bed, our hands remaining linked as we watched people find homes—something I'd never really had and never would have.

25

Isaac

As the car drove off, I pushed and shoved against Jack, but somehow the left wing managed to keep me in place. Maybe because the fight had burned out of me, leaving me drained and miserable.

"Fuck, man!" he exploded as soon as they were gone.

"Fuck, man," I agreed, hanging my head.

"You fucked up bad," he said. "What did you even *do*?"

"I fucked up bad," I repeated. "I tied her naked to the founders' statue and hid in the shadows. And then when some asshole showed up and tried to touch her, I lost my shit and beat him nearly to death."

Jack blinked.

"Don't even act like you haven't done worse," I growled.

He lifted a shoulder. "Oh, I have done worse. Way worse. But I never expected you to do something so awful. Desperate to prove she doesn't mean anything to you, right?" He nodded like he understood. "But this shit isn't like you. Not Dr. Dimples. Not Isaac Jones, Good Guy."

I was learning that Isaac Jones, Good Guy didn't really exist. It was a hard pill to swallow, but nowhere near as difficult as facing what I'd done tonight. The monster had won, after all.

"I'm not sure you really know me," I admitted. "I'm not sure *I* really know me."

The only person who knew me was sitting in the passenger seat, headed to Jack's house. And fuck, I'd hurt her. The terrified, devastated look on her face was something that would haunt me for the rest of my damn life. It didn't matter what I did to try to fix it, every time I closed my eyes, I'd picture the tears running down her face. I'd have nightmares about the way she'd yelled, the way she'd shivered.

Fuck, was she cold? She was only wearing my shirt, and it wasn't much.

Jack watched me. "Aviva will take care of her. Although she may hide her from you or change the locks on our doors so even I can't get inside."

"Sorry, man."

He shook his head. "Like I said, I get it. Wanting someone so much, caring about them so much—*loving* them—it's the scariest shit in the world."

"I don't love her," I interjected so quickly, even *I* doubted myself.

A small, sad smile appeared on his face. "Even so. Feeling things—it's a whole nightmare," he continued. "So much easier to get angry at them, to blame them, to take that fear out on them. To try to push them away and prove you don't give a fuck. But here's the problem with that. When you catch your breath and the fog lifts, you have a new nightmare to deal with, because she's gone and you don't know how to get her back. If you think you're desperate to throw her away now, imagine what it's like not having her within reach. And yeah, you can force her to stay—but emotionally, forget it. That shit..." his eyes looked haunted. "...losing her is the worst thing you'll ever experience."

"I...fuck."

He was right. Seeing Tovah drive away had hurt like nothing in my life. Like someone had reached into my chest and ripped out the heart I never knew I had, only to drop it in a food processor and press start.

"I don't know how to fix this," I said.

"I know. And I don't know what to tell you, because even though apologizing is a start, it doesn't cut it. Remember man, it's not about redemption, it's about atonement. It's about living every goddamn day of your life like your only purpose is making it right."

We stood there as I digested his words. He slapped me on the back.

"Okay, where's this guy you beat the shit out of? You can't make it right if you're in prison. Even if both of us belong there."

I led him to the statue. The guy was still lying on the ground, but he was breathing. His eyes opened, and he tried to crawl away when he saw us.

"I'm sorry, I'm sorry, I never was going to actually touch her, I swear. Please don't kill me."

Jack and I didn't have to speak out loud to know what the other was thinking. Being hockey teammates was a benefit right now; we were used to communicating practically telepathically.

Simultaneously, we crouched down before him.

"I won't kill you, as long as you never speak a word about this to anyone," I said slowly.

"But if you do talk...well, you won't make it to graduation," Jack added smoothly.

"Got it?" I finished.

"Yes, yes, yes," he said quickly, trying to nod his head and then groaning from the pain. "I won't tell anyone, promise."

We both stood. "Good," I said shockingly easily, given that this was completely unfamiliar territory for me.

"You'll find your own way home, right?" Jack added, and then without waiting for an answer, we turned and walked back into the night.

When we arrived at Jack's, I turned off the car.

He glanced over. "I don't think you should come in with me. Aviva might rip your head off."

I shrugged. "I can handle it. I'm not sleeping without Tovah in my arms, man. I don't care how much she fights."

A slow grin spread across Jack's face. "That's what I hoped you'd say."

We exited my car, and I hit the lock button on the remote key. Jack opened the door to the lobby, waving at his doorman sitting behind the desk.

"Hi Robert," he said.

Robert stood. "He's not allowed here," he said, jerking his head at me. "Your fiancée made me promise."

Jack waved it off. "I'll take care of her."

Robert squared his shoulders. "With all due apology, I'm more afraid of her than I am of you, Mr. Feldman." To me, he said, "Mr. Jones, I'm going to have to ask you to leave."

Fuck.

Well, my father had taught me to deal with obstacles in my way, too. You either killed them or you paid them off. And Robert was a good guy, and I wasn't a killer, so the latter it was.

"What about an all-expenses-paid vacation for you and your wife to the Maldives?" I asked.

He froze. "With business class seats?"

Fuck. This was going to be expensive.

Worth it, though.

"How about first class instead?" I offered, ignoring Jack's smirk.

"You have a deal," Robert said. "But if Ms. Gold asks, you snuck past me while I was in the bathroom."

"You have my word," I said solemnly. "Thank you, Robert."

He tilted his hat at us, and we passed him, headed toward the elevators. Once inside, Jack pressed the button for the penthouse. I inhaled, fear and anticipation warring within me. I didn't know what I was facing, or exactly how I was going to handle it, I just knew what I'd said to Jack: I wasn't sleeping tonight without my little journalist in my arms.

When the elevator doors opened into the apartment, Aviva was standing there in pajamas and a robe, arms crossed over her chest.

"Nope," she said as soon as she saw me. "You aren't here. You're leaving, now."

"You have to give him a chance to apologize, little fury," Jack cajoled her.

"An apology isn't going to cut it," she said flatly. "Not after what he did."

"I know you never forgave me, but you kept me," he

pointed out. "Don't you have to give Tovah the opportunity to make the same decision?"

"I don't have to do shit," she said mutinously.

"Aviva," I said. "I fucked up. I know I fucked up. Please, please—let me make it right."

"How?"

"By giving her every damn thing she wants," I said, meaning every word.

Aviva exhaled, staring at me.

"You promise?"

I nodded.

"If it kills me," I said seriously.

"Fine. But if you hurt her again, I will end you. And I'll make Jack bury your body," she warned.

Jack chuckled, scooping her up in his arms and carrying her to their bedroom.

"They'll be fine," he told her. "It's you who has to worry..."

They disappeared down the hallway, leaving me alone. Taking another deep breath, I headed to the guest room, quietly opening the door.

The lights were on. On the muted TV, some couple was touring an apartment.

Tovah was curled up on the bed, head cupped in her palm, eyes closed, breathing slowly and easily. For a moment, I stood and watched her, taking in how innocent and vulnerable she looked. And as I stared, I realized just how badly both I *and* the monster wanted to protect her. Because she'd been right. I had been jealous. I did care. She was mine, and I was keeping her.

As I moved in closer, I spotted a wet spot on the pillow.

She'd been crying.

I'd done that.

I'd made her cry.

Never again though. The only time she'd cry from now on was from too many orgasms, or choking on my cock. Otherwise, I was going to learn how to make this gorgeous, smart-assed, brilliant and courageous woman smile. I'd make it right. I'd atone for every single tear I'd caused, until the day I died.

Shit, did I *love* her?

I shook it off. I couldn't love her. But I could keep her. I wasn't sure how to have her and make sure she was safe, but I'd figure it out. Because she was mine, and that was never, ever changing.

Careful to not wake her, I scooped her up in my arms and carried her out of the bedroom, down the quiet hallway, and out of the penthouse.

I was taking her home, where she belonged. She'd sleep in my arms, like she was supposed to. And tomorrow, I'd start making it right.

26

Tovah

Something shook me out of sleep. I opened my eyes to see Isaac in the seat next to me as he turned onto his street and pulled into the driveway.

I shot straight up.

No. This wasn't happening.

I unbuckled my seatbelt the moment he stopped the car. I couldn't breathe the same damn air as him.

He clicked the locks shut, and tears I thought I'd run out of spilled from my eyes. I didn't even bother wiping them away.

"Tovah," he said into the silence. "I..."

"You *what,* Isaac? You *what?* What fucking excuse do you have for what you pulled back there? And no," I said, holding my hand up. "I don't care that you warned me you were going to do it earlier. You literally tied me *naked* in *winter* to the goddamned founders' statue at night for anyone to see me. That's not funny. That's insane. And what's more insane? When someone did see me, you descended on them like you were protecting me, when you know what, Isaac? It wouldn't have happened if you hadn't *put me there in the first fucking place!*"

I was screaming now, tears pouring faster down my face. Isaac was lucky his closest neighbor was half a mile away, or they would've come out to see what the issue was.

"Tovah, you have every right to be angry—" he started.

"Angry? I'm enraged. Livid. *Furious.* Take your fucking pick, Isaac Silver! God, you're no better than your father."

Out of the corner of my eye, I could see his jaw set, a vein throbbing on his forehead. I'd pissed him off with the last.

Good. He deserved it. I refused to feel bad about what I'd said, either.

"Now, let me out of the car," I said.

He didn't.

"Isaac! Let me out of the *fucking car!*" I cried, desperate to get away from him.

But he didn't unlock the car. Instead, he pulled me toward him while I struggled. Capturing my head in his hands, he kissed me. His mouth moved against mine, desperate and sad, angry and remorseful, and his emotions threatened to swallow me into whatever deep, dark pit he'd climbed into himself.

But I wouldn't let him drag me down with him, even if the feelings he poured into the kiss made my heart hurt.

What happened to you, Isaac Silver? What broke you?

And why do I even care?

I sat there, stiffly, not opening my mouth to his, and finally with a broken snarl he pulled back.

"You're still cold," he said. "Let's get you inside."

"I can get myself inside," I said, and he didn't respond, just went around the car to the passenger side door and finally unlocked it, lifting me back into his arms like a child or a bride and carrying me into his house the same way he'd carried me out of the hockey house.

Although it had only been hours since we'd left, it felt like I'd aged a million years. I didn't fight him as he carried me upstairs and through his bedroom into the bathroom. I let him set me down on the sink, watching him as he turned on the water in the shower, testing the temperature.

I only spoke when he started stripping out of his clothes.

Did he really think he was going to join me?

"I can shower on my own," I told him.

He paused, looking at me, his eyes dark and tortured, with demons roaming in the shadowed depths.

Inhaling slowly, he relaxed his shoulders, looking down at the tile floor.

"I'll be in the bedroom if you need me," he said, passing by me and shutting the door softly.

"I won't," I said once the door was closed, hating the way my voice trembled.

Pulling Isaac's shirt off my body, I hopped off the counter and stepped into the shower, closing the glass door. My whole body, which had been stiff and cold, began to tremble, the hot water bringing me back to life. I sobbed, my eyes burning as I sank down to the floor of the shower, pulling my legs into my chest and wrapping my arms around my knees, burying my head against them. Rocking back and forth, I let myself cry, let the water pour over my head.

I wasn't only crying because of what Isaac had done. No, I cried, angry and helpless, about the ways that men had hurt me over the years, and how helpless I'd been to stop them. How I'd been helpless as a young girl to stop my stepfather from beating my mother, and then later, me, as his threats to kill us got worse and worse. How I'd been unable to do anything but run ever since that fateful day. It didn't matter that Isaac had untied me from the statue. Not when the danger from his family kept me trapped in this state of desperate fear forever. I'd never be free.

Not from Abe Silver. And not from Isaac, either.

I was so lost in my grief and rage, I didn't even notice when the shower door opened and I was lifted from the floor of the shower and deposited on Isaac's lap. He was still in his clothes, but they quickly grew wet as warm water still poured over us.

Now it was *him* rocking me, and even though I shouldn't have let him, I accepted the comfort my tormentor offered me as he wrapped me tight in his strong arms and buried his head against my neck.

Gomen'nasai, he was saying. *Mujhe kshama karo. Mi dispiace tanto.* I didn't recognize the languages, or the words, but as he kept speaking, I relaxed against him, letting the soft sound of his remorse settle and soothe me until the water turned cold and he turned it off, carrying me out of the shower, drying me off in a fluffy towel before finally removing his soaked clothes and wrapping another towel around his body.

I watched him, curious. Now he was the one who was cold. I wasn't sure what he was doing, and honestly, I didn't care. Suddenly, I was bone tired, and all I wanted to do was sleep.

Passing him, I entered his bedroom, grabbing a shirt out of a drawer and pulling it over my head, dropping the towel on the ground listlessly. I walked out of the bedroom and turned right, opening doors until I found a guestroom with a bed. I entered, locking the door behind me.

I'd be sleeping here tonight. And I'd be going home in the morning.

I fell asleep the second my head hit the pillow, and then I dreamed. I dreamed that Isaac entered the room, picking me up and carrying me back to his bedroom, handcuffing our wrists together again, except this time, the handcuff wasn't metal but was a soft fur and leather bracelet, bracketing my wrist in warmth and an ownership that felt safe. That made me feel achingly whole.

In my dream, Isaac kissed the back of my neck, holding me tight and saying, "I'm so sorry, Tovah. I'm so sorry for the way I hurt you. But I can't—I won't—let you go."

Since his words were absolutely absurd, it had to be a dream.

When I woke in the morning, I was still in the guest bed, alone.

So it had been a dream. He had not, in fact, carried me back into his bedroom, cuffed me to him, and whispered a heartfelt apology and declaration of caring into my ear while I'd slept.

The disappointment I felt at knowing it was only a dream made me even more sour toward the asshole.

I headed into the bathroom, only to be blocked by boxes upon boxes of hair dye lined up on the floor. They were in every color imaginable, and some I couldn't have even imagined if I'd tried. There must have been sixty boxes there, all in the brand I liked.

On top of a, yes, millennial pink, box was a note:

Pick whatever color you want. I'll love it, regardless.

> **FOR WHAT IT'S WORTH—AND I KNOW IT ISN'T WORTH A LOT—I'M SORRY.**
> **I'LL BE HOME LATER.**
> **THE ASSHOLE**

Love.
Sorry.

My heart squeezed tight in my chest. He was right, his apology wasn't worth much. But seeing the word "love" in his handwriting, knowing that even though he hated me dyeing my hair, he'd made it easy for me to do it as much and any way I wanted, realizing he was giving me back this piece of agency and control over my life...it meant more than any lengthy apology could have.

No, I didn't forgive him. Yes, I still loathed him. No, I didn't trust him an inch. But I had to be honest with myself—even if I could leave, I wasn't going to.

Running my hand over the boxes, I chose an electric blue and got to work.

27

Tovah

The peace between us lasted about a week before it came to a grinding halt.

"You've completely lost it if you really think I'm coming to your hockey game," I told Isaac angrily.

It was the Friday after Statuegate and we were facing off in his kitchen, glaring at each other. For the past week, we'd existed in a state of...not quite a quiet truce, but more of a temporary armistice. Isaac's teammates walked me to class every day and walked me home, and Isaac was barely around. I'd focused on schoolwork, snooping around Isaac's house—which proved fruitless—and worrying endlessly about my mom.

I'd also used a library computer to search the news and see if there was a report about a guy being beaten nearly to death on campus, but both *The Daily Queen* and the local papers were silent about it. Part of me, the part that needed to speak truth to power, wanted to write an article about it. But whoever had cleaned up the issue for Isaac would probably do worse to me if I wrote a piece about it. But I was worried; I wanted to make sure he was okay, and I had no way of knowing if he was or not.

I was helpless, and angry. And on top of all of that, I had to deal with Isaac and his nonsense idea that I was going to go *support him at his hockey game as his fake girlfriend.*

Fuck that. *No.*

"No," I said out loud. "Besides, I thought I was just your fuck buddy."

He shrugged as he grabbed eggs out of the carton for an omelet. "Not fuck buddy. Girlfriend. And you're coming. Besides, as senior sports editor, don't you have to go?"

I glared at him. "I don't actually have to go to every single one of Reina's sporting events. I can send a staff writer instead."

"No," he said, imitating me, before adding, "I want you there. As my *girlfriend.*"

I scoffed. He couldn't be serious. And the word girlfriend, fake or otherwise, shouldn't make butterflies dance around in my chest like that. "You think I trust you enough to come to your game? What are you going to do, strip me naked, tie me to the Zamboni, and let everyone take photos?"

One of the eggs Isaac was holding cracked, yolk spilling onto the counter.

"I think you're supposed to usually have a bowl for that," I said.

He glared down at his hands like he didn't trust them. "No one is fucking taking a photo of you. And I wouldn't do that."

I rolled my eyes. I was still pissed. "You kind of already

did. Speaking of which, did that guy even survive? Do you not care?"

Another egg cracked and spilled out everywhere. At this rate, someone was going to have to go back to the store.

"He's fine," Isaac said shortly. "I don't want to talk about that asshole. I want to talk about the hockey game and what you're wearing. You need clothes. Actually, you need one of my jerseys."

I bit my lip.

He couldn't know, could he?

"We'll make a trip to your apartment after breakfast to get your stuff," he decided. "And you can wear one of the extra jerseys I have here."

"I can go to my apartment by myself."

He snorted. "Like I'm letting you go anywhere on your own. You're a flight risk."

He wasn't wrong.

I HAD TWO GOALS WHEN WE GOT TO MY APARTMENT.

One was to grab one of the burner phones I had hidden under the floorboards. My mom hadn't heard from me in days and I needed to both alleviate her fears and also make sure she was okay. That was my main priority.

The second was getting clothes from my closet without Isaac seeing what was hanging in there. If he found out, he'd never, *ever*, let me live it down.

I wasn't sure how I was going to pull either goal off, though. Especially as Isaac loomed behind me as I unlocked the door to my apartment.

"The only thing I like about your place is the locks," he grunted.

"Well, you can thank Jack for that," I said. "He had them replaced when he first started stalking Aviva."

Isaac chuckled. "You know, I'm not even going to defend him. I don't blame him, though."

I looked up at him in consternation. "You don't blame him for being a creepy asshole without any respect for boundaries or like, the law?"

"It got him Aviva, didn't it?"

Damn. I couldn't contradict him; Isaac was right.

I used to think my best friend needed to get her head examined, but then here I was with the man who'd kidnapped, blackmailed, and then humiliated me. Maybe I owed her an apology.

Unlocking the door, I let us into my apartment.

I thought I'd miss it. I *should've* missed it. But my apartment looked unfamiliar and strange, like it belonged to someone else. There was nothing comforting about it anymore.

I headed into the bedroom. "You can wait out here," I told Isaac.

He snorted.

"Sure, sounds good," he said, following me into my bedroom.

I'd never had a guy in here. My bedroom had always been small, but with Isaac in it, giving off heat and so much energy, it felt almost claustrophobic. Having him in my space felt vulnerable in a way I hadn't before.

Especially when he made his way to the closet.

I had a split second to decide: preventing my embarrassment when he discovered what I was hiding in there, or letting him get distracted so I could grab the burner phone without him noticing.

I chose to be embarrassed.

Isaac opened the door to the small, dark closet and disappeared inside.

Immediately, I kneeled beside the bed, lifting the loose floorboard and removing a burner phone, only to quickly replace the floorboard and tuck the burner phone into the pocket of Isaac's hoodie I was currently wearing.

I did it just in time, because the closet door opened all the way, and Isaac stood there, an amused and bemused expression on his face. In his hands were hockey jerseys.

Three hockey jerseys.

Three hockey jerseys that had *Jones 37* written across the chest and back, to be precise.

"You know, I was going to make you wear one of my jerseys I have at home, but it looks like that wasn't necessary." He grinned, dimples annoyingly and adorably on full display.

I didn't want to think he was cute. I was still too pissed at him.

I also didn't want him to think I had a crush on him, or anything stupid like that.

"I didn't buy them," I lied. "The newspaper gave them to me."

He shook his head, smirking, dimples showing. "Sure. And you had to take all three."

"No one wanted them," I told him. "No one was interested in wearing your number. I felt bad. It wasn't the jerseys' fault. So I decided to give them a home."

"How charitable of you." He was still grinning.

"Don't make this something more than it is," I said. "Don't turn this into some huge thing in your head where

I've liked you in secret forever and have been doodling 'Tovah Silver' in my diary. I know who you are, Isaac, don't forget that. I'd never have a crush on someone like you."

His dimples disappeared. He stepped toward me, reaching down with his hand and gripping my chin in between his forefinger and thumb, tilting my head back to look at him.

"Oh, little snoop. I'm not making this more than what it is, because I know exactly what it is. You can pretend to hate me all you want—hell, you can actually hate me all you want—but it won't change what's between us. It won't change that you're mine, body and soul. That you've been mine since the day we met. You know it, and I know it." He nodded to the jersey in his other hand. "And you're going to wear my jersey to the game tonight so everyone else knows it, too."

With that, he released me, stepping back.

"Pack your clothes," he said. "You won't be coming back here for a while."

I found an old suitcase and started stuffing clothes into it, heart racing like I was being chased. Because as much as I hated it, in a way, Isaac was right. I had been his since we'd first met—as young children in Brooklyn on his family's compound. But he didn't remember me from back then, and I wasn't his now.

I wouldn't let myself be.

And I wouldn't let him—or anyone else—think so, either. Not after what he'd done to me on the quad the other night. I wouldn't put up with his bullshit, and he was going to see exactly who *Tovah Lewis* was.

28

Tovah

In my time at Reina, I'd been to more hockey games than I could count. Always as a reporter or editor, and, more recently, as the captain's girlfriend's best friend. I didn't mind my reporter or sidekick role, because it let me be there as an observer.

But as I'd been discovering, being attached to Isaac "Jones" meant I was no longer an observer. Instead, I was the one *observed*.

"Can they all stop staring and whispering?" I complained to Aviva as we took our seats in the row behind the penalty box. "Seriously, it's going to give me hives."

Aviva laughed. "They all want to know who their star forward's new girlfriend is," she teased, before sobering. "How are things between you two? You were gone in the morning when I woke up."

"Yeah, he still...has my phone."

Which was beyond frustrating—and worrying. What if my mom had tried to get in touch with me?

Aviva continued with her questions. She would've made a good investigative journalist. "Did he apologize? Or try to make it right?"

"He bought me like, fifty boxes of hair dye, even though he hates me dyeing my hair. He's been...nicer, but distant. Honestly, I don't know where we stand. I want to hate him still, but there's a connection between us, this crazy, no, insane chemistry. And even though I wanted to run away from it...it caught up with me. Ever since, it's like something is tying me to him. I couldn't get away from Isaac or say no to him, even if I wanted to."

Aviva's face softened. "Yeah," she said. "I get that." A stern look played over her face. "But if he hurts you again, tell me."

Fortunately, I didn't have to answer her, because we were interrupted by someone screaming, "Hey, hey, hey girlies hey!"

Lucy and Leslie, two of our friends from Tabb University, stood in the aisle. Lucy was a tall, voluptuous blonde who swore like a sailor, was more outspoken than even *me,* and also had a doomed crush on the Tabb hockey coach that she'd sworn us all to secrecy over. Leslie was a sweet, petite black-haired ballerina who got along with everyone. You wouldn't think the two would be best friends, but they balanced each other perfectly. Leslie was also engaged to Tabb hockey's left wing, Mason Calloway. Because of their connections to the team, they came to all their games—but they broke the unspoken rules and hung out with us on our side of the arena for at least part of the game.

We hugged them, then scooched over to make space.

Lucy eyed me up and down.

"I think it's warm enough in here that you can take off

that parka, Tovah," she said finally. "Unless you're embarrassed to show us what you're wearing underneath?"

"Troublemaker," I said, reluctantly unzipping my coat and revealing Isaac's jersey underneath.

Leslie giggled. "That's what Coach Samson calls her."

Lucy's cheeks flushed. "Whatever. We don't have to talk about that. Not when you're wearing Isaac's jersey. So the rumors are true?"

I pasted a smile on my face, aware that the staring and whispering around us had just gotten worse. "Depends on what the rumors say."

"They say that you and Isaac are dating. Not even dating. *Together.* Apparently, he's been making it *very clear* to all the guys at both Reina and Tabb that Tovah Kaufman's taken now. And that jersey just drives the point home."

I smiled to myself, brushing my hands over the three rolled up posters I was holding upright between my legs.

The jersey might.

But I had my own point to make.

"Uh oh," Leslie said, watching me. "I know that look. I've seen that look. I've *made* that look. Whatever you're up to, seriously think through it. Or if Isaac's anything like Mason, he'll take it out on your ass later."

This time, it was my turn to flush.

"I have no idea what you're talking about," I said primly, even though I remembered in graphic detail what Isaac's punishment had felt like when he'd spanked me.

Leslie and Lucy exploded into laughter. Aviva just watched me.

"You're hiding something from me," she said quietly. "Tovah, you don't have to tell me right now, but if Isaac is doing anything to hurt you…"

"I have it under control," I said firmly.

Because at least for now, I did.

The players lined up, Isaac facing off against Tabb's center for the puck drop.

Tabb's center lifted his stick and pushed Isaac backward off the line, while Mason, Tabb's left wing, picked up the puck with his stick and carried it off into the offensive zone.

"That's my man," Leslie said dreamily.

"You dork," Lucy teased.

Isaac chased Mason into the offensive zone, pinned him to the boards and took the puck back. He passed the puck to Jack, who drove in toward Tabb's goal. Isaac was close behind, followed by Tabb's defense. He skated around the back of the goal until he was open for Jack to pass the puck to him. A few moments later, the horn sounded—Isaac had scored a goal.

The game paused as the ice crew members used shovels to clean up and smooth out the ice. Isaac looked up, scanning the arena, his eyes catching on mine—and it felt like everyone was watching us.

Which was what I wanted.

Knowing Isaac's eyes were on me—and everyone else in the arena's, apparently—I stood, unrolling the first sign and holding it up so everyone could see.

"Holy shit," a guy near us said.

As luck would have it, the jumbotron's camera was on me, so everyone in the arena could see me and the sign I was holding.

The sign that said:

37'S A BENDER

So many people gasped, the sound echoed the stadium.

Someone stood up and yelled, "No one talks about Isaac Jones that way!" and then they were all yelling, "JONES, JONES, JONES," so loudly, it was like the arena itself was roaring.

I barely noticed. My eyes were on the player in the #37 jersey himself as he pulled his helmet off and spun around on the ice, scanning the stands until they landed on me. And held.

So much passed between his dark eyes and mine. Anger, frustration, lust, remorse, ownership, and something else, something terrifying that I refused to put a name to.

Finally, he smirked. *You'll pay for that*, he mouthed.

I smirked back, dropping the first poster and revealing the second.

If you want more ice time, 37, I hear they're hiring a Zamboni driver.

There were more gasps, more yelling. I probably should've been worried that a fan was going to take me out. But I ignored all of it, focused entirely on the way Isaac was staring at me.

"He looks like he wants to kill her." Leslie sounded worried. "Maybe we should stop her."

"Nah, he looks like he wants to *eat* her," Lucy corrected. "And in the fun way. Let her do her thing."

The ref blew his whistle, and the game resumed. Isaac and Tabb's forward faced off on center ice. This time, Isaac won the puck, and pushed toward Tabb's goal, only to be stopped by Mason, who stole the puck and drove toward our goal. Mason was fast, gliding across the ice, but when he shot the puck, Lawson, who was in the crease, caught the puck right before it hit the net, leaving us at 1:0, Reina : Tabb.

Just as the first period ended and the horn sounded, I let go of the second poster, revealing the third and final sign.

I should've worn a different player's number—one who can actually score.

This was a lie, of course. Isaac had the most goals in the league. But still, I was proud of myself. And like any good journalist, I loved a good em-dash.

The entire stadium went silent, the jumbotron still showing off me and my signs.

If they were going to stare, at least they had something legitimate to stare at.

Isaac shook his helmet as he stopped in front of the penalty box, looking up at me. I didn't have to see his face to know he was probably torn between laughing and spanking me. The idea got me hot and bothered, my heart racing. I knew I was taunting him, waving a red flag in front of a bull. But I didn't care. He'd hurt me, emotionally, when he'd tied me to the statue in the quad. I wasn't about to take it lying down. He'd gotten into this with me, and he knew who I was —sass and all. And if he didn't, well, I'd reminded him.

I was Tovah *Lewis*. I was no one's doormat.

Someone tapped on my shoulder, and I glanced away from Isaac and at an irate looking middle-aged man with a red face.

"You fucking bitch," he seethed. "Didn't anyone teach you manners? You don't come to one of our games and insult our star player."

He grabbed the neck of my jersey and pulled, still ranting. "You don't deserve to wear Jones' jersey, you cunt."

"Sir, get your hands off me," I tried to say as calmly as possible, while the girls yelled at the man to go away.

They needn't have bothered. Because one second, the man was there, his beer breath in my face while he leaned over me, and the next, he was flat on his back on the stairs, getting the shit pummeled out of him.

By Isaac.

29

Isaac

She was the most aggravating, annoying, offensive and frustrating woman I'd ever known.

And I was motherfucking obsessed with all of it.

As I stood on the ice, spinning in a circle and watching her insult me with each of her posterboard-created chirps, I couldn't help but laugh. I wanted to pick her up, carry her somewhere dark and quiet, and go to town on her ass for daring to, well, dare me in this way, but at the same time, it made me laugh harder than anything had in a long time.

The horn sounded, signaling the end of the first period. Jack skated over to me, followed by Judah, Levi, Asher, and Lawson.

"She's not fucking around, is she," Jack observed.

"She's a hell of a chirper," Asher laughed.

"She could teach us a thing or two," Lawson agreed.

Asher slapped him on the shoulder.

Lawson was our other goalie, and although Jack had once beaten him up during a game because he thought

Lawson had made a move on Aviva, the two had buried the hatchet. It was pretty obvious that Lawson wasn't into Aviva; he'd had some girl back in high school he'd never gotten over, even though he wouldn't give any of us details.

I couldn't focus on my team's ribbing, though. I was too busy staring at Tovah in the stands, her face above the sign. She grinned at me, a little sassy and a whole lot sexy.

"Isaac, come on, Coach wants us in the locker room," Jack said.

"He's too busy eye fucking Tovah to listen to you," Judah laughed.

Judah was right. She was beautiful, there in my jersey, a little sweaty, her bright blue hair curling up around her temples, her face bare of makeup, nose stud sparkling under the lights.

And there was a man next to her.

Some older guy.

Touching her.

I watched, my vision going from a normal clear to a red mist as the asshole tapped on her shoulder and started shouting at her. I didn't have to be able to hear him to know the words were vile.

"Isaac, man, breathe. Breathe, brother," Judah was saying. "Tovah can handle herself."

Except that asshole had grabbed hold of the collar of her jersey and was yanking on it.

The monster, who had been happily chilling out while I played, sat the fuck up and growled. And before I even fully realized what I was doing, my hands were on the boards and I was vaulting over them, running up the stairs in the stands until I reached her.

And then I—or the monster, or maybe even both of us—was grabbing the bastard by *his* collar and ripping him off

Tovah, throwing him on the ground and straddling him so I could punch his fucking face in. I was yelling something at him, I wasn't sure what, but there were definitely words coming out of my mouth. I kept hitting him, even though he curled into a protective ball and begged me to stop, even though people were shouting, even though Jack was grabbing my shoulder and trying to pull me off him.

I didn't care. Because someone was trying to hurt what was *mine*, and that someone was going to pay for even thinking of touching a goddamned fucking blue hair on her perfect head.

"Isaac," a husky, feminine voice said. *Her* voice. "Stop. You need to stop." Then: "I'm okay."

The red mist cleared and the roaring quieted. I realized where I was—kneeling on top of some random fan, my gloves off, my hands covered in blood—his blood.

I rose on shaking legs, looking down at the man groaning underneath me. I'd broken his nose, for sure, maybe some teeth, too.

All I felt was satisfied.

"You don't talk to my girl that way," I told him, my voice low and shaking with leftover rage. "You don't touch her, either. I don't care what kind of insulting sign she's holding in the stadium. You ever get near her again, I'll kill you."

"But I'm your number one fan," the man sobbed in some kind of confused pain.

"Isaac." Coach said. "You're out of the game. Locker room. *Now.*"

"Yeah," I shrugged. "I figured." I grabbed Tovah's hand. "She's coming with."

Coach started to argue with me, then sighed. "Ms. Kaufman can wait in my office while I talk to the rest of you," he agreed.

With that, I tugged Tovah by her hand and she followed me and the rest of the team down the stairs and through the hallway toward the locker room. I was aware of the whispering, the shocked silence of the crowd during what should've been a chaotic intermission, but I ignored them. I ignored everything but the comforting assurance of her small, soft hand in mine as I led her into the locker room and away from anyone else who could possibly hurt her.

"He's lost his fucking mind," Asher muttered to Lawson.

"Happens to the best of us," Lawson laughed ruefully, following us inside.

30

Isaac

After Coach reamed me out for my behavior in front of the whole team and I nodded along and pretended like I felt remorseful—when all I wanted to do was take my skate blade to that fucker's neck—the rest of the team filed out for the second period.

"Not you, Jones: You're suspended for the next few games. If I can't make a good argument for you, you might be out for the rest of the season. Beating up a fan; Jesus fucking Christ," Coach said, shaking his head.

"Sorry, Coach," I said, hanging my head.

"No you aren't," he sighed, but he slapped me on the shoulder and then he was gone.

"You can come out," I called to Tovah in the office.

She stepped out into the locker room, leaning against the wall and crossing her arms.

"You know, for someone who hates violence, you've gotten pretty violent lately."

I stood, keeping my eyes on her as I peeled my jersey off over my head and stripped out of all my gear above my waist until I was shirtless, feeling a warm satisfaction in my chest when her eyes caught on my chest and held. I trained and stayed in shape for hockey, but having the kind of body that kept Tovah entranced was a nice perk.

I advanced on her slowly, pleased that she had nowhere to go. Even more pleased when her breathing picked up as I grew closer, until I placed my hands on the wall above her head, effectively trapping her there.

The move worked; her eyes dilated, eclipsing the dark brown of her irises.

"Isaac?" she said sweetly, breathily.

"Yeah, little snoop?"

She wrinkled her nose. "You stink."

Chuckling, I leaned in further. "Comes with the territory."

Standing, I held out my palm for her. "I'm taking a shower. And you're gonna watch."

She hesitated.

"Tovah," I warned.

"A deal's a deal," she sighed, but her hard nipples gave her away.

Tugging her behind me, I led her to the showers, positioning her on the edge where she'd have the perfect view of me without getting wet—from water, at least.

"Eyes on me," I ordered, as I removed my remaining gear, tossing it on the ground before stepping into the shower and turning the water on. I'd clean it up later. And I didn't reprimand her when her eyes dropped from my face to my hardening cock, which grew thicker under her appraisal.

"You like it, gorgeous? He's hard for you. You made him

that way. You *always* make him that way," I crooned as I slowly stroked my dick, pointing in her direction. "He knows you're about to make him really fucking happy. Aren't you?"

Breath shallow, mouth open in a small "o," she watched me. Smirking, I continued with slow, easy strokes. If I hadn't been keeping such a close eye on her, I wouldn't have noticed the way her legs pressed together, thighs clenching.

Yeah, she wanted my cock. Bad.

And I'd give it to her, which meant leaving it alone for now.

Releasing my protesting dick, I filled my hands with body wash, lathering my neck, my chest, my arms and abs, before reaching down to do the same to my cock, my legs, my ass. As I washed my body, I paid special attention to the parts of it Tovah took the most interest in, spending extra time on my pecs and the area between my abs and my hips that formed a V. I'd never noticed it, but she always seemed to get distracted by it. She licked her lips, her eyes glazing over.

"I didn't take you for an exhibitionist," she said, and even though her words were dry, the lust in her voice gave her away.

"Only for you, sweetheart," I said, rinsing the soap off my body before quickly washing my hair.

Once I was done, I wrapped a towel around my waist, drying my hair with another.

"Come," I told her, knowing I'd be telling her that again soon.

She followed me back into the main part of the locker room. Dropping my towel on the bench, I sat on it, spreading my thighs wide.

"Pants and panties off," I said.

She glanced around, worried. "But anyone could come in."

I growled at the idea. "No one's coming in right now. No one's going to see you. Clothes off, Tovah. I want to see those thick thighs, those delicious dimples in your hips. That dripping pussy. *My* dripping pussy. *Strip.*"

She stripped slowly, almost awkwardly, leggings off, then red lace panties that matched my jersey she was wearing.

"Hand them over."

She did. And when our hands touched, I swear to fucking god, my whole arm tingled. It wasn't even sexual, but something about skin to skin contact with this girl set my whole body on fire.

Mine.

There was a big wet spot on the front of her panties. Without taking my eyes off her, I lifted them to my nose and inhaled.

Somehow, her lemon and sugar scent was stronger here. Sharper, sweeter. And woven in was the musky, earthy scent of raw fucking pussy.

"So fucking delicious," I growled, before tapping my thigh. "Sit."

She eyed my cock, which was sticking straight up at that point.

"I'm not fucking you."

"Who said anything about fucking? I want to finger your sweet little cunt to orgasm."

She moaned, the sound so soft and perfect, I almost came on the spot.

Slowly, almost hesitantly, she came toward me. The second her thighs touched my knees I reached forward, lifting her by those delectably dimpled hips and dropping her on my thighs so she straddled me. Placing a hand between her thighs, I traced her pussy lips, instantly rewarded by the wetness that greeted my fingers.

"This pussy's mine," I told her on a rasp, as I drew circles on her slit before slowly pushing one finger inside her up to the knuckle. Her pussy immediately clenched around it.

"Goddamn, you're so tight," I said in a voice I hardly recognized, pulling out my finger and replacing it with two. She felt even tighter like this, and when she shut her eyes and whimpered, it was like sparks flew between us, lighting on my lower spine and making my cock thicken. As I pushed my fingers back into her pussy, I lifted my hips, my bare cock sliding against her stomach.

She looked down at me and moaned.

"That's right, you like that cock, don't you?" I crooned as I played with her.

Eyes on the digital clock across the room that tracked the period, I did some guy math. There were fifteen minutes left to the period, plus whatever pauses and penalties there were. Given how responsive Tovah was, I had time to get her off this way before using her sweet body anyway I liked.

Fucking perfect.

Withdrawing my fingers, I gave her a moment of reprieve before working a third inside her. I could feel her pussy stretching around them, unused to their thickness and length.

"Isaac," she said, her eyes already watering. "It's too much."

"Never, baby," I crooned. "You're going to take my fingers up your cunt like my bad little cum slut, aren't you?" I punctuated my words by thrusting my fingers deeper into her pussy, exulting in her resulting cry.

"Shh," I admonished, even though no one was around.

"I don't want anyone else hearing the sweet sounds you make."

With my free hand, I wrapped my hand in her hair, tugging her forward so I could catch her cries with my mouth. Her taste exploded on my tongue, sweet and sharp, lulling me with softness and waking me up to a world beyond anything I ever could've imagined. Every kiss was like this. Her mouth was made for mine.

She was made for me.

And I was made for her.

There would be no one else for me, ever. The idea of ever setting her free was so unimaginable, I denied it with everything in my being, biting her lip in punishment even if she hadn't been the one who said or thought it. I shoved my fingers deeper, ignoring the way she struggled in my lap as I continued to stroke the inside of her pussy.

"Oh, oh fuck," I groaned, overwhelmed by the way her tight cunt squeezed the sides of my fingers. I rocked my hips, shoving my cock against her stomach, barely aware of the precum leaking from the tip. She wasn't even touching me, but there were still waves of pleasure shooting up my spine. She didn't need to touch me for this to feel so fucking good. Not when I controlled every fucking bit of her, not when she tried to fight and lost as I gripped the back of her head with my free hand and kept biting her lips, not when her spread thighs trembled and her goddamned beautiful fucking pussy clenched and clenched and *clenched* around my fingers, drenching them in wetness that was spilling onto my bare legs.

I released her lower lip, pulling back so I could speak.

"You're close to coming, aren't you? I can feel how tight you're getting. Get used to the feel of them, because they're the only fingers you're ever going to know in your pussy.

This pussy? Fucking mine. All of you? Fucking mine. And no one better get near you to hurt you or touch you in any way or I will fucking *end them.*"

I wasn't sure where the words were coming from. It should've just been hooking up; she shouldn't have been anything more than a sweet mouth and a tight pussy. But I knew better. Tovah wasn't just pussy.

She was goddamned *everything.*

I felt her coiling tighter at my words, and god knew my cock felt ready to explode. So despite my cock and fingers' protests, I withdrew my fingers from her pussy again, drawing gentle circles on her slit.

Whining at my withdrawal, Tovah slapped my thigh.

"I was close, Isaac," she said.

"I know, little snoop," I said, stroking her trembling cheek. "But neither of us get to come yet."

I soothed her, waiting until her breathing slowed and she retreated from the edge. "Ready?" I asked, although I didn't wait for her reply. Instead, I dragged her head back to mine, kissing her as I thrust my fingers back inside her empty, grasping cunt. I turned them toward me, hooking my fingers and rubbing them against her G-spot as I started drawing teasing, barely there circles on her engorged, pulsing clit with my thumb.

She cried out desperately, the sound swallowed by my mouth. I rolled my hips back and forth, rubbing the side of my cock against her stomach as I continued to stroke the inside of her pussy and added more pressure with my thumb, forcing down the urge to come so I could enjoy her as long as possible. Wet sounds echoed in the locker room and even more of her arousal drenched my thighs.

"You're so fucking wet, aren't you, bad little girl? But you're only bad for me, aren't you? This pussy only gets wet for me from now on. You don't even get to touch yourself with your own fingers unless I tell you to. I can't wait until it's my cock in that tight, pulsing pussy."

Tovah moaned my name against my lips. I could've gotten lost there, in her kiss, our tongues dancing intimately, but my cock reminded me it was getting lonely. It was going to have to wait its turn. The longer it took to come, the longer I had her here at my mercy—and the longer I could ignore the outside world that would take her from me one day.

Withdrawing my fingers again, I played gently with her pussy, pulling her back from the brink.

"Isaac, please," my perfect bad girl begged, her eyes glassy and pleading.

"What do you need? Tell me," I said, as I traced a figure eight pattern around her clit.

"I need to come, please let me come!"

"You come when I let you come," I told her. "You *only* come when I let you come. And I may not let you. How would that feel, keeping you on edge for the rest of the night? Tomorrow, too? I can keep you this way for as long as I want, tie you down and play with you for hours until you've lost track of time and all sense of self, you're so desperate for me. And then, only then, maybe I'll let you come."

She liked that. Even without my fingers in her, I could tell the way she was clenching, and her little nipples were so hard, I could see them in my jersey.

"Isaac, please...."

"I love how you beg," I said. "And bad girls like you deserve rewards."

Besides, I loved how hard she came, and I wanted her spasming around my fingers.

My eyes caught on the clock. Five minutes left in the period.

Just enough time.

Once more, I thrust my fingers inside her pussy. I thrust my fingers in and out quickly, rubbing hard circles around her clit, not caring if it was too much. My balls were heavy, my cock was beyond thick and hard, and it was time.

Rubbing my fingers over her G-spot, I pressed down hard on her clit.

"Mine, Tovah. You're fucking *mine*. For goddamned ever," I growled.

That was all it took. With a scream, she came, pulsing tight, hot, and wet around my fingers and absolutely *soaking* my legs as she goddamn fucking squirted. I barely stopped myself from following her.

Instead, I rose, my arms around her waist, her legs dangling, carrying her over to the bench in the middle of the locker room. Placing her on her hands and knees, I made sure she was steady before moving behind her, my legs straddling the bench.

"Ass up," I told her.

"Wh-what?" she asked, drunk and hazy off her orgasm.

Chuckling, I put my hands on her hips, positioning her. Once she was where I wanted, I grabbed my hard, desperate cock in my hand, sliding it between her bare and shaking thighs, so it rubbed against her soaked pussy.

"Ahhhhh, fuck," I moaned, as I gripped the outside of her thighs and pushed them together, creating the perfect tunnel for my cock.

"Isaac," she cried. "It's too much, it's—"

"It's not too much," I said as I began to slide back and forth between her thighs. "There's no such thing as too much when it comes to us."

I pumped my hips, needing this, her bare, wet skin, her trembling, her cries. Needing to feel this connection between us, a closeness I knew I'd never feel with anyone else. It wasn't about my cock, about getting off. It was about the tie between us, winding tighter and tighter, closing a loop between her body and mine, her heart and mine, her soul and mine, until I felt like I was about to explode.

"You're everything, you know that? More than hockey, more than my team. More than my life. The goddamned sun could fall out of the sky and the world would still burn bright as long as you're in it. Fuck, Tovah, you've changed how I *see*. I'm not giving you up."

She cried out at my words, her thighs squeezing even tighter as she came.

I followed her, my balls releasing, aware I was bruising the shit out of her and not caring as I came and came and came—harder than I had in my whole life, shooting hot cum between her thighs and on the bench.

It could've lasted a second, it could've lasted forever. I didn't know, and I didn't care.

Finally, I began to soften. I slid from out between her thighs, wanting to collapse, and catching her by the waist before she did.

I glanced at the clock. Thirty seconds left of second period.

Lifting her and putting her back on her feet, I tracked down her clothes and helping her into them before I threw on my own street clothes. Technically, I was supposed to stay through the end of the game, but I was already in plenty of shit—what was a little more? I wanted to get Tovah home, in *our* bed, so I could play with her some more—and get her away from my teammates. She was mine, and the less than human part of me wanted her alone and safe and yeah, locked up. I was pretty fucked in the head, but I no longer cared.

"Isaac, we need to stay," she protested, as I scooped her up in my arms and carried her out of the locker room.

"Fuck that, I want you home and naked," I told her as I carried her out of my arena, back to my car, and drove her home.

31

Tovah

By the time I got out of the shower, I'd regained my equilibrium.

Mostly.

What Isaac had done had completely shaken me to my core. Sure, he'd threatened Veronica and Toby at the editors' meeting, but I'd never expected him to defend me—or punch the hell out of a stranger for being an asshole to me. Although I hated myself for it, it softened me toward him, making something warm spark in my belly. No man had ever protected me before. I didn't remember my birth father, and my stepfather had been an abusive nightmare. So to have Isaac's protection, not just of my physical self, but for my emotional safety—it meant something.

More than it should.

And then the locker room. It should've been humiliating, the way he'd used my body. I should've hated the way he edged me, playing me like a musician and not letting me come even though I needed to. But not only had I come, hard, I was more satisfied than I'd ever been in my entire life. Isaac didn't know, of course, that he was the only man who had ever touched me that way. But when he'd told me in that deep growl that I was his and no one else would ever lay a hand on me, part of my heart had detached from my body and spilled out onto his hand. When he'd called me "everything," even more of it defected to join his team. Maybe they were the parts that had always been his, since we were young children and he'd promised to protect me then, too. I didn't know. All I knew is that I was losing pieces of myself to this man, even though he'd hurt me.

Possibly because instead of getting angry at me for challenging him at the hockey game, he'd been amused, even impressed.

And then had stood up for me.

Even though he supposedly still hated me.

The goddamned sun could fall out of the sky and the world would still burn bright as long as you're in it.

God.

I had to face him.

And say what?

Exhaling, I opened the bathroom door. In the bedroom, Isaac was stripping out of his clothes. The lamp beside the bed lit his body with a copper glow.

His eyes landed on me, and they warmed. Opening his arms, he gestured me forward.

I stared at him.

Did he...

...did he want me to hug him?

"Come here," he said gruffly, and slowly, like I was stepping on eggshells or possibly landmines, I made my way over to him. Once I was within arm's reach, he grabbed my wrists, pulling me against his body, wrapping my arms around his back, and then wrapping his own around my waist. Isaac was so tall; I barely came up to his chest. As he held me, the world and all my fears and confusion and worries receded, until all that was, was him.

"Do we hug now?" I asked his chest.

It vibrated with his laughter. "I guess. I don't fucking know. I'm not going to even pretend I know what I'm doing with you anymore, Tovah."

"Me neither," I admitted, and the way he laughed again warmed something in my soul, something that had been slowly, cautiously defrosting since the night he'd tied me to the statue.

We stood there for a while, quiet but together, warming each other, protecting each other. Caring about each other, maybe. Although I couldn't entirely let myself trust that, or him.

Could I?

Deciding to be brave, I pulled away from his chest.

"I'm not done holding you," he grumbled, but I was already grabbing his hand and tugging him to the bed.

Shockingly, he let me guide him.

"Lie down," I said, pushing at his arms, and he did.

I climbed onto the bed and over his body, straddling his stomach, still in my towel. His eyes grew hazy.

"This looks fun," he commented, reaching for my waist.

I stopped him, pulling his arms off me and lowering them to the bed.

Once again, he surprised me by letting me.

I swallowed. "Will you tell me about your tattoos?"

He blinked. "You climbed on top of me in only a towel so you could ask me about my tattoos?"

I nodded. "Almost everything I know about you, Isaac, I know from investigating."

"Snooping," he interjected.

"Whatever. I want to know more about you because *you* told me. So, tell me about your tattoos."

After a moment, he nodded. Taking my right hand in his, he linked our fingers and guided it to his tricep.

"I started the sleeve when I was fourteen. Didn't even know it was going to be a sleeve back then. Most Jewish people—well, you know why we don't get tattoos. But my father likes to be a rule breaker, so he made all his sons get tattoos. Liza got them too, so she wasn't left out." He smiled at that. "Anyway, my brothers and I all got a tattoo of a typical-looking gangster from the 20s. We all thought it was pretty badass."

I leaned down, kissing the tattoo of the gangster. "I'm sure it was—to a fourteen-year-old boy."

He snorted. "Don't you start, Millennial Pink."

"What about this?" I asked, dragging our fingers over the huge pool of blood.

His smile disappeared. "I've had nightmares for years about my mother's death. Reuben—stupidly—thought if I tattooed it to my body, it would be cathartic somehow. Stop the nightmares from coming."

"Did it?" I asked softly.

Isaac shook his head. "No. I had the nightmares multiple times a week—until you started sleeping in our bed."

"Oh," I said.

The implication was almost too much to digest. That I might be the reason he wasn't having nightmares anymore, that he might be healing...it couldn't be true.

That the bed was *ours*.

"Oh," he mimicked, and a dimple popped.

It was the first time I'd ever seen him dimple naturally when it was just us. I wanted to photograph it. For evidence, and later, when this was all over, for the memory.

I swallowed, changing the subject. "And this one?" I asked, trailing our fingers lower.

"The snake. It's a constant warning not to fall for my father's tricks."

I nodded, finally asking the question that had been plaguing me. "And what about the tattoo on your back?"

Isaac closed his eyes. "The wall is a symbol for my fate. The dying vine is a reminder that no matter how hard I try to climb over it, I'll never be able to get out."

Oh, god.

God.

Isaac had told me as much when he'd first kidnapped me, hadn't he? That he was trapped? Trapped, like I was. By the same man. By his father. We both wanted our freedom from Abe Silver.

And neither of us would ever get it.

My heart rose and fell, rose and fell, from the breathtakingly sweet and devastatingly sad knowledge. We were both that dying vine.

Was there any way I could bring it back to life?

"We're not so different," I murmured to him.

"Yeah?" With his free hand, he reached up to cup my cheek, slowly dragging me down until our lips were only a breath apart.

"Yeah," I breathed against them, and he kissed me.

It was different from any kiss we'd ever had before. There was no ownership in it, no dominance or demand. We met as equals, not opponents. Instead of a power struggle, there was kindness, tenderness. An understanding that said, *I see you. Even with my eyes closed, I see you. I know you.*

We kissed, and kissed, and kissed, some hidden magic

between us casting a spell and weaving us together, changing us in ways I wasn't sure I was ready for.

Overwhelmed and gasping from the intensity of it, I pulled away.

He opened his eyes, and there was humor in them.

"There's no such thing as 'too much' with us," he said, like he'd read my mind.

Unable to respond, to verify or validate, knowing that doing so would abandon everything that mattered to me, I asked instead, "Any other tattoos?"

He scanned my face, before shrugging. "Yeah. Remember that little girl I told you about? She had a birthmark under her left armpit in the shape of a crescent moon. I was drunk last year with the team and we all went to get tattoos; for some reason, I asked the artist to put a crescent moon tattoo under my armpit like hers. Don't really know why."

He lifted his arm, showing me. It peeked out from the hair, angry and accusatory.

There was something stuck in my throat; I couldn't breathe.

He'd gotten a tattoo of a birthmark.

My birthmark.

I'd hidden it so well, was careful not to lift my arms too high. But it never occurred to me that he remembered. That he would've memorialized it.

That he cared so much about that little girl—the one he claimed he hated.

The one I left behind.

"You okay?" he asked, concerned.

"Just tired," I said.

And I was, suddenly. Bone tired. Drained and exhausted by the reminder of who we were and what really kept us apart. There was no future for us. We were both dying vines on a wall, unable to ever climb to freedom.

Isaac, unaware of my morose thoughts, pulled me into his arms, stroking my back with his free hand, and murmuring something in Spanish:

"He intentado detenerme, pero no puedo. Me estoy enamorando de ti, amor."

I knew some Spanish, but before I could try to translate the romantic-sounding words, I was already asleep on his chest.

32

Tovah

Isaac didn't give me my phone back. He did, however, edge me to the point of insanity for the rest of the week, care for me afterward, and then cuff me to him every night and make me sleep in his arms.

They were the leather and fur cuffs from what I thought was a dream. Apparently not.

"Not going to hurt you again," he'd said. "Got rid of those other goddamn handcuffs after they rubbed your wrists raw."

God help me, but I was beginning to grow addicted to it —both his torture and his care.

That didn't mean I forgot what mattered to me, though. So even though he and his teammates were still shadowing me to all my classes and newspaper meetings, I had to find a moment alone so I could call my mom.

I found my moment after my sociology seminar one day. Dave Lawson, or Lawson, as he went by, was my babysitter that afternoon. It was a bright, sunny day, warm for early spring, and the sun streamed in through the trees that surrounded the quad, dousing it with light and making the old snow sparkle.

Lawson wasn't much of a talker. It was an easy silence, but we were both lost in our own thoughts. Lawson, thinking about god knew what, probably goalie stuff. Me, about how I was going to manage to call my mom. My phone was burning a hole in my purse.

Until Lawson stopped in the middle of the quad, almost tripping over his own feet as he stared into the distance.

"What's wrong?" I asked.

"Just saw some—not possible. Stay here, I'll be right back," he said, not even bothering to look back at me and make sure I stayed like a good little prisoner as he practically sprinted down the path and out of sight.

Perfect.

I hurried in the other direction, back into the building toward the women's bathroom. I could always say I needed to pee, and the sound of running water would cover up whatever conversation I had.

Entering the bathroom, I locked the door, apologizing silently to anyone who might have to pee between classes. But they could go up a floor.

Flipping open the burner phone, I pressed the buttons for my mother's number, letting it ring three times before hanging up. I did it two more times. It was my signal to her that I was calling when I couldn't use my own phone.

Finally, on the fourth call, she answered on the first ring.

"Tovahleh?"

"Hi mom," I said, trying to hold back the tears at finally hearing her warm if worried voice.

"Oh honey, thank god. I haven't heard from you in days. How are you? Why aren't you responding to your texts?"

Shit, how did I explain this without terrifying her?

"I lost my phone," I finally said. "And I haven't been able to afford a new one. I'm so sorry."

She exhaled. "So you're okay?"

I choked on a laugh. "Yes, I'm okay."

If being okay meant being sexually edged and denied orgasm for days by your former and maybe current greatest enemy who claimed he knew your secrets but only seemed to know some of them and spent the same amount of time tormenting you as he spent protecting you. And wondering if you were falling in love with him, each time he opened up to you more. Then sure, I was okay.

But I needed to lie.

"Are you okay?" I asked. "Wait, why do I hear other cars? Are you on the road?"

"Honey, I'm fine," she said, clearly trying to keep me calm. "The neighbors told me some strange men showed up outside the house I'm staying in and asked some concerning questions. I packed up our things and changed the plates on the car. It's time to go on the run again. I think San Diego might be nice for a while."

She laughed, but she also sounded like she was crying.

The room started spinning around me. "Did you see the men?"

"No. But I wasn't taking the risk. Maybe you should take a leave of absence and come meet me here, Tovah. Warm weather will be lovely. And then I'll know you're safe."

I clenched my teeth. As scared as I was, as much as I'd like to see my mother, I had to see this through. Had to get to the root of the Silvers' crimes and expose them once and for all. I couldn't go to her, not when the most important thing for me to do was protect her.

Besides, I doubted Isaac would let me get away that

easily. If I tried to run, he'd chase me, and all I'd end up doing was lead him and his family directly to my mom.

And, if I were honest, the thought of leaving him made my heart feel like it was ripping apart.

"I can't, mom," I told her. "I have too much to do here."

"School doesn't matter as much as your safety, darling," she argued.

She was right. But there was nothing else I could say. "I'm being safe, I promise."

"Tovah—"

"Mom, I have to go," I lied. "Someone's coming. You be safe, too, okay? Let me know when you're safe. Make sure no one is tailing you. Switch the car out as soon as you can."

"I know, honey," she said. "I taught you those tricks, remember?"

I did remember. All the times we'd been on the run together were embedded into my brain, a lifetime of cautiousness and fear and never, ever feeling free.

"I love you," I said.

"Love you too, Tovahleh. Check in with me in a couple days, okay? Or I'll worry."

So would I.

"I will," I promised, before hanging up.

Pocketing the phone, I planted my hands on the sink in front of me, staring into the mirror. A woman, angry, desperate, and determined, stared back at me. Her dark eyes promised perseverance and retribution. Her lips were set in a firm, resolute line.

It didn't matter how complicated my relationship with Isaac had grown. Or that I had feelings for him, real and confusing. My mother always had and always would come first, and that meant I would do every goddamned thing in my power to protect her. She was going to be sitting in the audience at my college graduation, safe and worry free. Even if I had to go against my own morals and hurt Isaac to make it happen.

Exhaling slowly and releasing the guilt that my thoughts had caused, I turned away from the mirror and pulled back out the phone, sending a text to Sebastian, who had one of the few phone numbers I'd memorized.

> Does your Fire and Hail brother have any Vice left?

Sebastian responded immediately.

> Probably. Why?

> I need it for something.

> Something? Or someone?

> You know the answer to that.

> Just be careful. I don't want you getting into more than you can handle…

> I can handle this.

> I'll leave it in a hollowed-out book for you at M Libe's check-out desk.

He always thought of everything. Malek Library, or M Libe, was the social sciences library, where we both spent most of our studying time. I had every excuse to be there.

> Thank you.

With that conversation done, I hid the phone at the bottom of my purse, going to the bathroom door and unlocking it.

Lawson was scanning the hallway.

"There you are, damn it, Tovah. You disappeared on me."

"I had to pee, and you were gone a while," I fibbed. "Where did *you* go?"

"Thought I saw someone I recognized. Wasn't her."

The investigative reporter in me that could sense a good story glanced at him. "Her?"

He shrugged. "She's from a long time ago. Better left in the past."

"Really?"

He sighed. "No, not really. But there's nothing I can do about it, so I'm forcing myself to leave it in the past. Saw someone who looked like her and I had a flashback to ... well," he said ruefully, "I was a different man back then. He's better left in the past, too."

That was interesting.

He spotted Asher in the quad.

"Okay, handing you off to your next bodyguard," he said.

"Don't you mean babysitter? Or warden?" I said.

He paused to look at me. "No, I mean bodyguard. I know you think we're just here to keep you from doing whatever it is that Jones doesn't want you to do, but he's made it explicitly clear that our first priority is to keep you safe."

With those shocking words, he handed me off to Asher, leaving me with questions I was afraid to ask.

"I don't know why the fuck I'm doing what these assholes want," Asher said as we walked through campus. "But here I am, doing it."

"It's nice to have friends," I told him. "Even if those friends are completely—"

"Unhinged assholes?" he offered, and we both laughed.

"Your sister loves Jack," I said. "So I guess that means we're stuck with them."

We walked a bit in silence, before Asher asked, "What about you?"

"What do you mean, what about me?"

"What are you doing with a charmer like Jones? I wouldn't have thought he was your type."

"Oh, yeah? And what is my type?"

"Scholarly. Slight. Nice. Probably a little bit of a doormat."

I considered this for a minute. Asher was right, in a sense. Once upon a time, I thought that was my type. But either I had changed on my own or Isaac had changed me, because now my type was big, tall, bossy jock dickhead with dimples that made my heart squeeze.

And I didn't think that was changing anytime soon.

"I need to go pick up a book from the library," I told him.

He smiled at me affectionately, rubbing the top of my head.

"Of course you do, nerd."

33

Tovah

When Isaac got home, I was waiting for him in the kitchen, a beer in my hand. Isaac's favorite kind of beer, to be precise. Which I'd doctored slightly by dissolving the pill of Vice that Sebastian had left for me in the fake library book.

I wasn't planning on taking sexual advantage of him. First of all, I wasn't a fucking psychopath. Second, Vice didn't even work that way. While Vixen, the pill for women, could double as a fancy roofie, Vice was like the most intense Viagra someone could ever take.

That was all I needed, though. I wasn't going to touch Isaac, but I was going to torture him until he had no choice but to tell me all of his family's secrets. And it wasn't that I didn't feel guilty for drugging him, but every single time I'd considered abandoning my plan, I pictured my mom, driving across the country with only the stuff she'd had time to pack, worried someone was following her. I was doing this for her.

Sometimes you did horrible things to protect the people you loved. Or at least I did. And if that made me bad?

So be it.

"What is this, a truce?" he said, looking at the beer in my hand.

"Peace offering," I told him, hopping off the counter and advancing toward him, making sure to sway my hips. "I was pissed at you for edging me, but I realized you can't help what a possessive asshole you are."

He snorted. "You're right, I can't."

Taking the beer out of my hand, he tipped it against his lips and chugged it back, his throat working. An Adam's apple had never been so attractive in my life.

"You aren't drinking?"

I hadn't planned to. But it would look weird, wouldn't it?

"I don't really like beer," I told him.

"I know," he said. Of course he did. "There's wine."

Walking around me, he trailed a hand over my back, making my whole body come to life.

"Red or white?" he asked.

"Red," I said.

Nodding, he wandered into the pantry, coming back out with a bottle of Malbec.

"What's a college guy doing with a wine cellar?" I asked teasingly, even though my heart was pounding.

From what I'd researched, it took a few hours for Vice to take effect. I needed him to drink the whole bottle of beer before I could enact my plan.

"My father raised me with the finer things in life, but I'm sure you found that out when you were investigating me. I know it makes me seem like a snob, but I prefer things finer. I never really was a fan of shitty keg beer." He made a face. "Parties like that never really do it for me."

"But you go to them all the time. You *host* them all the time," I pointed out.

"Yeah," he shrugged. "But that's just part of the Isaac Jones veneer. The fun, easygoing party guy with a heart of gold. I figured you more than anyone would realize it was just a front."

I couldn't help but feel sympathy for him. After all, I knew all about pretending to be someone you weren't just to get what you needed.

That didn't mean I'd veer away from my plan. Isaac poured me a glass of wine, handing it to me. We clinked glass against glass, and I sipped my wine as I watched him finish his beer.

"To showing someone our truest selves," I said.

He shook his head. "How about, 'to honesty.'"

I swallowed, my heart pounding harder. "To honesty."

HOURS LATER, I PRETENDED TO STUDY IN THE BEDROOM, listening to Isaac's groans as he masturbated in the shower for the third time. He hadn't yet realized what had happened to him, and I felt a horrible mix of incredibly guilty and incredibly turned on.

Finally, I heard a not particularly satisfied moan, then the sink turned.

Isaac exited the bathroom, his eyes almost black, his pupils were so dilated.

"On your knees, Tovah," he growled. "I can't get my cock to go down, but I bet your tight little throat will help."

"Why don't you get on the bed?" I suggested, patting the spot beside me. "It's more comfortable."

Usually he would've been suspicious that I was being so agreeable. He should've been suspicious. Instead he climbed onto the bed next to me. I turned, straddling him, and his hard cock, encased in gray sweatpants, settled between my thighs against my pussy, sending waves of heat through my body.

God, I wanted him. It would be so easy to abandon my whole plan and swallow down his cock, or dry hump him, or—

—But that would make me just as bad as he was. He might be mostly in control, and fully aware of what was going on, but it would still be taking advantage, and I refused to do that.

Still, I kneeled over him, running my hands up his arms, listening to him gasp.

"So sensitive," I murmured. "What if we play a little game?"

"What kind of game?" he asked, his voice a low, lusty rasp.

Shifting his wrists, I reached for the cuffs that were currently attached to the headboard. Before he could realize what was happening and stop me, I cuffed them around his wrists, hopping off his body and off the bed, putting distance between us in case the cuffs didn't hold.

They did.

"What the actual fuck, Tovah?" he growled, pulling at his wrists. But try as he might, he couldn't rip them off the headboard. The wooden slats would hold.

Relaxing slightly, I moved closer to him, tracing little circles over his bare abdomen near his hip bones. He shuddered beneath my touch.

"Here's how the game goes, Isaac. I dosed you with Vice—"

"You what?!" he roared.

"—and from what I've heard, it takes between twelve and eighteen hours to wear off. I'm not going to touch you, and I'm going to keep you tied up so you can't touch yourself. That is, unless you answer my questions. If you answer all of them satisfactorily, I'll uncuff you so you can handle your cock until its rubbed raw, for all I care."

He glared at me, his eyes promising retribution. "Funny that the woman who was going to expose me for distributing Vice and Vixen ended up using it herself."

"Yeah, well," I tossed my hair. "Fight fire with fire."

"I'm not going to give you anything," he said. "I can deal with having a hard cock for a while. But can you handle seeing it so hard without getting your pretty mouth on it? Fuck!"

His cock pulsed at his words alone, staining his sweats with precum. Or maybe actual cum. I couldn't tell at this point, and I wasn't going to risk getting close and checking, as badly as I wanted to. Because he was right, he'd trained me well, or I'd imprinted on his cock or something, because I wanted it badly, in my mouth, thrusting between my breasts, or sliding between my thighs. I wanted it places I'd never had a cock before.

Unable to resist, and aware that there was no reason for me to have to, anyway, I slowly removed the dress I was wearing and dropped it on the floor, taking off my bra and panties until I was naked in front of him. Crawling up on the big armchair that faced the bed, I started plucking at my nipples, staring at Isaac's straining, desperate body.

"Maybe you can deal with having a hard cock, but what about having a hard cock and not being able to use your little cumslut to work it off with?"

The words did their job. Isaac moaned, deep and almost frantic, writhing against the cuffs as he stared at me.

"Are you admitting you're my little cumslut, Tovah?"

"I was," I said. "But right now I'm going to be my own little cumslut."

"Tweak those pretty nipples for me," he ordered. "Get them hard, and I'll tell you what you want to know."

Hell yeah. Triumph, and his hot words, lit me up like a sparkler. I got to work tweaking my nipples, and the awareness of his attention on me made them stiffen quickly. I moaned, throwing my head back, my gaze on the ceiling as I made myself feel good.

But I had a job to do.

Lowering my head, I looked at him as I played with my breasts. "What illegal businesses are the Silvers involved in, beyond Vice and Vixen? Arms dealing? Human trafficking?"

"Fuck no," Isaac growled. "My father might be a bastard, but he—we—would never traffic people."

I hid my smile. I knew that the Silvers weren't involved in human trafficking, but I needed evidence that Isaac would break and talk about his family. And by denying their involvement in trafficking people, he'd basically admitted that they were involved in arms dealing.

"Who supplies the Vice and Vixen to your family?" I asked.

But Isaac had clearly realized he'd given too much away, because he shut his mouth and shook his head, glaring at me.

"Isaac, baby," I lowered my voice. "If you tell me, I'll release you. It can be so simple. And doesn't your cock need a little attention?"

"What my cock needs," he enunciated slowly, "is to shove its way between your thighs and into that hot tight pussy that belongs to me. Or maybe into your tiny asshole. Have you ever tried anal, Tovah?"

I couldn't stop the blush that spread across my face and chest.

He laughed, dark and dirty. "That's what I thought. I'm glad I'll be your first, when the time comes."

"There are seventeen men who went missing from your father's organization over the past ten years. Do you know what happened to them? What did your father do to them?"

"They left."

"Left? Or were killed?"

"How the fuck do you expect me to know? I stay out of that side—*damn it,*" he swore, realizing a little too late that I'd caught him again.

Unfortunately, nothing he'd said so far was usable. I wasn't recording this because I'd implicate myself, too. But although he was giving me helpful information, I needed to ramp up the game and play harder and dirtier to get the confession I wanted.

Climbing off the chair, I walked toward Isaac, standing over the bed and trailing a hand down between my breasts, over my round stomach, between my hips, touching my mound, my slit, and finally circling my clit. I slowly slid a finger inside myself, and my touch didn't do what his eyes on me did. I clenched around my finger, but it wasn't enough.

It wasn't *his.*

Still, I popped my finger into my mouth and licked it like a lollipop.

"*Fuck, Tovah,*" Isaac said, his voice strained with desire.

"I'll let you taste next, if you tell me if you've ever seen your father murder anyone. Or maybe your sister, Liza? She's always seemed pretty violent."

"What do you mean, always seemed violent? How would you know?"

Shit. I'd almost given myself away.

"It was obvious from all the tabloid coverage," I said, switching back to the important topic. "Have you ever seen your father kill anyone?"

"Yes, fuck, damn it!" Isaac was sweating, his chest heaving, as he tracked my fingers circling my clit. "He made me watch when he killed one of our enemies. I was seven. The sound of the gun going off—I'll never get it out of my head. Half his head was gone, and there was blood everywhere." His throat worked, and I glanced down to see if he'd lost his erection, but the Vice was hard at work and so was Isaac. "Do you know what it's like, seeing a dead man when you're that young?"

I did, in fact. Sometimes at night, in the dark, I could still see my stepfather's lifeless eyes as he lay crumpled over the kitchen table.

"My father looked me in the eye and said, 'One of these days, Isaac, you'll be the one holding the gun.'" Isaac looked disgusted. "I think about that all the time, you know. How no matter what I do, no matter how good at hockey I am or how kind and helpful of a guy I try to be, I'll never be able to escape my fate. He's right. One day, I'll be holding the gun, and seventeen more men will go missing because of me."

I froze, shocked. Isaac had given me what I needed. Maybe not all of it, but admitting his father was a murderer was close. But I couldn't focus on that. Not when Isaac sounded so broken, so hopeless. This time I didn't bother to fight the sympathy I felt for him. It was futile, anyway; there was no way the sympathy wouldn't win out.

"I've tried so hard to keep the darkness at bay," he told

me. "I've done every fucking thing to be the complete opposite of my father. And I was succeeding—until I met you."

I paused with the circles on my clit, looking at him. He was stretched out on the bed, chest heaving, cock hard and leaking cum all over his sweatpants, his hips twisted. But his eyes were on me and there was a rage in there I didn't fully understand.

Until he explained.

"You showed up that day in the student center, your hair this bright, puke colored green..."

"Thanks," I snorted.

He shook his head, "With those big brown eyes and those huge tits and hips and ass, looking more delectable than any dessert I'd ever eaten. And you were laughing at something some other guy was saying, so hard coffee came out of your nose. And this overwhelming urge came over me."

"What urge?" I asked, even though I knew better. I needed to know.

"The urge to stomp over there, beat the shit out of him, and carry you away to somewhere quiet and private and secret where no one could ever take you from me. I was shocked at myself—I'd only ever kicked someone's ass on the ice, and even then, I was considered the team's pacifist." He snorted. "And yet here I was, seriously considering violence and kidnapping and god knew what else. I told myself I had to stay away from you, but you were everywhere: games, classes, all over campus, your byline on the newspaper every goddamned day, and then you even showed up for the hockey party the night Jack met Aviva. And you were writing articles mocking the team, and *me*. It was like you knew what you'd done to me, and you were fucking *baiting* me."

"Is that why you hated me?" I asked, staring at him, eyes wide in shock. I'd never known. He'd hated me because—

"I wanted you that badly," he admitted. "More than I'd ever wanted anyone or anything else, even hockey. And I *hated* you for it. You bring out this monster in me, and I've fought him so long. But I'm done fighting him. Done fighting it. I may be a monster, Tovah Lewis, but I'm *your* monster. And the monster has a message for you."

I was so caught up by his words, his story, I wasn't paying attention. Wasn't ready. Not when he lifted his hands, only to pull them down—hard.

The chains holding his cuffs to the headboard snapped like they were nothing more than a silly pair of pink fuzzy handcuffs.

He slowly rose off the bed, towering above me, his whole body tense and powerful and terrifying in its beauty.

"*Run.*"

34

Tovah

I ran like wolves were chasing me. Like if Isaac caught me, I'd die.

And maybe I would. He'd never seemed as angry as he'd seemed in the bedroom. They called orgasms "the little death" for a reason. But, little death or big one, I wasn't going to wait to find out. Barefoot and naked, I raced out the bedroom and down the stairs, my feet pounding on the wooden floors as Isaac's feet pounded behind me. If there was ever a time for my track team skills to kick in, it was now.

It didn't matter that part of me wanted him to catch me, to toss me to the floor and drive into my pussy with his thick cock. No, even though Isaac was fully mentally present, he was so desperate for a fuck that it would still be taking advantage.

At least that's what I told myself. I couldn't admit that I was terrified of giving myself to him completely, about how much I wanted that, about what that might mean.

When I got to the front door, the real problem presented itself: I didn't know the alarm code.

I was trapped.

And god, part of me, so badly, wanted to be trapped. Loved the feeling of being trapped by him. I loved it, the safety from knowing I had his protection, in these four walls and everywhere. And I loved the freedom of giving myself over to him, letting him take control, so I could explore the dark and dirty and scary parts of myself that loved what he did to me, without guilt or recriminations or questioning.

I was grateful to him, and I could never tell him.

Even when he appeared at the bottom of the stairs, advancing toward me, the chains still hanging from his wrists where they'd snapped in two...

...but he just passed me, going to the alarm system and typing in the code to disarm it.

"Run, bad girl," he repeated. "Run."

35

Isaac

I'd never been so desperate to fuck in my whole goddamned fucking life. I needed to shove my cock in wet, tight cunt and pound into it until it squeezed all the cum out of me. And not any wet, tight cunt. *My* wet, tight, cunt.

Tovah.

For months, I'd been battling with the monster within, trying to ignore his demands so I could keep being Isaac Jones, Good Guy, Moral Compass of the Kings. I hadn't wanted to give into him or accept the truth: that he was me.

But when Tovah drugged me with Vice, it didn't make me lose my mind—it did the opposite, it clarified things for me, forced me to reckon with that truth. The monster was me. I was the monster. I could finally let go and claim both sides of me, the hero *and* the villain.

I could let go of the tight control I'd tried and failed to keep over myself, and finally, *fucking finally*, be free.

And god, that felt good.

Maybe I should thank her for that, someday.

But first I needed her to run.

She was trapped by the door. Locked in. And as tempting as it was to take her down here, the monster wanted to chase, and so I was going to fucking give him what he wanted.

Passing her, I went and turned off the alarm, before turning to her.

"Run, bad girl. Run," I ordered.

She was moving before I could say "run" for the second time, slamming the door open and sprinting down the steps, past the driveway, and into the trees.

My property butted up against the state forest Gehenom was known for. It shrouded my house in privacy, but it also meant that, except for some hikers who'd show up in the summer and fall, there was no one around for miles. Just me, Tovah, and hundreds of trees cloaking us in shadows and silence.

Which made it perfect for chasing and fucking. She could scream as loud as I wanted her to, and no one would hear her.

"Fuck yes," I muttered, taking off at a lope, letting the scenery pass me by as I chased her into the woods.

At first, I couldn't find her. The trees were silent, and no one was there. But when I stopped and listened closely...

...there. Panicked breathing.

And the barely-there scent of lemons and sugar.

"Got you," I said, turning right and racing through the trees.

I spotted her ahead of me, a flash of lightly tanned, bare skin and blue hair in the dark. I raced faster, gaining on her foot by foot. She must have heard the twigs crack under my feet, or maybe just sensed me chasing her, because she picked up her pace. Even as I chased her, I marveled at how fast she was, how determination and focus coalesced somewhere in her brain and made her almost superpowered. It wasn't just with running. I'd learned, both from stalking her and from spending time with her, that Tovah was 40% focus, 40% persistence, and 20% sass. That combination made her a force to be reckoned with, and I admired her for it.

And right now, I was going to enjoy the fuck out of it and the way she was challenging me. Catching her was going to be all the sweeter for it.

My cock bounced, hard and heavy as I ran, but instead of being angry at how much I hurt from the need to fuck and to come over and over, I reveled in it. I was becoming a primal beast whose mission was to hunt down his woman and get inside her, and giving in was exactly what I needed.

Maybe Tovah's goal had been to get me to talk—and I had talked—but she'd given me something unexpected.

Myself.

I was gaining on her, her breath rasping through the trees as she ran. A small part of me worried if she was cold, or hurting, or tired—I didn't want her to ever be cold or hurt or tired. But as the lemon and sugar scent grew, I realized the truth: she was getting off on this, too.

"You want this, don't you?" I taunted her as I ran, my words echoing through the night. "You want me to grab you from behind and shove you to the ground and hold you down in the dirt while I fuck you. I bet if I touched you, you'd be wet and slick, wouldn't you? So wet that, as small and tight as that pretty pussy is, it would be easy to shove my cock all the way into you with one thrust. Are you ready for that? To be dragged to the ground and fucked like the animals we truly are?"

She whimpered, a sweet, scared sound that made my cock even harder.

Only a few feet between us now.

I stopped speaking, relishing the sound of her gasping breath and the quiet of the night, the headiness of knowing we were alone and could do whatever the fuck we wanted without anyone telling us we were wrong to do it. This was about us, Tovah and Isaac, woman and monster, with none of the bullshit that pulled us apart.

"Mine," I growled, just as I reached her, grabbing her around the waist, the chains of my cuffs slapping her tits.

She fought me, scratching, kicking, and clawing, but it was like a kitten fighting a lion. I easily subdued her, shoving her to the ground and falling on top of her, holding her face in the dirt like I'd said I would.

"Isaac," she cried.

"This is what you wanted, isn't it, bad girl? You might pretend you wanted answers from me, but what you really wanted to do was unleash the beast and see what happened when he caught you."

"No," she cried.

"Yes." I used my knees to shove her thighs apart, and the second my hard cock came in contact with her bare, and *yes,* wet pussy, my balls clenched and I came, my release splashing on her pussy, stomach, and the forest floor.

There was barely any physical relief, and I was still hard. Still ready. Tovah's pussy was there for the taking. I'd resisted before, like if I fucked her, actually fucked her, it would be surrendering not only to the monster but to my true feelings for her. But with the Vice and Tovah herself freeing me, I no longer cared that fucking her would make me vulnerable. I wanted to be vulnerable. Wanted to expose the hidden parts of myself and surround them with the softest, most fearful, secret part of hers.

And so that's what I was going to do.

But not when I couldn't see her face. Not without those brown eyes telling me everything she was feeling when I finally got inside her.

Snarling, I gripped her waist and flipped her onto her back.

She tried to scoot away, but I trapped her between my hands and knees, so all she could do was stare up at me.

Well, stare up at me and beg.

"Isaac, please, you don't want to do this," she cried.

I lifted a hand, balancing on one arm, so I could swipe at the tear on her face. "Little snoop, why would you ever think I don't want to do this?"

"Because this isn't you."

"Maybe it's not Isaac Jones. But it is Isaac Silver. And I wouldn't have realized that, if it weren't for you. Thank you for that."

"Maybe I don't want this."

"Don't you? Fine. Tell me that, truthfully. Say, 'Isaac, I don't want you to stuff me full of your cock while I writhe in the dirt.' Tell me you don't want me to take the pussy that was meant for me, because you were meant for me."

She didn't speak.

"Tell me, Tovah," I barked.

"I can't," she cried again.

Something settled in my chest. "And why can't you?" I tapped her lips. "Tell me."

"Because I want you. Because I want you to stuff me full of your cock while I writhe in the dirt."

"Why?"

"Because my body only makes sense when it's with

yours," she said, and it was the most honest thing she had ever said to me.

"The world only makes sense when we're together," I agreed, wrapping my hand around my cock and pressing it between the lips of her pussy.

She was so fucking wet I slid in easily, the feeling of her tight cunt surrounding the crown of my cock so fantastically unfamiliar yet so ecstatically right that I came right then and there.

"Isaac?" she asked, her eyes huge and dark in her beautiful face, looking lost and confused. "Did you just?"

"Yes, I just," I admitted, and maybe I should've been embarrassed, but I wasn't. "Your pussy feels so damn good I came the moment my cock entered it."

"Oh, then—"

"No," I told her gruffly, as I pulled back and surged forward, pressing further and further in. "Whatever you're thinking, stop thinking it. We're not done here. I won't be done with you until the sun rises, and I probably won't be done fucking you then, either."

With that, I surged forward the rest of the way.

36

Tovah

I stared up at him, caught in his arms, buried in dirt, surrounded by trees, held captive by his eyes, as he pushed his way into my body.

I was wet. So wet. The days of edging already made me constantly ready for him, and between teasing him in the bedroom earlier and his filthy words when he chased me, I was needy and desperate for him. I hadn't lied, I wanted to be fucked by him, to be torn in two by his cock. In a world of confusion and chaos, it was the only thing that made sense.

But as my body stretched to accommodate his massive girth, that mix of pain and pleasure I was beginning to recognize made me cry out. My pussy burned from the way his thrusts pulled at my skin, and I wasn't sure if I wanted to fight him off and make it stop or beg him to fuck me harder.

He pushed in, impossibly deeper, before pulling out and pushing back in again. The feeling of him inside me was somehow both completely alien and new, and yet familiar— like we'd done it a million times before. On his next thrust, he changed the angle of his hips, hitting my G-spot and making my core coil tight. Pleasure melted my body, hot and sticky and sweet like taffy, and I got lost in it—in him.

"Oh, god, Isaac," I moaned, completely overwhelmed by how good he felt inside me.

"You only say my name. You know how jealous I am," he growled as he shoved his cock deeper, pushing me so hard against the ground, a twig snapped under my ass.

"Isaac," I moaned again.

"Better. Let's see if I can make you scream it."

I stared at him, and he stared back, so many unspoken words being shared.

My eyes said:

Isaac, this is my first time.

Isaac, we've known each other since we were children.

Isaac, I loved you when we were young, and I might still love you now.

His eyes said:

Tovah, I've been searching for you so long, I didn't even know I was looking.

Tovah, I'm the first and last man you'll ever fuck.

Tovah, I've loved you and will love you forever, I'm just waiting for you to catch up.

Except his eyes didn't say that, because he didn't know any of those things, because he didn't feel any of those things.

Right?

Because at the moment, it felt like he knew it all. Like he knew me down to my very soul, and he liked all of it.

He kept moving in and out of me, hitting that same spot *every. Single. Time.* And as he did, he shifted his hands. Before, they were on both sides of my shoulders, trapping me in. But he moved them, so one circled my throat, and the other shoved between his hips and mine, finding my clit and oh god, oh god, oh god, *goddamn pinching it* in time with his thrusts.

"I'm gonna—" I began on a gasp.

I could feel the orgasm coming on a wave that threatened to drown me.

Isaac gently squeezed the sides of my throat as he began to fuck me faster. Dots appeared in my vision, making the dark trees look above me waver.

"I know, bashert, I know. Let it happen. It's time."

Bashert.

My destiny. My soulmate.

The nickname did it. With a crash, the tidal wave drowned me in out of this world pleasure, and I sank, sank, sank down with it, lost as it dragged me forward and backward, trapped in its undertow. My whole body was singing and sparking, and as I writhed in the dirt, as Isaac continued to fuck me through my orgasm, I didn't know which way was up anymore, who Tovah Lewis was, and I didn't fucking care.

Only this, *we*, made sense.

Bashert.

This was our destiny. We were each other's destiny.

"Ah fuck, you're squeezing my cock so tight, bashert. You want me to come again? Want me to fill up this pretty pussy, fill it so full it spills out of you and makes mud out of the dirt?"

I moaned at his words, and the juxtaposition of the filth of the image he created with the tenderness of the nickname made another orgasm crash over me.

This time, I must have screamed, because Isaac released my throat and yelled, "Fuck, yes, you scream my name and only mine," before kissing me and swallowing the sound.

His hips stuttered, and then sped up, smashing against mine over and over, as his balls slapped against my ass and he pounded into me, making me come a third time. This time, when I screamed his name, he roared mine, the sound echoing in the trees as he came, filling me with his release, full, so full, just like he'd promised.

He didn't stop, though. Didn't pause for one goddamn second. No, he pulled out of me and flipped me over, lifting me onto my knees, shoving my head into the dirt, before thrusting back inside my pussy and continuing to fuck me as he surrounded me with his body and dark, earthy, surprising scent.

I lost track of how long he fucked me for, of all the filthy things he said, of the number of times he made me come. I had no sense of time or space, completely focused on the feeling of him inside me and the sound of his voice in my ear.

When the sun finally rose, we were on our sides, spooned together, my top thigh on the outside of his, as he slowly slid in and out of me. I felt rubbed raw and sore, and I couldn't imagine how he felt. But the idea of him leaving my body was intolerable, and Isaac clearly felt the same way, because he'd been inside me for hours and didn't seem to be stopping anytime soon.

"The sun's up," I murmured into the ground.

Isaac heard me. "The sun can go fuck itself. I'm not stopping."

Except he paused, pushing up on one arm to scan my face from the side.

"No, you need a break. Shit. Okay." Slowly, he withdrew from my pussy, his cum—so much cum, from so many hours of fucking—spilling out of me and onto the forest floor.

I whined, protesting at the loss of him.

"I know, bashert, I know. But we need to go inside before someone finds us."

Lifting me off the ground, he swung me up into his arms and carried me out of the forest like a groom carries his bride. The thought made my chest—already aching at the endearment—go tight with longing at something I wanted but would never have.

Gold and orange light dappled the trees, making the forest glow. As he walked with me, I had to bite my lip to keep myself from begging him to stop, to go back to where we were safe. The forest now felt like our place, and the world outside, even his home, brought the certainty of trouble with it. I wasn't sure how long this peace would last between us, but I doubted once Reina and his family intruded, we'd be able to continue like this. And I didn't want to lose this. Didn't want to give up what we'd found as we'd fucked like beasts all night on the forest floor.

But I would've sounded crazy, or needy, and besides, we couldn't actually stay in the trees, so I didn't say anything as we left the trees behind, back on Isaac's property as he carried me up the path to his home.

37

Isaac

My control had snapped like a twig. I was determined to leave it behind in the trees. To be this new, maybe not improved—okay, definitely *not* improved—version of myself. Because that version of Isaac Silver, as villainous and monstrous as he might be, had one thing Good Guy Isaac Jones didn't have: Tovah.

Every moment from the night before replayed in my head as I held Tovah tight to my chest and carried her back inside. The way she'd tricked me, chained me, teased me. The way I'd chased her through the house and outside. How she'd run and run, and run, until I caught her. How she'd protested at first, until she'd admitted how badly she wanted me, too.

My body only makes sense when it's with yours, she'd said.

And then I'd fucked her. I remembered every moment of that, the feeling of her impossibly snug pussy squeezing my cock, her gasps, her moans, her cries, the glassy look in her eyes as she'd come for me again and again. I'd fucked her in a dozen different positions, filled her with cum more times than I could count, and even though my body ached and my cock felt raw from all the friction, I wasn't done. I wanted, needed more.

My body only makes sense when it's with yours.

Maybe I could freeze time while I was inside her, so I could fuck her for all of eternity without worrying about the outside world trying to destroy us.

But I'd seen the hint of pain in her eyes this last time. It had been too much, and I needed to take her home, warm her up, bathe her, feed her, let her rest. And then, only then, could I fuck her again.

Sounded like a good plan to me.

I carried her, my bashert, into the house, leaning down to sniff her hair and luxuriate in the smell of lemon and sugar, pine and dirt. She smelled like *mine*.

My bashert.

My destiny.

My soulmate.

I'd called her my bashert. I'd only ever called one other person bashert. And while part of me fought against the word and what it actually meant for me and for us, it felt so damn right. A voice in my head, quiet and resigned, reminded me I couldn't have a bashert, not with the dark, violent future that loomed before me. But for now, I was ignoring that potential nightmare, choosing to lose myself in Tovah.

"You don't have to carry me," she said, sounded worn out.

"I like carrying you," I told her. "You feel good in my arms, so that's where you're staying. Are you really going to fight me on it?"

She sighed, snuggling in closer. "You fucked the fight out of me."

I grinned into her hair.

Hell, yeah, I did.

Once inside the house, I locked it behind me, making sure my precious cargo stayed safe from whatever might threaten her. Then I headed up the stairs, bypassing the bedroom and the temptation of the bed with the broken chains for the shower.

Placing her carefully on the tile floor, I turned on the shower, testing the water and playing with the hot and cold faucets until the water was the perfect temperature—hot enough to warm her but not so hot it would burn that perfect, lightly tanned skin.

"Come on, let's get you cleaned up," I said, leading her into the shower and placing her under the spray. As I did, I glanced down for a moment at my own body...

...and spotted what looked like dried flecks of blood on my cock.

What the fuck?

My breathing froze, a nightmare coalescing in my head.

I'd fucked her so hard, I'd hurt her. Tore something, ripped her up inside. Was she in pain and hadn't told me? Had that not been pleasurable for her at all?

Trying to keep my breathing even, I gently said, "Can you open your legs for me, bashert?"

She sighed. "I love when you call me that. But why?"

I swallowed, trying to get the choking feeling out of my throat. "I want to check something."

"Okay." Her face was wide, soft, and trusting. She smiled, stepping wider.

Hands shaking, terrified of what I would find, I stroked her inner thighs, looking down.

Dried blood stained her thighs, her pussy. I jumped back, as if she'd burned me.

"What's wrong, Isaac?"

"I hurt you," I said flatly. "Why didn't you tell me? I tore you and—"

"Oh." She blushed and looked away from me. "There's something I didn't tell you."

"What?"

"I'm—I was...a virgin. Until last night, at least."

I wasn't sure I'd heard her clearly at first, my heart was roaring so loudly in my ears.

"What?"

She turned her head back to me, and although her face was solemn, there was a small, almost rueful smile on her face. "Yeah, I was a virgin. The reputation I have—" she waved her hands, "—it's just rumors. None of it was true."

Without realizing it, I sank to my knees in the shower, putting a hand on her calf, partially to steady myself, partially because I needed the physical contact.

"None of it?"

She shook her head. "None."

"So I was your...first."

"First everything. Well, I'd been kissed before, but that was—"

"I don't want to hear about other guys," I barked, making her flinch. "No, I'm sorry, I—"

I didn't know what was going on inside of me. My heart had started racing, was still pounding in my ears. Did I want to yell in triumph, beat my chest? She was mine, completely mine, had only ever been mine. Did I want to go destroy whoever had kissed her in the past, for daring to even touch what belonged to me? I'd never *judged* Tovah for her past—

that would have been hypocritical as fuck. But I'd always been jealous.

And now? Now I didn't have to be.

I had so many questions for her. Like why she'd lie about something like that, about what had been going on with Sebastian and those other men if she hadn't been fucking them. But one question shoved all those others out of the way.

"Did I hurt you? If I'd known, I would've—"

I was so fucking worried. Would I have been gentler, if I'd known she'd been a virgin? God, her first time was a rough fuck in the woods...

"You did." She didn't mince her words, and this time, I was the one to flinch. "But you also made it feel so goddamn good. I didn't want some gentle, soft, bed of roses first time, Isaac. Maybe I couldn't admit it to myself before, but what I wanted was you." She reached down, stroking my hair. "The real you, the caring side and the scary, controlling, animalistic side. I know I've called you a monster, but..."

"But what?" I needed to know, needed something to quell the shame that dragged me down like a weight.

"...but you're *my* monster."

And then I was nuzzling and kissing her ankles, her calves, her thighs, her stomach. I looked up at her.

"Thank you," I said. I'd lost the battle with my throat, and the sound that came out was choked. "For making me come to grips with who I really am, and for accepting him. For giving me you. I fucking promise I'll never let you regret it."

And then I was dipping my lips between her thighs, kissing her pussy, circling her clit with my tongue, gently nipping her lips with my teeth, licking her slit and sliding my tongue inside.

"Isaac, I can't—" she whimpered, starting to shut her legs, but I stopped her with a grip on her inner thighs.

"No," I said. "I need to taste you, us together. Know what my pussy tastes like after the first time it took my cock. Don't deny me this."

"But I'm so sore."

"I'll be gentle."

Without giving her more of a chance to argue, I started fucking her with my tongue. I could taste my cum, which honestly, I didn't love, but then the taste of her own arousal came through, and the combination of us together, of what we'd made, was the best fucking flavor I'd ever consumed. Suddenly ravenous, I fought myself to give her tenderness, to give when all I wanted to do was take. I started swiping my thumb over her clit, and it didn't take long until she was clenching my tongue with her pussy, thighs tensing as she came with sweet, high-pitched moans and sighs.

"Again," I demanded.

"Isaac—"

But I was diving back between her legs, my eyes on her face, taking in every perfect, beautiful expression as she surrendered to me, melting into my hands.

I couldn't help it anymore, the need to be soft with her unable to keep the monster at bay who wanted to soak himself in her, drown himself. I hungrily ate her pussy, sucking and licking and working her clit until she came again with a shriek, just as sweet as her sighs, and I swallowed down her cum.

Rising to my feet, I caught her around the waist, lifting her and dropping onto my pounding hard cock. Once again, I tried to be slow, to be gentle, but with her eyes on me, she begged, "harder, Isaac," and I wasn't going to deny her, was I? So I bounced her, over and over again, keeping her pinned against the wall with my right hand and hips alone as she wrapped her arms around my neck. I bit and sucked at her nipples as we fucked, her pussy squeezing around me.

"Isaac," she moaned, and I abandoned her breasts temporarily to see the look in her eyes.

"I'm so close..." A shocked, desperate, expression, filled with pain *and* pleasure, turned her brown eyes gold. She was squeezing my damn cock so tight, her cunt slippery wet, and god, fuck, there was no better feeling in the whole goddamned universe than being inside her.

"Fuck, you feel so good," I groaned, and, barely aware of what I was saying, added in Yiddish, "Dayn neshemah iz mayn, bashert."

"Isaac," she cried out, and I swallowed her pleasure and her pain with my mouth as I fucked her, and fucked her, and fucked her.

38

Tovah

Dayn neshemah iz mayn, bashert.
Your soul belongs to mine, destiny.
He'd groaned those profound words into my ear over an hour ago, but they continued to play on repeat in my mind. It was surreal that we'd come so far in such a short period of time, hating each other to being...whatever we were now.

"You're thinking too much, bashert," he muttered from behind me, dropping a kiss on my neck. "Stop."

"You can't tell me to stop thinking," I said.

He chuckled, his laughter moving through my back and making me arch against him. "Fighting with me again. Do I have to fuck you back into submission? You're so sweet after I've given you multiple orgasms."

"Absolutely not," I told him immediately. "There's no way I'm letting your dick anywhere near my vagina again. I think you broke it."

He kissed my neck again. "I can wait. I'll give your poor little pussy a break—for a little while. Because now that I've had her, I'm not going to stay away for long."

Hopefully, I asked, "Does that mean no more edging?"

"Nope." I could feel him grin against my neck. "It's the best punishment, and it's so fucking hot to hear you beg."

My pussy clenched at his words, sending a shockwave of soreness through me. "Ow, ow, ow. No dirty talk, either."

"Okay," he said. "There are other things we need to talk about."

I tried not to tense in his arms. Was he going to probe more into why I had tried to blackmail him? My history with his family?

With him?

Fortunately, he asked an easier question. "Why did you let people think you were sleeping around?"

I sighed. "I didn't exactly *let* them. Vicious assholes and bitches started the rumors, and while I hated it at first, I couldn't fight it. You can't ever fight those things, you know? People are going to believe what they want to believe about you, and the more you fight it, the more they think you're lying. So, instead of being helpless and angry, I decided to see it as an opportunity I could use to my advantage. Let people think when I was meeting with sources, it was for sex, not for information."

He stiffened slightly. "So Sebastian?"

"Is just a friend who knows a lot about what happens on campus."

"Right." He paused. "He clearly didn't tell you this, but I almost beat the shit out of him. Threatened him in his apartment. It's how I found out about your real last name."

"Ugh," I groaned. "No wonder why he's mostly been avoiding me."

"Mostly?" there was a low, possessive snarl in his voice as he squeezed my waist.

"You can't hurt him," I said.

"I can do whatever the fuck I want to him, if he touched you," Isaac said back.

"He didn't. I didn't even see him. He's the one who... procured the Vice for me, since the team is no longer dealing."

"Hmm." Isaac laughed again. "Maybe I should thank him, instead. I should be pissed at you, for what you did, but it...made me free."

Free.

What I wasn't.

What my mom wasn't.

My mom.

I needed to make time to check my burner phone and make sure she was okay. And decide what I was doing with the information Isaac had given me. I didn't want to hurt him, now, didn't want to betray him, but what choice did I have? Would my mother ever be safe, if I let it go? Worse, what would she think if she knew I was sleeping with the enemy?

As if Isaac had heard my thoughts, he added, "I still have more questions for you, Tovah. I know there's a lot you aren't telling me, and I won't push for the information now, but I will get it out of you. Even if *I* have to resort to giving you Vixen to get it."

I stiffened in his arms.

"You wouldn't."

His voice was solemn. "I would. I don't want to hurt you, but I refuse to let anything or anyone take you from me. We're together now, and nothing will separate us."

His next words were ominous as he wrapped his arms around me, tight, trapping me against his front.

"Not even you."

39

Isaac

The next night, I entered the house after hockey practice, resetting the alarm and hiding my car keys—and a secret package—where Tovah couldn't find them. I needed to trust her, but I...didn't. I'd been going over and over our conversation the day before in my head all throughout practice, making me play like shit. I'd been so distracted, it had been obvious, and both Coach and my team had let me know they were pissed about it.

But how could I not be? Although Tovah and I had turned a corner, in a good direction, I knew she was still hiding something from me—something important as fuck. The fact that she refused to tell me what it was, that she had secrets, kept us from getting close the way I wanted us to. I could feel the other shoe waiting to drop, and I knew it was going to fuck shit up when it did. I wanted her to talk to me, to trust me, but part of her clearly still thought of me as her enemy.

I needed to smash through her walls, but short of giving

her Vixen like I'd threatened, I didn't know how. And regardless of her giving me Vice, that was something I refused to do to her.

Checking my phone, I noticed multiple missed calls from my sister. I was about to call her back, when I heard low, pained moans coming from upstairs.

The bathroom?

Dropping my phone immediately, I ran up the stairs two at a time. When I reached the bedroom, I found Tovah curled up into a ball, hugging a pillow and whimpering.

I sat on the bed, checking her over. "What's wrong, bashert? What happened?"

"It's nothing."

"It's clearly not nothing," I said, calculating how long it would take to get her to a hospital.

"It's nothing, Isaac, I just have really bad PMS." She said the words into the pillow, like she was embarrassed.

I glared at the wall. I was going to kill her doctor.

"What do you usually do for it?" I asked.

"Just try to get through it. I've been dealing with this for years, it's nothing new."

"If you're in pain, it's not nothing," I stated as I got on the bed, sliding in behind her, opening up the group chat with my teammates.

"Isaac, what are you doing? I don't want to have sex right now—"

"I'm not trying to have sex with you. I just want to hold you and rub your back," I said, wrapping my body around hers.

"Oh, you feel so good," she moaned, and I had to remind my dick it wasn't a sexy moan.

I typed a quick text.

> Me: can one of you do me a favor and make a run to the grocery store? I need supplies

Jack: What kind of supplies?

Jack: If it's for sex, the hardware store might be better.

I rolled my eyes. The sociopath always used proper capitalization and punctuation.

> Me: its not for sex, you unhinged asshole
>
> Me: Tovah has PMS and I need to get her stuff
>
> Me: its bad tho

Asher: OVERSHARE

Judah: chill the fuck out

Judah: women menstruate

Judah: its biology

Lawson: what do you need?

I really liked this guy.

> Me: motrin, midol, something with codeine in it for the pain

Jack: That's going a little overboard, don't you think?

> Me: shut up, you asshole
>
> Me: youd do the same if it was Aviva
>
> Me: heating pad, chai, books
>
> Lawson: what kind of books? and she might want a hot water bottle instead. my ex girlfriend has PCOS. it always helped her.
>
> Me: yeah, get the hot water bottle
>
> Me: And memoirs from journalists if you can find them
>
> Lawson: i can go pick it all up. give me half an hour
>
> Me: thanks man
>
> Me: owe you one

I closed out of the text, pulling Tovah closer.

"Rest," I said. "I'll be downstairs if you need me."

I left her and went to the kitchen, pulling out ingredients to make soup. As I cooked, I watched the clock. It was quiet upstairs, hopefully she was sleeping. My body ached. I'd heard about sympathy PMS, but really, I just freaking hated that Tovah was in pain and I couldn't take it from her. If PMS were a man, I'd pummel the shit out of him and then take my skate blade to his throat.

The doorbell rang. I left the soup simmering on the stovetop, going to the front door, disarming the alarm, and opening it.

Lawson stood there, a bag in his hand.

"Thanks, man," I said. "Really appreciated."

He shrugged. "Used to take care of my girlfriend all the time. She got horrible cramps, had to stay in bed for days. I'd skip school and practice to be with her."

"Girlfriend?" I asked, curious. "Or ex-girlfriend?"

"Oh, she'll be my girlfriend again," he said, a sly grin on his face. He looked wolf-like in the shadows. "She doesn't know it yet, but she will."

"I know how that goes," I laughed.

Lawson didn't leave yet. "Look, I know how you guys operate. I know how *I* operated. It feels like things are perfect right now, but there's going to come a moment where they aren't, and you're going to want to be an asshole, to push her away, to punish her for something that's outside of her control. My advice? Don't. Or you'll fucking regret it."

With that concerning advice, he nodded at me and turned, heading back to his car.

I closed the door, both on him, and on what he'd said. I was still pissed Tovah was hiding shit from me, but I wasn't going to let it come between us. I'd been a complete asshole to her in the past, but I was done with that now.

I hoped.

When the soup was done simmering, the scent of chicken broth in the air, I poured some into a bowl, grabbed a spoon, and headed upstairs with that and the bag of PMS recovery shit.

Tovah was sitting up in bed against a pillow, rubbing her stomach.

"I have food. And supplies," I told her, setting the bowl and spoon down on the nightstand and opening the bag, handing each item to her.

"I've got Motrin, Midol, Tylenol with Codeine—"

"How did you get Tylenol with Codeine?"

I ignored her, glad that Lawson had come through. "A heating pad, a hot water bottle—"

"Isaac, I'm fine."

"—tea for later, a biography on William Randolph Hearst—"

"William Randolph Hearst?" she wrinkled her nose in confusion. "The newspaper magnate?"

"The guys thought you might like it. Also Anderson Cooper's and Anthony Bourdain's memoirs."

"Well, those I'll read. Thank you, Isaac, but this is too much—"

"No such thing," I said, sitting on the edge of the bed and picking up the bowl. It was so hot it burned my fingers, but I didn't give a shit. "Here," I said, scooping up broth in the spoon and lifting it to her lips.

"Isaac—"

"Eat." There was no room for argument in my tone.

She complied, opening her mouth and swallowing the broth. I repeated the process, and some part of me hummed in contentment that I was providing for her this way. Torturing her had felt good, in some ways—but taking care of her felt much, much better.

Finally, she pushed my hand away. I handed her a water bottle and some pills, which she took with some grumbling about how *she had her period all the time and none of this was necessary*, which I ignored.

"Heating pad or hot water bottle?"

"Hot water bottle," she said, and I silently thanked Lawson for coming through.

After filling it up in the kitchen, I came back out, climbing back into bed with her and pulling her against my chest.

"What do you want to watch?" I asked, looking at the TV.

"You're going to think it's stupid."

"Nothing about you is stupid," I said emphatically.

"House Hunters International."

I raised an eyebrow, not expecting that, but I grabbed the remote and turned the TV on, locating the show on a streaming app and starting it up.

We settled in, watching for a bit as Americans and Canadians traveled to foreign countries and tried to find apartment rentals, complaining about how small everything was, how there was no air conditioning, or asking why the fridges were college dorm sized. Clearly, none of these idiots had done their research before they'd moved.

"My favorite part is when they say they need an oven to cook a Thanksgiving turkey. Like, why are they cooking a turkey in Thailand?" she giggled in my arms, making something in my chest ache at the easy happiness in her voice, and the absence of pain.

I'd done that. I'd made her feel better. She was happy, because of me. That heart I'd been so sure I didn't have, that had shattered so long ago, when my mom had been killed… slowly, it began to stitch back together.

"Why do you like this show so much, then?" I asked her.

She sighed. "It's the combination of them finding a home, a place that's theirs, a place to just be safe in, and the freedom to go wherever they want. I've never had any of those things. It's all I've ever wanted."

Fucking hearts. Maybe I didn't want one after all, because mine squeezed painfully. It was insight into her life she hadn't given me before, but she sounded so sad, I didn't want to push. So instead, I held her, watching this dumb show, determined to give her a home and freedom—even if I'd never, ever, give her freedom from me.

"Where would you want to live if you could?" I asked her.

She brightened. "Oh, that's easy. I have a whole bucket list. Paris, London, Kathmandu, Lima, Ushuaia, Jackson Hole—" she glanced over at me, "What? I love a mountain."

A smile played on my lips.

"Noted. Where else?"

"Todos Santos, Melbourne, Tokyo, and Prague."

I stroked her hair. "Why those cities?"

"They seem equally like places you could get lost in and find yourself."

We were quiet for a bit, before she asked, "So, why major in linguistics? Why so many languages?"

Fuck, this hurt to confess. Emotional intimacy was a pain in the ass.

I cleared my throat. "My mom studied linguistics in college. She spoke like, ten languages. She'd wanted to be an interpreter, but instead she met my dad, and..." I shrugged, clearing my throat again, but the tightness didn't go away. "Well, he wouldn't have let her. And she never got the chance, anyway."

Tovah kissed my shoulder. "I'm so sorry you lost her," she said. "You have no idea how sorry."

I blinked a few times, willing the tears away. I never got emotional like this, but her sweetness was doing me in.

"I'm sorry you lost your parents, too," I said. "It really sucks."

She looked troubled, but all she said was, "It really does."

Wrapping my arms around her, I pulled her in tight and settled in to watch the show that embodied her dreams.

Dreams I couldn't make real for her if I was going to keep her.

And I was going to keep her.

Once she was asleep, I carefully moved her off me, glancing at her and taking in her soft, sleeping form before quietly leaving the bedroom and heading down the hall. I felt uneasy, and I couldn't determine why. Unlocking my office, I went to check her phone, hoping it might give me some answers she wouldn't give me herself.

Other than texts from Aviva, Tovah's phone had been largely silent, which was kind of weird. I couldn't unlock it to see any of her emails, except for when I supervised her in the evening when she checked it herself.

Tonight though, there was a text, from someone saved as LOML.

LOML.

Love of my life?

It seemed they'd texted a few times. With a sinking feeling in my gut, I read the only text that showed on the home screen.

> Worried about you. Love you. Call me.

Who the hell was LOML, and why the fuck was he telling Tovah he loved her? Aside from Aviva, there was no one in Tovah's life that she had a close relationship with, according to my sister and her snooping.

Which meant she'd hidden a guy from me.

A boyfriend?

Fuck, no. It might technically be fake between us, but I was the only boyfriend my little snoop was allowed to have.

My hands fisted, and I had to restrain myself from going in there, waking her up, and forcing her to tell me who LOML was. I could do it—

—and I could also make her retreat even more into herself, to hate me.

Maybe she'd tell me on her own.

And if not, well...

...I'd learned a little about snooping from spending so much time with her, hadn't I?

So I downloaded a phone cloning app on her phone—one that also tracked its location. I'd give her back her phone and some of that freedom she wanted so badly.

But I'd see everyone she called, and everyone who called her. Be able to read her incoming and outgoing texts. See where she was at all times. One way or another, I was getting answers.

There was a small voice in my head that pointed out that trust had to be earned, that it was a two-way street. That if I spied on her, and kept secrets from her, our relationship would never progress the way I wanted it to.

That voice could go to hell.

40

Tovah

Isaac was acting weird.

In some ways, he was more himself than he'd ever been—demanding, almost needy in bed, insisting on walking me to class, forcing me to go to hockey practice with him, not leaving me alone for a second. In other ways, he was distant, almost cold, giving me gruff answers when I asked him questions and not being nearly as emotionally open or intimate as he had been.

But when I asked him what was wrong, he brushed me off easily, kissing me, telling me everything was fine, and that he was just focused on hockey right now. He also gave me my phone back. That, alone, should have signified we were okay.

But it didn't. And even though I told myself everything was fine, I knew it was bullshit. Fortunately, I had gotten a moment to myself—once again in the bathroom—to call my mom, this time from my real phone. I felt guilty, keeping this secret from Isaac, but the risk was too high to tell him the truth. My mom, for her part, was only worried about *me*. She insisted she was fine in San Diego, she'd found an apartment and a job cleaning houses, and so far, no one had seemed to have followed her. It settled my anxiety, somewhat, but it felt like there was danger waiting in the wings, and I felt completely paralyzed by it.

The team had a game tonight, and Isaac's suspension was over. He'd been so eager to get back on the ice, I hadn't pushed him about where things stood between us. Currently, he and the team were stretching, and even though Aviva and I were sitting in our usual seats, behind the penalty box, both wearing our respective boyfriends' jerseys, Isaac hadn't looked up at me once. It was completely opposite of every other game I'd gone to since we'd started this thing with each other, and I tried to keep the smile on my face and pretend his lack of attention wasn't affecting me, even though it was.

It continued throughout the entire game. Isaac was on fire, scoring goal after goal, with assists from Jack and the rest of the team. It was a blowout. We were on the bleachers, screaming as the horn blew for another goal of Isaac's, while I tried to ignore the woman two rows over.

She was beautiful. Tall, lithe, straight black hair, blue eyes, and pale skin. And she was holding a sign that said JONES with hearts around it. It shouldn't have meant anything or mattered to me. There were plenty of girls holding signs or cheering for Isaac. He had a huge fanbase, after all.

Except he'd glanced over at her. Twice. He'd seemed surprised the first time, but the second time he'd smiled at her, and she'd smiled back.

Hi, she'd mouthed.

He'd waved.

"I'm sure it's nothing," Aviva said, seeing where I was looking. "And if it's not, I'll kick his ass."

I shrugged. "I don't care."

"Bullshit. You do. And I swear it's nothing. He only has eyes for you, Tovah."

But if that was true, why hadn't he looked at me?

As second period ended, Isaac skated up to the boards, tapping on the glass right in front of her seat.

I got up.

"I need some water," I told Aviva.

"I can come with you," she offered, looking worried.

I waved her off. I needed time to myself, even in a crowd. Maybe to shut myself in a bathroom stall and silently cry. I was so frustrated, and hurt, and what was worse, he wouldn't tell me what was wrong.

As I headed up the stairs and out to the main corridor, I spotted her ahead of me. She was checking her phone as she brushed her hair behind her ear.

Unable to stop myself, I tapped her shoulder.

"Oh god, hi," she said, jumping. Her voice was high and clear. Pretty like the rest of her. I hated myself for it, but I wanted to punch her in the throat.

"Hi," I said. "I'm Tovah."

She was clearly surprised that a complete stranger was introducing herself, but I needed to know who she was.

"Hi, I'm Eliana. Why—" she scanned my jersey, and a half smile slid onto her face that didn't reach her eyes. "Ah, a fan of Isaac's."

"Fan?" Even though Isaac had never verbally cemented us this way, I didn't care. "I'm his girlfriend."

She flinched. People streamed into the corridor on either side of us to get snacks and drinks and go to the bathroom. "Girlfriend?"

With a sinking feeling in my stomach, I nodded. "Yeah."

She bit her lip. Even *that* was pretty. I hated how jealous I was, but if Isaac was allowed to be a possessive asshole, so was I.

Someone elbowed her, and she fell backward. Without thinking about it, I grabbed her arm to steady her.

"Come on, let's get out of the way," I said, leading her to the wall by the bathroom.

She turned to me. Her smile seemed tentative, but it was genuine now. "Thank you. I don't usually go to hockey games, are they always this wild?"

"Always," I said, and she laughed.

"I guess I better get used to them."

With a sinking feeling in my stomach, I asked the question I was terrified to learn the answer to.

"Why do you need to get used to them?"

"Oh." She brushed her hair behind her ear again. "I... god, this is awkward. My dad didn't tell me Isaac had a girlfriend. And Isaac really should've been the one to tell you this, and he's kind of an asshole—no, really an asshole—for keeping it from you."

I could walk away. Pretend I'd never spoken to her, noticed her. Continue to fuck Isaac and sleep in his arms like everything was okay and the small, isolated world bubble we'd built wasn't about to shatter into pieces and come crashing down around us. But I was Tovah *Lewis*, the same girl who'd survived despite everything. The journalist who never shied away from hard questions and harder answers. I wasn't about to start now, even though I had a feeling whatever she said next was going to *hurt.*

"What should Isaac have told me?" I asked, already dreading the answer.

She shook her head. "That we're engaged. I'm so sorry."

41

Tovah

I didn't go back to the game. I walked blindly through the crowd, ignoring Eliana as she called after me with concern, shoving around people and running down the stairs and out of the arena, unable to breathe.

Once I was outside in the dark, chilly night, I doubled over, puking up bile. My mouth tasted rancid, and I gasped for breath, feeling dizzy and nauseous. I refused to cry, and as badly as I wanted to scream—at Isaac, primarily—I wasn't going to lose my shit in public like that.

So instead, I walked. I walked around the parking lot, in circles around the arena, zigzagging across the grass toward the construction site where they were rebuilding Hallister Hall after it had burned down a few months ago. I lost track of where I walked, and of time, only cognizant of the aching in my chest and the tears spilling down my face after I lost the battle with them. There was a barrage of texts from Aviva; I ignored all of them.

Finally, maybe an hour or two later, I found myself back where I'd begun, outside the arena, near the parking lot.

Isaac's car was there—and so was Isaac.

With Eliana.

She had her hand on his chest, and she was speaking to him urgently. He didn't look happy, but he didn't move her hand, either.

And on her hand—her *left* hand—was something I hadn't noticed earlier. I'd been too desperate to get away.

An engagement ring sparkled in the night, a beacon of devastation in the form of a diamond so huge I could see it in the dark.

This was it.

This was everything I should've dreaded but hadn't known to.

The world rocked underneath me. Spun. Bile filled my mouth. I wanted to puke, scream, sob. Beat my fists against his chest. Hurt him.

But all of that would only make me hurt more.

I had to get out of there.

I had to find somewhere safe to go. Somewhere he wouldn't find me. Somewhere I could nurse this pain and figure out what my next steps were. Maybe I would go to San Diego and stay with my mom. What did I have left here? I could become a remote student, finish my courses that way, and still become a journalist. But I couldn't deal with the pain of listening to his lies, or worse, his truths, and then watch him marry someone else.

No. I refused.

I refused.

Almost blind with tears, I didn't notice at first that they'd spotted me. But then Isaac was shoving her hand away and walking toward me quickly.

"Tovah," he said.

"No. No, Isaac. Stay away from me," I gasped, backing away. "Leave me alone."

"That's the last goddamn thing I'm going to do. Tovah, you don't get it. Eliana just—"

So he did know her. She wasn't some crazy woman who had made this up out of nowhere.

I nodded. "Yeah, I met Eliana. I heard what she had to say. And that's fine. I hope you're happy together, you goddamned liar," I spat, and then turned and ran.

I heard him behind me, chasing me, calling my name. I ignored him. But I put everything into my breathing and my pace, speeding up and—probably because he was tired after his likely win, or maybe because he just didn't care enough—Isaac didn't catch up to me as I raced through campus in the dark, alone.

All alone.

Like I was meant to be.

42

Isaac

What a fucking clusterfuck.

Even though I desperately wanted to chase Tovah down, I still had to deal with the woman behind me. I jogged back to where she waited, a disappointed look in her eyes.

Eliana Rabin was the daughter of one of my father's... business colleagues. The Rabins were another crime family in New York, and while they didn't have the power of the Silvers or the prestige of the Golds, they had plenty of wealth and control over various industries, which made them an important player in my dad's world. And, soon to be, mine.

"You just let her go?" she asked.

I crossed my arms. "That's not really your business, Eliana."

She smiled a sad smile. "It is if we're getting married."

I shook my head at this bullshit. "We aren't getting married."

"Isaac."

She stepped up again to put what she thought was a comforting hand on my shoulder, but I stepped out of the way. I never should've let her touch me in the first place.

Sighing, she dropped her hand. "I don't like it either. But our fathers decided it was a good idea to grow both our families' holds over the city. We don't have a choice, so we should make the best of it, shouldn't we?"

"Why the hell am I only hearing about this now?" I asked. "Why did you think it was a good idea to come to my hockey game instead of, I don't know, calling me?"

"Your sister called you multiple times," she said. "According to Liza, anyway. And you spoke to your father, didn't you? He said he told you you'd have to marry soon."

Fuck.

Fuck fuck fuck.

I'd spoken to my father, and he *had* mentioned it. But I'd been so enraged at him, and the idea of getting married had been so absurd, I'd blocked it from my mind. It didn't fucking matter though; I wasn't engaged to Eliana.

There was only one person I wanted to marry.

And she'd run from me.

"I'm not marrying you," I told her.

She shook her head. "Your father sent me. He says this is happening. No one says no to your father. You know what he does to people who ignore his commands." She shivered. "He's not...entirely sane, is he?"

He wasn't. He was a maniacal asshole, who of course had sent her here without warning. And I had missed some of Liza's calls. Abe loved to fuck with his children. This was more than just messing with my mind and my life though. This was a reminder of his power over me and my fate, and how I had no say in my future.

But I was going to have some goddamn say in this.

"I don't think your father knows you have a girlfriend," Eliana told me.

"He doesn't. And it's going to stay that way. I refuse to let him fuck with our lives. Starting with this sham of an engagement. Where did you get the damn ring, anyway?"

She shrugged. "Your father gave it to me."

"Do you do everything my father tells you to do?"

Her eyes flashed, a little bit of the fire I knew she had peeking out behind the reserved polish. "I do when my family's safety and well-being is on the line. We're not getting out of this, Isaac. So I suggest you break up with your girlfriend and save her, and yourself, a lot of heartache. She deserves better than being a mistress."

Mistress? I gaped at Eliana.

"Don't talk about Tovah that way. She's not going to be my mistress; she's going to be my *wife*."

Eliana gasped, but I was done with her. Getting into my car, I told her, "Send my regards to dear old dad," before slamming the door shut and starting the car. As I drove away from the parking lot, not even caring that my team was blowing up my phone, wondering why I wasn't there to celebrate our win, I checked the cloning/tracker app to see where Tovah had run off to.

Her dot was at the newspaper office, not home.

Of course. She'd gone somewhere that felt like hers, and where she assumed I wouldn't look for her, like I would at Aviva's and Jack's, or her old apartment. Plus, I didn't have keys.

Was she calling "LOML" to ask for help?

Didn't matter. She didn't know I'd always know exactly where she was as long as she had her phone with her, and I had no problem at this point with a little light breaking and entering. And another kidnapping, if it came down to that.

And if LOML tried to contact her, I'd kill him.

I PARKED IN THE LOT BEHIND THE NEWSPAPER OFFICE, CHOOSING a spot in the shadows so Tovah didn't see me in case she was looking out the window. I wasn't giving her the opportunity to run again. Walking around to the back of the building, I picked the lock. It was one of the first things my older sister had ever taught me. The alarm beeped once, but didn't go off. I walked through the quiet, dark building, searching for her.

The only light that was on was in the editor-in-chief's office. Was Tony or whatever his name was here?

For one, insane moment, I worried that she'd asked him to come. That she was writing the exposé against me and my family, after all.

No, she wouldn't.

Fuck, would she?

Not bothering to knock, I threw open the door to his office. Tovah and that asshole were behind his desk, looking at something.

What were they looking at? Were they plotting against me, or was I being paranoid?

"Get the fuck out," I barked.

"Isaac!" Tovah looked up at me, eyes wide, before they narrowed into slits.

"*You* get out," she said.

I didn't look at her. "Tony, get the fuck out here, before I fulfill my earlier promise of tossing you out a window."

"I believe the term is defenestrate," he said snottily. "And my name is Toby."

"I know what the term is, and I don't care. I know what your name is, and I *also* don't care. I'm still going to *defenestrate* you if you don't leave *right now.*"

Even though he was a complete asshole, he wasn't a complete idiot, so with one last look at Tovah, he gathered his things and was gone a moment later.

I advanced toward Tovah, who shut off the computer.

"Working on anything interesting?" I asked, my tone bland.

Her tone wasn't. "Where's your fiancée? Waiting nicely in the car for you?"

"I don't *have* a fiancée."

"The ring on her finger would suggest otherwise," she spat. "Seriously Isaac, how the hell could you not tell me you were engaged to someone? I know you were fucking with my head, but this is low, even for you."

God, the accusation hurt. So did the pained, distrustful look in her eyes. Coming around the side of the desk, I grabbed her out of the chair and pulled her around to face me.

"Get. Your. Hands. Off. Me," she hissed.

Hell no.

"I can put my hands wherever I want. You're mine, remember?"

"Right. Your little fuck toy. I'm sure you'd love to keep me around after you get married."

I glared at her. What was it with everyone thinking I wanted a mistress?

"Oh, I'll keep you around after I get married," I threatened. "Keep you tied to our bed and my cock inside you until you get sweet and submissive again. Sounds like a good idea, actually."

She wiped frantically at her eyes. "Your *wife* might have an issue with that."

"That would be weird, since *you're* going to be my wife," I said, satisfied when her eyes bugged out of her head. I should be remorseful, but the distrust was messing with that.

"But—"

"I'm not marrying Eliana. My jerk of a father is trying to arrange a marriage between us to fuck with me. I didn't even know about it until Eliana showed up at the game tonight."

Tovah's hand dropped away from her face, and I finally saw the tears she'd been hiding.

My heart, that fucking thing, squeezed.

Shit.

All the distrust and anger fled, leaving guilt behind. I hated, hated, hurting her now.

I tilted her chin up with my fingers, making sure she was staring straight at me.

"Tovah, bashert, I promise you, I'm not engaged to her. It's not real. The only person I'm ever marrying is you."

She was my soulmate after all, my destiny. I'd only ever called one other person that, but the way I'd felt about that little girl didn't come close to how I felt about Tovah.

Fuck.

I loved her.

I felt like I'd been punched by a goalie with his gloves off. It shook me to the core, but it was true. The truest thing I'd ever felt.

Tovah must not have realized what I had. She shook her head. "Do you really think you have a choice? Forget the fact that I never agreed to marry you, Isaac. You're the one who told me that your father has already decided your future, and you can't get out of it. No hockey. No Tovah. Just a career as the head of the Silver dynasty, and a pretty mafia princess to go with it." Her voice broke. "Can you tell me honestly you won't have to marry her?"

Tears were spilling down her cheeks. I hated watching her cry. The only time I wanted to see her cry was when I was fucking her face and she was choking on my cock. And knowing I'd put these tears there right now...

"Tovah, baby, bashert, don't cry," I demanded, or tried to. But all she did was cry harder. I gently wiped away a tear with my finger. "I will *not* marry her. I'll give everything up to make sure that doesn't happen. The one thing I'm not giving up is you. That's non-negotiable."

She shook her head. "Admit it, Isaac. You and I are on borrowed time. There's no way this works. Your family is my enemy, and you don't have control over your own life. We need to end this thing between us. We never should've started it in the first place."

I froze. I could feel my jaw going hard, my eyes going flinty. She was trying to take the wheel of our relationship and probably drive us into a tree. She wasn't wrecking what we had.

I wouldn't allow it.

"Never say that," I said, as I towered over her, and moved around behind her, kicking the rolling chair away from the desk.

"Isaac, what are you—"

"Reminding you who you belong to, and who I belong to. You don't talk that way, and you certainly don't try to end this thing between us. Don't think I forgot how I just found you. What were you doing in here, so late, with your weasel of an editor?"

"Nothing," she said, turning her head to watch me warily. "He was here when I got here."

"Yeah? And what were you two working on so diligently?" I asked silkily.

She shivered, just like I wanted her to. "Don't change the subject. We were talking about your fiancée."

"Until you're wearing my ring, I have no fiancée. That conversational topic is over. What I want to know is what you and Tony were working on."

"Toby."

"Tell me, Tovah."

"I was giving him notes on the editorial," she said.

"Editorial? Not, say, an exposé on my family? One that we agreed you'd drop?" Even I could hear the danger in my voice.

She flipped around. "First, we never *agreed*. You threatened me with death by your family's hand if I wrote it. Second, I dropped it. The article's *dead*, Isaac. Just like our relationship."

"If you say that again, Tovah, I'll go out there, drag Toby back in, and throw him out the window like I threatened. And you can be an accessory to his murder. If you're so interested in death right now."

"Isaac, stop."

"No."

Stepping behind her, I gripped her by her hips and bent her over the desk, even as she fought me. Keeping one big hand on her back to keep her in place, I pulled her leggings and panties down with the other, until her ass was bare and presented to me.

Without warning, I slapped her right cheek hard, then her left, right, then left again, relishing in her shrieks and the way she fought me as I reminded her *who she belonged to and who I belonged to,* just like I'd said.

I didn't really care about the article at the moment. I cared about reminding her she was mine. She was wearing my jersey right now, but that wasn't even close to what I needed.

"It's not enough for you to wear my jersey in public," I told her. "I thought that would quiet this fucking beast inside me, but it doesn't declare my ownership enough. Not to the world, and not to you. No, I'm going to make sure you never, ever forget who owns you. You don't belong with LOML, whoever the fuck that asshole is. You belong to *me.*"

"How do you know about LOML?" she cried.

"Who the fuck is he?"

She turned her head to glare at me. "What's your plan, spank me until I can't sit? Been there, done that, have the handprints to match."

"Oh, little snoop, that doesn't even come close to what I'll do to you," I said as I continued to turn her ass red. "I'll tattoo my name to your tits. That way, I won't even need you to wear my jersey to remind you you're mine—it'll be written on your skin. Permanently."

"Don't you fucking—"

I covered her mouth with my free hand so all she could do was scream her pain and denial against it.

Finally, the spanking did its job, because she was wet and trembling in front of me, begging me to stop.

I did, testing her pussy to make sure she was wet enough for me.

"You love this, don't you, perfect girl? You were made for me, like I was made for you."

Unzipping my pants, I pulled out my cock, lined it up

with her pussy, and shoved all the way in on one, perfect thrust.

Tovah screamed at the top of her lungs. She'd been ready physically, but not mentally. I didn't give her time to catch up, setting a furious, frantic pace as I fucked into her, again and again, my hands gripping her bare hips tight so she couldn't get away. As always, being inside her cunt was like coming home. Her pussy must have felt the same way, because it squeezed me each time I withdrew, like it didn't want me to leave.

Releasing her hip with one of my hands, I shoved it under her so I could finger her clit and play with her pussy.

Tovah cried out, writhing against me as she moaned my name, over and over, only making me that much thicker and harder. I quelled the urge to come, because I wasn't coming in her pussy tonight. No, I was going to explore the one hole I'd left as virgin territory so far. Claim her in every goddamned way I could, until there was no doubt in her head that she was mine, that I was hers, and that no one—no fake fiancée, no secret boyfriend—would come between us.

I slowed my pace, enjoying her gasps and pleas for more as I kept her from coming, edging her over and over, her tits smashed up against that fucker's desk. Glancing up, I noticed a mirror over the door.

That perverted asshole. Well, I'd use it to my advantage, like watching Tovah's face as she tried to contain how good it felt to be fucked by me. Her mouth was open, her eyes glazed and glassy, her cheeks and chest flushed.

"God, you're so beautiful, bashert. Made to be fucked by me, made to come."

"Isaac—" she moaned, and I could feel her body clenching tight as it prepared to make my words come true.

"Nuh uh, not yet," I scolded as I withdrew from her pussy, leaning down to admire how pink and swollen it was as it clenched on empty air, desperate to come.

Inspiration struck. If that pervert had a mirror facing his desk, he probably also had lube somewhere.

Leaving Tovah panting on the desk for a moment, I opened a few drawers, spotting it.

Perfect.

Thanks, fucker. Don't mind if I help myself to some.

Grabbing the chair, I dragged it back over to the desk, my cock standing straight up. The horny fucker was desperate and hard, pissed that it hadn't released in its favorite place. But he had to be patient because it was about to be better.

Uncapping the lube, I squeezed some onto my fingers, before I rimmed her asshole.

"Wait, Isaac—"

"No, no waiting," I interrupted. "You don't get to keep any part of you from me." I slid one finger in up to the knuckle, circling it around, before withdrawing it, adding more lube, and sliding in two fingers this time. Tovah moaned and squirmed, but she liked it, couldn't hide it, not the way her little hole was clenching around my fingers as I stretched and prepared her.

I withdrew again, adding more lube, before inserting three fingers this time. She was hot, and tight, and I couldn't fucking "wait to get my cock inside this tight little hole, little journalist," I told her. "Then you'll really know what it's like to be owned."

Once I felt she was adequately prepared, I withdrew my fingers, lubing up my cock.

Holding it steady, I lifted her, lowering her onto my lap —and her little asshole over my cock. Lifting my hips, I slowly edged inside her, careful not to go too far, too fast. Just the feel of her squeezing the tip was more than I was ready for. She was tight and hot, and the triumph over knowing I'd been first *everywhere* made my balls throb.

"I'll be last everywhere, too," I said out loud, not caring if I made sense or not.

"Isaac, I can't do this, it's too much," she whimpered, like she always did.

"It'll never be enough," I corrected her, like I always did, as I slowly pushed her down over my cock, letting her ass swallow me up a little at a time.

Oh, fuck, fuck, nothing had ever felt like this before. But that's always how it was with her, wasn't it? It was like I was the one who was the virgin. Sex had never felt like this with anyone else.

"Just you," I said. "It's out of this world with you, and it's only going to be with you. You aren't going anywhere."

"Isaac, I caaaaan't," she whimpered.

"Yes you can," I crooned in a voice I hardly recognized. "You're my Tovah, aren't you? My good girl. You're going to relax that sweet, tight hole and bear down and open up for me, inch by inch, as I take you, because you want to be a good girl—just for me. Yes, that's it. That's my pretty little journalist. You're doing so well, taking me like this." I caught her gaze in the mirror and held it, and the blind, confused passion in her eyes made my legs practically shake with the effort not to come.

But I wasn't fucking done with her yet.

Grinding my teeth, I forced myself to continue to go slow, thrusting up as I pushed her down, adding lube until she slid the rest of the way onto my cock and she was sitting on my lap.

I was as deep as I could go.

And, crazy as it is, I wanted to get deeper. Wanted to be so far inside her, she forgot where she stopped and I began.

"I never thought anyone would have this kind of power over me," I confessed, not moving and just letting her clenching ass massage my dick as she adjusted to me inside her. I kissed her head, then lowered my chin onto it so I could continue watching the reluctant ecstasy on her face. "I never wanted anyone to. But you do. You own me. I don't care if you're lying to me. You could probably try to kill me, and I'd hand you the knife. That's how torn up I am over you. That's how much I belong to you, bashert. All I want is for you to belong to me right back. *I love you.*"

"Isaac, what? I don't? What are you?" she gasped, her moans confused and lost by my words. I didn't give her time to consider them, because now I did need to move, as I rose to stand and bent her back over the desk so I could thrust. Slowly at first, and then more steadily, I pulled my hips backward and pushed them back in again, tunneling into that hot, tight, virgin hole, letting it squeeze me again and again. My balls were boiling and I needed to come, but she was going to come with me. With my clean hand, I started playing with her again, strumming and then pinching her clit, determined to make her orgasm as violent as mine was going to be.

"Isaac," she cried, "It's so much, it's too—"

"What did I tell you? It'll—"

Thrust.

"Never—"

Thrust.

"Be—"

Thrust.

"Enough."

I caught her eyes with mine in the mirror and growled,

"I'm in love with you. And no matter what you do, that won't fucking change. You aren't going anywhere."

Gripping her clit, I pinched it tight, not releasing it until she screamed my name so loud the windows could've shattered, gripping my cock tight as her ass and pussy clenched, milking my cock so hard I came with her, my vision going white, my own roar echoing off the walls as I shot cum deep into her ass, filling her up with everything I had.

And still, it wasn't enough.

It would never be enough.

43

Tovah

I was a mess by the time Isaac brought me back to his house. As always, he carried me out of his car, into the house, up the stairs to the ensuite bathroom, seating me on the counter and handing me a glass of water. Thirsty, throat still dry, I chugged it while he tested the shower temperature. Once the temperature was to his liking, he swooped me back up in his arms and carried me into the shower, gently placing me on the bench. Grabbing body wash, he lathered his hands and cleaned me, slowly, carefully. I was so overwrought that his touches made my pussy throb, but there was nothing sexual in the way he washed me, only a single, focused, almost devout care.

Once my body was clean, he stood me up, his chest to my back so I could lean against him, as he lathered up my hair with shampoo and then worked through the tangles with conditioner, holding his hand over my eyes so the spray didn't sting them, like I was a child. I relaxed into his arms, forgetting to be pissed at him, and soaking up the tenderness in his touch.

Sitting me back down, he quickly washed and rinsed off his own body, before carrying me out of the shower. As he dried me with a towel, I could barely look him in the eyes.

What had happened between us had been so *much*, so *intense*, and I didn't even know how to look at him or talk to him. Why had he accused me of being a liar again? Of writing the article? The article I'd abandoned, even knowing it was possibly the only thing that was going to save my mother? We had so much to talk about, but I was exhausted, and all I wanted to do was sleep.

I wanted to sleep with him, to have his arms around me. But if Eliana were right, if they were engaged, then all I was doing was sleeping with another woman's man. All I was doing was prolonging the inevitable, and if Isaac was going to break my heart, I'd rather it happen now than later, when the break was irreparable.

"Let's go to bed," he said, kissing me, carrying me to the bed and tucking in before climbing in after me. He didn't bother to cuff us together, and I was grateful for that as I waited for him to fall asleep.

Once his breathing had deepened and slowed, I gently, carefully lifted his arm and crawled out of the bed, grabbing a sweatshirt and heading to the guestroom. I closed the door and locked it, and then, only then, did I let the tears flow again.

Flopping onto the guest bed, I sobbed into the pillow.

How had we gotten here? How had we gone from a month ago, when he'd been nothing but my enemy, and a means to an end, to here, where he meant more to me than my own life, as much—if not more—than my own mother?

How had we gotten to this place where he had the ability to break my heart, if he wanted, if he cared?

God, and he claimed he wanted to marry me! I bit the pillow to withhold the frustrated scream that bubbled up in my throat. Didn't he understand we weren't meant for each other? That we were destined to destroy each other, not love each other? It didn't matter that he'd said he loved me, or that my stomach had dropped out of my body when he had. It didn't matter that I loved him back, because I did. Anything between us was destined to end in tragedy.

I had to figure out how to end this, and if he wouldn't let me, then to get away.

The door opened, and he was there, lifting me off the guest bed and carrying me back to his bedroom.

"You don't leave me, not in the middle of the night, not ever," he said gruffly. "I sleep like shit when you aren't in my arms. Away games are torture. I refuse to let you out of my damn sight."

He grabbed a new pair of cuffs, closing one around my wrist and the other around his.

"How did you even get into the bedroom?"

He laughed. "You think a locked door can keep me from you? Tovah, god himself couldn't keep me from finding you and bringing you home."

With those jaw-dropping words, he wrapped me up in his arms, not saying anything else. I didn't know what to say, either. We both lay there in silence, skin touching skin, breathing in sync, lips inches apart. I couldn't see him in the dark, but I knew he was watching me.

"I hate you," I told him, my eyes burning from all the tears I'd already cried over him. "I love you, but I hate you, too. You hurt me. You keep hurting me. When does it end, Isaac?"

"It doesn't," he told me, his voice thick with emotion. "I'll do my best to stop hurting you, I promise. But it will never end, because we'll never end, bashert. I love you. My heart knows yours. My soul recognizes yours. Like we've known each other forever."

He didn't even know how right he was.

We lay in the dark like that, silent but not sleeping, our bodies wrapped around each other, a wall keeping the world out, like we could keep it from destroying us.

But as each second ticked by, I became more and more sure we couldn't.

44

Isaac

When her breathing finally evened out, I gently unwrapped myself from her and headed downstairs. I felt like an asshole for what I was about to do, especially when she'd been crying, but the urgency to get this done was building inside me.

Downstairs, I grabbed the package I'd hid the night she'd had PMS and headed back up.

Jack had sourced a microchip for me. He'd put one in his own girl's body, and she still had no idea. I felt bad for the poor fucker when Aviva found out, because there'd be hell to pay. But even knowing that, I was going to do the same thing to Tovah. I'd gone back and forth about this all week, questioning such an unhinged choice, but now I was decided.

She was hiding shit from me; she'd changed her last name—obviously she wasn't safe. And then there was the possibility of the article...I loved her, but I didn't trust her. And with the bullshit engagement, she was too much of a flight risk. In case she ever ran, or someone took her...well, I needed to know where she was at all times, didn't I?

Grabbing what I needed—the microchip, surgical knife, and needle and surgical thread for stitches, I climbed back up on the bed, kneeling over her to prepare the area. I watched her for a bit. She looked so soft and vulnerable in sleep, and I couldn't help but drop a tender kiss on her lips. Fortunately, she didn't wake up, although she did moan my name softly. The sleeping powder that I'd dissolved in her water earlier had done its job.

My cock stirred.

I smacked it in reprimand.

Then I lifted her arm, because I wanted to put it under her left armpit where she wouldn't look—and where she'd hopefully assume the sting was from razor burn.

I looked down.

And sucked in a breath like I'd been punched.

"What the actual fuck?"

There was a birthmark in the shape of a crescent moon.

A birthmark.

In the shape of a goddamned crescent moon.

Oh, I remembered that crescent moon. I'd never forgotten it.

The girl from my childhood appeared in my mind's eye. Short, dark, curly hair, a feisty grin. She'd lived on our compound, the daughter of one of the staff. I'd even *told* Tovah about her. About the birthmark. She'd been afraid, and I'd sworn to protect her...until she disappeared.

The same day that my mother had been killed.

Blood. Death. Loss. The memories, the feelings, they came back in waves that threatened to drown me. To take me under and never let me free. Like my father, like my fate, and now, like Tovah—who, by lying to me, had stolen our future and any chance I'd ever have at happiness.

No. Everything in my body rejected what I was seeing. I fell to the floor, my legs no longer holding me up.

It all made sense, didn't it? Tovah was on the run from my father, she'd gone into hiding. She kept changing her hair color, not out of rebellion, but because she didn't want to be found. Who else could she be? And the evidence in front of me was irrefutable.

I flashed back to that day in the kitchen where I'd told Tovah about my mom's death and the little girl. She'd defended her, hadn't she? I'd thought that was odd at the time but blamed it on her journalism dreams and her big heart.

She was just a kid, wasn't she? Do you really think she'd plot against you that way? Or was she just an innocent bystander with no control of her own?

For a moment, just a moment, I considered what she'd said was true.

But if that were the case, why lie to me?

Because you would have thrown her to the wolves, my inner voice argued.

No, fuck that. She'd betrayed me.

Maybe Tovah was right, and I couldn't blame her when she'd been a child. But still, she'd lied to me, hidden the truth. What else was she hiding, while she slept in my goddamned bed?

Denial roared within me, and then betrayal. My goddamn chest felt like someone had taken a sledgehammer to it. I'd been beaten up, shoved into the boards, gotten concussions during hockey. But none of it, not a single second, had hurt like this did.

My stomach roiled, and my dinner threatened to come

back up. I couldn't even stand, so I crawled to the bathroom, barely making it in time to the toilet before I leaned over it and puked my guts out. It felt like it lasted for hours, and when I was done, there was nothing left inside of me.

I was empty.

Tovah lied to me, hidden our connected past from me, fucked me, planned to expose me and my family...had she even let that go? Or had she been plotting against me this whole time? She'd been in the office with Toby earlier—and although she'd told me the exposé was dead, why should I believe her? She'd lied about who she was, she could be lying about that, too.

What kind of viper had I allowed into my heart?

Mine, the monster roared, stopping me from doing anything I might regret.

It was right. She was still mine. I might not be able to trust her, but I was keeping her, all the same.

Slowly and methodically, I finished cleaning the area, quickly cutting the skin, placing the microchip, and stitching it back up. Tovah didn't stir.

When I was finished, I stared down at her, this stranger in my home.

And I hated that my heart had partially healed, that I even had one. Because the fucker *hurt*. So much, it was hard to breathe.

I'd never known you could love and hate someone so intensely.

Because I did. I still loved Tovah, with every part of me.

And hated her, equally.

I didn't have a heart, after all. She'd stolen it from me.

And I wanted it back.

I didn't sleep at all. The next morning, I was an exhausted mess. It was a major problem, because we had an away game that night.

Without saying a word to her, I grabbed her by the arm and dragged her into the shower. She glared at me, arms crossed, also not speaking, as I washed my body and hair, for once not bothering to wash her. It was a ritual I'd come to love, but I didn't trust myself to not be rough right now. I was too angry.

I stepped out of the spray so she could step under it. I tried not to watch, but it was impossible, and I finally gave up the battle, eyes on her hands as she lathered that perfect body with soap.

"Why are you staring at me like that?"

"I own that sweet body," I told her. "I can stare as much as I want."

"You aren't staring like you want to fuck me," she pointed out as she backed away. "You're staring like you want to stab me."

"I might," I said nonchalantly. "But I'm going to use your body to get off first. That's all you're good for, isn't it, little hack?"

Her eyes widened. "What the hell, Isaac? Why are we back to this? I'm the one who's mad, remember?"

"I don't give a shit if you're upset about some girl I might be engaged to—"

She interrupted. "Might? It's might now? What happened to 'the only person I'm marrying is you?'"

"—I don't care about how you feel," I spoke over her. "All I care about is how *you* make *my cock* feel."

Her face turned white. "Fuck you," she snapped.

"Speak like that to me again, and the only time you'll be opening that mouth is when *I* fuck it. On your knees."

She shook her head.

"I don't understand what the hell has gotten into you, but I'm not putting up with it."

"You will," I told her. "Or I'll call my father right now."

"You wouldn't," she shook her head once, twice, then stopped. "Or maybe you would." I hadn't seen hatred or anger like that in them before, not even before we started this whole thing.

"I'm not kneeling for you, Isaac Silver. Not now. You get your cock near me and I'll stab you."

"You certainly felt differently last night."

"Last night was apparently a mistake. I was right, wasn't I? This whole," she gestured, "thing between us has been one giant mistake."

Although I kept my expression blank, her words felt like she'd stabbed me in the heart and then twisted the knife.

I hate you, she'd said.

I hated myself a little, too.

But not as much as I hated her, hated that I loved her.

I stepped forward so I was looming over her, crowding her against the tile. The water poured over her head, her face, practically drowning her.

"Why were you really at the newspaper office last night, Tovah? I saw you working with Toby on something. I saw you close out of whatever it was so I didn't see. I didn't press you on it, because like always, I got distracted by your fucking body." My voice was getting louder and louder, but I couldn't bring myself to care. "You have some hold over me, and I'm getting sick of it, when you won't give me more than your body. So tell me, Tovah, are you still planning on publishing a story that will destroy my team, my family, and me? This whole time, have you been planning on betraying what I thought we were building together?"

Her throat worked.

"Fucking admit it. Admit that you betrayed me! You've been playing me this whole time!" I was shouting now.

She shouted right back. "No, you asshole. Toby was showing me something else, and I was going to tell you about it, but last night wasn't the time, and now clearly isn't, either."

I paused for a moment, considering this. But no, she was just hiding more shit from me.

I advanced on her, looming over her, aware that I was so angry, the veins were popping in my neck.

"I don't believe you. You've been lying to me this whole time about who you are."

She blinked. "You know who I am, you know my last name..."

"That's not what I meant, *bashert*." I snorted. She didn't deserve the fucking endearment, not when we were children, and certainly not now. "I called you that, when we were children, didn't I? That's right, I saw the fucking birthmark. I know who you truly are. Who you were. The little girl I trusted who disappeared when my mother was killed. That was you, wasn't it?"

Her chest heaved. "Isaac—"

"Wasn't it?" I roared, slapping the wall next to her. She flinched, lifting her hands like she needed to protect herself from me.

Gulping, I stepped back. I would never hit her, ever. Clearly, she didn't know that. Because we didn't know each other.

Not at all.

"It was me," she said quietly. "I grew up on your family's compound. My mom was a maid there for a while. But we didn't leave because we were involved in your mother's death. We left because it wasn't safe for us anymore. My stepfather...he was important to your dad, but he was abusive. Murderous, even. We disappeared and have remained hidden for years. That's who LOML is on my phone, by the way. Not some other man. My mother. We're always looking over our shoulders, terrified your father will catch up with us. Do you know what that's like, never feeling safe? Knowing your loved one is never safe? That's why I escalated things, that's why I was going to write the article, that's why I need evidence against your father to put him away for good—"

I tried to digest her words, to understand her fear, but all that mattered was that she'd lied to me, she'd tried to hurt me, that I couldn't trust her. And all I could see was my mother's unmoving body, her eyes blank, forever, my father screaming with her in his arms, both of them covered in blood.

Tovah couldn't be trusted. I couldn't trust her.

I'd been right. I couldn't have a woman in my life.

We were a mistake.

I leaned over her, putting my lips to her ear, relishing the way she leaned into me. She still responded to me, still wanted me, and it would make hurting her all the sweeter.

"You know what the mistake was, Tovah? It was trusting you. It was believing you. It was forgetting who you really are: a lying, conniving hack who will do anything for a story."

She shuddered, like I'd truly hurt her.

Good.

But then she turned her head, so our lips almost touched.

"You're no better than your father, Isaac Silver," she said against them. "My mistake was forgetting that. You are a monster, and not, never, mine."

She'd twisted the knife again. The words sliced through me.

Angry as fuck, I slammed out of the shower, wrapping a towel around my waist.

"If you really feel that way, you can leave. Take your shit and get the fuck out of my house. When I get back from the game at Cortland, I want you gone."

She stared at me, her shoulders heaving, water still sluicing over her face, so I couldn't tell what was shower water, and what were tears.

A small part of me fought to go back to her, to apologize, to do anything to make sure she didn't cry.

I buried that part six feet under.

"You know what? Maybe I will marry Eliana. She's beautiful, kind, and most importantly, I know her and can trust her."

"I hope you're happy," she shot back.

"I will be," I lied, storming out of the bathroom and ignoring Tovah's quiet sobs as I got dressed and headed out to go meet the team at the bus.

I had hockey.

For now.

That had to be enough.

45

Tovah

When he slammed out of the bathroom, I sank down, my back rubbing against the tile as I slid down the wall, hitting the shower floor with a painful thud. Water poured over my head, making it hard to breathe, and for a while I gave in, because what was the point? I hurt so badly, I could barely breathe, anyway. I might as well drown here.

I'd told Isaac everything except for what my mother and I had done to my stepfather. I'd taken a huge risk, confessing that my mother was alive, and instead of listening to me and understanding me, Isaac had thrown it back in my face. He didn't believe me, didn't trust me. He still thought I was writing the exposé.

I snorted. Toby had wanted to talk to me about an exposé last night, but it had nothing to do with Isaac's family. No, it was about me. Turned out someone had taken photos of me dressed in that slutty maid uniform and when I was tied to the founders' statue. Toby had told Veronica about it, who proposed an article about a kinky journalist who got involved with the subject of her article. *Is Journalistic Integrity a Thing of the Past? Sex, Kinks, and Tovah Kaufman* was the headline.

It was going to ruin my entire career. But I had no idea what to do about it. Toby had said if I had something *better*, he'd kill the piece, but the only thing I had was the exposé about Isaac's family.

It would be so easy to finish writing the article I'd started, load it up onto *The Daily Queen* website, and hit publish. To choose my mother over him.

But I couldn't. As I sat there with Toby, all I could see was Isaac's face when he discovered I'd betrayed him that way. Seeing him dragged away in handcuffs—the scary kind —and knowing I'd destroyed his life. I couldn't do that to him. Couldn't hurt him that way, because it would be like ripping my own heart out.

In that moment, I chose Isaac over my mom. In my head, I'd promised her that I'd find another way to free her. I didn't know how, but I would.

It just wouldn't be by hurting Isaac.

But here I was, soaking wet in his shower. I'd seen his face, and it had been more horrible than I'd ever imagined. He'd been so angry, frightening enough that I'd flinched and protected myself when he loomed over me, soaked and livid. I knew, of course, that he'd never hit me, but it made me flash back to times my stepfather had been angry.

Isaac would never hit me, but he had hurt me, and his words would leave bruises.

So had him dumping me. He'd never left me before. Even at the worst of our battles, I'd never imagined him kicking me out of his house, which had been beginning to feel like a real home. He'd been so emphatic that I was his and he was mine, I'd believed him.

Tovah, bashert, I promise, the only person I'm ever marrying is you.

He'd said those words just last night, even when we were fighting, but clearly he didn't mean them.

I thought I'd run out of tears, that there were none left. But as I sat there in the shower, hugging my knees, my tears mixed with the water pouring over me, until I didn't know which was which. The water turned cold, and still, I didn't move. I welcomed the cold, the pain, hoping it would numb my heart so I'd stop *feeling* so much.

It didn't work.

46

Isaac

I barely made it out of the bathroom before everything in me started screaming to go back.

Especially when I heard Tovah's sobs.

Fuck, what was I even doing? Leaving the woman I loved crying in my bathroom? Breaking her heart because I'd never dealt with my past trauma, or my anger over my future fate? None of this was her fault. None of it. Not giving up hockey, not going to work for my father, not my violence, not my pain. Certainly not my mother's death. I'd blamed her, because she was the closest thing to a target I had. I'd bullied and tortured her for the same reasons.

I'd promised myself I'd change, but I was acting like the same asshole who'd tied her naked to the founders' statue. I rubbed my hands over my face, slowing my breathing and trying to calm my racing heart.

I caught a glimpse of myself in the mirror. I looked ravaged, crazed, and cruel. I shook my head. I wasn't Dr. Dimples, and I wasn't a monster. What I was, was hers.

Forever. Even when I was a fucking jackass.

Who was I? This was not the man I wanted to be. This was not the man she deserved.

Tovah deserved better.

A different man would recognize that and let her go, give her her freedom and the opportunity to meet someone kinder, peaceful, easy to be with. But I wasn't a different man, and I wasn't giving her up. Which meant that I had to be a better man—the best version of myself.

But there was no best version of myself, without her by my side.

Starting now.

47

Tovah

My whole body felt like ice. Worse. Like ice after a whole period of a hockey game, scratched and broken. And there was no one to clean me up and dust me off—but me.

Shivering, I began to stand, planning on shutting off the shower, finding a towel, and drying myself. I tried not to think about what it felt like when Isaac was the one to dry me off, the care he took. The towel, so soft before, would feel like sandpaper on my raw skin, I knew it. Because I was raw all over, vulnerable in ways I hadn't been before.

But then the bathroom door opened, and Isaac was striding toward the shower.

"What are you doing?" I asked with a voice scratching from crying.

He opened the shower door and stepped inside. He was fully dressed and the freezing shower water immediately soaked through his jeans and shirt.

"Isaac—"

He wrapped his arms around me, pulling me against his chest and laying his head against my wet hair.

"I'm sorry," he said. "I'm sorry. I'm so, so sorry Tovah. You have no idea how much."

"You hurt me," I told him. "You hurt me so much. How could you hurt me like that? How could you doubt me like that? How could you say you love me, and hurt me like that?"

There was a raw vulnerability in my voice, an honesty I hated. But I was too worn out to hide it, and I deserved better.

"I know," he said. "Fuck, you're freezing. I hate when you're cold. I never want you to be cold."

He pulled me out of the shower, still ignoring how wet his own clothes were, or that he was also shivering. He grabbed a towel like he was going to wrap me in it, like he always did, but I stopped him, pulling away.

"You can't," I told him. "You can't do this to me. An apology isn't enough."

He nodded. "It's not enough. Nothing is enough to fix my cruelty. But god knows I'm going to try. Please, Tovah, let me warm you up. I can't think clearly when you're shivering like that. My brain wants to break at the sight of you hurt."

"Even when you were the cause?"

His eyes were as raw as my body felt. "Especially if I was the cause. Once, bashert, I told myself that no one was allowed to hurt you but me. But now, no one is allowed to hurt you, *including me. Please, let me make you warm again.*"

His words alone helped eradicate the cold, but I wasn't about to tell him that much. Instead, I stood and let him dry me off, the towel less like sandpaper than I'd expected.

"You're still cold," he muttered, picking me up and carrying me into the bedroom, where he proceeded to layer me in sweatpants and sweaters before grabbing the duvet off the bed and wrapping it around me. There wasn't much funny about this moment, but I cracked a smile when I saw myself in the mirror.

"I look like a burrito."

"The prettiest burrito I've ever seen," he said solemnly.

And then he knelt in front of me, wrapping his arms around my hips.

"I'm so sorry. I'll give you everything you want. Everything you need. The evidence that the team was distributing Vice and Vixen. You can take us all down, I don't care. The evidence that my father was involved. There's a bottom drawer in the office, the code is 0914." He looked up at me. "September 14. It's the day we met."

I swallowed.

"In that drawer, you'll find everything you need to destroy the Silver family and get freedom for you and your mom. Dates, deals, money exchanged. Texts and emails. Liza and I have been keeping all of it as insurance against my father, in case we need it. But it's yours. All of it is yours. I don't care if they drag my entire family away in handcuffs, if you have the life you want."

I stared down at him, stroking my hand through his wet and curling hair.

"You mean it," I said. "You'd really do all of that to give me my freedom."

He chuckled. "I mean, freedom with caveats. Even if I spend my life in prison, you're still marrying me."

I raised an eyebrow, but my heart was about to burst in my chest. "Am I now?"

"Yup. That's non-negotiable, Tovah Silver."

For years, I'd had to live with a name that wasn't mine. It

had always felt like a too-tight sweater. But hearing my name *this way*...it felt like it fit. It felt right.

It felt like coming home.

"Stand up," I said, voice hoarse.

He shook his head against my blanketed stomach. "No. Not until you know that I'm not leaving you. That I'd never leave you. I mean it, Tovah. Please. Trust me. Even at my angriest, my stupidest, I'd still keep us cuffed together every night."

I sighed. "I believe you," I said. "But I don't forgive you."

His eyes, dark, were wet with pain, regret, and gratitude. "You don't have to forgive me. You only need to know how sorry I am. I don't blame you for my mother's death, or for keeping it and your mom a secret from me, Tovah. I understand. I was just afraid, and angry, and being a dick."

He slowly unwrapped the blanket. I let it fall.

Lifting the sweatshirts he'd put me in, he placed gentle kisses on my rounded stomach and the dimples on my hips.

"You don't have to forgive me," he murmured against my skin. "You just need to love me, bashert."

"I do," I said. "I do love you, bashert."

And then he was rising to his feet, and lifting me in his arms, and kissing me, and I was kissing him back, and even though the world outside still threatened to destroy us, for now, we felt strong enough together.

We felt invincible.

If only that were true.

48

Tovah

Isaac stood by the kitchen counter, keys in hand.

"You'll be at the game?" he asked. "I know it's a few hours away, but I need you there."

There was worry in his eyes. I'd never thought it was possible that Isaac Silver could be insecure, but right now he seemed more like a boy than a man.

"I'll be at the game," I assured him. "I can't promise not to chirp though."

"As long as you wear my jersey."

I smiled. "I'll wear your jersey."

He grabbed my hand. "And you'll—"

"I'll be at the game, Isaac. I mean it. I'm in this with you. You don't have to throw me in your trunk again, promise." I scratched my head. "Although now that I think about it, I've spent more time in the trunk than in the cab."

"I should apologize for that, but if I hadn't kidnapped you that day, you wouldn't be here." He glanced at his phone. "Fuck, I'm already late. Call me if you have any issues, okay?"

I nodded.

That must not have been enough for him, because he said, "promise me."

"I promise."

With one last kiss, and one last look, he left me in the kitchen.

I grabbed my phone to text Aviva to ask if she could pick me up on her way to the game.

My phone rang. I glanced at it.

LOML.

I swiped it open and lifted it to my ear.

"Mom? Why—"

But it wasn't my mom who answered. Instead, a man's deep, scratchy voice, one I sometimes heard in my nightmares, responded.

"Oh, Tovah. Just the person I was hoping to speak to," said Abe Silver.

For a moment, I forgot how to breathe.

"Don't hang up," he said. "Your mother wants to talk to you."

At least that meant she was alive.

"Tovah," she said, sounding desperate. "Don't listen to him. Get out, get somewhere safe. Don't come—" her words cut off on a scream.

A scream that continued. And continued.

"There you go. She's alive and...well, maybe not well. But alive. For now," Abe said when he got back on the phone. I could still hear her screaming. Every part of my body rejected this reality, what was happening. Her screams shattered my heart, which raced as I tried to figure out what to do.

"Don't you dare hurt her. Stop it," I seethed into the phone.

"That's really up to you, Ms. Lewis. See, I once had a second in command who mattered a great deal to me. I found him dead the same night my wife was killed. And his wife and stepdaughter? Nowhere in sight. I've been searching for both of you for some time now. It was quite fortunate that my son was the one to find you. When he had my daughter look into you, she called a PI, who then reported it to me."

"Get to the point," I growled. I could still hear my mother screaming, the sound so high-pitched and desperate.

He sighed. "Always in such a hurry, your generation. I'll tell you what—come to the compound and I'll stop hurting your mother."

"And you'll let her go?" I asked. I was already throwing clothes on and grabbing my bag.

"Maybe. Maybe not. But it's your best option, isn't it? It should take four hours to get from Gehenom to our part of Brooklyn, four and a half if there's bad traffic. Five hours, and she'll be dead."

Oh god, that was barely enough time. I wanted to hurl.

"Oh, and Tovah?" he added, as if it was an afterthought. "Don't tell my son, or I *will* kill her now. After all, it'll spoil the surprise." His voice going hard, he said. "You have five hours. Don't be late."

He hung up. I fought not to hurl at the thought of my mother's suffering. I didn't have goddamned time to puke. I needed to get the hell out of here and find a car and—

I immediately called Sebastian. "I need your car," I told him the second he picked up.

"Why?" he asked, alert and concerned.

"Because Abe Silver has my mom."

"Fuck."

I didn't bother to agree. "I need your car."

"It's yours," he said immediately. "Where are you?"

I gave him Isaac's address.

"I'll be there in five minutes. But Tovah, I'm coming with you."

"No, you aren't," I told him firmly. "I don't know what he'll do if I show up with backup. It's better if I go alone."

"Absolutely not," he began, but I cut him off.

"Sebastian, she was *screaming* in pain. He was hurting her. The man is a sociopath, and I'm not taking that risk."

"And what's to say either of you get out of there alive?"

I exhaled. "Nothing. But she won't survive if I don't go."

"Got it. On my way," he said, and hung up.

Rushing downstairs, I grabbed my shoes, lacing them up, and ran outside, just as Sebastian pulled to a stop in his Maserati. Running down the steps to the driveway, I opened the driver's side door.

"I still don't like letting you go alone," he said.

"No time."

He nodded, climbing out of the car and handing me the key fob.

"Thank you, Sebastian." On impulse, I hugged him.

"Stay as safe as you can," he said, when he released me, his eyes troubled, and I knew in his mind, this was goodbye.

And it very well might be.

49

Isaac

I was playing like shit, and I knew it.

But where the hell was she?

Cortland was up, 3:0. As hard as I tried, I couldn't focus. All I could see, all I could hear, was Tovah crying under the shower spray as I laid into her. Had she lied to me? Changed her mind? Was she running away, even now? If so, I'd deserve it—even if I'd kidnap her back, if I had to.

Jack kept passing me the puck, and I kept missing it. Finally, he gave up on me, shoving into me and growling, "Get your damn head in the game," before shooting the puck into the goal himself.

But seconds before it passed the goalie and hit the net, the horn sounded.

Second period was over.

Dejected and pissed, our team headed into the guest locker room.

The moment I got inside, the whole team turned on me.

"What the fuck, Jones? What has gotten into you?" Nick McPherson shouted, shoving me against one of the lockers.

Fuck that.

I shoved him back, raising my hand to deck him, when I was being dragged away.

Judah and Levi shoved me down on the bench, holding me there. Jack got in my face.

"What the hell are you doing out there, asshole? And where is Tovah?"

"That's what I want to fucking know," I growled, making my way over to the locker where my bag—and phone—was. I needed to see her location for myself, know she was at least safe, even if she was leaving me.

Judah snorted. "Of course. Girl trouble."

Coach slammed into the locker room, rounding on me. "Jones, I don't know what's going on with you, but you're playing like you can't even stay on your skates."

"Girl trouble," Judah offered.

"I don't goddamned care what kind of trouble it is. We look like clowns out there, and it's because of you. I'm benching you for the rest of the game. Gavin, you're up," he said to my backup.

"Oh, shit, sir, yes sir," Gavin said, jumping to his feet and saluting like a complete dipshit. I would've laughed, if I wasn't such a damn mess.

"See you out on the ice," Coach said, and slammed back out of the locker room, probably to give interviews and try to explain why I was playing like a kid who'd just learned how to skate.

"Alright, fucker. Talk. Tell us what's going on," Asher, who'd been watching the whole thing, said. "And if you hurt Tovah, I'm going to take my blade to your neck."

I glared at him, but then slumped, covering my face. I *had* hurt her. Maybe she wasn't over it after all.

"I thought we worked our shit out, but then why is she not here?" I groaned into my hands.

Jack raised a hand. "Hang on. I know what it's like to fuck up with a woman."

Asher grunted.

"Isaac, we can't help you if you don't tell us what's going on," Jack said, his tone calmer.

Sighing, I did exactly that.

I told them everything. My obsession with Tovah from the day we'd met, the monster I'd try to banish by hating her. Stalking her for months, the interview, her blackmailing me and me blackmailing her back. Fucking her. Falling for her. And then the fallout over the past few days, ending with the blow-up in the shower this morning, and the make-up after. I even told them about me, how I was secretly crown prince of the Silver dynasty, and I'd been hiding from it for years so I could play hockey and pretend my violent inheritance wasn't real.

When I finished, Judah clapped.

"What the fuck man?" I said.

"I didn't think anyone could make more of a mess than Jack did with Aviva. But you deserve a crown for this shit." Judah shook his head.

Asher was stuck on something else. "You're Abe Silver's son?"

I nodded, watching him warily.

He brushed a hand over his head. "I guess that makes us mortal enemies."

"Guess so," I said.

He put out a hand, and after a moment, I shook it.

"Fortunately," he said, "I have no contact with that part of the family, so you're good."

Judah shook his head again. "It's like we've been living *The Prince and Me*, except it's *The Mafia Prince and Me*," he said.

Levi, however, didn't say anything. He hadn't looked surprised, either.

"You knew," I guessed.

He shrugged. "I know more than any of you realize."

I didn't want to touch that.

"How did you leave things with her?" Jack asked. He already knew who I was, and didn't care.

"We were fine," I said. "We worked our shit out."

"So then where the hell is she?" Judah asked logically.

Levi smacked him on the head. "That's what he's trying to figure out."

Grabbing my phone out of my bag, I pulled up the tracker app. Tovah's phone was still at home, thank fuck.

But a bad feeling made my scalp tingle, so I pulled open the other tracker app—the one that was tied to the tracker I'd put in her armpit.

The dot that showed her location was *not* at home. It was moving down I-278 East. Headed toward Ocean Parkway.

Toward Flatbush, Brooklyn.

No.

There was no fucking way.

But I couldn't deny that she was headed in the direction of my childhood home in Brooklyn. Where my family lived.

Without a thought, I unlaced my skates, leaving them on the floor as I slid on my sneakers, not even bothering to change back into street clothes. I was going to pay for this. I'd be benched for sure, maybe for the rest of the season, maybe kicked off the team.

I didn't fucking care. All I cared about was getting to Tovah.

I scrolled through my phone until I found my father's number and hit the call button as I dressed.

He picked up after three rings.

"Do you know what today is, son?" he asked.

His voice sounded hoarse, like he was in pain, but I didn't have the time to wonder why.

"Why the fuck is my girlfriend headed to the house?" I asked.

"Ah, so you admit you have a girlfriend now. Tovah Lewis, is it? I've spent some time getting acquainted with her mother..."

Which explained why Tovah was headed in that direction. How the hell she'd gotten her car back, I had no idea. Nor did I care at this damn moment.

"Don't you fucking touch her. Don't you fucking touch either of them, or there will be hell to pay."

My father chuckled, the laugh making the hair on my neck stand up. "I don't think you're in the position to be giving orders, son. At least not yet."

Seething, I forced out, "What do you fucking want."

"Ah," he said. "I'd like you here for Shabbos dinner. We'll have some special guests, and it's in your best interest to attend. Sundown is at seven. Don't be late."

He hung up before I could say anything else.

"What the fuck just happened?" Judah said, and the guys crowded around me.

"What's going on?" Asher asked.

I couldn't even respond. My whole body felt like it was on fire. The last time I'd felt fear like this was when I'd watched my mom's car get shot up and seen her body. I'd never thought I'd feel fear like this again, because I never thought I'd care again.

My father had her. Was doing god knew what to her. She might not even be alive.

I could've lost her. Could lose her still. She was mine, and we'd finally worked our shit out, and my father was trying to *take her from me.* And knowing Abe Silver, he would do everything in his power to succeed. My body felt like it was tearing itself apart.

I didn't even realize what I was doing until the pain drove through my hand and up my arm.

I'd punched in one of the lockers. There was a huge fucking dent, and my hand was bleeding.

"Holy fuck," Judah exploded. "Isaac, you need to breathe. Breathe."

"What I need is to get the fuck out of here. My dad has Tovah. I don't know how much time she has left before—"

I punched the locker again, barely registering the pain.

"Isaac, this isn't helping," Jack said. "Get your shit together. She needs you."

I shook my head, clearing it. He was right. There was no time for emotion.

"Go," Lawson said. "We'll cover for you."

But was there time? It would take four hours to get to Brooklyn. My father could do anything in that time.

I tried my sister's phone, but it rang and rang.

I texted her.

> Call me. I need you.

I ran out of the locker room, keys in hand. I had no idea what tonight would look like, or what was happening to the woman I loved.

I only knew one thing.

If my father had touched a single hair on her goddamned head, it didn't matter who he was to me, or that I'd never wanted to become a murderer.

Because I would kill him.

50

Tovah

Abe Silver had Isaac's eyes. They were the same brown, the same shape. But where Isaac's eyes could be warm, or cold, depending on his emotions, there was something off with Abe's. I didn't remember him that way; when I was young, he'd been scary, but he'd seemed sane. Not so much now.

He was waiting in the foyer when I arrived. I'd broken a million traffic laws on I-81 South to get here, and then a million more in the city itself, but I'd made it in under four hours.

"Impressive timing," Abe said when he opened the door. "I like punctuality."

I ignored his attempt at cordiality. "Where's my mom?"

"Oh, don't you worry about that," he said easily. "You'll be joining her promptly. But first, I'd like to talk to you about my son."

"And I'd like to see how my mother's doing." I responded

in the same easy tone, even if inwardly, I wanted to punch this asshole in the balls.

His easy tone disappeared. "Let me explain something to you. You are not in control here, I am. You have no power, no leverage, no nothing. I will tell you what to do, and you will do it, understand me?"

His son had said something similar to me, once. I was sick of men thinking they were in control, thinking they could say jump and I'd say how high. In that moment I decided that I wasn't only getting my mom out of here alive, I was getting myself out, too.

But Abe would die.

I fingered the blade in my pocket. Isaac shaved with a straight razor, and I'd pocketed one before I'd left.

After all, I'd killed a tyrannical asshole once, and I'd been a young kid.

I was bigger now, stronger, smarter.

I could do it again.

I didn't say anything though, other than, "after you," and followed him through the hallway into the sitting room, which looked exactly the same as it had when I was young.

"Take a seat," he said, all affability and cordiality again. Warily, I sat in a white armchair my mother had probably dusted and spot cleaned multiple times.

My mother. She was somewhere on the compound, and I had to get to her.

He joined me in the opposite armchair, taking a seat and crossing his leg over his knee.

"Tovah, my son is a man at war with himself. Part of him is ruthless, ambitious, and will do anything for the bottom line, whatever that may be. I'm sure he'd even kill for it." He laughed. "But the other part of him? It resists it. That's why he's always so charming, so kind, so gracious to fans. He's too much like his mother that way. She always hated the violence in our world, too. Isaac tells himself he can't fall prey to it, that if he embraces his dark side, he'll lose himself. He doesn't realize he's already found an outlet for it in hockey."

Abe shook his head. "No, he doesn't see it. But it's important he...make peace with his dark side, because one day he'll pick up the mantle and take his place as the head of this family, and he'll need to use that violence and ruthlessness to protect this family and everything we've been building for two generations."

I already knew this. Most of it. Isaac had told me parts, and the other parts I'd seen for myself.

"The problem, you see," Abe continued, clearly not caring at my lack of participation, "is that Isaac is grasping the softer side of his persona too tightly. His caring, his concern, his protectiveness. And while he's grown darker, and I do believe I have you to thank for that, he also has too much keeping him tethered to the light. I need to cut that string, so he fully embraces his role in this family."

He eyed me up and down, and my skin crawled. It wasn't sexual, it was worse. It was like he could see my corpse already.

"That string, Tovah, is you. And it's time for me to cut it. I'm delighted because it does kill two birds with one stone, since you and your mother took someone very important from me. Your stepfather, you see, was like a brother. And while I know your mother was the one who killed him, you were an accessory to the crime and should be punished as such."

He rose. I rose, too.

"You don't know your son," I told him. "He is fiercely

loving; he is obsessively caring. He's protective. He's the best man I know."

"Then you clearly haven't known good men."

"I didn't. But I do, now."

The moment stretched between us, and then he finally nodded, acknowledging it, before changing the subject.

"Now, would you like to see your mother?"

It was so tempting, to get close and slide the blade across his neck. But I had no idea where my mother was, and there were probably armed soldiers everywhere. No, I needed to wait for the right moment.

I followed Abe out of the house, down a path in a huge garden that I sometimes saw in my dreams. I'd played out here with Isaac, played "he loves me, he loves me not" with dandelions, and hid from my stepfather. There was no time for memory lane, though, when he stopped in front of a large building that looked like a garage.

A silent garage.

"In here," he said.

I hesitated on the threshold. I had no idea what waited for me in there. It may not even be my mother. Most likely what waited for me was excruciating pain, maybe even the death Abe had threatened earlier.

But I had to find my mother. Had to save her.

Squaring my shoulders, I opened the door.

It was a torture chamber.

Sharp implements everywhere. Hooks hanging from the ceiling. Dried blood.

And my mother, at the center of the room, tied to a chair. Bruises covered her face, her body, and there was blood around her mouth.

She cried out as soon as she saw me. "Tovahleh, why are you here? Run!"

The man beside her cuffed her ear, and she yelped from the pain.

I took a step forward, only for Abe to stop me.

"Not so fast," he scolded.

"Let her go. What will it take Abe?" I spoke through clenched teeth, fingering the blade in my pocket. "What will it take to let her go?"

He tsked. "That was never our deal. I'll tell you what though, I won't kill her, if you're a good girl and go sit in the chair next to her. I have no need to kill either of you for now. I need to make sure my son sees it."

"What makes you think he won't kill you?" I asked him.

A strange look appeared in Abe's eyes. "A father's job is to sacrifice for his children."

Oh god, he was insane.

But he was also distracted enough for me to do what I needed to do next. I pulled the blade out of my pocket...

"You know what, I won't kill your mother," he mused. "Instead, I'll make the murderous cunt live with the grief. That's a much better punish—"

He didn't finish the sentence, because I'd reached out and sliced his throat with the blade.

Blood appeared, and he staggered backward.

For a moment, triumph and hope bubbled in me, effervescent—and possibly naïve. Had I solved our problems? If I could get mom and I out of here, would we finally be free?

But things were happening too quickly to indulge in that thought, even for a second. Especially when the man near my mother yelled and charged me. Charged with adrenaline and possibly the help of angels, I ducked below his arm and raced over to my mother.

Men filled the torture garage, crowding around Abe and barking orders at each other as they tried to staunch the bleeding. I wanted him dead. But I couldn't finish the job, not when my mother was still tied to a chair and the easiest next target.

Running to her, my chest burning from fear, I worked on the knots keeping her trapped. The rope had been tied to tight, and there were red marks on her skin. I ignored them, trying to loosen the knots themselves. The rough rope burned my hands, rubbing my palms and fingers raw as I tried to find a slack spot to loosen them.

"Tovah, *run*," my mother coughed.

I shook my head, not bothering to reply to such a ridiculous request.

"Tovah," she insisted. "I didn't live this life to lose you. *Go.*"

"No! I'm not leaving you," I insisted, finally getting one knot undone and starting on the other.

And then there was a big hand squeezing my throat, grinding bones and skin. I couldn't breathe. I was lifted into the air and dragged backward, my toes dragging on the ground.

I tried to scrabble against the floor, struggling to free myself, but I was no match for the stranger's strength.

An unfamiliar voice whispered in my ear, "Oh, you shouldn't have done that, little girl. No one touches the boss. Now we're going to play."

He squeezed my throat harder, choking me so hard my vision swam.

The last thing I heard was my mother screaming my name.

And then everything went dark.

51

Isaac

Three and a half hours later, I pulled up to the gates to our family compound. I'd driven like a maniac, and it was by sheer luck that I hadn't been pulled over. At one point, my father had called me. I'd answered immediately, and the sound of Tovah's helpless screaming would haunt me for the rest of my life.

Especially when she screamed my name.

Me. I had done this. I had made the mistake of leaving her alone for even a second.

If she didn't survive, neither would I.

Tick tock, son, my father had said. *The sun is beginning to set.*

So I shoved my foot down on the gas pedal as hard as I could. Even though it still didn't feel fast enough.

But I was finally here. The guard waved me in, and I drove through onto the paved brick driveway, parking in front of the house. I hadn't been home in months, not since the High Holidays. I used hockey as an excuse, but really, I didn't want to see my asshole father.

But I had no choice.

Leaning over, I grabbed the gun out of the glove compartment and tucked it into my hockey pants. I'd stopped on the way to purchase it from one of my sister's friends. I'd never owned one. Never wanted to use one. I didn't care anymore. I'd sell my very soul to the devil if it meant Tovah was safe and free.

Getting out of the car, I shut the door and jogged up to the front door, ringing the doorbell. My father didn't let us have keys, too paranoid that one of us might lose them and someone could get in. Instead, he kept maids and butlers on rotation 24/7 so there was always someone to answer the door.

Olga, one of the many housekeepers, was the one to open it.

"Oh, Isaac! You're here." She twisted her hands in her pristine white apron, fretting over something. "Your father is waiting for you in the dining room. He won't be pleased about what you're wearing, but...oh, go in. There are... guests."

Guests. Plural.

Tovah was safe. For now.

I stretched out my hand to stop the shaking, heading in the direction of the dining room. Each step felt necessary; each step felt like it tightened the noose that was always around my neck. But I forced myself forward.

And froze in the doorway.

My father sat at the head of the table, a white gauze bandage on his neck.

My sister Liza sat next to my brother Reuben, their backs to me. On the other side of the table, my brothers

Sasha and Jordan sat. Everyone's eyes, however, were on the two women at the foot of the table.

I stared at Tovah. She was next to an older woman who looked a bit like her. Tovah's mother. One of my father's men stood behind Tovah's mother, holding a gun to her head.

In the middle of the table, the Shabbat candles burned. Everyone's plates were full, but no one was eating. Except of course, my father, who was chewing on brisket like there was not a worry in the world—until I saw him wince and touch a hand to his throat.

I split my attention between him—the bomb ready to go off at any moment—and Tovah, who sat there, alive.

Alive.

I almost fell to my knees from relief, until I looked more closely at her.

She was covered in bruises. Her arms, her face. She had a black eye, and her cheek was swollen. Blood had dried on a cut under her chin.

Those screams.

They'd hurt her.

He'd hurt her.

"Which one did it?" I asked her.

"Hello, Isaac, it's nice to see you," my father said, voice thick with pain. "Thank you for joining us for Shabbat dinner." He tsked. "But wearing your hockey gear? That's inappropriate."

I ignored him, my eyes on Tovah. "Which one?"

Tovah shook her head. "Isaac, you shouldn't be here," she said. "This place is bad for you."

Bullshit.

"Which. One," I asked, gritting my teeth.

It was her mother who pointed at one of my father's

soldiers standing in the corner, sipping a whiskey without a care in the world.

I didn't hesitate or consider the fact that I'd never wanted to kill. Just pulled the gun out of my pants, lifted it and pulled the trigger.

A moment later, blood bloomed in the middle of the man's head and he slumped against the wall behind him, sliding to the ground, dead.

"Anyone else?" I asked Tovah's mother.

"No," she said.

The man behind her cocked his gun.

I shot him, too.

My father pushed back from the table and rose to his feet. I expected him to call for more guards, but instead he clapped.

"Oh, Isaac, my boy. My son. I always hoped you had it in you. I worried you were too much like your mother, but you do take after me, don't you?"

"Drop the bullshit," I growled. "You're going to let both of these women go."

"Now, why would I do that, when we're having a nice family dinner and getting to know each other?" He gestured at Reuben and Jordan, who sat, shoulders stiff, not willing to intercede, the cowardly bastards. Sasha was slumped sideways in his chair, looking bored with all of us.

Liza, for her part, caught my eye and shook her head. She didn't have to say what she was thinking.

Don't. Don't aggravate him further. Don't escalate this.

"Sit, Isaac," my father said, patting the empty chair next to him.

Fuck that. Not when my girl wasn't safe.

I moved toward Tovah.

Another one of my father's men lifted a gun and shoved it against her temple.

She froze.

So did I.

"*Sit*," My father repeated.

I sat.

"And I'm going to ask for you to hand over the gun. We don't bring weapons to Shabbat dinner—it's supposed to be a time of rest, of peace."

Sasha rolled his eyes. "If that's the case, why do your peaceful henchmen all have Rugers in hand?"

"Sasha," Liza hissed, her eyes still on me. "Drop it."

Sasha shrugged.

"Dad's never going to give you control of the 'family business,' sister dearest," he said. "I fear bossing us around is going to get you nowhere."

"I'm the oldest," Liza began.

My father glared at my siblings, taking his attention off me for a moment. I contemplated shooting the man holding the gun to Tovah's head, but I couldn't guarantee her safety.

"Children. Not at dinner," he admonished, before his eyes flitted back to me. "Isaac, whatever you're thinking, I promise it won't end well for her. Gun. Please."

I passed him the gun, forcing myself to release my grip on it.

Placing it next to him, so it faced out, my father picked back up his knife and carefully sliced off a bit of brisket as he spoke. The smell of brisket usually made me salivate. Now, with Tovah in so much danger, the cooked, dead flesh made my stomach roil.

"You see, Isaac, there are things you *don't* know about your girlfriend here. I'm disappointed in you, by the way.

Eliana is such a good match for you. Not like this violent criminal," he said with disdain.

"Funny you of all people should call me that," Tovah said, sounding calmer than she should've with a gun pressing to her temple.

The way she slurred her words with pain made the monster in me rage. I wanted to let him out, but I couldn't. I had to be smart. Had to outthink my father.

My father, who scoffed at Tovah. "You know, Isaac, she tried to slit my throat? I was almost impressed. But she's not the girl for you. You need someone with a...cooler head," he finished, like he'd read my thoughts. He always had an uncanny ability to do that.

"What you don't know," he continued, "Is that Tovah here aided her mother in killing my second-in-command. You remember your uncle Mordy, don't you? He was my very dearest friend, and he died the same night as your mother. They found him keeled over at his kitchen table, over a half-eaten piece of cake." My father shook his head. "Such a loss. May his memory be a blessing."

I glanced at Tovah, and she didn't look away.

"Is it true?" I asked.

"Yes."

"Good," I said. "I'm glad you both protected yourselves."

She blinked, like she was surprised and relieved I didn't hold murder against her. All I cared about was that she'd lived.

And she'd live, now.

"I—" she began, but she was cut off when my father's man shoved the gun harder against her temple.

Love you, she'd been about to say.

I swallowed the monstrous growl, following my sister's

unspoken advice. Instead, I forced a pleasant smile on my face and faced my father.

"What do I need to do to make you lower those guns and let them go?"

The grin that took over his face was pained.

"Ah, yes. I have a bit of a laundry list, you see. First, you'll stop playing that silly stick game and focus on learning how this family operates. The second you graduate, you'll come home—and marry Eliana."

Once upon a time, these demands had been my biggest fears. Give up hockey. Take over the family business. Now, even though they all hurt—and the idea of marrying anyone but Tovah hurt most—they didn't matter. Nothing did.

Nothing but her. I'd sacrifice all my dreams, live all my nightmares, if it meant she got to live, period.

"Isaac, don't," Tovah tried to say.

"Done," I told my father. "Now let her go."

"I don't think so," he said. "I think I'll keep her around until I'm sure you won't renege. We don't break promises, Isaac. Remember that."

"You. Will. Let. Her. Go," I told him.

He chuckled. "Who are you, Moses? No. In fact, I think they're lucky. I loved Mordy deeply, and they took him from me. They should die for that. You know what?" he tapped his chin. "Maybe I'll kill the mother, and the daughter can grieve. I need my vengeance somehow. For him."

"No," Tovah said. "If you want your vengeance, take it from me."

"Tovah," I said sharply, at the same moment, her mother said, "Don't, please don't, honey."

But Tovah ignored both of us, instead lifting her gaze

and staring my father down. My heart began to beat so loud it could've shaken the floorboards.

"I remember that day," she began. "I remember when we mixed the poison into the cake. Red velvet, my stepfather's favorite. But see, it wasn't my mother who killed him, because I was the one who served it to him. I was the one who made sure he ate *every single bite*," she enunciated. "And I was the one who watched, with relief, with happiness, when that bastard keeled over on the table and we were finally free. So Abe, you can have your vengeance, but you'll want to take it against *me*. Because *I'm* the one who killed him."

52

Isaac

What happened next happened fast, too fast.

My father's face turned red.

He grabbed my gun from the table, and stood, cocking it and aiming it at Tovah.

I stood, too, turning to him, my arms reaching out to stop him.

My chair crashed to the floor.

"An eye for an eye," he said.

And pulled the trigger.

It happened too fast.

53

Isaac

In that moment, everyone else disappeared. My siblings, her mom...it was like my father, Tovah, and I were the only ones in the room.

I launched myself at my father as he pulled the trigger, knocking him out of his chair and onto the floor.

The shot went wide, the bullet hitting the window behind Tovah. Glass shattered, high pitched and eerily musical.

"You fucking shot at her?!" I'd hated my father for years, for causing my mother's death and trapping me in a life I hated. But I'd never, ever felt rage like this toward him before. I'd never felt this kind of rage toward anyone, not even myself.

He struggled against me on the floor, gun still in his hand. I reared back and punched him square in the throat—right above his bandage.

"Don't you ever—" I began.

He choked, eyes bulging. Blood leaked, staining the

bandage and my knuckles. An inhuman satisfaction filled me.

So I punched him again.

"Fucking—"

And again.

"Hurt—"

And again.

"Her—"

He coughed over and over, choking on blood and his own sins, as my monster unleashed his unholy anger on him. My father fought to free his hand, but I just kept whaling on him.

"You fucking asshole, you've done so many horrible things, and I've accepted all of them. Would've let you get away with this shit. Until you tried to take the woman I love from me."

"Isaac!" Tovah yelled from across the table. A warning.

I wasn't fast enough. My dad raised the gun he was still holding and pistol-whipped me with it. Pain shot through my head, turning my vision grey. Holding my head in my hands, I rolled off him, and he crawled away and clambered up the chair until he was standing.

As my vision cleared, I saw him aim the gun again.

"This is the man you were always supposed to be, but your loyalty is in the wrong place," he croaked.

"I'm not a man, dad. I'm a monster," I slurred. Dizzy, woozy, and sick, I stumbled to my feet and launched myself at him again, this time grabbing him from behind. We grappled for control of the gun, my hand slippery from his blood, his own hand shaky from the pain I'd inflicted on him.

Tovah was still yelling my name, but I couldn't concentrate on her. I needed the gun. Needed her safe. Needed this nightmare to end. Because everything I feared was happening; loving someone only for her life to be at risk because of my family.

With a surge of energy, I grabbed the gun, but I couldn't get it out of my father's hand. The most I could do was turn his wrist around, so the gun was pressed against his chest.

All it would take was me pulling the trigger, and he'd be dead.

But I was behind him, holding him in place with my arm locked around his neck. I'd learned how guns and bullets worked at a young age. If I shot a bullet into his chest, there was a 70-30 chance it would pass through his body—directly into my heart.

The world slowed back down in that moment, as my father tried to turn the gun back around.

If I shot him, and I miraculously didn't die, I'd be forced to take on a life I loathed.

If I shot him, I'd probably die.

But if I didn't shoot him...

...I lost everything that mattered. Because she was everything.

Tovah was on her feet now, my father's man still pressing a gun against her skull.

"Lower the gun," I told the man. "Or I shoot him."

"Ignore him," my father said. "Kill her."

The man cocked his gun.

"You kill her, I kill him. I'm your next boss. Who do you think dies next? And not only you. I'll take out your entire family, everyone you love, until there's no one left," I told the man.

After a moment, he lowered his gun.

One problem solved. But my father still had a grip on the gun and battled me for control of the trigger.

Fuck.

No time.

"I love you, bashert," I said. "Any time with you, however short, was worth a million lifetimes."

Tovah's eyes widened as if she understood what I was planning.

"Isaac, don't, please," she begged.

"I love you, bashert," I said. "I'll see you in another life."

I stared into those big brown, terrified, loving eyes, committing them to my soul.

I pulled the trigger.

The shot was deafening. My father's scream even louder. A moment later, a fireball of pain tore through my heart—the one my bashert had brought back to life.

As my father slumped against me, as I fell to the ground, as my father's man raised his gun again and pointed it at me to finish the job, Tovah's voice rose above the cacophony, an enraged battle cry. She elbowed him in the side, knocking the gun out of his hands and running toward me—

—and then there was another hellish slap of a gun firing and a bullet hitting skin.

Through blurred eyes, I spotted a red spot bloom on Tovah's chest and grow.

Watched her fall to the ground.

Helpless, trapped under my father's body, I roared my rage and anguish, at a world that would accept my sacrifice and take her from me anyway.

With the little strength I had left, I shoved my father's body off mine and rolled over, crawling toward where she lay. Somewhere, far away, Liza was barking orders. Somewhere, far away, a woman was wailing.

When I reached Tovah, she was on her back, gasping for breath.

"Isaac, why—please, be okay, please be okay," she was trying to say.

And, "Tovah, bashert, you're okay, you're okay," I was saying back, or maybe thinking, I wasn't sure. Were those tears on my face? "Tovah, you're okay," I kept repeating, weakly reaching forward like I could staunch the blood seeping out of her chest, but I could barely move my arm.

Around us, people were moving, there was yelling, maybe someone called the family doctor, I wasn't sure. Everything disappeared again but the woman lying inches from me, as I tried to touch her and couldn't. Tried to hold her and couldn't. Tried to save her and couldn't.

I heard a choked laugh.

I strained my head to look over at my father. His legs were hidden by the table, but I could see his face.

"Now you have no choice," he said, with a strange gleam in his eye. "You'll take over this family. And I can join your mother."

With one final gurgle, he went still.

There was more yelling around us, guns being cocked. I ignored all of them. I didn't care about anything. What else mattered?

"Tovah, please," I begged. "You're okay. Be okay."

"I need you to live," she was crying, reaching an arm toward me. "Live, please. *Live*."

I reached out my arm and felt cooling skin as my fingertips touched hers. It was barely contact, but I grasped for it like it was the only lifeline left.

"Isaac," she whispered, her eyes shutting. "I'm so—"

And then she stopped breathing.

Someone roared with so much anguish, it shook the house. I didn't even realize it came from me.

Someone was trying to drag her away from me. I grasped

onto her hand, but the barely-there sensation of her fingers disappeared from under mine, like she'd never been there at all. Like she was already a ghost, and god, please fucking god, let her haunt me forever, let me not be alone for long.

Someone was pressing down on my chest, trying to staunch my bleeding, speaking to me. I didn't hear them.

I didn't pay attention to any of it. Didn't respond to any of it.

My hand was empty.

She was gone.

Tovah, my bashert, was gone.

My own eyesight was going, my heart was stuttering, I was losing the will to breathe. To live. My father had the right idea. I'd go with her.

My eyes shut and I saw her face in front of mine.

Live, she said.

Not without you.

And then finally, thankfully, it was quiet.

54

Tovah

When I was a freshman, I wrote an article about guns for *The Daily Queen*. I'd learned that in close quarters, there are about 1.5 seconds between the moment a gun fires and it hits its target.

A lot can happen in 1.5 seconds.

A lifetime can flash in front of your eyes in 1.5 seconds.

Or the same person, from a million different angles.

1.5 seconds.

1500 milliseconds.

1500 moments with Isaac, flashing in my mind, as I tried to grab his hand.

1500 moments, as he slipped away from me.

1500 moments, as I slipped away, too.

And then they were gone.

55

Isaac

Breathing fucking hurt.

Actually, everything fucking hurt. There was a vise gripping my head in its claws, and brick covering my face. And I clearly had been run over by a Zamboni, and then run over again for fun.

Where the fuck was I?

And more importantly—where was Tovah? My last memory was of her hand leaving mine.

Of her no longer breathing.

It was a struggle, but I finally managed to wrench my eyes open, only to spot my sister sitting on the edge of my hospital bed, a worried look on her face.

Tovah wasn't in sight.

"Oh, thank fucking god," Liza said, shutting her own eyes for a moment in what I assumed was relief. "I wasn't sure if you'd make it, and there was no one left to kill."

No one left. Which meant my father had died.

Good.

I tried to swallow, to speak, but the words were weak when I croaked, "Where the *fuck* is my girlfriend?"

Liza's face fell.

So did my heart.

"Liza, where is—"

"She's in surgery," she said quickly. "So were you, by the way. Marcus flew The Doctor and his team in to operate on both of you."

Marcus was Jack's billionaire half-brother, and The Doctor was one of his partners. No one knew his real name.

"It was touch and go with you. Luckily, the bullet didn't lodge itself in your heart. The Doc was able to repair the rest."

"And Tovah?"

"The bullet pierced her lung. Doc put her in a drug-induced coma, completed multiple blood transfusions, and has been trying to rebuild her lung for three days now. But he's not ready to close, and the risk of infection is high... Isaac, you need to prepare yourself for the worst."

No.

No.

"No," I said. "I'm not preparing myself for shit. Doc better save her, or I'll kill him."

Liza looked at me. "And how are you going to do that?"

"Dad's dead, right? I killed him. Last I checked, that made me the head of this family and the Silver organization, and I will use every goddamn bit of power we have to destroy that man if I don't get her back, alive and whole."

A bitter look flitted over my sister's face, disappearing quickly like it was never even there. I ignored it. "Now, take me to wherever Tovah's being operated on."

"You can't leave your bed, Isaac. You aren't recovered. At least let the other doctors come look at—"

"Take me to my fucking girlfriend right now," I roared at her, not caring that she was my sister.

Her eyes widened. "You *have* changed."

She was right. And even though I hated everything about who I'd had to become, and who I'd continue to become in the future as the new head of this family, if it meant protecting Tovah, it was worth it.

Sighing, she went to the corner of the room where there was a wheelchair.

"C'mon, little brother. Your ride awaits."

THE WHEELCHAIR RIDE DOWN THE HALLWAY WOULD HAVE BEEN disconcerting, if I'd had any attention to spare. My father's people treated me with a newfound respect, calling me "sir" and telling me how glad they were to see me. And when I had time, there were business things to—

"Not now," I growled, Dr. Dimples forgotten. My sister chuckled as she wheeled me past various doors in the family hospital.

Finally, we reached a set of locked doors, guarded by one of my father's men.

"Mr. Silver, sir," he startled when he saw us.

"Let us through," I told him.

"But she's in surgery—"

"It's okay, Ari. You can let us through," Liza interrupted, and with a look of utter loyalty on his face, he swiped his card, unlocking the doors for us.

Down another hallway, and we reached the operating room. I tried to stand, looking through the glass. Tovah was barely discernible on the operating table, surrounded by

The Doctor and other surgeons and nurses as they worked on her. Heart in my throat, I watched, praying to any deity that existed, bargaining—no, begging—that they save her. I'd give up anything, to have her sass me. To see that bright-colored hair and that bold smile. To smell lemon and sugar again.

But as the hours ticked by, and the doctors continued to work, my hope began to dwindle, and darkness hung over me like a permanent cloud. And through it all, a voice whispered in my head: *This is your fault, Isaac Silver. You knew better. You knew that loving you was signing a death warrant, but you were so selfish, you let her, anyway.*

"I can't live without her," I told my sister in a choked voice.

She placed a hand on my shoulder. "I know, Isaac."

"No, you don't understand. I will burn this world down to get her back. I will make a deal with the devil himself."

"We don't believe in the devil," she reminded me gently.

"I'll do it anyway."

The physical pain from my healing wound, my exhaustion—none of it compared to my fear of losing her, the weight that pressed down on me and made it hard to breathe. A life without her was unacceptable. I'd told her once that god himself couldn't keep her from me, and I meant it. I'd find her and drag her back, kicking and screaming—and if I couldn't, I'd go wherever she went.

"I don't like the look in your eyes," Liza murmured.

"You shouldn't," I admitted.

Because if Tovah died, my heart would die with her—for good.

At that moment, The Doctor glanced up, and our eyes met.

And he lifted his hand...

...and gave me a thumbs up, and the only smile I'd ever seen on his face.

And thank fucking god, suddenly, I could breathe again. I was still in charge of this goddamned family. I had to deal with a life I'd never wanted, earlier than planned. I'd have to figure out breaking off this fucking engagement and figure out how to keep Tovah safe—even if it meant not having her with me. But none of it mattered right now.

Because she was still breathing. As long as she breathed, the rest of this shit was just annoying details.

56

Tovah

Something beeped. My head pounded in time with the incessant sound.

Where was I?

I struggled to open my eyes; they were so heavy. Finally, on the third try, I cracked them open.

"Oh my god, she's awake!" an unfamiliar woman's voice said. "I'll go get the doctor."

I heard a door open and then shut.

"Oh, honey." My vision swam, but when it settled, my mother was in front of me.

She gripped my hand.

"You've been out for days," she said. "I thought I'd lost you. Oh thank god, you're okay."

My last memories came back to me. Shabbat dinner at the Silvers, guns trained on me and my mother. The deal Isaac and his father made. His father threatening to kill my mother—and me confessing that I'd been the one to murder my stepfather.

Abe trying to shoot me.

Isaac fighting him for the gun.

Isaac shooting his father, knowing the bullet would go through him, too.

Isaac, falling to the ground.

Knocking the gun out of the guard's hand and running to Isaac.

And then the gunshot, the pain, and Isaac's eyes on mine as everything faded to black.

Isaac.

Only my mother was in the room with me.

Where was Isaac?

"Where is he?" I asked my mom. "Where's Isaac? Is he okay? Did he make it? Is he—"

I could barely voice my fears out loud.

She laughed again. "He's fine. He didn't leave the room for days, except, I hope, to use the toilet at some point. His brothers finally dragged him out of here so he could shower." She lowered her voice in a false whisper. "He was beginning to stink."

"Oh," I said, settling into the bed I was lying on, relief allowing my strained muscles to relax.

"Oh," she mimicked. "You've been hiding things from me. I'll admit, I'm...concerned about your involvement with the next head of the Silver family. I don't want you anywhere near their violence or criminal activity. But he does seem to truly care about you, and wants to protect you, and I do like that."

"Mom, I think—" I began, before I could finish the sentence the door slammed opened. A tall man in a white doctor's coat entered the room, Isaac right on his heels.

The man gave me the chills. Isaac did not seem concerned.

"— a second to check her over," the doctor was saying.

"Fuck that." Isaac moved around him, crossing with long strides toward the bed and pulling an IV stand behind him. He stopped, leaning down and pressing a hard, possessive kiss to my lips.

"Ow," I complained.

"Shit." He lifted his head, pressing a softer, gentler kiss to my forehead. "I just—fuck, Tovah. I thought I'd lost you. I thought you were gone. I thought—"

"We know what you thought," my mom said, dryly. "You haunted the halls of this hospital while she was recovering and yelled at so many doctors, I'm surprised they didn't kick you out."

Isaac shrugged. "It worked, didn't it? Your daughter's alive, and safe." He looked at me. "And you're going to *stay* alive and safe." A look passed over his face, one I couldn't read. It scared me a little.

"You're okay," he said again, kissing my forehead.

"I'll be the judge of that," the doctor said. "If you'll give me some space, sir."

Sir. Why was he calling him sir?

And then it came back to me.

If Abe Silver was dead, that meant Isaac was now in charge of the family.

The exact opposite of everything he'd ever wanted.

"Isaac," I said urgently, tugging on his wrist. "I'm so sorry. This is all my fault, I—"

"Quiet," he ordered, kissing me again. "Nothing's your fault. There's nothing for you to be sorry for."

"Sir," the doctor repeated.

He moved out of the way, still hovering, as the doctor checked my vitals, looking me over.

"You're lucky," he said, when he was done. "Incredibly

lucky. The bullet missed your heart by only a few inches and almost destroyed your lung. And then you were in surgery for days, and there could've been a terrible infection, or you could've gotten stuck in the coma I induced. It's a miracle you pulled through. You're going to have quite the scar, and you'll need bedrest for weeks and physical therapy, but you'll be okay."

He straightened, glancing at Isaac. "Sir, I recommend no...strenuous activities for the next month. Including that kiss you greeted her with." He smiled slightly. "But then you should be fine to...proceed as normal."

That same strange look flitted across Isaac's face, here, then gone.

"Marcus says you owe him a favor for this," the man said.

"Got it, Doc," Isaac said, and with one peculiar look at me, the doctor left.

Once he was gone, Isaac glanced at my mom. "Hana, can I have a minute alone with your daughter?"

She rose. "Of course." Kissing my cheek, she said, "I'll be right outside."

Alone, Isaac, sat on the bed, holding my hand carefully. "Tovah, I don't know where to start. I've fucked up, from the beginning. Didn't trust you, treated you horribly. Put you through hell I wouldn't wish on my worst enemy. I said awful, horrible things to you, words I'll always regret, because I was so—"

I interrupted him. "You were a fucking asshole."

"I know," he said. "I was terrified about what it meant that I couldn't control myself around you, and then later, what it meant to love you. I was broken at the possibility that I couldn't keep you, so I took it out on you. It was dick behavior after dick behavior, and I'm going to do everything in my power to make it up to you. For every single horrible thing I've done. For the rest of my life. I promise."

What it meant to love you.

He loved me.

He'd said it before, but I'd never been able to truly believe it. Not until now.

"The things you went through," he swallowed, continuing. "If you hadn't killed your stepfather, I'd kill him right now, slowly and painfully. I want to bring him back to life just to rip him apart, piece by little piece."

My eyes were wet. My throat, still dry, stung from the tears.

"Oh, god, bashert, don't cry," he said. "I hate when you cry. I want to tear the world apart and rebuild it, bit by bit, into something that will never make you cry."

"I'm okay," I told him. "I never thought I'd have someone want to protect me like this. Who would care so much. It feels overwhelming."

He nodded, not speaking.

"I love you, too, you know?" I said. "So much. I didn't know it was possible to feel this way about anyone."

"Like you suddenly have a heart when you never think you did, and that it exists outside of your chest now, and you want to wrap it in bubble wrap and put it in an indestructible glass case and surround it by barbed wire so no one can get near it or ever hurt it?" he asked, his eyes troubled.

I squeezed his hand and laughed a little. "I mean, maybe not that exact imagery, but something like that."

"Then I feel the same way. I love you, bashert. I'm going to give you the life you deserve."

Leaning over, he kissed me again, sweetly, gently, protectively, like I was the most wonderful, important thing in the world to him. There was a desperation in his kiss, the way his mouth moved on mine, like he was memorizing my lips and my taste.

Like this is the last time.

But why would I think that?

Finally, he pulled away.

"I'm giving you the life you deserve, Tovah. Starting with letting you go."

"Isaac, what are you talking about?" I asked, my heart starting to beat faster in fear.

He sat up, rising off the bed. "You told me how much you wanted freedom; you wanted to live a life without looking over your shoulder. But I can't give you that, not if you're with me. Now that my father is dead, I'm in charge of the family. The whole business. And it's not safe for you. It'll *never* be safe for you. You almost died next to me, and I couldn't save you. I refuse to let anything to happen to you. I *refuse* to be the cause of your death. And if you stay with me, if I let you love me, if we spend the rest of our lives together, you will end up dying. Someone will take you from me, and I can't live with that. So I have to let you go."

"What kind of White Fang bullshit is this?" I asked furiously, but behind my anger, my heart was beginning to break.

"It's not bullshit," he said emphatically. "If I do one good thing with my life, before I get fully entrenched in the darkness, before I become my father, it'll be this."

"Isaac," I reached for his hand, but he was already backing away from the bed. "I'm sorry. I never should have told you that you were like your father. You're *nothing* like him. You are *nothing* like that man. He was soulless, heartless, dead inside long before you killed him for me. Don't do this."

He closed his eyes, like it hurt to look at me. "I'm already becoming my father. It's the sacrifice I made, to save you—and I'd do it a million times over."

"You aren't saving me, Isaac," I said, devastation, anger, and shock all fighting each other as I felt myself falling off the side of a cliff. I thought we were about to have everything, and he'd ripped it all right out from under me. "You're letting your fear control you."

When he opened his eyes, they were as broken as I felt. Worse, the light in them looked like it was dying. Like he *was* becoming his father.

Never. I'd never let him.

He turned to go.

Furious, I sat up, trying to rip the IV out of my arm.

"Don't you fucking leave, Isaac Silver. I swear to god, I will follow you and I will torment you, every second of every day, to make you pay for doing this to us."

He whipped back around. "You think I'm not already tormented? You think anything you can do will hurt more than letting you go? It's going to kill me, Tovah. It's killing me *now*. The monster in me wants to keep you, cuffed to my wrist forever, but I'm not giving into him this time. I promised that I'd atone for everything I've done to hurt you, and this is me doing it. I transferred the deed to the house in your name. You and your mom can live there. I'm going to give you everything else you ever dreamed about, too."

"But what if what I dreamed about is you?"

He shook his head, like he wanted, no, *needed* to reject my words. "You'll finish up school," he continued. "You'll go on to be a journalist and do brilliant, incredible things with your life. And you and your mom will be free of the Silvers and all the ways we've hurt you over the years. That's what I want for you. To be safe, and happy, and *free*. Be happy, bashert. And know that I will never, ever stop loving you."

And with that, he left the room, ignoring the way I cried his name.

And even though I kept crying it, he didn't come back.

57

Isaac

Given my pacifist nature during hockey games, I'd never known a very basic fact—getting blood out of fabric was practically impossible.

I glanced with an almost numb disdain at the blood stains on my white button-down as I beat the shit out of the traitor tied to the cement wall in front of me. Every punch, every kick, pulled on the skin on my back and chest. I was still healing from the gunshot, and moving hurt.

Good. It should fucking hurt. Everything should hurt.

I was grateful to my father for making the garage a good spot to torture people, even if looking at it reminded me of Tovah's screams that terrible day.

The man in front of me was worse for wear—way worse. Blood poured down his face, and his nose was practically caved in from the number of times I'd punched him. Behind me were torture implements in case I needed them. Once, I'd have hoped I wouldn't. Now, they were tools to help me reach my goal: making sure Tovah and her mother were safe, forever.

I'd lied that day, when I'd left her. It was the hardest thing I'd ever done, but it was necessary, even when the heartbreak on her face broke me. My father still had men loyal to him, even after his death. There were other factions against the Silvers; even the Golds waited in the wings to take us down and take over Brooklyn. I had to distance myself from her. I wouldn't risk her life, but I wouldn't leave her either. No, I had a plan to get back to her and be with her for good.

The plan began with violence and interrogations; with wiping the family clean of anyone who might wish us ill. The plan started with the man in front of me.

As I beat him, a memory came to me—chasing a little girl through the backyard as she laughed with delight, air bursting through my lungs as I ran, determined to catch her.

I'm going to catch you, bashert.

Really? You better hurry up, slowpoke!

"Brother dearest, aren't you forgetting something? If you kill him, you won't get the information you need." Sasha said from where he sat, watching me.

Oh, right. I'd gotten so lost in my thoughts, I'd forgotten why we were here.

"I want names," I told my father's man. "Everyone who is still loyal to my father, everyone who's thinking of challenging me. Give me the list, or you die."

"Fuck you," the man said through broken teeth.

"If I were you, I'd stop cursing and start talking. Your daughter's name is Sarah, right? Only seven years old. It would be a shame if something were to happen to her."

Even at the age of seven, I'd known what caused the bruises on Tovah's arms. I just hadn't known who.

Who hurt you, bashert?
No one hurt me.
Then what are those?
I fell.

The pain hadn't done it, but the threat against his family did. "Alright, I'll tell you, I'll tell you," he said. "Please don't hurt my family. Please, sir."

I paused in punching him, wiping my bloody knuckles on my already stained shirt. "Talk."

Name after name bubbled from his lips. In the end, twenty-two men were against us. Twenty-two men a threat to my family, and the woman I loved.

Tell me, bashert. Tell me so I can protect you.

I can't tell you. If I tell you, how am I going to protect you back?

I'd blocked out so many memories of her, of us as children, but violence took me back to that innocent time, and to the little girl who'd loved me regardless of who my father was.

Who I would protect, no matter what it cost me.

"One more question," I asked. "Were you there when Tovah Lewis was tortured?"

The man didn't speak, but the fear in his eyes told me everything.

Grabbing a scalpel off the tray behind me, I rewarded his cowardice with a slice across the throat. He'd been witness to Tovah's pain; he died. As simple as that.

When we were done, I turned to my brother.

"You're a mess," he said, his own shirt pristine. "You know, Dad would never have gotten his hands dirty like this. He had people to do it."

I straightened my collar, staring dispassionately at the

dead man hanging from chains. "Yeah? Well, I'm nothing like Dad."

"Come in," I called.

I sat in what had been my father's office and was now mine. There was no memory of him here, no ghost. I'd exorcised his hold on me when I'd killed him.

Eliana and her father entered my office, standing at the threshold and staring at me.

"It's good to see you here, Isaac," Donny said. "Even better when my daughter joins you as your wife."

I saw Eliana flinch.

"Ah yes, about that." I cleared my throat. "I won't be marrying your daughter."

Brown eyes stared at me. "Did you just say we're getting married, Isaac Silver?"

I smiled at her with a gap in my teeth. "That's right, bashert. One day, you'll tell me your name, and then we'll be together forever. I promise."

In the present, Donny stiffened, his chest puffing out. "I had an agreement with Abe..."

I gestured around me. "In case you forgot, Abe Silver is dead. I make the decisions now, Donny. You either get in line, or I'll make sure your family starves."

"Is this about that little slut?" he sneered. "Because—"

Reaching under my desk, I pulled out the gun I'd become familiar with and shot him between the eyes. He slumped forward in his chair.

I expected Eliana to scream or faint, so I was surprised when she smiled.

"Thanks," she said.

I blinked.

"We'll have to unite our families in a different way," she continued. "I'm not opposed to marriage, but since you're not an option, can I suggest one of your brothers?"

I laughed in shock. "We'll discuss it," I told her.

Rising, she cast her eyes at the dead man beside her. "I look forward to doing business with you," she said. "And I hope I'm invited to the wedding."

I grinned at her, dimples on display. It was the first time I'd smiled in weeks. "I'll make sure you get an invitation."

IF YOU THOUGHT ABOUT IT, REALLY THOUGHT ABOUT IT, THE human body was an amazing thing. It kept breathing, kept moving, kept walking and talking and even pissing and shitting, even if you were completely dead inside.

I was completely dead inside. It had been a month since I'd walked out of Tovah's hospital room and out of her life.

Well, *technically* out of her life. I hadn't talked to her so much as once, but that didn't mean I'd left her alone. If anything, I spent more time with her than I had when we were together. I watched the tracker all the time to see where she was. I wired the house with cameras and mics (except for the second bedroom her mother was staying in), so I could watch her 24/7. I wired the newspaper offices too, which was...illuminating. I had guards on her whenever she left the house, to make sure no one got close to her or could hurt her.

And in the time I wasn't busy lining up the dominoes or going to class—I was still a college student in the midst of all of this mafia shit—I stalked her myself, hiding in the trees with binoculars and watching her through the windows, which the damn woman never closed. Did she not care she was giving any creep in the woods a peep show?

Of course, the only creep in the woods was me.

But right now, I wasn't in the woods. No, I was in Toby's fucking dorm room, wearing gloves, waiting for him to get home from the newspaper office. He and I had an appointment with a window, a window I'd opened to let the night air in. I might not be able to be with Tovah, but I'd fucking make sure no one tried to ruin her career or her future.

A key turned in the lock and the door opened. Toby stood there in skinny jeans and a tweed jacket. He didn't notice me at first, his head buried in his phone.

I cleared my throat.

He jumped.

And then he saw me and jumped again.

"Isaac, what are you doing in my room?"

"Oh, Toby, I have a bone to pick with you. Well, several bones. And honestly, they may be picking your bones off the ground in a bit."

He blanched, then lifted his phone, probably to call the cops. Fortunately, I had hockey reflexes, and the phone was out of his hand and in my pocket before he could dial 911.

"I didn't do anything," he cried.

"No? You weren't planning on publishing an article with naked photos of her calling her journalistic integrity into question?"

"How...how did you find out about that?" he practically choked on his question.

I'd bugged his office, that was how. But I wasn't about to say that.

"I don't think you should be worried about my sources. I

think you should be worried about your own skin. Because if you don't kill the article, I'm going to...well, do I have to finish that sentence?" I asked coldly.

"You fucking hockey players think you run this damn school. And your little whore is just as bad—"

Rage filled me. He had no right to call her a whore. No one called her that and lived.

"Wrong answer," I said, dragging him toward the window.

"What's that word for throwing someone out a window?" I asked casually.

"You won't get away with this," he spluttered. "I'll call the cops. You'll go to prison—"

I paused, staring down at him, knowing there was death in my eyes. "Toby, I'm now the proud owner of an entire criminal empire. The cops are in my pocket. The judges are in my pocket. *Everyone* is in my pocket. Now, tell me the word, or you're about to experience a four-story drop."

His eyes practically bugged out of his head, making him look particularly froglike.

"Defenestrate," he said weakly.

"That's a really big word for a hockey player. Spell it for me."

"Isaac, I swear, I'll never—"

"Spell. It. For. Me." I repeated, glaring at him.

He swallowed.

"D-E-F-E-N-E—"

He didn't get a chance to say the "s"—I'd already lifted him up and tossed him out the window.

Moments later, I heard a loud thump, then screams.

I texted one of the men who was loyal to me.

> Need cleanup on the newsie job. Let our people in the Gehenom police department know.

That done, I left Toby's dorm room, no fingerprints, and moved my way through the chaos in the hallway, spotted the emergency exit, and headed down it and into the night.

I THOUGHT TAKING CARE OF THE TOBY PROBLEM WOULD GIVE me at least some peace.

It didn't. Not when Tovah was so close, but still out of reach.

But she'd be back in my arms soon, I promised myself. Soon.

I stood in the shadows, watching Tovah as I toyed with the ring box in my pocket. I'd bought it in the city after killing Donny Rabin. It was perfect for her: a rose gold band and something called a halo diamond. One day, soon, it would be on her finger. I kept it on me all the time, taking it out to look at when I really wanted to hurt.

As I reached into my pocket to stare at the ring some more, a twig snapped.

Someone was here.

Without a thought, I pulled out a gun. If there was a single goddamned motherfucker who thought they could touch a hair on either woman's head...

"God, you've become a paranoid asshole. Put that gun down," my older sister said as she came out from behind a tree.

"Oh, good. You're here," I said, lowering the gun.

"I'm here," Liza acknowledged. She scanned me. "I have to say, being head of the family does *not* agree with you. You look like you've been run ragged, although I guess that bespoke suit is flattering."

I shrugged. I missed my hockey uniform. But not only did I not have the time right now for hockey, I'd been kicked off the team after running out of that game. Jack and my friends had fought for me, but Coach was adamant that I was out. I hated it, not playing, and I missed my teammates —but it was worth the sacrifice. She was worth the sacrifice.

"This job isn't easy, or for the faint of heart," I told her.

"You think I don't know that?" The bitter jealousy flashed in my sister's eyes.

I hid my smile. I'd been counting on it.

"I have an offer for you," I told her.

"Listening."

"You've always wanted to be the head of this family. Since we were kids. It went to me because I was the boy, but it's 2025. Way past time to shake things up. And fuck, I don't want to do this shit."

Her eyes tracked me, and her breathing sped up. "What are you saying?"

"I'm saying it's all yours, if you want it. The family, the money, the power—no one deserves it more than you. No one has your ability to play this game, negotiate, and wield violence when necessary. You were made for this, Liza, and I'm happy to—"

She raised a hand to stop me. My heart lodged in my throat. Was she going to turn it down? Had I been wrong? Had all this work been for nothing?

"You realize," she said, "That if you pass it to me, no one is going to be okay with you being half in, half out. *I'm* not okay with you being half in, half out. You'll still be a part of the family, but the money, the power, the resources to protect you when you're throwing someone out a window—yes, I heard about that—it's all gone."

Hell yeah. Relief filled me. She wanted in. Still, I spoke. "One of these days, you'll fall in love. And you'll be willing to sacrifice everything else that matters to you to be with them."

Liza wrinkled her nose. "I fucking hope not."

"So, is that a yes?"

"They aren't going to make it easy," she said.

"You love a challenge," I pointed out.

She quirked a smile. She'd always been calm and composed, but this was the most excited or happy I'd ever seen her.

"You sure?" she said.

I fingered the ring again. "Never been more sure about anything in my life."

"Then it's a deal," she said. "I hope she's worth it."

"She's worth more than you could even imagine," I said, squaring my shoulders. "Now, if you don't mind, I have somewhere to be."

"Good l—"

But before she could finish, I'd already taken off through the trees.

58

Tovah

Taking One for the Team: Isaac Jones Sets Standard for the Kings

On Reina University's campus, he's known for his charming smile. On the ice, he's known for being a team player and his wrist shot. But behind closed doors, Isaac Jones has a depth, loyalty, and conviction of character his devastating dimples and playful wink hide from the rest of the world.

And that's deliberate. Jones is the epitome of the complicated hero (or antihero), the type of man who would sacrifice anything—including his self-image—to protect the people who are important to him. That's true in his personal life, and true in his hockey life, too. And although the Kings have gone through upheaval over the past year, his guidance as the team's forward saw them through this season to the Frozen Four. And when Isaac and his fellow seniors graduate, his legacy of putting his team and everyone who matters to him first will continue on.

"Well." Coach Philip placed the tablet back on his desk and sat back in his chair, steepling his hands. "That was quite some piece on Isaac and the team. Not an interview, but still. Impressive work."

I smiled at him, even though my heart was racing. "Your husband thought so, too."

A brief smile came to the coach's face. "He speaks very highly of you. Between us, you're his favorite student. He says you have quite the journalism career ahead of you."

That was good to hear—but I wasn't here about my future. I was here for Isaac's. He was deeply entrenched in his new life, and I had no idea if he'd ever be able to play again. But he'd sacrificed so much for me, and I wanted to at least give hockey back to him.

"Speaking of careers…" I began.

"Ah, you're here about Isaac specifically. You know, I've kept tabs on him. He's missed more classes than he's made. If he graduates, it will be by the skin of his teeth. But then, someone in Mr. Silver's position may not care about graduating anymore."

I gaped at him.

"You know."

He nodded. "After Isaac ran out of the game, and his teammates tried to cover for him, I had a feeling there was more going on than anyone was telling me. Combine that with your own odd behavior this semester, and well…" he shrugged. "As it so happens, I'm married to quite an impressive journalist myself."

"He won't—"

"He won't do anything to put Mr. Silver or his family in jeopardy. We both know better than that. Isaac's a good player and an even better teammate, with a great deal of potential in hockey. It's a shame he won't be ever be able to see that through."

I lifted my chin. "That's actually why I'm here. Like you said, the article is good. It puts Isaac—and the team—in a good light. Which is what the Kings needed. As interim editor-in-chief of *The Daily Queen*, I'd love to publish the piece—as the lead story on our website. But."

"But you want something in return," he guessed.

Of course I did. I might not have Isaac anymore, but I wanted him to be happy. To have everything. Even if I wouldn't be there to witness it.

"You have a lot of sway with the university, Coach Philip. And with the NCAA. You can get Isaac back on the team. Let him play in the Frozen Four. Please. Or at least give him the option. And if you do that—I'll publish the article."

"Hmm." He considered for a moment, his gaze on the photo of his husband. "And what if I do all that work to get Isaac back on the team, but he decides not to accept it?"

"Then I still publish the article," I assured him, even though the thought of Isaac not playing hockey hurt almost as much as his absence. "I don't want to—I can't—decide his future for him. I want him to get to decide for himself."

Coach Philip shifted his gaze back to me. "He's lucky to have you."

My throat, my chest, my whole body—those five words made me ache with longing.

"I wish he knew that," I said quietly.

The coach rose out of his chair, holding his hand out for mine. I placed it in his, and he shook it—once. "I promise you, he does. He'd be a complete idiot not to, and Isaac is not an idiot."

Later, I sat in front of my laptop, re-reading the email for the third time. I still couldn't believe it.

Dear Ms. Lewis,

Isaac Silver has purchased ten properties around the world for you. We'll need certain information from you to set up a property portfolio and make sure we're managing the apartments and houses to your expectations. Here are the various locations:

Paris, France
  London, UK
  Kathmandu, Nepal
  Lima, Peru
  Ushuaia, Chile
  Jackson Hole, Wyoming
  Todos Santos, Mexico
  Melbourne, Australia
  Tokyo, Japan
  Prague, Czech Republic

Please schedule a meeting with one of our assistants at your earliest convenience.

Thank you,
  Ilana Brandeis, Esq.

Heartless Game

EVERY TIME I REREAD THE EMAIL, MY HEART SANK A LITTLE more.

"Why do you like this show so much?"

"It's the combination of them finding a home, a place that's theirs, a place to be safe in, and the freedom to go wherever they want. I've never had any of those things. It's all I've ever wanted."

He'd remembered. Down to each individual city I'd listed.

And he'd bought homes for me in all of them.

It hurt, knowing how much he loved me, and how he still insisted on staying so far away.

He'd saved me from Toby's exposé, too. Toby was in the hospital with broken bones, but he was alive. Everyone on campus was talking about the editor-in-chief falling out of his window. No one seemed to suspect Isaac—but then why would they, when he had the power of the Silver family behind him? Besides, no one but me and the Core Four knew who he really was or what he was capable of. And I'd make sure to keep it that way. To protect him, too.

I should've felt guilty about Toby, but I didn't. Instead, it just made me love Isaac that much more.

You wonderful asshole, why do you keep breaking my heart? I thought, closing out of the email and picking up my phone to text him for the thousandth time—knowing it would go unanswered like all the rest. Two months of complete silence from him.

Putting my phone down, I lay down on the floor and did my PT exercises and stretches. The doctor had pronounced me completely healed from the gunshot and cleared me to return to all normal activities. But I wasn't healed. How could I be, when half my heart was missing?

At that moment, the security alarm went off.

My mom had changed the locks and reset the system

after we'd moved in, insisting that we didn't know who else had it. She liked having an alarm system. I think after years of feeling unsafe, that fear still never went away.

The alarm was blaring.

Could someone be after me?

My mom was out of town—she'd gone to the city to see old friends she'd fallen out of touch with years ago—and I was alone in the house.

Fuck, what did I do?

I called Isaac immediately, but he didn't answer.

Hanging up, I called 911.

"What's your emergency?" a kind woman said on the line.

"Someone's just broken into my house," I told her in a whisper. "My address is—"

The door to the bedroom began to open.

Oh god, after all of this, I was *going to die.*

But it was Isaac framed in the doorway, chest heaving, covered in dirt and leaves. In the light, I could see his dark eyes, but unlike the last time I saw them, they were no longer filled with devastation.

Instead, they were filled with hope...

...and love.

"Never mind, false alarm," I told the protesting 911 operator, and hung up.

"Why are you here?" I asked him.

"I've never not been here," he told me. "I've been about a hundred yards away every second I could get. I can't think, can't see, can't fucking *breathe* if I'm not near you, Tovah."

Oh, god.

"Then why did you stay away?"

A dark look crossed his face. "I had to make sure you were safe. That we were safe. I had enemies, Tovah, and watching you get shot haunted me. All I could see while you slept in that hospital bed was blood pouring from your chest and not being able to get to you in time if you were with me...so I made sure you weren't. I lied, and broke your heart in the process, and I'm so sorry for that—but not sorry that it was what I had to do to get back to you. I'm here. And I'm not going anywhere, ever again. I'm too selfish of a man to let you go."

I blinked rapidly. This man always made me cry.

He saw, his throat working as he came toward me.

"Oh god, bashert, please don't cry. Please, every time a tear falls from your eyes, it's like I die a little inside."

"Then fix it," I told him. "Fix it."

"That's what I'm here to do." There was a soft determination in his face, as he knelt down on one knee.

"Isaac, what the hell are you doing?" I wasn't even sure how I was able to form words.

Was he about to—?

"Tovah, I told you once that the only woman I would ever marry was you. It's still true. After my mother died, I thought love couldn't, wouldn't, exist for me. I was sure I didn't even have a heart. But the day I met you, even though I resisted, that heart came back to life, and it's been beating for you and only for you ever since. You are the sole reason I was put on this earth, and I will exist entirely to love you until the day I die, and then I will love you forever after. That's why I call you bashert, Tovah Lewis. You're my soulmate. My destiny. You're it for me."

"Isaac," I said softly, my eyes still filled with tears as my heart came back to life, too. "I love you so much."

Utter devotion moved over his face as he pulled something out of his pocket.

It was a small black velvet ring box.

He flipped open the top.

A rose gold halo diamond ring sparkled in the light.

"Then marry me," he said fiercely. "Be my wife, be mine forever, like I've always been yours."

Of course he demanded I marry him. Of course he didn't ask.

But would I want it any other way?

No.

I wanted him, all versions of him.

"Yes, Isaac, I'll marry you," I said, moving toward him and holding out my hand so he could slide the ring over my finger.

"Good," he told me. "Because I wasn't giving you a choice."

"But what about the family? What about—"

"Liza is taking over, thank fuck," he said. "I'm giving up all of it. None of it means anything if I have to live without you."

"I can't live without you either," I said.

"Good."

And with that, he kissed me, a kiss that made every other kiss he'd ever given me pale in comparison. The room spun around us, gravity gave up the fight, and it was like I was floating in his arms as they tightened around me. What once felt like a prison was now my safe haven; nothing and no one would ever, ever, tear us apart again.

Finally, he pulled away. And a dark smile spread across his face, popping out his dimples.

"You know what I want you to do next, don't you, little journalist?"

I nodded, already feeling breathless.

"Good." He rose, setting me on the floor, and crossing his arms. "I'll give you a sixty-second head start, and you better move fast, because the second I catch you, I'm going to shove my dick inside that tight cunt so hard and so deep, you'll feel me forever. Now, *run.*"

My feet pounded down the stairs as I raced to the first floor and out of the house, ripping off my clothes as I went. The driveway passed behind me, Isaac close behind, and then I was in the trees, darting through the forest, bare feet catching on rocks and twigs, but I didn't care, didn't care, didn't feel the pain, because all I felt was elation as I ran and the love of my life chased me.

And then he caught me, shoving me down in the dirt and following me down. I was already so wet, and he grunted in pleasure as he shoved my legs apart. And then he was inside me, as hard and deep as he promised, no, harder and deeper, fucking me and fucking me and making love to me and loving me, and I fucked him and made love to him and loved him right back, forgetting everything but the hot, hard, thick feeling of him inside me, his body covering mine, until nothing existed in the world.

Nothing but my monster and me.

EPILOGUE ONE

Isaac

It felt good to be back out on the ice. Especially now that the name displayed on my jersey was SILVER. My redone tattoo on my back—of living, thriving vines climbing up and over the wall on my back, vines that spelled out *bashert*—may have been hidden by my jersey, but I was always aware of it—just like I was always aware of *her*.

I had Tovah to thank for all of this. Not only for giving me back my life, but myself, as well. The tattoo was a reminder of what I had in my life now—freedom to choose my own fate with the woman I loved by my side. I thanked her, multiple times, mostly with my head between her thighs as she cried my name. It was my favorite way to show my gratitude. And even though I'd missed the draft, I was a free agent and could still join the NHL. According to coach, recruiters had been asking around. It was good, and not only because I would finally get to play hockey professionally. Liza had followed through on her warning: I was cut off financially from the family, and I was determined to make sure Tovah and her mom grew accustomed to the best life possible.

For now though, I no longer had the weight of my father's crown hanging around my neck. Liza was having some difficulties bringing the family around, but my sister was smart, resourceful, and always had a plan. That was her business—mine was winning the Frozen Four for my team—and my fiancée.

She sat in the stands next to her mother, hair a radiant millennial pink—a color I'd grown obsessed with—her fingers typing away at her phone as she wrote an article—her last ever article—for *The Daily Queen*. She was still the same distraction she'd always been, but it was easier to focus, knowing she was safe, and more importantly, that she was mine.

The Kings were playing the best game we'd ever played. It was like we were one on the ice, flying across the rink and passing the puck, not letting the opposing team get close to it. The puck was ours. The game was ours.

The cup would be ours, too. Especially now that I was fully healed and not only allowed, but able to play.

Jack passed me the puck, and I slapped it into the net.

After the next puck drop, I passed the puck to Jack, only for the other team's defense to slam him into the boards.

But he regained control of the puck, and the two of us skated in sync toward the goal, and I watched as my best friend executed the slapshot of his life, and the puck flew into the net, right past the goalie.

The horn sounded.

We'd won.

We'd won the cup.

My team was screaming, and so was the crowd, exhilarated and celebrating the win, but I only cared about one

Epilogue One

thing—my woman, engagement ring on her finger, waiting in the stands.

I skated toward her, and without a thought, jumped the boards, running up the stairs on my skates as she ran down to me.

I caught her in my arms.

"You won!" she said, elated.

"Yeah? What did you think of the game play, little snoop?"

"My investigative reporting tells me you're about to get really lucky," she teased.

"Oh, bashert," I said, kissing her. "I'm planning on it."

Hana had, thankfully, found somewhere else to be after the game. Which was good because I planned on making Tovah scream so loud the windows shook.

Parking my car, I hopped out, going around to her side like the gentleman I still pretended to be and then grabbing her and throwing her over my shoulder like the monster I truly was.

"Isaac, what the—"

I slapped her ass. "No sassing from you, or I'll change my plans and spank your ass black and blue instead."

She grumbled something against my back.

"What was that?"

"I said, you're a fucking tease."

I snorted. She wouldn't be thinking that soon.

To entertain myself, I smacked my fiancée's ass as I jogged up the steps and into our house. I continued spanking her as I headed up the stairs to our bedroom. As she struggled against me, my cock got thicker and thicker.

"So eager," I taunted, although it was debatable whether I was talking to her or to myself. "You're leaving a wet spot on my shoulder, aren't you? I'll make you lick it up later."

She whimpered, delighting me.

In our bedroom, I dropped her on the bed, not giving her time to catch her breath as I grabbed her wrists and locked them in the cuffs. I didn't make us sleep locked together anymore, but I kept them on the headboard for times like these—times when I wanted complete control over her. That first task complete, I grabbed a few other items out of the nightstand—a spreader bar, a rabbit vibrator, a feather, and a butt plug.

What could I say? The sleazy sex shop had a sale.

She glanced down at the items on the bed, her eyes wide with fear—and desire.

"Isaac—"

"Yes, bashert?" I asked as I cuffed the spreader bar to her ankles before opening it so her legs were forced wide.

"What are you planning?"

I flipped on the rabbit vibrator, and as it began buzzing, Tovah tried to clench her legs. She couldn't though; she was trapped, forced to take whatever I wanted to give her. And like always, what I wanted to give her was everything.

"It's been a while since I've edged you," I told her casually. Her eyes widened further. "I miss the sound of your helpless whimpers and the way your cunt twitches when I've forced you to take it for too long."

"Oh god," she moaned, her eyes going glassy at my words alone.

Dropping the vibrator on her belly, I climbed up on the bed, shoving my head between her gorgeous thighs and latching my mouth to her clit. I didn't bother to work her up gently. I just sucked hard.

"Isaac!"

She went from zero to sixty in about three seconds flat. So did my cock.

"Good, you're wet enough," I said, lifting my head, picking up the vibrator and then shoving it in her pussy without any of the care or tenderness I felt for her. But then again, she wanted me this way—rough and demanding, like nothing mattered but what I wanted from her. As the rabbit buzzed, I made sure its ears covered her clit. Leaning down on one elbow, I watched for a bit, entranced by the way she wiggled and writhed, her cunt pulsing with need. Absently, I pumped my cock with one hand.

Just as she grew close to coming, I shut off the vibrator.

"Fuck, I hate when you do that," she growled.

I laughed. "Don't lie."

Flipping it back on, I turned it up to a higher frequency, stroking myself in time to her moans, gasps, and jerks. But I watched her, in tune with how close she was, and just as her body stiffened, I shut it off again.

She struggled again, mindlessly humping the air, trying to shove her thighs together—anything to get friction. Anything to get off.

"Please, Isaac, please," she begged in a thick whine.

Ah, fuck. Her voice alone almost made me come.

"What do you want, bashert? What do you need?" I crooned.

"You," she said, and even though my plan had been to play rough with her, I couldn't help but prowl up her body and drop a few, tender kisses on her perspiring face.

"I love you," I told her as I kissed her nose, her cheeks,

her lips. "I could say it a million times a day, and it still wouldn't be enough."

"Then let me come!"

I pretended to consider it.

"Nah," I said instead. I wasn't going to go sweet on her. No, she needed this side of me—craved the darkness within me. Which was good, because I craved it now, too.

Drawing back, I stroked her face with a finger, murmuring, "You know, there's something we've never done. Something I've always wanted to do with you."

Her eyes grew wary.

"Am I going to like whatever this is?"

I grinned, aware that even my dimples looked feral.

"Probably not at first. But you'll love it after a while."

Reaching over her, I grabbed the bottle of lube we kept in the nightstand.

She blinked. "Anal? We've done that plenty."

"No, baby," I said, kissing her again before whispering in her ear. "I love this cunt so much, but I've never gotten my whole fist inside it. Doesn't she deserve my whole hand? She's been so good, I think she does."

"Wait, Isaac."

I squeezed lube onto my right hand all the way up to my wrist, working it over, and then squeezed more and spread it inside her cunt.

"I'll go slow," I promised.

"I—" I could hear her hesitation.

"Do you want to come tonight? Do you want my cock? Because this is the only way you're getting either." I was serious. I'd keep her on edge for days if I had to—I had before. "Besides," I added, suddenly inspired, "I feel like I also deserve a treat for winning the championship for you."

"Oh, god, fuck—" she began, and I slid a finger inside her, hooking it toward me and rubbing her G-spot.

"Yes," she cried.

"Is that 'yes' consent? Because I can stop..." I teased.

"Yes, please, *do it*," she begged.

I played with her like that for a bit, getting her ready, before withdrawing my finger and adding a second, making sure to rub her walls and work her G-spot each time. She started writhing again, humping against my hand. Adding a third finger was more difficult: I'd done it before, but no matter how many times we fucked, she was still tight. I spent more time with three fingers, playing her pussy with the same patience I practiced stick work during drills. As I worked her cunt, I listened to her moans, her pleading turn to gibberish. She was begging to come again.

"I'll let you," I promised. "Just not yet. Now, take a deep breath and exhale when I tell you."

She inhaled loudly, almost gasping, as I slowly and carefully worked a fourth finger into her cunt. Even though my cock was thicker than my four fingers together, the angle made it so tight, it was practically impossible. I couldn't get past the first knuckle. But I was determined.

"Exhale," I demanded, and as soon as she did, I withdrew my fingers.

She jerked on the bed.

"Oh god, oh god," she cried. "Isaac it's—"

"We aren't done, little snoop," I said as I added more lube to my fingers. "Deep breath."

As she inhaled, I pushed my fingers back in, using more force this time. The lube helped too, and I was able to get all four inside her the whole way this time. She was squeezing them so tight, my cock was jealous. But he'd get his turn.

I continued to stroke and play with her, using my thumb

to rub hard, firm circles against her pulsing clit and carefully opening my fingers to widen her pussy as much as I could, to prep her for the last part. As she moaned and cried and humped my hand, I told her sweet nothings in every language I knew, and some I didn't. I told her how much I loved her, how beautiful she was, covered in sweat and desperate for me, how perfect she looked with her pussy spread open around my four fingers, how every part of her was made for me, was made to take me—and she would.

"Isaac, Isaac, Isaac," she chanted my name. "Isaac—"

Her whole body tensed again. She was about to come.

"Give me your eyes," I ordered. "I want to see you. Oh, and exhale."

She may not have heard me, but as she released her breath to cry out, I shaped my hand like a duck bill, pressing my thumb to my fingers, and slid my hand inside her.

My whole. Goddamned hand.

I could feel her pussy, all of her pussy, from the inside. The walls and ridges, where it was puffier and swollen, where it was tighter. The best fucking part was the way I felt her try to clench around me, over and over, as she came with a gorgeous, stunning scream I'd replay in my head forever. Her cunt continued to clench, loosening slightly, as I worked my fist inside her, pumping it, rubbing my knuckles against her G-spot, and twisting my hand, careful to avoid her cervix. Surrounded by her this way—wearing her cunt like a fucking hand puppet as she pulsed around me, forced to take me—made my balls draw up, and I had to take my own deep breaths so I could control my own need to come.

"I love you," I said, still working my fist inside her slowly. "I love you, bashert."

"Isaac, it's so much, it's so—"

"No such thing," I interrupted her.

Epilogue One

"—good," she cried, then choked on her words as she came again.

Fuck.

"I told you you'd love it," I growled. "Your little cunt is too greedy not to."

I wasn't done though. There was one more thing I wanted out of her, before my cock could have its turn. With my free hand, I pushed down her stomach, right above where my fist was. It served the purpose to keep her in place, yes, but as I began shoving my fist in and out of her faster and harder, the pressure from both sides got to my poor girl. She screamed again, coming so hard she squirted, soaking the bed, the sheets, my legs, herself.

Ah fuck, my cock. I didn't have much longer, and I wanted to come inside her pussy, not on the bed.

"That's it, that's my good girl. That's exactly what I wanted from you," I praised her. "Now, inhale one more time, hold your breath—"

My good girl listened to me, following my instructions. Turning my hand and making the duck bill shape with it again, I said, "Exhale, Tovah."

She released her breath—and the loudest scream of all —as I carefully pulled my hand out of her pretty pussy, so red and swollen, and more open than it had ever been before. I stared for a moment, entranced by the mess she'd made of us, my cock threatening to release the cum I'd been saving for her.

"Fuck, fuck, fuck, so goddamned pretty," I said, quickly removing the cuffs from her ankles before dropping the spreader bar on the ground.

Tovah stared at the ceiling with unseeing eyes, limp as a ragdoll. I grabbed her right leg, lifting it over my shoulder, lined up my cock, and pushed inside her. My fist had loosened her up some, and I was able to shove my cock the whole way inside her with one thrust.

"Isaac, I—"

"Come again for me, bashert," I demanded as I began a fast and brutal pace, using the lube and my earlier work to my advantage as I stuffed my cock deep in her, again and again and again. "Come for me and show me how much you love me. I'm not stopping until you do. I'll fuck you all night if I have to. Be a good girl and give me one more."

As I shoved deep, she came, her walls trembling around me in weak little pulses, and the wetness of her pussy, the feeling of her—and knowing that this, that she, was mine forever, and no one would ever take her from me, ever again—snapped the little control I had left. The monster in me roared as I came deep inside her, coating her poor cunt with my cum as my vision almost went black.

Finally, I came down from my high, reluctantly withdrawing from her pussy, and releasing her leg where it dropped onto the bed. She was trembling, moaning from aftershocks.

Even though all I wanted to do was collapse next to her, I rolled off the bed and stumbled to the headboard, undoing the cuffs and rubbing her wrists back to life. Usually, I'd shower her as aftercare, and this had been intense, but instead I got back in the bed with her, pulling her into my arms and stroking her hair, murmuring to her as I soothed her.

"You were so beautiful, so perfect. You're okay, I've got you," I said. "I love you." I continued stroking her hair, her back, wrapping her up tight in my arms and keeping her warm.

After a while, her eyes drifted open, a soft, satisfied smile on her face.

"Oh my god," she said, sounding fuck drunk.

"Oh my god good, or oh my god bad?"

"Ask me tomorrow," she said. "I've never felt anything like that before. I've never felt so vulnerable before."

"I know," I said. "That's why I did it. I want that kind of intimacy with you. I want every kind of intimacy with you. There's nothing I won't do to feel closer to you."

"Thanks for warning me," she teased.

"Anytime."

"And for blackmailing me."

"You're welcome."

"Although no thank you for throwing me in your trunk—"

I kissed her to shut her up. Because I didn't regret it. Not one fucking bit.

EPILOGUE TWO

Lawson

I'd fucked up a lot in my life.

Truly. My list of fuck ups was a mile long.

I'd fucked up when I hadn't defended Asher, I'd fucked up when I had flirted with Aviva, and that was just the start of it. The team, and the Core Four—now Core Five, including Asher—had grudgingly forgiven me and accepted me into the fold.

But none of it came close to my hugest fuck up.

When I'd fucked up with *her*.

As my team celebrated the win, taking turns skating around the rink with the Cup in our raised hands, my eyes caught on someone in the back of the stadium.

Someone I thought I'd seen a couple months ago when I'd been watching Tovah, someone I'd chased after, only to come to the conclusion I was seeing things.

She couldn't be here. She was supposed to be at Oxford.

But my eyes weren't lying to me. Because in the stands sat a beautiful girl with big blue eyes and a blonde pixie cut, and even though she looked older and her hair was different, I'd recognize that smile anywhere...

...as she laughed at something the bastard next to her was saying.

Asshole. I didn't even know him, and I had no right to, but I still was going to rip him away from her.

Because he was talking to the only girl I'd ever loved, and even though I'd fucked up expeditiously, even though she'd told me she never, ever wanted to see me again, she was here, at my game.

At my university.

Which meant she was still mine. That she'd always been and would only ever be mine.

All I had to do was set the right kind of trap.

As I watched Emma talk to the soon-to-be-dead idiot next to her, I smiled a grin, scary and wolf-like.

"Game on," I murmured.

Game the fuck on.

***

Can't wait to read Lawson and Emma's story? PREORDER NOW! >>

Want more Isaac and Tovah? Read the bonus epilogue here. >>

And you can get more dark hockey romance right now with Jack and Aviva. Remember Isaac's best friend, who warned Isaac about bullying the woman you loved? And Tovah's best friend, who wasn't willing to back down and let her get hurt again? Jack and Aviva's romance is so hot, it burns. Read BRUTAL GAME right now. >>

Want even more dark hockey romance? What about a stalker stepbrother? Mason and Leslie's romance was a seriously spicy ride. Read BUTTERFLY right now >>

Desperate to know more about Jack's older brother, Micah, his wife, Kara, and their other husbands, Conor and Luke? Their story is about three ex-Navy SEALs turned hitmen, and the woman who got away, but not for long... Their dark, why choose trilogy is beyond filthy and absolutely *wild*. Kara's men are feral for her (and each other) and don't take "no" for an answer. Read YOU CAN FOLLOW ME right now >>

Want to know more about me, and get publishing updates, sneak peeks, and other news? Join my newsletter! >>

And finally, reviews make all the difference to an author's career. If you loved *Heartless Game*, review it here!

***

Want free signed SFW/NSFW art of the primal scene mailed to you? Fill out this form here! Or scan the QR code below:

Epilogue Two

AUTHOR'S NOTE

I'm going to admit to something I probably shouldn't admit to: There was a point at which I wasn't sure I could even write this book.

I remember texting with my friend Liz, as I stared at a blank Word document, and asking: *Given the state of the world, can I write dubcon and noncon anymore? Is that ethical, given that so many of us are fighting for the ability to make our own choices for our own bodies? Young men are yelling, "Your body, my choice,"—so what the fuck am I even doing thinking of writing that shit into a book?*

And Liz, who is always brilliant and often my favorite, pointed out that if anything, stories that pushed boundaries, that didn't play by the rules, and that allowed people to explore their fantasies safely and without consequence, were more necessary than ever.

And even though it took me a while to get there, she was right. For me to abandon Isaac and Tovah's story, to abandon the ways in which I confront and challenge what consent actually means, and, in doing so, abandon my readers...well, that would be the same thing as me lying down, belly up, and surrendering. Surrendering to this bullshit that surrounds us right now. Surrendering to the men who don't want me to make my own choices.

And so I wrote it. And while I wrote, Isaac and Tovah fell in love with each other's monsters. And fought, so hard, for everything that was important to them. They did not lie down, belly up. They didn't surrender. *They did not comply.*

And neither will I.

There's a monster inside of each of us, something deep, something scary, something we try to bury and ignore for fear that it will get out and we won't like what we see. But a divided self never leads to peace, or joy, or self-acceptance... or love. Isaac's monster was the dark violence inside, the willingness to do whatever it took to protect the people he loved, no matter how wrong. Tovah's monster was the quiet voice inside her that wanted, desperately, to belong to someone—to have a home. My monster loves to read dubcon and noncon, even as it abhors the idea of losing my ability to make my own choices. My monster is unhinged, obsessive, and at times, feral. My monster is violent and angry, and sometimes wants to do horrible things to horrible people.[*] My monster also wants to crawl under the covers and hide from the world. (My monster is kind of a mess.)

And I am working, every day, on growing to love her.

I don't know who or what your monster is. Here is what I do know: That those deep, buried parts of ourselves deserve to be loved. And if you dig them up and let them see the light, you might realize they—you—aren't so scary, after all.

Isaac taught me that.

Tovah, too.

---

[*] Not actually, FBI agent reading this book.

There's a fuck ton to fear right now. I'm not even going to go into it, because if I do, I'll spiral, and if I spiral, I can't do what I need to to help. I will tell you this: They want us afraid. They want us to comply in advance, to give up, to lose hope.

They want us to fear our monster. To not accept ourselves for who we are. They don't want us to recognize how deserving we are of love.

"Love turns men into monsters." But what if those monsters aren't as scary as we think they are? What if they're exactly what we need to meet this moment?

Isaac said it himself:

I may be a monster, but I'm your monster.

So let's embrace our monsters.

Together.

ACKNOWLEDGMENTS

This one really took a village. There were so many people who helped with feedback, with brainstorming, with holding my hand, with cheerleading, and with talking me off the many ledges I ended up on throughout the process of writing this book.

Brittney: I haven't forgiven you for moving across the world, but your help, support, and relentless encouragement with this story has (almost) made up for it. Thank you for your editorial prowess, your ride-or-die friendship...and finally convincing me to write the noun version of "cum" instead of "come." (I'm sure my readers are also thanking you.)

Sierra, Skye, and Kenya: There's a reason why the three of you are displayed in the middle, most prominent part of my bookshelves, where my mentors go. Thank you for your endless generosity, guidance, and wisdom. I would be nowhere without your help.

Pepperidge Farm Cookies: Thank you for the jokes, the tea, the TV watchathons, and for not murdering me when I complain about not being able to fall asleep and then falling asleep two minutes later.

Rachel: Thank you for personally testing out multiple car trunks to ensure I chose the right one for Isaac to stuff Tovah into. Not all heroes wear capes.

RFC: I do not know what I would do without y'all. Truly. Really, really, truly. Being in community with you is one of the highlights of this author experience, and I'm so glad we get to be on this journey together.

Liz and Alex: You're both my favorite. Deal with it.

Mikaela: I don't know, woman. I appreciate your help and your friendship, and am afraid to say you're stuck with me. Please get some sleep.

Diana: I love you. Thank you for reading my books, and for always being in my corner.

Jasmine: Thank you for going above and beyond with everything. No thank you for the surprise Urban Dictionary drops.

To my alpha and beta teams: This book would not be what it is without your thoughts and insights. Thank you for being so generous with your time; I hope I did y'all proud.

Alphas: Demi, LeeAnne, Justine Y-D, Justine G, Bekah, Madison, Marina, Michelle, Kendra, Alex, and Liz

Betas: Joey, Aimee Hardy, Brooke, Jaime, Lakshmi, Fiona, Abby, Emily, Nathalie Pilon, Taylor Wittman, Rory Drake, Gemma, Caitlen, Ashley Bolan, Lauren Odermatt, Cindy Lokken Kator, Lisa, Kali, Mia Gray, Samantha, Kristan, Jane, Jess Van Buren, Somya Surendra, Sierra, Brittney, Paige Willerick, Alicia, Tabatha Hawkins, Angie P, Sheelan McIntosh, L.B. Martin, Erin Rougeau, Logan, Tori, Autumn H., Alissa, Leanne, Jennifer Ross, Ashley, Dana, Tara Macoguillen, Brittney Carroll, Amanda M, Sammy, Amber Adams, Jenn, Amoy, Tânia Pinto, Kinga, Ebony, Nesma, Jess, Brittany, Nikki Grant, Skylark Melody, Buriedwithinpages, Alexandra Gibson, Heather Kearns, Abigail Hayden

To my ARC, Influencer, and Street Teams: I can't describe how much light and joy your excitement and enthusiasm brings into my life. Thank you for all of your energy, your posts, your jokes in and out of my DMs. I love you all very, very much.

To my mom: What are you even doing with this book? Put it down, please. You aren't allowed to read it.

And finally, to my readers: I'm not exaggerating when I say you have changed my life—for the better, times a million. You've made it possible to do this very hard thing that I love so very much—not only practically, but also emotionally. Every DM, every email, every post, every page read…you give this job meaning and give me purpose. Even on the hardest days, when it feels practically impossible to write, I think of you, lost in the world I created, turning page after page. It gives me the power to put aside everything else, open the document, and begin to write.

From the bottom of my very soul: Thank you.

Printed in Great Britain
by Amazon